CREATING CHAOS

Claire Dowie is a writer/performer/poet/comedian, and pioneer of 'stand-up theatre'. After starting out on the comedy circuit, she switched to writing plays 'when the punchlines ran out'. Her first major work, *Adult Child/Dead Child*, won a Time Out award in 1988 and *Why is John Lennon Wearing a Skirt?* won a London Fringe Award in 1991. Other works include *Death and Dancing*, *Easy Access (For the Boys)* and *All Over Lovely*. She wrote *Came Out, It Rained, Went Back In Again* for BBC2, *Kevin* for Central Television, and *The Year of the Monkey*, *From the Bottom of a Well*, *The Barnes Originals* and *Bonfire Night* for BBC radio. *Designs for Living* was produced by Ruby Tuesday, and *Sodom* by The Living Room. Claire is currently writing a new play for the Drill Hall, *H to He*, and a series of five plays for BBC radio. This is her first novel. Claire Dowie's website is at www.clairedowie.co.uk.

D1464515

Also available from Methuen
(plays)

Why is John Lennon Wearing a Skirt?
and other stand-up theatre plays

Easy Access (For the Boys) and
All Over Lovely

The Year of the Monkey
and other plays

CREATING CHAOS

CLAIRE DOWIE

Methuen

Published by Methuen 2004

1 3 5 7 9 10 8 6 4 2

Methuen Publishing Ltd
215 Vauxhall Bridge Road
London SW1V 1EJ
www.methuen.co.uk

ISBN 0 413 77417 1

Methuen Publishing Limited Reg. No. 3543167
A CIP catalogue for this title is available from the British Library.

Typeset by Servis Filmsetting Ltd, Manchester

Printed and bound in Great Britain
by Mackays of Chatham, Chatham, Kent

Dedicated to Colin Watkeys (of course)

Prologue

God, it's hard being an anarchist at thirteen. Especially when you're not on the Internet *like every other person in the whole school, street, city, country and western hemisphere! And* you've left your mobile phone upstairs. *And* you've decided to wear multi-coloured nouveau-hippy grunge, which is *not* black, *not* dramatic and *not* right. But *mostly* you've just discovered that Frog is the greatest band in the whole world, and their lead singer dies. How tragic is *that*?

Sally Field sat cross-legged on the floor of the living room, head in hands, three feet from the TV screen, in a mixed mood of pissed off and mourning. She watched the death of Chaos being dissected on GMTV while taping *BBC Breakfast News* and flicking over to Channel 4 during the adverts. It still wasn't enough. God, parents! The greatest tragedy of the century and all they had was terrestrial!

Sally Field allowed the tears to roll down her cheeks. She wasn't going to wipe them away; she was just going to sit, in silent shock, staring as the images and words unfolded before her. She looked, and felt, a tragic (but colourfully clothed) figure. It's got to be black for school, definitely. *If* she was going

1

to school today. *If* her mum was *ever* going to do the usual barking and bellowing – what was the matter with the woman? Did she want Sally to be late? Sally noticed that her mum was standing in the doorway, in silent shock, staring as the images and words unfolded before her. 'For Christ's sake!' Sally wanted to shout. 'This is *my* band; Chaos is *my* hero – don't do tragic attitude better than me, mate!' Except it wasn't tragic attitude. Sally realised with some alarm that her mother was genuinely white-faced, hand-over-mouth, oh-my-God shocked.

Sally returned to the TV screen. She'd only really been into Frog for about a month. They'd come with Damon and his Internet. Without the Internet Frog would be a hard band to get into, since they'd been pushed so far underground they'd been all but buried – as Damon liked to say. Damon was a seventeen-year-old in the sixth form who Sally was embarrassed to call a boyfriend because it wasn't like that. Anarchists didn't do conventional. Damon spent every evening on the Net. He'd also been to Frog gigs and spoken to Chaos personally. Damon had the entire catalogue of Frog CDs, played them all to Sally and lent her a book, *From Tadpoles to Frogspawn*. He said *Tads to Frogs* was the new bible. Sally thought Damon was way cool. Her mum was suspicious and Dad didn't like him at all, but all Damon wanted to do was talk about Frog, and Sally was honoured that he chose to talk to her. She would phone him soon, during a suitable gap in the broadcast or on the way to school, whichever came first.

A suitable gap in the broadcast. There would be no school today, it was obvious. Sally's younger brother, David, was still in his pyjamas and playing with his Game Boy; Mum hadn't even noticed. Mum hadn't noticed *anything* except the television – and the front door, which she kept glancing at for no apparent reason. She was mainly watching the TV, though.

David too, his thumbs were moving but one eye was on the news. The scenes on the TV showed the beginnings of madness. So many people with differing reactions to the news – *so many*. Sally was quite disappointed to see how popular Chaos had been – practically mainstream, it seemed. People in tears, people angry and shouting, people almost celebrating, people silent and numb, a few rent-a-gob celebrities trying to out-grieve each other. Sally watched them all, taking in their appearance and attitude, trying to work out what the correct conventional anarchist alternative Chaotic way of mourning was. Trouble was, the Chaotics – the ones who looked like Chaotics, anyway – simply stared inscrutably at the cameras and said, and did, nothing. Sally couldn't just stare inscrutably and say and do nothing; her mum was doing that.

Sally watched the latest lingering shot of the mangled car wreck in the field by the motorway, before GMTV went live to Tadley Hall, the headquarters of Frogspawn and Chaos's home. Nothing was happening. There were just locked gates and a waffling reporter so she flicked over to Channel 4 for *A Life of Chaos*, a brief biography of the band and their lives, their involvement with Frogspawn, what it stood for, how it all started and, as always, Ewan Hughes.

Sally waited for the usual picture of Ewan Hughes, chief Tadpole, founder of Frogspawn, creator of Chaotics and probable father of Chaos. The picture mesmerised her, it was so familiar. Nobody had seen *him*, though – he'd disappeared years ago – but his face was the symbol of Frogspawn. His face, the one image, as famous and recognisable as the face, the one image of Myra Hindley or Che Guevara. The face was an icon. The image spoke volumes. The poster on the wall or the badge on the lapel said more about a person than a shelf of manifestos or a month in the pub. Sally thought the face looked awfully familiar. And her mum taking a step towards the TV and David looking up from his Game Boy showed she wasn't the only one who thought so.

Ewan Hughes. Channel 4 had other photos. Grainy snapshots from the *Tads to Frogs* book. Sally had seen them before, of course. She'd pored over the book for hours, giggling at the coincidences, fantasising about the consequences and squirming with embarrassment while reading and rereading the sex bits.

But the photos on the TV looked clearer. The face in the background digitally enhanced, the little figure in the field made bigger, brought closer. No reason to squint, no need to peer with a magnifying glass; these photos were clear. He *was* familiar – give or take thirty years and a month of wishful thinking.

Sally heard a low, almost imperceptible moan. It was her mother. Sally stood up, rushed past her and left the room. She hurried upstairs to get her mobile and Damon's book. Sod what was on the TV. It was beginning to make sense. He was more than familiar. The reason Sally's mum kept glancing at the front door was because she was expecting Dad to come home. And although Sally's dad was more a pain in the arse than a mythical icon, he was the spitting image of Ewan Hughes. Well, he would be, if Ewan Hughes was twenty/thirty years older – which he would be. And Ewan Hughes was the probable father of Chaos. Which meant . . .

'Don't talk such rubbish,' Damon sneered. 'Ewan Hughes is the greatest revolutionary there's ever been, not some thick brickie who spends every evening slumped in front of the telly, watching garbage like *EastEnders* and *Brookside*!'

Sally rearranged herself on the floor, three feet from the TV, book in lap, phone to ear. Her dad wasn't that bad. In fact, Sally thought her dad was lovely really, in a lumpy, lardy, couldn't-care-less kind of way. But it seemed the correct Chaotic way of mourning was anger and insult, so Sally chose to ignore the attack – just this once.

'But the pictures on the telly . . .' Sally said, awkwardly flipping the *Tads to Frogs* pages with one hand.

'Forget the telly; the telly's lying. When did you last see Chaos on the telly? When were Frog last on the telly? Or the radio? Or in a newspaper? They're only on the telly now because the Establishment's warmongering. The Net, Sally, the Net. Ewan Hughes is right in front of me now; he is on my screen and it's happening. The revolution has started.'

'What revolution?'

'Don't you get it? Hasn't your *dad* explained it? Or is he too busy scrabbling around on dodgy building sites because he can't be bothered to get a proper job?'

If it wasn't for his Internet, information, books and CD collection, Sally would dump Damon. Tragedy or no tragedy.

'We're talking about assassination. Chaos was murdered. His death is a corporate, capitalist, Establishment propagandist plot!' Damon bellowed in her ear. 'Now, I'm going to Whitehall. Are you coming?'

'Why Whitehall?'

'Because Ewan Hughes says so.'

Sally was thoroughly confused. Life had been so much easier with Oasis. She held the phone to her ear as she watched her dad come home and stumble up the stairs, muttering something about flu to her mum. He looked terrible. Sally looked back at the TV screen. A woman was shouting, telling people to go home. She looked familiar too.

'No, I can't come to Whitehall. My dad wants me to stay at home.'

Sally was beginning to wish Ewan Hughes didn't look familiar at all. If Chaos *was* murdered, then . . . what next? The news had moved on to the beginnings of riots and gathering angry crowds. Chaos's death a corporate, capitalist, Establishment propagandist plot? Why, for Christ's sake!

Chapter 1

May 1970 – thirty years earlier

The knocking in Ewan's dream continued for a couple of seconds before he heard Sarah's voice and realised it wasn't a dream at all.

'Ewan, get up and open the door, you lazy sod!'

Sarah. The beautiful creature with big green eyes and long, thick, tousled blonde hair, and sexy, arty-tart clothes and a perfect body, almost boyish (small breasts, thin hips, nice legs, not much bum – just the way he liked 'em), was knocking on his door.

Oh my God! he thought. Ewan sat up too quickly and screwed up his face. He hated mornings – mornings hurt. He opened his eyes. Panic set in. Self-centred, stuck-up, snobby, sexy, stunning Sarah would want to come in. Or rather she wouldn't. His student room was a *pigsty.*

He glanced over at Birmingham Dave's bed. Dave was already up and off and doing something clever. Ewan was alone. He'd never been alone with Sarah before.

He'd fantasised, though.

Ewan threw back the bedclothes. He had approximately ten seconds to jump out of bed, have a bath and a shave, wash and cut his hair, clean his teeth, spring-clean the room, change his personality and his life story, *and* find his lucky underpants.

Why was she knocking?

Or he had approximately ten seconds to remember that she was *Jonathan's* girlfriend and banish all thoughts of underpants (lucky or otherwise) to the nether regions of his disgusting and treacherous mind.

Ewan pulled the bedclothes back round him. She wasn't knocking for him. She hated him. She was just knocking. Bitch. Treated him like shit because, to a shopkeeper's daughter, 'son of a miner' didn't have the same ring as 'son of a lord'. Treated him like shit because she was too unimaginative to read *Lady Chatterley's Lover*, see the error of her ways and fall into his arms where she belonged. Ewan snorted at the image of Sarah falling into his arms – he'd drop her, of course. He was only obsessed with her because he couldn't have her. Only obsessed because he wasn't good enough. *He* wasn't the kind of person universities were built for; he didn't know the rules, had no right to be there and was supposed to be *grateful* for the privilege. Or so *she* thought. But *she* hadn't worked so hard to get somewhere she didn't belong, mixing with friends she felt socially inferior to. *She* wasn't studying dull-and-full-of-morons geography and being the laughing stock of the rest of the student body. *She* was a bitch. History of art – what kind of an acceptable and laudable subject was that? Ewan looked around the room and shook his head. There was *no way* she was going to come in – to his room *or* his life.

He stared at the door as Sarah knocked again. Obsessed? No. He was totally *crazy* about her. He creaked out of bed and struggled into his beloved greatcoat, opened the door a crack and squinted blearily at Sarah standing in the harsh light of the halls of residence corridor.

'What?' He scowled.

Sarah pushed past him and barged her way into his room. He smelt of stale sweat and sleep. She blinked, blushed, and knew this was a mistake. She should have told him the news at the door, left him to dress and waited for him downstairs, or outside. She and Ewan had *never* been alone together; they went out of their way to avoid it. But this was a crisis. Nothing could possibly happen in a crisis.

Sarah sat gingerly on the bottom of Ewan's bed, her hands held up like a scrubbed surgeon warding off germs as her eyes scanned the shambolic room. It smelt. It smelt of two lads who were only on nodding terms with the launderette. It smelt of stale fish and chips, stale bodies and stale air. She grimaced at the filthy cups, overflowing bin, layers of dust and dirt and rubbish, and tried to ignore the growing excitement between her legs.

'Jonathan's dad's died,' she said.

'So shouldn't you be with Jonathan?' Ewan said.

Sarah looked up with instant irritation. He was still standing by the door. His untidy hair, almost curly, almost black, pointing a wayward west. His normally animated and intelligent face sleep-creased and sullen, with two sunken, dark-ringed buttons where sparkling, get-away-with-murder brown eyes should be. His amphetamine-thin (naked?) body hidden in the depths of that familiar, overlarge, horrible, itchy grey coat. How could that possibly be sexy? How could that possibly turn her on? God, he annoyed her. Everything he did and everything he said. And he was *Welsh*, for God's sake!

'Jonathan's gone mad,' she said. 'He's destroying his flat. He wouldn't let me in.'

'So you came to me?'

'I need you.' Sarah looked fully into Ewan's face, reddened and crossed her legs. 'Jonathan needs you,' she corrected herself.

9

Ewan stood two feet away and hugged his coat close to his body. It was reasonable to get an erection when you'd just woken up. Easily explained should she ask, should she notice. Of course, if she did ask, if she did notice, it was also reasonable to lose the power of speech and die of total embarrassment. Ewan's head pounded as he tried to concentrate on the news, not the length of thigh on display when Sarah crossed her legs. Tried to concentrate on poor old Jonathan; the last thing he needed was a mate worrying about premature ejaculation, worrying about shooting his spunk all over the gold-digging bitch – don't even think about that!

Ewan needed to get dressed. Sarah seemed rooted to the bed (*his* bed – God!) so he turned away, one hand holding the coat like a lifeline while the other picked up a shirt. He looked at it, she looked at it, they both saw it: the black line of dirt round the frayed collar. Ewan had never seen such a disgusting shirt; this wasn't his, was it? Sarah stared at it, then shifted position and crossed her legs tighter. Ewan looked at her face, the disdain on it clearly showing. He felt judged, felt her scorn for everything he was and everything he couldn't be. If he didn't hate her so much, he would swear that he fell in love with her the first time he saw her.

Then she said the worst thing possible.

'We have to be quick.'

Ewan wasn't sure if she meant quick to comfort Jonathan or quick to fuck. He didn't have time to ask. Who started it, who made the first move, neither of them knew. Ewan was surprised to find Sarah's face against his, her hands pulling his head towards her mouth, and Sarah was surprised to feel Ewan's hand up her skirt, pushing her already wet knickers aside.

It was quick. But they'd had six months' foreplay.

★

Jonathan picked his way over the shattered glass of the coffee table, ripped books, wrecked record collection and redundant table leg, rested his elbows on the window sill and looked out over Ridgmount Gardens. The quiet little street was deserted. That was how it should be: Jonathan alone in the silence, stuck in a bubble, while a hundred yards away in Gower Street, in Tottenham Court Road, in the centre of London, life was going on without him. The rage was gone now. All that remained was a ruined flat, a feeling of injustice and the spectre of Tadley Hall looming large.

Jonathan turned from the window and looked about him. No reason to clear up; once he was back in Ludlow playing the new lord, he doubted he'd return. He unthinkingly righted the overstuffed armchair and noticed a pile of papers lying beneath it; they were remarkably unscathed. He picked them up, scanned them, and remembered how normal life had been an hour ago. He automatically hand-combed his sweat-damp sandy-brown hair, smoothed down his clothes, sat in the chair and started reading, started studying. It was a waste of time, but it felt better – it felt much, much better.

Jonathan opened the door to Ewan and Sarah half an hour later. All three appeared their usual selves. A little pale perhaps, a little dishevelled, but their usual selves nonetheless.

It should have been awkward. The prospect of embarrassed silence or stilted words of regret hovering on the threshold. Sarah waiting for Ewan to throw a gleeful spanner in the works. Jonathan waiting for the platitudes of sympathy. Ewan not knowing what to say, or when or how. But Jonathan's raised eyebrow invited them in, so Ewan stepped over the debris of the trashed flat, shook his head with a mix of disbelief and admiration, grinned at Jonathan and said with matter-of-fact irreverence, 'The old man kicked the bucket then, has he?'

Jonathan collapsed in hysterical laughter. His best friend always knew exactly what to say.

Ewan exchanged a brief guilty glance with Sarah, and decided to say nothing. Yet.

Chapter 2

Tadley Hall, the grotesque monster of a place, loomed larger as Jonathan drove nearer, the sudden silence of his four friends palpable. Parapets and porticoes, columns and steps, windows and windows and windows, the Palladian symmetry and simplicity trying to soften the screaming, neurotic opulence. Built by an ancestor on an ego trip and embellished and enhanced by sons proving their superiority over their fathers. Jonathan hated it, and a quick glance in the rear-view mirror confirmed that Ewan hated it too. Jonathan felt ashamed.

Sarah whispered, 'Wow!'

'Bloody hell, Jonathan, your heating bills must be enormous!' Birmingham Dave said.

Dave never saw what the others saw, or felt what the others felt. Dave didn't see the house – he saw the structure. He didn't see the politics – he saw the plumbing, and the wiring, and the use or misuse of energy. It was what Birmingham Dave was good at: seeing things sideways. Dave was a natural born mechanic. A solid bear of a chap with a sad-dog face, an innocence and honesty that Ewan said bordered on criminal, and a genius for physics. In ordinary, everyday life, though, Dave was the most *stupid* person Jonathan had ever met.

Jonathan smiled grimly as he flashed a glance at Miriam, the cleverest person he'd ever met. Miriam nodded her head and smiled back in sympathy. Miriam understood. She knew how Jonathan felt, sitting in the car, Tadley Hall in front of him, Ewan Hughes behind him. Miriam understood everything as far as Jonathan was concerned. Well, she understood *him*, anyway.

'Enormous, Dave, but still cold,' Jonathan said, checking the rear-view mirror. Ewan stared at the house and Jonathan wanted to die.

Fuck, was all Ewan could think. He'd known what to expect but Tadley Hall was . . . *fuck*. It was unreal. It was a house in a film or on the television. It was a house he'd point to in a magazine and sneer, '*That's* what's wrong with capitalism.' And he was now supposed to go into it. The thought scared him to death. He stared at the stern-looking elderly woman at the top of the entrance steps and prayed it wouldn't be Jonathan's mum. She wore a severe black dress that looked almost Fascist and stood with rigid back and perfect posture, flanked by two younger women in black skirts and white blouses. A Benita Mussolini posing with soft heavies. Jonathan got out of the car.

'Is that his mum?' Dave whispered.

'I think that's the housekeeper, Margaret,' Miriam said.

Ewan watched Jonathan, awkwardly formal, in conversation with Margaret the housekeeper, and hoped Sarah wouldn't turn round and look at him – he was convinced he was shrinking.

'His mum lives abroad somewhere, with her fourth husband,' Sarah said, keeping her eyes on Jonathan.

'*Fourth*?' Dave queried.

'Or fifth, something like that.'

Sarah got out of the car and Miriam followed, turning hastily to the lads to whisper, 'Just treat it like a posh hotel.'

14

Dave and Ewan exchanged clueless shrugs. They'd never been in a posh hotel – or any kind of hotel for that matter. Ewan shrank down in his seat as his nervous laughter erupted.

'Oh Christ,' he said, 'hasn't he got a shed we can sleep in?'

Once the staff were out of sight, Ewan and Dave quietly disappeared. Though they'd experienced neither, for them Tadley Hall was more like a boarding school than a posh hotel, and therefore required sly muttering, idiot giggling and sneaking off somewhere for a smoke.

All Jonathan could find was their shoes.

The place was *so* unwelcoming. Some rooms looked like stage sets, formal and theatrical, and definitely out of bounds, so they'd settled on an empty, cold, neglected room at the end of a long corridor of empty, cold, neglected rooms. It seemed private and out of the way but . . .

Ewan and Dave jumped off some tea chests and almost stood to attention a second after Miriam's head appeared round the door.

'Bloody hell, Miriam, can't you knock?' Dave complained, trying to calm his thumping heart.

'There is a smell of dope all down the corridor!' Miriam hissed.

As she joined them Ewan noticed that she too was barefoot. So even well-to-do Miriam was tiptoeing like an intruder. That surprised him. Ewan didn't think Miriam was scared of *anything*. With a face too intelligent to be pretty, and sensible clothes, sensible shoes and shapeless frizzy black hair, Miriam was too intelligent for men, too sensible for women, and far too clever to care. But when Ewan once called her a humourless frump the outrage of her reply silenced him for a week, and Ewan had respected and feared her ever since.

15

She took the joint from behind his back and, annoyed though she seemed, sucked in a couple of drags. She was also alone, which meant Jonathan and Sarah were alone, which meant . . . Ewan took back the joint and sucked hard, itching to finish it in order to roll another.

'How on earth can people live in these places?' Miriam wondered. 'I expected to be impressed but I just feel . . .' She scanned the room; it was large, empty apart from tea chests and packing cases, nice ornamental cornices, cut-glass chandelier – cold, neglected, weird. Miriam looked at Dave and Ewan. *'Alone,'* she said. 'Jonathan doesn't want to be here *alone.'*

Dave and Ewan nodded, understanding their duty over the next couple of days.

'Jonathan hates this place more than I do,' Miriam muttered as she sat down on a packing case.

Dave nodded.

'Yeah, but not as much as I do,' Ewan said, hogging the joint.

Sarah loved it. But then Jonathan was being very selective in what he showed her. Jonathan's father had been antisocial at the best of times and in the final years of his life he had been reclusive, tolerating only Margaret as his live-in staff, so ninety per cent of Tadley had been uninhabited. Jonathan thought that might give the impression of impoverished gentry, which was fine for Miriam, fine for Dave, perfect for Ewan, but for Sarah? Sarah needed the Gainsboroughs and the Turners; she'd want the sixteenth-century Italian furniture, rococo panels and Queen Anne legs. And that was what Jonathan was showing her. And it was working.

As Sarah moved from room to room she became more elegant, her voice more polished. Jonathan relished Sarah's enthusiasm, his spirits lifting as he accompanied her.

'Maybe the place isn't so bad after all.'

'Isn't so bad? Jonathan, it's beautiful!'

He smiled. Isn't so bad with Sarah in it, swanning up the stairs pretending to be Grace Kelly. Isn't so bad with his friends in it, somewhere, shoeless. With ghosts and memories temporarily on hold. No, not so bad. Maybe this was all Tadley needed. Friends injecting some life and transforming it. Helping to make it his own. He could live in it then. Maybe.

Jonathan followed Sarah into the master bedroom. He stood awkwardly as she sat on the bed, his father's bed, now his own. She bounced slightly, then lay on it, luxuriating, her hands smoothing the eiderdown, her head pressing into the softness of the pillow.

'Come and join me,' he wanted her to say, wanting the impetus to move. He was supposed to want her, *did* want her, loved her, but his father's bed – this was where the feeling of alienation was strongest. This was where the feeling almost hurt. His smile faded. He jammed his hands into his pockets and turned towards the window.

Think about something else, Jonathan, think about death – that'll cheer you up. He did. It didn't.

There was Ewan, though. And Ewan definitely did cheer him up. Ewan Hughes and Birmingham Dave running around the grounds. Running, screeching, laughing. Stoned, I bet, thought Jonathan. His smile returned, but this time a slight one, the sort he got when he was lost in some pleasant, private thought.

Sarah saw it and knew he was watching Ewan. Jonathan only ever got that strange sort of smile when he was watching Ewan. If Ewan wasn't watching Jonathan, of course. She got up, joined Jonathan at the window, and wordlessly watched what Jonathan was watching. She tried to create the scene, delicately resting her hand on his shoulder. Master and mistress of all they surveyed. Her clothes weren't right, of course; she needed something long and flowing.

Then Birmingham Dave fell headlong into the rose garden and that was their cue. A shared laugh, eye contact, sudden sexual stirrings, followed by the slow, romantic kiss and the manoeuvred stumble towards the bed.

Later Jonathan slept while Sarah went on another tour of the house, this time more fleeting. She found Ewan in one of the bathrooms, sitting on the floor rolling a joint. The look on his face suggested the hash was an attempt to top up his humour.

Ewan stopped rolling and stared at Sarah for a few seconds. Jonathan's name wasn't mentioned but the argument was brewing in his eyes. Sarah flickered her attention to the bathroom's decor and tried to change the subject.

'Where's Miriam?' she asked.

'Don't know. Skulking around somewhere being serious, I imagine.'

'She's not always serious.'

'She's always serious.'

'She just likes to—'

Ewan interrupted her. 'Did you come to talk about Miriam?'

'No.' Sarah blushed. 'What about Dave?'

'Having his grazes looked at by what's-her-name the housekeeper.'

'Margaret.'

'That's the one,' Ewan said. He stuffed the rolled joint into his coat pocket and stood up.

Sarah giggled nervously. 'We saw him fall into the roses; we watched you from—'

'Yeah, enough about that,' Ewan interrupted again. 'Get your knickers off and tell me what he did.'

18

Sarah's face tightened as Ewan roughly pulled at her clothes. She could have asked him to stop, told him to smoke the joint and mellow out first, not be so rough. But his mood was strange, half dismissive, half vengeful, and Sarah thought she understood why. Yesterday he'd thought he couldn't compete with Jonathan, and today he was confronted by overwhelming proof that he couldn't. She could have told him otherwise. She could have told him that Jonathan made love to her with consideration, with tenderness, almost tentatively. She could have told him that it was nice but it wasn't hot and hard and angry; it wasn't explosive. She didn't think about it later and get turned on all over again. She didn't want to fuck and fuck and fuck with Jonathan the way she did with Ewan. She didn't itch with excitement every time she looked at him, thought about him, touched him. She could have explained all that, but she didn't.

Ewan sloped into the dining room later than the others, not willing to admit he'd got hopelessly lost. He made his way across the imposing, wood-panelled room, walked the length of the long, highly polished table and pulled out an elegantly ornate wooden chair at one of five cutlery-laden, plate-cluttered, silver and bone china place settings. His mother's voice screamed, 'Don't touch! Don't touch!' He sat down and grinned at Jonathan sitting at the head of the table. He glanced fleetingly at Sarah. Her eyes were fixed on her hand, clasped round Jonathan's, emphasising their lovey-dovey togetherness. Ewan felt the rising bile of jealousy and dismissal but swallowed it. Argument or not, Sarah *was* right: normality was what Jonathan needed. The stab in the back could come later. Although Ewan doubted the knife would be in *Jonathan's* back.

'I made it you know; I helped make it,' Birmingham Dave enthused. He smelt strongly of TCP, his hands and face were covered in Elastoplast and a bandage was wound round his head for no other reason than Dave thought it looked good. Nobody mentioned it.

Ewan wondered how to appear normal when he felt anything but as he patted Dave's shoulder in mock congratulation.

'You helped prepare dinner, Dave?' Jonathan asked.

Ewan watched Jonathan blink rapidly, as though caught off guard. He smiled as Jonathan glanced with a slight, almost worried expression in Ewan's direction.

'Something wrong with that, Your Lordship?' Ewan asked, a sly glint forming in his eye as he realised that the most normal thing in the world was to take the piss out of Jonathan – and, hopefully, get in a few digs at Sarah at the same time. That was normal. That was what Ewan did. That was what Jonathan loved.

'No, not at all. Just . . . no, nothing wrong.' And, trying to ease his embarrassment and change the subject, Jonathan added, 'And please don't call me that, Ewan; I really do hate all that lordship nonsense.'

'Okay, Your Eminence,' Ewan said.

'*Just* what?' Dave asked.

Jonathan faltered. 'I'm just surprised that Margaret . . . a guest helping to . . .'

It took Ewan only a split second to realise: Margaret, kitchen, Dave, downstairs, upstairs. Dave's battle with the rose bush was a godsend. Jonathan would love the embarrassment and Sarah's social ladder would lose a couple of rungs. Ewan jumped in.

'You know what I'm thinking, Your Worship?' He grinned. 'It strikes me that if upstairs went downstairs then downstairs should come upstairs.' Ewan's grin broadened, goadingly. 'Or is she going to just stand there and watch us eat?'

Ewan knew he'd hit the spot as Jonathan's smile turned into a grimace and his eyes sparkled with watery embarrassment.

'Have I done something?' Dave asked.

'I think Ewan wants Margaret to join us for dinner,' Miriam explained.

Dave thought for a second and nodded his approval. Ewan gleefully noticed Sarah's petulant frown as she let go of Jonathan's hand, sat back and folded her arms.

Jonathan said, 'She wouldn't want to.'

'Ask her, Your Holiness,' Ewan challenged.

'It's not –'

'Done?'

'– as simple as that.'

'What's complicated about it?'

Jonathan opened his mouth to speak, realised it *wasn't* that simple and closed it again. He liked Margaret, had known her all his life, knew her perhaps better than he'd known his own mother and father. As a child he had, like Dave, gone down and helped, made cakes mostly, biscuits, been allowed to lick the bowl. She'd had time for him, patience. Elastoplast, like Dave was now wearing, Jonathan had worn. 'Let's put a plaster on it,' Margaret would say, making him feel special, turning a cut knee into something to be proud of, something worth having. And her late husband, Jack, showing Jonathan how to plant seeds, helping him water his sunflowers, standing together admiring their height. His own father had never had the time or the inclination to stand and admire the height of Jonathan's sunflowers. His own mother had never put a plaster on Jonathan's knee.

'What's complicated about it, oh great Toad of Toad Hall? Oh great Tadpole of Tadley?' Ewan asked again.

Jonathan knew full well that *nobody* could beat Ewan in the socialist, egalitarian, 'come the revolution, brother' argument that he was so fond of having. He also knew that saying he didn't know *why* but the thought *horrified* him would be like giving Ewan a loaded gun. So Jonathan said nothing, looked up, maintained eye contact and fixed a smile.

'Must be incredibly complicated then,' Ewan goaded.

'Leave it, Ewan,' Miriam said.

Ewan turned to Miriam and felt his sense of humour ebb. Miriam had that look in her eye. It meant the joke was wearing thin and she'd cut him down to size if necessary. Ewan hated that look. But he hated Sarah's snobbism more.

'Nothing complicated about it at all.' Ewan tapped his leg impatiently. 'It's simple. You just want to be lord of the manor don't you, Your Frogness? You want to maintain the status quo, with yourself firmly at the top of the pile, having your servants and lackeys running around for you. All that garbage you spouted, it's just bloody hot air, isn't it?'

'I think you're being unfair, Ewan,' Sarah said.

Ewan turned on her with a sneer. 'Why? You think this is right, do you? Having servants waiting on us? Yes, you probably do.'

'I think Jonathan needs time to—' Sarah started.

Ewan interrupted, all trace of humour vanished as their private argument spilt in. 'What? Get used to it? Learn to live with it?'

'Why not? What's wrong with it?'

'Oh, do you want a list?'

'It's only because you're jealous!'

'Of what exactly, Sarah?'

Ewan glared at her. Sarah was still sitting, arms folded, solidly obstinate, her face set and her eyes blazing, daring him to push it. He would have done, but he could feel the others' eyes on them, waiting with the usual impatience as he and Sarah fired off at each other. Trouble was, it wasn't the usual fight.

'Ask her, Jonathan,' Ewan demanded, his eyes still on Sarah's as he sat back in his chair.

'I'll ask her; she likes me,' Birmingham Dave said, springing to his feet and disappearing through the door before anybody realised what was happening.

Ewan wondered what had possessed him to come up with such a stupid idea. He'd wanted the argument, not the woman sitting at the table. The *last* thing he'd wanted was the woman sitting at the table. He stared into his bowl as Margaret and Dave served the first course, soup. The silence was unbearable. And he knew it was going to get worse. She was going to start chatting. As soon as she sat down it would be like back home in Maerdy, the neighbours and the aunts and his mother's friends. Sitting around, wittering on, drinking cups of tea and talking small-minded, small-town small talk. Perfectly contented with their draggy, tedious, TV and gossip-filled lives. Shot in the foot, Ewan thought to himself. I've just shot myself in the bloody foot. He glanced furtively at Margaret as she worked her way round the table. She was old and starchy, her white hair pulled back so severely it looked as though it might induce a permanent headache – she certainly looked pained, her lips pursed as though laughter were a foreign language. And she hovered. Clutching a bowl and debating which side of the table to sit on.

Margaret sat down next to him and Ewan prayed for death as everybody started eating their soup. The only sound was the unusually loud, echoing clatter of spoons.

What seemed like half an hour later Ewan heard Miriam's voice. 'Have you worked here long?' 'Yes,' Margaret said.

Three hours went by. Ewan's soup bowl wouldn't empty. Nobody's soup bowl would empty. Ewan wished his mother was there with her friends and wittering neighbours; they'd know what to talk about. The time was *dragging* and it was all his fault.

'Were you here when Jonathan was born?' Sarah asked.

'Yes,' Margaret said.

There was still soup in the bowl. The soup wouldn't *go*. Hours went by and it was still soup. This was stupid, this was awful, and all because Sarah was a bitch and Jonathan was rich and Ewan couldn't handle it.

'That must have been . . . interesting,' Sarah commented desperately.

'Yes,' Margaret said.

Ewan risked a peek at the others. They were either willing their soup to disappear or throwing pleading, surreptitious glances at Jonathan. Birmingham Dave obviously thought the whole affair would appear splendid if he just kept a broad smile plastered on his face throughout. Don't, Dave, you're making me laugh, Ewan begged silently. His leg waggled beneath the table. Look at the soup; nothing funny about soup.

'Yes,' Jonathan said, his voice cracking as he realised it was going to be wrong even before he said it. 'Yes, Margaret has been with us for ever, it seems.'

Everything seemed to stop. Ewan glanced up. Jonathan looked like he'd been shot, his face frozen, fearfully wondering if anybody else had caught the double meaning. Ewan's leg waggled furiously as he saw Dave's smile broaden. He watched Miriam put a hand elegantly up to her mouth and bite it. Sarah wouldn't look at him. She wouldn't look at anybody. She was looking at her soup. Nothing funny about soup. Ewan's shoulders started to twitch, then shake. His head slumped onto his arms and he started giggling hysterically. The others followed suit. Jonathan struggled to rescue the situation.

'I believe you were employed by my grandfather when you were, what? Younger than us even?'

'That's right, sir, younger,' Margaret said. 'But I believe your friends are sharing a joke that you and I have missed. Perhaps one of them would care to explain it?'

Ewan fought desperately to get himself under control. The kicks from Dave and muffled snorts from Sarah were not helping.

'Yes, well, it's been a long day, Margaret, the drive from London and so forth. I think we're probably a little bit . . . tired,' Jonathan suggested lamely.

That didn't help either.

'Perhaps this young man here? I've not had the pleasure of speaking to him yet,' Margaret politely persisted, turning to Ewan. 'Could you explain the joke?'

That helped. Ewan's thoughts shrank to the eight-year-old caught out at school, singled out as the ringleader responsible for whatever pranks he and his friends had been up to. He had the urge to say, 'It wasn't me, miss, it was Jonathan,' in that childish, half-surly, half-defensive way he used to. Instead he muttered, 'I don't know.' Managing, just, to omit the word 'miss'.

'Well, no matter,' Margaret said. 'Whatever it was, it doesn't seem to be funny any more.'

Ewan recognised contempt when he saw it, and he saw it in the smile Margaret gave him before she rose to collect the soup bowls and make her way back downstairs.

'Students,' Margaret thought. So stupid, so easy.

She bustled about in the kitchen, preparing the dishes for the main course and trying to keep her mind blank. At sixty she found change daunting – retirement was frightening, and the thought of new employers and stiff, starchy servitude made her back ache. But those were the only options. Jonathan would sell. She knew it. Tadley held nothing for him but memories of a lonely child, gentle and sensitive and out of place. Becoming more aloof and introspective as he was packed off to prep school, boarding school and university. Rejecting the Oxbridge route because he wanted to be with 'real people'. Real people didn't live at Tadley. Real people were like the bunch upstairs, know-nothing twenty-year-olds, no doubt wanting to discuss Bob Dylan and the Beatles and expecting her to listen and be grateful. Trying to change the world by stripping her of her uniform and her purpose and her reason for being there.

Margaret didn't want her world changed. She wanted dignity and respect; she wanted routine and ritual. She wanted what she had. She didn't want stupid students with stupid ideas invading her house and feeding her fears. *Her* house. Margaret smiled slightly and sat down for a moment as a feeling of grief and tiredness engulfed her. She did think of it as *her* house. She loved every inch of it and she had a say in none of it. Not now, not any more.

Margaret forced herself up and loaded the dishes onto the dumb waiter. She tried to wipe away her memories, her grief and resentment, and tried to remember her place. Jonathan was the boss, at the moment, and Jonathan's friends were real people. And Dave seemed a nice lad. And the others were probably nice too. She should have been friendlier. She should have chatted. She knew nothing about Bob Dylan, but she liked 'Eleanor Rigby', and that was a Beatles song.

★

'I knew it was a bad idea,' Jonathan lectured. 'I said from the outset that things were complicated, but no, you had to embarrass the poor woman, humiliate her in an awkward situation.'

Dave and Miriam sat silently and waited for the storm to pass. Sarah tugged at Jonathan's sleeve but he wouldn't sit down. He was up and angry – a bit too angry, Sarah thought, but Ewan wasn't helping.

Ewan sat, arms folded and obstinate, stubbornly scowling. 'You've always said you hated the situation.'

'I have to think of others, Ewan! I have to think how Margaret might feel. She's been here years; it's her home, her life. How do you think she'd feel if I said, "Oh, Ewan thinks I shouldn't have servants, so off you go, toddle off, pretend you don't exist till he's gone"?'

Ewan and Jonathan rarely argued, and if they did it was only intellectually or politically; it was never personal. Sarah felt that this argument was personal, and somehow her fault. She gave up on Jonathan's sleeve and stared guiltily at the table instead, concentrating on the plates, white with silver trim – she wondered if it was real silver.

'I never suggested she "toddle off" or "pretend" anything, Jonathan. I suggested she join us for dinner. I think that's perfectly reasonable. And I still do. And I wasn't talking about a couple of days – I was talking about you and her eating up here permanently.'

'She doesn't want to!'

'Or you don't.'

Jonathan threw his arms up in exasperation. Sarah thought he was going to sit down, but instead he leant over the table and jabbed his finger at Ewan.

'You know nothing about Tadley, Ewan, so shut up. If you want to change the world I suggest you go home to your little mining town in the Rhondda and start there. Bulldoze the bingo halls perhaps, blow up the TVs during the soap operas, educate the peasants, teach them to think, but do it somewhere where you know what you're talking about!'

Jonathan straightened up and sat down. 'Now, can we please declare this subject closed,' he said.

Sarah glanced up as Ewan stood and left the room. Followed by Dave and Miriam. Sarah hesitated, not sure what to do. Finally she patted Jonathan's arm gently and said, 'It was the word "peasants".' She shook her head. 'That was going too far.' And she left.

They were all in Ewan's room. Jonathan listened at the door and tried to make out what they were saying. Their voices were muffled, nothing distinct, occasional giggles. Smoking hash. He could smell it. He wanted to go in to apologise to Ewan. But he wanted Ewan alone. It had to be tonight. Tomorrow he had solicitors, accountants, meetings, the estate to sort out, the funeral, his mother. His mother was flying in from Belize in a couple of days, and Jonathan was dreading it. Everything was too much, but the worst thing was that Ewan wasn't his friend. Jonathan couldn't handle that. He listened; they giggled. Were they laughing at him?

He should just walk away, go to bed and hope to catch Ewan at breakfast, or before. Or knock. Knock on the door and ask to speak to him alone. Sounds formal. Too formal. They'd laugh. Ewan would be awkward, refuse to come. He'd sit there cross-legged on the bed with that challenging light in his eye. Make me, he'd think. Make a fool of yourself first, Jonathan Jo.

Jonathan dithered. He started to walk away. He came back, listened at the door. Walked away, came back, burst into the room.

Everybody jumped.

'Just wanted to say good night,' Jonathan blurted before backing out. He quickly closed the door and held it shut. His knuckles turned white on the handle and his head leant heavily on the wood. He listened to the silence before the eruption of giggles, then he went to bed.

They hadn't been laughing at him. They'd talked about him, briefly, but only long enough for Ewan to say that he wasn't really bothered about what Jonathan had said. The walking-out business had only been a gesture, a convenient excuse to avoid another eternity around the table with Margaret. 'And besides, his dad's just died. No point in getting sensitive when someone's dad's just died.'

They all agreed, muttered words like 'shame' and 'grieving process' and got out the dope. They fully expected Jonathan to join them. Somebody mentioned at one point that someone ought to go and get him, but no one noticed that nobody moved. And the conversation changed, things got forgotten, time disappeared and before anyone knew it, the munchies had taken hold and the Mission to Invade the Fridge was on. It was in the middle of Strategy Planning that Jonathan burst in. By then they'd forgotten about the earlier incident and thought it was going to be Margaret announcing (with an evil laugh) that she'd got wind of their dastardly but ingenious plans and was writing letters to their parents. Cause for hysterics, naturally. It was only while Brave Dave and Maverick Miriam were engaged somewhere downstairs in enemy territory raiding the fridge that Sarah thought seriously about Jonathan.

She'd waited ages, expecting Ewan to make a move as soon as they were alone. She'd expected one hand down her jeans, the other grabbing at her breast, expected to be pushed up against the door, rough, wordless, passionate.

She'd nearly died earlier. Her hips had jerked forward in an involuntary twitch of anticipation when Miriam had suggested they all go and Ewan had said no, he had to stay and guard the ammunition. What ammunition? 'Sarah. Sarah's the ammunition.' And he'd given her an 'I'm going to fuck you' look and half laughed, as Miriam had glanced suspiciously between the two of them. Miriam knows; Miriam's guessed, Sarah had thought as her groin throbbed and her face reddened.

But that was ages ago and Sarah was now *aching* to be fucked.

'I can always go to him, you know,' she said.

Ewan didn't reply. He lay on the bed and stared at the ceiling, miles away, ignoring her. Sarah felt like a desperate slag. Since yesterday, all she and Ewan had done was snatch time, create the opportunity, seek sordid seclusion and obsessively grab for each other. While Jonathan was making arrangements to return home, while Jonathan was packing, while Jonathan was sleeping. Most of the day and all of the night they'd fucked and argued and fucked and argued. And now Jonathan was safely next door and the others were downstairs, the time had been snatched, the opportunity created, and the bastard was staring at the ceiling, ignoring her.

'Jonathan. I can always go to Jonathan, you know. Right now,' she said again. She wanted to hit him. He wasn't supposed to behave like this; he was supposed to want her. Miriam and Dave were going to be back any minute; now there was not even enough time for a fumbled quickie with the added danger of being caught.

'Bastard,' she spat. 'Do something or say something, you bastard.' She finally hit him, punched him on the shoulder.

Ewan blinked and looked at her. He sat up, climbed over her to get off the bed, pecked her briefly on the cheek and ruffled her hair. 'I'm going to see Jonathan.' He grinned.

As he left, Sarah wanted to shout, 'Don't you dare fuck it up!' but thought if she tempted him, he might. Instead she hissed, 'I might just start to hate you!' as she threw a pillow at the closing door. 'If I don't already,' she muttered petulantly, grabbing another pillow, thrusting it between her legs and squeezing hard.

Jonathan was almost asleep, or had already been asleep, he wasn't sure which. All he was aware of was a presence in his room, a sudden heaviness pressing down on the side of the bed near his feet. His father. Jonathan didn't believe in ghosts but he knew it would be his father. He decided to keep his eyes shut and hope that the old goat got the message and departed properly like the departed were supposed to.

'You told me you hated this life.'

Jonathan stopped breathing for a second or two. His father with a Welsh accent?

'Told me you wanted to change it, turn your back on it, something.'

Jonathan was about to sit up and put the bedside lamp on, but thought better of it. Arguments weren't so easy in the dark, and he didn't want another argument. He relaxed back into his pillow and let Ewan continue.

'I wasn't trying to get at you, Jonathan. I don't want to put you down. So if I made you feel awkward tonight, I'm sorry. And if I made Margaret feel awkward tonight, I'm sorry for that too. But you did say you hated it; you did say you wanted to change it.'

Ewan wasn't trying to fight. Jonathan was surprised. Ewan was being quiet, gentle even, apologising. Jonathan was glad he hadn't put the light on; he liked this mood.

'I do hate it, Ewan. I've always hated it, but I don't know, it's not . . .'

31

'As simple as that?'

Jonathan paused. There'd been no edge to it, no cynicism. Ewan wasn't goading now.

'I'm sure it's not,' Ewan finished for him. 'You know, when you used to talk about Tadley Hall, when I took the piss and called you Jonathan Jo and everything, I used to think, What a wanker; he's got everything and still he moans.'

'I liked you calling me Jonathan Jo.'

'Did you? Well, it was sort of affectionate, I suppose.' Ewan laughed slightly. He sounded almost embarrassed. 'Anyhow, now that I'm here, can see what it's like . . .' Ewan hesitated.

Jonathan sat up, interested. 'What?'

'Well, I know it sounds daft, but – it's not cosy, is it?'

'Cosy?' Jonathan thought it strange that a word like 'cosy' should come out of Ewan's mouth.

Ewan backed off as though Jonathan had taken offence. 'Look, Jonathan, I'm stoned, I don't know what I'm talking about, and I'll have forgotten all about it in the morning. I'll wake up tomorrow and hate you again for calling me a peasant.'

'I didn't call you a peasant, I—'

'Whatever. It's not important. Half my friends and family are peasants, so what? I don't want to argue.'

'Neither do I.'

'So. What was I talking about?'

'The house,' Jonathan offered. 'It's got no life in it; it's too big, no character, no warmth, no people.'

Ewan paused slightly before adding, 'It's just that the rooms echo when you talk. You feel like you're being watched all the time. In a smaller house, everybody piled into the one room, you *know* you're being watched. But here . . . it's weird.'

'Do you think I should sell it?' Jonathan asked.

'Are you thinking of it?'

'Don't know.'

Ewan hesitated, then shrugged. 'Early days yet. Give yourself time to . . .'

'What?' Jonathan prompted. 'Get used to it? Learn to live with it?'

Jonathan started now. In Ewan's present mood he felt the urge to speak, wanted to talk, wanted to keep Ewan here on the edge of his bed – intimate.

'Look at me, Ewan. My father's just died and what am I doing? Having fun with my friends. I feel nothing. Nothing, except that it's a pain having to sort out the funeral and the estate. I'm sitting here and I've inherited all this – all these bricks and wood and furniture and . . . meaningless, meaningless crap. Is it right? Is it right that I'd rather be at college, doing something else? Is it right that I don't care? No, I do care. I do care because I feel trapped here. And you going on about Margaret sitting with us – that didn't even occur to me. That should be what I want. It wasn't, but it should be. And I want it to be, because the other way . . . I hate it. I loathe and detest it.'

'So change what you hate and stop feeling guilty,' Ewan said.

Jonathan burst into tears. A sudden explosion of grief poured out of him. He tried to stop, waving Ewan away in the darkness, trying to turn away, wanting to hide. Ewan moved forward, grabbed him, held him, and allowed him to cry. Jonathan buried his head in Ewan's neck, felt Ewan's body against his own, Ewan's arms around him. He felt safe, warm, loved. He desperately wanted Ewan to love him. Desperately wanted Ewan to stay.

'I don't want you to go,' Jonathan heard himself pleading through the sobs. 'I can't handle this on my own.'

'I'll be with you, Jonathan Jo,' Ewan gently replied. 'I'll be with you till it's over.'

Ewan woke and scratched his cheek. He pulled off the note Sellotaped to it and stared at Jonathan's pyjamas folded neatly on the pillow next to him. Jonathan himself was gone. It seemed quite late in the morning and Ewan was lying fully clothed on top of the bed. He felt exhausted already and all he'd done was scratch. He read the note:

Change what you hate and don't feel guilty. Yes. Thanks. J.

Ewan hadn't a clue what the note meant but the massive guilt and self-loathing he'd felt for the last couple of days steam-rollered back. Jonathan wasn't talking about Sarah, though. Folded pyjamas wasn't the action of a man consumed by jealousy, rage and murderous intent.

Folded pyjamas. Ewan snorted a slight, affectionate laugh and wearily closed his eyes. He felt like shit even before breakfast, terrible. He hated mornings. Mornings hurt.

Chapter 3

June 1970 – one month later

Ewan was shivering. He pulled his knees up to his chest, jammed his hands between his thighs, opened his eyes and took his bearings. The drawing room in grey metallic light, birdsong and heavy breathing punctuating silence – dawn. Ewan was curled, fully clothed, on a sofa. Sarah was about twelve feet away, semi-naked and wrapped in a blanket on a pile of cushions on the floor. Sarah was always about twelve feet away lately. It was nice. Sarah's eyes were open too, looking at him, smiling in a half-asleep, can't-be-bothered-to-pretend kind of way. That was nice too. Ewan returned the smile. He raised his arm, closed one eye and squinted at his watch.

'What time is it?' Sarah whispered.

'Quarter past dawn,' he replied, squinting with alternate eyes and getting nowhere.

Sarah giggled. Ewan grinned, shivered and gave up on the watch. He pushed his hand back between his thighs and drew his knees closer as he watched a man's arm snake from behind Sarah's body and drape itself over her, the hand cupping her breast. Neither commented.

Other bodies scattered around the room were inert, eyes

closed, asleep. Ewan couldn't count how many there were. What had started as a party for a few university friends and old schoolmates had turned into a festive free-for-all of freaks, goons and weirdos (plus a few brain-sharp drug dealers supplying God knows what, but Ewan happily tried it all). And Sarah – so it seemed to Ewan – happily tried all the freaks, goons and weirdos. Free Love. Sarah had decided it and so it had happened – mostly when Ewan was too stoned to leave the room but not too stoned to watch. The result of the long-standing whispered venom of an argument that raged between them in linen cupboards, toilets and out-of-the-way private cubbyholes. Sarah refusing to give up Jonathan, refusing to go back to university, refusing to be a couple. Nothing free or loving about it, though. Not free because the cost for Ewan was crushing humiliation. Not to mention the confusion and guilt of intense arousal he felt watching Sarah writhing with a succession of strangers. The confusion only eased with help from the dealers, which in turn lessened his libido, increased his passivity, confused Sarah and created a vicious circle. Not loving because Ewan was reduced to a voyeuristic private dick amongst a queue of public dicks. Private only because Jonathan was still his friend and Sarah was still (officially) Jonathan's and both of them were cowards.

Sarah gently lifted the guy's arm off her, wrapped the blanket around her and crawled about twelve feet across the room. She wedged herself onto the sofa and around Ewan's body, sharing the blanket between them. She held him, said, 'Love you,' and planted a kiss on his forehead. Ewan smiled, felt a bit warmer and drifted back to sleep. It was nice.

Eric pushed his straggly blond hair off his face, snorted the amphetamine and hoped the map was where he left it.

Otherwise the speed would kick in and, looking for the map, he'd start tidying the place, and cleaning it, and before he knew it the squat would be immaculate but they'd be late for the gig.

Eric didn't really need a map; he knew exactly where they were going – 'Tadley Hall, Shropshire, you can't miss it; big place, ask for Jonathan' – but he liked to check. Eric was quietly neurotic about checking everything. Quietly neurotic about getting to gigs on time and, if the truth be known, quietly neurotic about living in a clean and tidy squat.

Eric's leg twitched as the speed kicked in. He banished all thoughts of cleaning (just in case) and got up. He found the map easily.

'You in there, Jim?' he called, banging on the bathroom door. Of course. If there was a bath and a mirror Jim would be there. Preening, practising the pout, teasing his long dark corkscrew hair into a perfect picture of hirsute indifference and reflecting on stardom. Jim was always in the bathroom. Except when he was in the pub. Or in some girl. Oh, and occasionally he got up on stage.

And occasionally Nick got up.

Eric kicked Nick's bed with his foot. 'Are you getting up or what?' he shouted.

Nick mumbled something indecipherable and turned over. Eric knew it was useless. The only way to rouse Nick was to pull the bedclothes off. That meant touching the bedclothes, and Nick's room was the worst and everywhere else was a pigsty. Let Jim get him up, Eric thought, taking Nick's bass.

Eric started gathering the gear to load into the van. Later on he would also drive the van. And set up the gear when they got there. And pack it away. And drive back. All for the hour or so of piano playing in the middle. Eric was keen. And the others were head cases. With Sean being the biggest head case of all.

Which was why Eric, Jim and Nick refused to live with him and Sean lived with his mum.

Sean twitched. His body jittered when he walked, his brown eyes darted, his dark hair suggested comic electrocution and he looked – and probably was – a madman. But he could drum. And good drummers were difficult to come by.

'Fucking stately home,' Sean muttered as he finished loading his kit into the van and climbed into the back.

'It's going to be a blast,' Nick mumbled beneath his lank, greasy hair as he concentrated on rolling a joint.

'I'd like to fucking blast them, fucking debutantes and chinless fucking wonders,' Sean complained. He almost broke Jim's neck as he leant over the front seats to roll down the window. He knocked the half-rolled joint out of Nick's hand as he leant over further to blow his mother a kiss.

Jim, Nick and Eric said nothing and waved sweetly to Sean's mum.

'I've never had a debutante,' Jim said thoughtfully. 'Might be interesting – a blow job with a plum in her mouth.'

'Hmm, Marianne Faithfull, far out.' Nick nodded dreamily, trying to retrieve his joint from the debris of the van floor.

All four fell silent for a moment thinking about Marianne Faithfull.

'They're paying pretty good,' Eric said, starting up the engine. 'Young, students, end–of–term party, I think.'

'I hate fucking students,' Sean complained.

Jim, Nick and Eric said nothing but collectively sighed and wondered how many miles to Shropshire.

Tadley Hall – floodlit like a beacon of decadence. Eric had visions of the Four Horsemen of the Apocalypse riding up in a blaze of fear and glory. But there was nowhere to park. The whole length of the driveway, from the gatehouse at the bottom to the paths surrounding the house, was full. The van was stuck halfway, unable to go forward and with no room to turn round.

Sean got out and left the problem to Eric. Jim followed suit. Eric watched Nick slowly slip out of the van and abandon him. Eric sullenly turned and looked at all the gear in the back; he looked at the house and its distance from the van. Tadley Hall mocked. Eric thumped the steering wheel in disgust and wondered what kind of moron had a place this size and no bloody car park.

Tadley Hall was teeming with people. Eric had lost the rest of the band but found Dave. Dave thought they'd be playing in the ballroom but wasn't sure and suggested that Eric wait there while he went to find Jonathan. So Eric stood waiting in the ballroom for Dave or Jonathan or a band member to turn up.

'Want a drink?' A girl by his side, holding two bottles of whisky, offered him one. 'You look lost,' she added.

'We're the band,' Eric said, feeling stupid as the girl looked around for the other members, or the instruments, or the stage, or any possible sign that he might be a band at all. 'The Horsemen.' Eric felt even more stupid. 'The Four Horsemen of the Apocalypse.' Whose stupid idea was that?

The girl nodded. 'Great name, yeah.'

Eric remembered it had been his stupid idea and nodded back. 'We're just preparing to set up,' he said by way of explanation. 'Getting organised.'

'Yeah, they had a band the other night, apparently.' The girl looked around again. 'They're still here somewhere. Never played.' She then added helpfully, 'You should have a word with Jonathan.'

Eric smiled and grabbed one of the whisky bottles as the girl drifted off. It was going to be one of those nights. He took a swig of Scotch, glanced at his watch, looked around at everybody noisily stomping and singing along to 'Give Peace a Chance', and wondered whether to search for Dave and the band. Fuck it, let them find me, he decided, and he left the ballroom.

By 1 a.m. Eric had forgotten about the band and was having trouble remembering his own name. It was a hell of a party. So many different people doing so many different things in so many different rooms. He found a room full of meditating people cross-legged and om-ing. A room full of candles surrounding two naked people making love. Glazed trippers painting psychedelic murals in otherwise empty rooms. Swathes of muslin and cheesecloth strung from light fittings, picture frames and banisters like Bedouin tents. The stench of incense, patchouli, cannabis and somebody standing next to him with a bacon sandwich. Dimmed light and bright light and candlelight and strip lights and strobe lights and no light and red light. And the obligatory bubble lights – but in the least expected places. Topless girls and bottomless boys having innocuous conversations about the weather and Edward Heath. Rooms of music bleeding into other rooms of music and creating weird sounds. And a man with a beard, wearing a dress, holding up a hookah and saying, 'I've fixed the toilet.'

Eric had been in every room, apart from the one in front of him. What was it? He opened the door – a study, two people arguing. Eric would have left them to it except he overheard one of them say, 'Oh, come off it, Jonathan.'

'Jonathan!' Eric beamed, throwing his arms out in greeting. 'Finally, at last. We're the Four Horsemen of the Apocalypse.

When do we get paid?' He then collapsed in a heap on the floor.

'Do you see my point?' Miriam continued, gesturing towards Eric's prone body. 'It's gone too far, it's out of hand.' She had only been away a week, but sitting her finals had been easy compared to the last two or three hours of 'sightseeing'. Either the madness at Tadley had increased tenfold, or her immunity had dissolved. Miriam was appalled.

'It's what we wanted, though,' Jonathan said defensively.

'Is it? Is it what you wanted?'

'What we all wanted,' he insisted.

'It's not what *I* want,' Miriam countered. 'Not what Dave wants, not what Margaret wants. The whole house is being overrun by . . . by . . .' Miriam struggled to find the words, as her finger waggled accusingly in Eric's direction. 'By deviants and drug addicts,' she managed to say.

'Yeah, but Ewan said—'

She interrupted him. 'Forget Ewan. Ewan is out of his skull, Jonathan. And as for Sarah – well!' Miriam shook her head in disgust. She stepped over Eric and marched to the door, waiting for Jonathan to follow. 'Come on, show me exactly what it is you wanted. And then give me one good reason why I should want to stay.'

Miriam stormed through the house, the mass of people fuelling her movement, her movement fuelling her rage. Jonathan followed, caught between apologising to the people Miriam knocked into and trying to appease her anger.

'Look!' she said at the entrance to the drawing room.

Jonathan obediently looked. Bodies. Stoned bodies, half-naked bodies, sexual bodies, seriously junked bodies. Strangers. And Sarah amongst them, between two men, talking, smiling, but their bodies close, their faces full of anticipation. If Eric had been awake he could have told them it was Jim and Nick. They often went in for threesomes: Jim doing most of the sex, Nick mainly watching, usually too stoned to manage anything physical.

'Is this what you wanted? Is this what you envisioned?' Miriam asked. The word 'envisioned' sounded like something dirty stuck to her shoe.

Jonathan saw Ewan in the corner, huddled amongst a small group of people all bent over something, burning something – another silver spoon being ruined. Ewan suddenly sat back, his eyes on Jonathan, as though Jonathan had called him. But Jonathan doubted if Ewan actually registered him, recognised him. Jonathan doubted Ewan was registering *anything*.

'No, of course not,' Jonathan managed to say, 'but . . .'

'But what?' Miriam asked.

'But . . . nothing.' Jonathan backed down: it *had* gone too far. 'You're absolutely right, Miriam. Something has to be done.'

'So do it!' she urged.

So do it. Do what? Ask them politely? 'Excuse me, old chap . . .' Threaten them? 'Miriam says . . .'

This was all Ewan's fault. Ewan Hughes was in heaven and all was wrong with the world. 'Let's have a party,' he'd said. He'd insisted. But for how long, Ewan? Weeks? Months? Till the money runs out? My money? Jonathan started to feel angry, cheated. He looked over at Sarah. And Sarah needs to be given less choice, he thought diplomatically as he watched Jim bend over her, kissing her, his hand fully up her skirt. Jealous? Me? No, not allowed. Jonathan's anger rose and he looked towards Ewan again. Ewan was watching Sarah too. Jonathan stopped, confused. Ewan watching Sarah, staring at her. No, not watching. Ewan's not watching. He can't be. He's just facing that direction.

42

'I'm sorry, Jonathan, I can't live like this,' Miriam said, calmer now, her point made. 'And I don't think Dave can, and I don't think you can.'

Jonathan looked at her. 'What if we do things properly, get rid of the hangers-on and freeloaders?'

Miriam jerked her head in Ewan's direction. 'All of them?'

'One way or the other.'

Miriam looked doubtful.

'It's just a question of finance.' Jonathan shrugged. 'If he hasn't got the money he can't buy the drugs. And, Miriam, I *know* he hasn't got the money.' He put on his most determined face but it convinced neither of them.

Margaret was mad at him as well, Jonathan could tell as soon as he entered the kitchen. She started stirring the sauce with more energy than was necessary. Dave lifted his eyebrows as he buttered the bread and gave his head a slight shake as if to say, 'You don't want to come in here, mate.' Jonathan dithered; he hated being in the doghouse – his permanent home lately. Margaret bustled about, purposefully ignoring him, until he had the audacity to pick at a bit of lettuce in a bowl. She moved across the kitchen and slapped Jonathan's wrist with such speed that even Birmingham Dave jumped. Margaret had long given up the master/housekeeper relationship.

'What do you want? What are you doing?' she asked tersely, distracted as a loud buzzing sound started up outside.

'I was thinking of having a meeting to—'

Jonathan stopped in mid-sentence as Margaret spun on her heel and marched out of the kitchen door towards the grounds, followed a second or two later by Jonathan and Dave, who collided in the doorway.

★

He looked monstrous. Standing in the middle of the floodlit lawn, wearing a protective helmet, protective overalls and protective gloves, with a huge chainsaw balanced on his hip. Half the rose garden had been decimated by the time Margaret arrived.

'Turn it off!' she bellowed above the noise.

He stood immobile, looking at her, the chainsaw buzzing menacingly in front of him.

'Turn it off!' Margaret yelled again, stepping closer. Dangerously close, Jonathan and Dave thought, clutching each other and inching forward.

The helmet shook its head and looked over the chainsaw, before holding it out towards Margaret. Jonathan and Dave moaned in fear as Margaret leant forward and found the *off* switch. The buzzing died as she grabbed the saw and waited for an explanation.

Sean lifted off the helmet and grinned. 'Nice bit of gear that. I just had to try it – it was begging me.'

Margaret turned furiously to Jonathan. '*Thinking* of having a meeting? No. We're *having* a meeting. And if it takes this chainsaw to shift those parasites, I'm using it!'

Eric opened his eyes slowly. His head hurt and he felt like shit. He was aware that he was on a floor, aware of a coat on top of him, aware of conversation around him, aware of the little plastic bag of pills that had just hit him on the nose and woken him. He slowly sneaked his hand out from under the coat and grabbed the bag, pulled it back under the coat, closed his eyes and listened to the conversation.

'That is the problem, don't you see? You're either up, down, high, low or just plain round the bend,' Jonathan was arguing.

'I'm only trying to get my head together,' Ewan replied. He muttered distractedly, 'Where'd they go?'

'Forget them, Ewan. It's got to stop. We need to talk, get things sorted out.'

'Okay, okay, Jonathan, but you shouldn't just knock things out of my hand. I can't find them now.'

'Forget them!' Jonathan bellowed alarmingly, making the whole room jump into silence and Eric clutch the little packet even tighter under the coat.

Ewan got up from searching under the desk and slumped back in his chair. He looked a wreck. He glared icily at Jonathan and glanced petulantly at Miriam, Dave and Margaret, taking in their disapproving faces.

'Well, let's get on with this meeting then,' he sneered, determined, if not to sulk throughout it, then at least to throw a spanner into it.

'What about Sarah? Isn't she coming?' Dave looked at the door.

Miriam coloured slightly. 'She was, um . . . busy. I didn't like to interrupt her.'

'Can't you have a word with her, Jonathan?' Dave asked.

'Yes, well, that was also the purpose of this meeting,' Jonathan began.

'She doesn't belong to Jonathan. What makes you think she belongs to Jonathan?' Ewan was demanding of Dave. 'It's her body; it belongs to her. It's got nothing to do with Jonathan what she does with it. Or you either, for that matter.'

Dave quietly defended himself. 'All I meant was it's worrying. I just worry about her, that's all.'

'Or you're just incredibly jealous because you're the only one in the whole place who hasn't had her,' Ewan countered.

Everybody winced, including Eric. Miriam had had enough. 'And what about you?' she asked.

'What about me?' Ewan scowled.

'You've "had her", have you?'

Ewan opened his mouth as though he were about to say something but he changed his mind. He jigged his foot a couple of times instead and stared at the desk and Jonathan's hands folded tightly on the top of it. The knuckles were turning white.

'Have you? Ewan?' Jonathan quietly asked.

Ewan looked away and turned his attention back to the floor and the search for his bag of pills, the leg jiggle increasing.

'Have you? Have you had sex with Sarah? Ewan?' Jonathan's question was slightly louder, a hint of anger creeping in.

'What Sarah does with her own body—' Ewan began.

'Have you?' Jonathan demanded, now fully angry.

'Is political,' Ewan finished. He sat up and stared straight at Jonathan with no hint of apology. 'The freedom to explore your own sexuality. Is there something wrong with that, Jonathan?'

'When?' Jonathan accused.

'When what?'

'When did you sleep with her?'

'Sleep with her?'

'Have sex with her? Fuck her?'

'As I already said, it's political.' Ewan could see that Jonathan was more than jealous. He could see that there was something other than anger in his face. Jonathan was losing it, badly. And Ewan was going to get punched any second now, he was sure of it.

'Women nowadays, well . . . Miriam would probably bear me out on this.' Ewan looked towards Miriam. 'You know, er . . . Women's liberation and stuff, sexual liberation, isn't that right, Miriam?'

Miriam said nothing, just glared back at him.

Bitch, he thought, she wants me to get punched. Ewan looked again at Jonathan, wondering whether getting out of his chair might help to avoid the punch or invite it. He decided to remain seated, go for broke, and cling to his belief that Jonathan hated violence more than he did.

'What's your problem, Jonathan? Yes, I've had her, loads of times. So what? What do you want? Do you want to own her? Do you think she's yours? Just because you've had sex with her? She was never yours. How can she be? It's her body, her mind, her choice, and her decision. Are you married to her or something? Is she your chattel? Your possession? I thought the days of the lord having his pick of the peasants were over, or are you just hoping to reinstate that one?'

Jonathan looked Ewan squarely in the eye and said, 'I loved you, Ewan Hughes.' He then punched him, stepped over Eric and left the room.

Good answer. Wish I'd thought of that, Ewan mused as his eyes watered and his face throbbed. The others stared in stony silence. Ewan stared at the desk.

'You're living in his house, wasting his money, and you've been screwing his girlfriend,' Miriam accused. 'I wouldn't have just hit you. I would have done more than just hit you.'

Thank you, Miriam. Next? Ewan thought as she left the room. He glanced at Birmingham Dave and Margaret sitting together, then standing together, then moving together. Like Darby and Joan, he thought fleetingly as he waited for their pearls of wisdom. Nothing. Just looks of disgust and a dignified exit, spoilt only by Dave gently squeezing his shoulder and muttering, 'Get yourself sorted out, Ewan.'

Ewan swallowed the urge to cry. Why is it always my fault? he thought before announcing sarcastically to the empty room, 'Great meeting, guys, thanks.' He laid his head on the desk. His face hurt. Good. His body ached. Even better. Sarah didn't want him any more. Wonderful. He'd lost his stash. Perfect.

'Where is that, anyway? Must be somewhere,' he said as he sat up and started looking around again. He noticed Eric lying on the floor. He got up, crouched down beside him and started feeling under the coat. Eric opened his eyes, looked at Ewan, and sheepishly handed him the little plastic bag.

'Is it my fault I love her?' Ewan asked, tipping out a few pills and shoving them in his mouth before handing the bag back to Eric. 'Is it my fault she's . . . well, I don't know what she's doing, but she certainly isn't doing it with me.' Ewan rubbed his aching face and sighed heavily. 'I can't tell them. How can I tell them? She's Jonathan's; she's always been Jonathan's. So what am I supposed to do? Why are they blaming me? Do they think I like it? Do they think I wanted this mess?'

Eric, not sure how to reply, sat up and said, 'My name's Eric. I'm with the band.'

Jonathan sat on the bench and stared at the lake. The sunlight bouncing off the water hurt his eyes and increased his head-ache, but what the hell, a bit of physical discomfort was bliss compared to his emotional state. Everything was going horri-bly wrong. Or rather, everything was coming to a horrible end. As it had to, really. Ewan on the edge of addiction, Sarah probably riddled with VD, Miriam packing her bags, Dave doubtless following, then Margaret handing in her notice, Tadley imploding to 'Revolution 9' at full volume, and himself alone and picking up the pieces. A month of madness was enough for anyone.

It *had* been fun, though. Ewan had been right about that.

'I loved you, Ewan Hughes,' Jonathan said morosely to a mallard bobbing by.

'You had an argument with someone?'

Jonathan jumped and jerked his head round. Nobody. Then somebody, a girl, a Beatle-cut blonde tomboy, appeared from behind a bush, zipping up her jeans and smiling.

'I was taking a pee,' she said, 'and I couldn't help overhearing. Was it your boyfriend or something?'

'Boyfriend? Oh my God, no, no, nothing like that. I just meant . . . platonically,' Jonathan blustered. He looked at the girl in alarm. She was only about fifteen or sixteen, way too young to know about queers, nancy boys, poofs, much less throw the question at him so openly, so easily.

'It's okay.' She shrugged. 'I sometimes think I'm a lesbian, so I know how you feel. It's difficult, isn't it?'

Jonathan turned away quickly and went back to staring at the lake. *Lesbian?* A young girl, a complete stranger, bandying words like 'lesbian' about without fear, loathing or self-hatred, like it was a weather report? Jonathan had never met a lesbian before. What a great party this was!

'I punched him,' he said.

'Oh,' she said.

'While I was telling him I loved him,' he added.

'Ah,' the girl said. 'You should have done one or the other, but not both.'

Jonathan nodded and smiled slightly. The girl smiled back. 'I'm Sally.'

'Hello, Sally,' Jonathan said.

Sally sat on the bench next to Jonathan. She shielded her eyes as she looked at the lake, deliberately not looking at Jonathan, since he was deliberately not looking at her. 'Is he queer too?' she asked.

'God no, not in the least. He'd run a mile if he knew.'

'So why did you punch him?'

'He was having sex with my girlfriend.'

Sally slowly nodded. 'Does the girlfriend have anything to say in all this?'

'No, she's too busy having sex with everybody else.'

Sally nodded again, but the nod slowly turned into a shake of the head and a grin. 'I've got a horrible feeling I'm going to love this story,' she said.

Miriam was amazed at the way Margaret took charge: no nonsense, no messing, just 'You do this . . . you do that . . . and what are you going to do?' And, hey presto, the madness was over. Or rather, sanity came into view and waved a flag.

Margaret embargoed the food. Dave cut the electricity supply. Jonathan was laying down the rules for Ewan. A girl called Sally was sweeping for drugs with a rubbish bag, in tandem with Eric (who was actually a very sweet guy, Miriam discovered), telling people politely that the party was over. A not so polite guy called Sean was bodyguarding Eric and Sally with a chainsaw in case people wanted to argue. And there was always a police bust if all else failed – Margaret said she'd be quite happy to arrange *that*. And Miriam? All Miriam had to do was talk to Sarah. All, Margaret? All?

'Get dressed and get out,' Miriam barked as she burst into Sarah's room, pointing her finger like a lethal weapon at Jim and Nick. Sarah looked wrecked, almost as bad as Ewan, which was more than just coincidence, Miriam reckoned.

There was no time to collect thoughts or arrange masks of righteous indignation. Jim bounded out of bed and grabbed his clothes as fast as he could, and Nick did the same but slowly, which was as fast as Nick could go. Sarah looked daggers at Miriam, but did not seem surprised. The rumours were rife and she'd been waiting for a knock. It was the reason she'd moved upstairs. What *was* surprising was Miriam's violation of the unwritten, religiously observed rule: bedrooms were private sanctums, no permission/no entry – and certainly no barging in like a bitch elephant on heat.

'Right, madam,' Miriam said as Jim and Nick disappeared. 'I want a word with you.'

'It's my body, my mind, my choice, and my decision,' Sarah said, pre-empting Miriam's attack.

'Yes,' Miriam said. 'Ewan said that.'

Sarah blinked. 'And if I choose to have sex with every male in the house, then that is my choice,' she insisted.

'Yes,' Miriam replied, 'and according to Ewan you *have* had sex with every male in the house. Well, every male except Dave, that is.'

Sarah glanced sharply, and suspiciously, in Miriam's direction, not quite daring to look her in the face.

'Why not Dave, Sarah?' Miriam waited a moment or two for an answer. 'Or would sleeping with Dave be pushing things – or rather Ewan – too far?'

Still no answer from Sarah.

'Right, okay, now let's talk about Jonathan, shall we?' Miriam said, settling down as though for a cosy chat.

Sarah thought for a second but broke into a knowing smile as she waved her hand dismissively. 'Oh, I don't think we need to worry about Jonathan, Miriam. I think Jonathan is perfectly happy with the way things are. Don't you?'

Chapter 4

July 1970 – three weeks later

It was late and Ewan wanted some hash, but the band weren't back yet, so he killed time working on his 'project'. He sat on his bed, scanning the notes he'd made. Farming. Basically it all came down to farming. Simple, really. No, not simple; it can't be simple, he thought, flicking through the pages.

'Fuck it,' he said aloud. 'They'll hate the idea.' He tossed the papers aside, stood up and went to the window. 'Come on, come home,' he said impatiently to the darkness. 'Put your dicks away and bring back some gear.' Ewan wasn't desperate, just bored. And after Jonathan's clean-up and clampdown the band's drug-smuggling games were amusing.

A knock at the door made him jump. It was Sarah. Ewan was only mildly surprised; he'd thought she'd been coming on to him all evening, but that was hours ago and he'd since assumed he was mistaken.

'You still awake?' she asked, peering round the door.

'Only just.' Ewan shrugged.

Sarah smiled slightly as she entered his room, but she looked awkward, unsure. Ewan stuffed his hands in his pockets, leant against the window sill and tried to look nonchalant, determined not to show the other reason why he liked Horsemen gigs.

'It's been a long time,' he said, raising his eyebrows slightly.

'No, it hasn't, a couple of weeks at the most,' Sarah replied. 'Anyway, what makes you think I've come for sex?'

'It's what you always come for.'

'No, it's not,' she said.

Something was wrong, Ewan knew it, but what the hell – she'd made *him* suffer. 'What's the matter, Sarah? You bored without your boys?'

'No.'

'Jonathan asleep then, is he?'

'Ewan, stop it.'

'Got the clap, have you? Want a cure for it? Or maybe you're thinking it's time you laid into Birmingham Dave; I mean, he's the only other male around here at the moment.'

'I think I might be pregnant.' Sarah said it hard, fast, cutting off his goading.

Ewan blinked and did nothing but stare for a few seconds. Then he looked out of the window, hoping to see the head-lights of the band's van in the darkness. Opium or acid would be good, he thought, before looking back at Sarah.

'My period's two weeks late,' she said as she brushed aside his papers to sit on the bed. 'And I do feel . . . sort of funny – different.'

Ewan couldn't think what to do, what to say. All he could think was, No, not acid, and he knew that wasn't helpful. Sarah was giving nothing away, sitting blank-faced on the bed, waiting – waiting for what? A proposal? From him? A pothead with no prospects and nothing to offer, fourth in line after Jonathan, Jim and Nick? Had she told them? He moved across the room and sat down next to her.

'So,' he said, trying to appear open and supportive.

'So,' she replied. Not helpful, no clues.

'Have you told Miriam?'

'Miriam?' Sarah looked shocked. 'Why would I tell Miriam? I'm telling you.'

'I just thought Miriam would . . .' Ewan tailed off, hoping the ground would open up. *She* wasn't thinking of abortion, but now she'd think *he* was. 'I meant, have you told the others?'

'No. I don't want them to know, not till I'm sure.'

Ewan nodded. Fourth in line with no prospects and nothing to offer except abortion – she'd laugh in his face and *then* gloat because the baby wasn't his.

'So,' he said again, 'what do you want to do?'

Sarah sighed, looked at him and smiled slightly. What she wanted to do was admit she was scared. Not for now, but for the future when Jim and Nick had gone and life with Jonathan would be loveless, dull. But that sounded mercenary and wasn't what she meant. What she wanted to do was try to be honest, drop the resentment, forget the slimy things they'd done to each other and start again. Start from the beginning and fall in love properly.

'I want to keep it and I want it to be ours,' she said.

'Ours?'

Sarah hesitated. She hadn't really expected him to propose. Why should he? It could be anybody's – Jim's or Nick's or Jonathan's, Sean's, Eric's – God knows whose. Or maybe his. It would be nice if it was his.

'All eleven of us,' she said.

'Oh.'

'Not just several fathers, but several mothers too.'

'Yes.'

'No ownership.'

'Right.'

'But shared responsibility. So that, whatever happens in the future, we'll all be involved. That's good, isn't it? Politically?' Sarah felt like an absolute fraud.

Both waited in silence for the other to say that it *wasn't* good, politically or otherwise. That it would be easier to swallow their pride, differences and distrust and just argue up the aisle.

But neither said anything of the sort.

'Yes, of course.' Ewan forced a wide smile. 'Politically it would be . . . a farm.'

Sarah frowned but Ewan waved his hand dismissively before putting his arm round her. 'Well done, congratulations,' he said. And then, because neither seemed to be celebrating, he added playfully, 'Not bloody surprising, though, is it, you old slag.'

Sarah laughed and punched his leg. 'Politics, Ewan, women's liberation.'

Ewan gave her a sardonic look. 'And does women's liberation stretch to us having sex tonight?' he asked.

'I've desperately wanted to have sex with you all evening,' she said, pushing him back on the bed and diving for his mouth.

For the first time they made love with defences–down honesty. Softer than the usual tit-for-tat, anger-fuelled snog and grab. More aware than the dope-addled half-hearted grope and faff. It produced a tenderness that was almost sad. Neither said anything, but both pretended *now* was the moment of conception, *this* was making the baby, and that would be enough. Anything else was just the bubble of Tadley Hall, and that had to burst – Jonathan couldn't keep providing; it was unseemly.

They could have stayed in love longer but Ewan bit Sarah's shoulder with playful spite and said, 'I can see why you sleep with Jonathan, I can even see Eric, at a pinch. I can even see the attraction of a five-minute Tom, Dick or Harry. But Jim? Why Jim? He's such a wanker.'

Sarah bit Ewan's nipple in venomous revenge and replied, 'Because he's going to be rich and famous and bigger than the Beatles.' Then she added, 'Besides, it turns you on.'

At which point the man himself barged in, held up a sweet bag and said, 'I thought we were meeting in Sean's room?' before tossing the bag to Ewan, making a dive for Sarah, and ensuring that Ewan and Sarah would be at loggerheads a while longer yet.

Jonathan was pleasantly surprised for all of a split second. One look at Ewan, though, and Jonathan knew he wasn't there for breakfast. Jonathan's heart sank.

'This is a bit early for you, isn't it?' he said, trying to sound cheerful as Ewan slapped a sheaf of papers on his side plate and insisted he read them. Ewan had clearly been up all night. And he was twitchy. Jonathan glanced at Miriam and Margaret, watched their backs go up and their expressions harden. He knew they were thinking the same thing he was. Drugs. This had been sorted out, hadn't it? This had been cleared up.

Jonathan picked up the papers. He tried to read but the words were a blur and the atmosphere was turning leaden. All he could do was stare at white paper and blue ink and worry about the Miriam and Margaret's waning patience and Ewan's growing instability.

Ewan paced the room. It was like waiting for exam results. He told himself it was only an idea, something for discussion. Nothing to lose (except his dignity, self-respect, Sarah and an eleventh of a baby). Ewan poured some coffee, drank it quickly, and paced.

'I do wish you'd sit down, Ewan. You're distracting me.' Jonathan smiled, straightening the papers and starting *again* at page one.

Jonathan's cheekbones were twitching – the teeth-grinding habit. Was that good or bad? Ewan didn't know but he hoped Jonathan's teeth would crumble. Page *one*? What was taking him so long? Ewan straightened the chairs around the table and poured more coffee before sitting down. His foot tapped. He gazed out of the window, studied the paintings on the wall, kept an eye on Jonathan and noticed that Miriam and Margaret were staring at him. He watched Jonathan pass the papers to Miriam.

'So your point is?' Jonathan asked.

Ewan glared at Jonathan. He hadn't read a word. 'We all work *here*,' Ewan said quickly, emphatically.

'Here?' Miriam queried.

'Yes. Dig up the land, get some animals, do it properly.'

Miriam's head was down, desperately scanning Ewan's notes. Margaret was peering at them over her shoulder. *They* were reading. He needed coffee.

'You're talking about farming?' Miriam looked bewildered and less than enthusiastic.

Ewan jumped up, unable to sit still any longer. It was obviously difficult to read. What was needed was an overview. 'It's simple.' Just keep it simple, Ewan told himself. Tadley – a self-sufficient community. Only using Jonathan's money to buy machinery and equipment to set it up.

'We've got to stop thinking that we've got – that *you've* got – millions . . .' Ewan glanced fleetingly at Jonathan – a touchy subject. Jonathan didn't bother. Good. Jonathan was listening, interested, or seemed to be. Ewan started spewing out words and ideas in no particular order. Forgetting what he'd said as soon as he'd said it. Solid foundation. Renewable infrastructure. An organic farm and alternative energy. Mention Dave.

'And Dave could bore you rigid about solar power – he did me, for years . . .'

Explain the freedom of a no-wage culture where everybody works for food, shelter, clothing and each other. *Nobody* works for money, the Establishment or false status. 'Sell that hideous Gainsborough for capital . . .'

Emphasise it's *not* Luddite. The latest technology – mention Dave. Dave knows all about alternative technology. Have I already mentioned Dave? 'Old ways too, but not Luddite . . .'

Books. There are a million books on a million subjects. 'If university taught us nothing else, it taught us how to look things up in books . . .'

Learn to be labourers, do-it-yourself. No employment. No money. No uniform. No bosses. A real community. What's mine is yours and what's yours is mine . . . Did I say self-sufficient? Did I mention the farm? Ewan rolled on. And on. And on. Till he was convinced it was a brilliant idea.

'Don't you think?'

Ewan stopped and stared at them. A sudden silence, nobody filling it. They just stared back.

Jonathan didn't know what to say. It was all too fast and too garbled. Luddite was mentioned a hundred times, and apparently Dave was a bore. Trouble was, with Ewan in his present state, it would be difficult to say anything. Miriam was seriously worried, Jonathan could tell, if not about living on a farm, then certainly about living with Ewan. Margaret was staring at Ewan's notes, her face like thunder. Jonathan wondered if she was reading them or just keeping her head down.

'Don't you think?' Ewan asked again.

Still silence. Ewan looked from one to the other, all frowning, all staring at him. Jonathan exchanged glances with Miriam and Margaret. Nobody wanted to be the first to speak.

'What? Say something,' Ewan pleaded.

Miriam cleared her throat and finally spoke, quietly demanding. 'Are you on something, Ewan?'

'What?' Ewan blinked at her. He couldn't believe what she was asking, couldn't believe his ears. After everything he'd said? He looked from Miriam to Jonathan to Margaret. They were all thinking the same thing.

'The rule is no drugs,' Margaret added.

'I know what the rule is!' Ewan snapped, the rage breaking inside him. All this work, all this effort − not to mention the massive fear of rejection. 'So, is that it? Is that all? Is that the only way you see me? Some kind of fucked-up babbling druggy?'

Ewan grabbed his papers from Margaret, tore them up, swept the breakfast things off the table, kicked his chair against the wall, then stood and attempted to out-despise all three of them. 'Have you any idea how hard this is? To want something so badly, to really want to . . . *do* something?'

He paced the room, throwing angry glares and trying desperately to calm down. 'Forget it; it doesn't matter. It's not important. Just forget it. What *is* important is Sarah . . .' Ewan realised what road he was on. He waved dismissively and quickly backtracked.

'I want Tadley Hall so badly, Jonathan. I've spent weeks thinking about it, working on it.' He gestured to the ripped papers strewn around the floor. 'From the day I got here. I sat on your bed and you talked about wanting to change things, wanting to do things differently. I think this could be perfect; it could be right for all of us. And I have absolutely no right to ask because it might go wrong, you might lose thousands, but I'm begging. I'm begging you to at least think about it, at least think further than a little bit of bloody speed.' Ewan stopped. 'Or whatever. Coffee. Just coffee and nerves.' He looked at them, sighed heavily and hoped somebody would shoot him.

'Sarah's pregnant,' he announced, and left the room in silence.

Eric was up and happy and ready to do what Eric liked doing second best to playing piano in a band – cleaning up after the party. Yes, it had been weeks since the party, but cleaning a place this size could take *months* – hopefully. Eric dragged the big electric floor polisher across the hall, the plug hanging from his hand as he searched for a socket. The hall floor was beautiful: ivory, cream, white . . . mottled. Marble, he reckoned. And it would look even more beautiful after a good clean. Of course, he'd swept it, several times. Mopped it, loads. But a polisher! Eric didn't know Jonathan had a polisher!

'Hey, Ewan, did you know Jonathan had a polisher?' Eric called as Ewan left the breakfast room and headed for the front door. Then he saw Ewan's face and decided it would be a good idea to flatten himself and the polisher against the wall and pretend to be an inoffensive mural. And maybe stop for a coffee break and see who else was in the breakfast room, and what the argument was about, and who won. Gossip was Eric's third favourite activity.

Coffee and speed. Bad mistake. Bad, bad, bad mistake. Ruined everything now. Ruined it all big time.

Ewan stood on the steps of the porch and looked out over the land. Beautiful land. He could run in the woods and the fields completely naked and tripping, having to hide from no one. Except Jonathan. Jonathan would be out in a minute, sidling up and saying, 'Ewan, may I have a word?' Margaret would have already packed his bag, and Miriam would stand with her arms folded, saying, 'Well, you *were* warned.' And then what? Back to London for the start of the autumn term. Without Sarah. That was the only drug problem Ewan had – an addiction to Sarah.

In the distance Sean, Sally and Jim were playing in a field, all speeding. Sean was chasing Jim with the lawnmower. A big petrol-belching unwieldy thing, it was like a truck. Sean bobbing on the top, Sally holding on behind him, laughing. Jim running for dear life, circles and figures of eight and dodging and weaving, and Sean bearing down on him and not really cutting the grass, just messing and the grass getting cut. Ewan laughed and thought about joining them. But no, he'd only end up *really* mowing Jim down, and that wouldn't be funny. Neither would arguing. And it was highly likely that he'd end up arguing. With Sean and Sally maybe, but Jim definitely. Bloody Jim. Ewan hated him.

Ewan walked round the side of the house. Round and round, back and forth, mindless and aimless. Where to go? There was nowhere to go. He didn't want to go anywhere else and he wanted to leave at the same time. Bloody Tadley. Part of him hoped Jonathan *would* throw him out. He hated the place. Oppressive and boring and much too big, and if it wasn't for Sarah he'd be out of there like a shot. Not true. But God, if he didn't feel so useless!

A walled garden, an overgrown vegetable patch. The place had looked good once, he could tell, laid out and organised and useful – a long time ago, though. It was the no-go, Margaret-only area outside the kitchen door, her sanctuary, an off-duty retreat. Ewan hadn't noticed he'd wandered in. He did notice the peas, though, and tomatoes, self-seeded and struggling for life amongst the weeds. The place was choking with weeds . . .

'What are you doing?'

The voice jerked Ewan out of the time-stealing, compulsive pulling of weeds. He'd been miles away.

'Nothing.' Ewan felt guilty straight away. He stood up, hid his dirty hands and came face to face with Margaret. He felt his head drag. She wasn't smiling and he was beginning to crash.

'This is my patch,' she said. 'And you're trespassing.'

Margaret looked him up and down like an irate teacher confronted with an idiot school kid. She waited for an explanation or a retreat. Ewan dithered.

'You've got peas and tomatoes,' he said.

'I know.'

'And I found a couple of onions.' Ewan's eyebrows raised with the excitement of a ten-year-old, but Margaret glared so the excitement (and the ten-year-old) died. 'And the whole plot needs weeding.'

'I know,' she said again, her glare increasing.

'Well then.'

'Well then what?' Margaret's face was stern, her body unbending, her arms folded – hating him.

'Do you want me to weed it?'

'No.'

'Well, fuck you then!' Ewan himself was surprised at the venom of his reply.

Margaret stiffened. 'I beg your pardon?'

In Ewan's head the words were: 'I'm sorry, Margaret, I didn't mean to say that. As you already know I'm a complete twat and not fully in control of my brain, my body or my manners.' But out of his mouth came: 'I was offering to weed; I was trying to be nice, and you slapped me in the face, so – fuck you!'

Venomous and way out of order. Oh God, was he crashing.

'Don't tempt me. If I slapped you in the face you wouldn't

be able to stand up for a week! Trying to be nice,' she sneered. 'By insulting me?'

Margaret stepped forward, her anger bursting inches from Ewan's face. 'Are you really so stupid? Do you think Jonathan *wants* you to leave?' She grabbed Ewan's arm and turned him towards the gap in the wall facing the fields beyond. 'There are acres, you could have seven hundred acres, if you didn't screw it up, if you didn't keep shoving stupid drugs into your system. Personally, I don't care what you do. Be as self-destructive as you like. Turn the whole estate into opium fields if you want. But I have this . . .'

Margaret yanked him back to the cottage garden, her free arm sweeping an arc across the unkempt tangle. 'It was my husband's, Jack's, and he loved it, so I love it. Every inch of it. And I know it's got peas and I know it's got tomatoes and . . . well, I didn't know about the onions, but . . .' Margaret paused, softening a fraction. 'I don't ever want to give up this garden.'

Ewan looked at her and began to see somebody other than a po-faced old housekeeper. He began to see somebody desperate to cling on to what little she had. He looked down and picked at the dirt beneath his nails. 'Margaret, I know I'm stupid, but I *am* trying. And I *was* only offering to weed,' he said by way of an apology.

Margaret made a 'humph' sound and, again in the irate teacher voice, she said, 'And all *I* was trying to say was that I don't want you to weed. I want you to rewrite your notes, because we are going to need them. And we are going to need you, but preferably sober and sensible.'

His project. She understood. She was on his side. She still hated him, but she was on his side.

'But in future . . .' she added.

'What?'

'In future, fuck you too, Ewan Hughes.'

Ewan looked up. Margaret was half smiling, challenging. Yes. Friendly dislike. Ewan could handle that.

Jonathan sat in his study and watched Dave rummage through the papers and cardboard models that he'd strewn over Jonathan's desk. He didn't want to be rude or impolite, or wipe the excited grin from Dave's face, but if Sarah *was* pregnant, then Jonathan felt he ought to be talking to her, not Dave.

'En suite bathrooms,' Dave announced gleefully, finding what he was looking for (an old sugar bag) and thrusting it under Jonathan's nose. There were lines, arrows, numbers and tiny writing on it, totally meaningless.

'What's this all about, Dave?' Jonathan asked, completely bemused.

'En suite bathrooms,' Dave repeated, as if that made it clearer.

Jonathan didn't really have time for this. Things were starting up again. Trouble brewing, with Sarah and Ewan, somehow joined, somewhere in the middle of it, and Jonathan no doubt required to sort it out. Somehow. Not Dave's fault, though. Dave was no trouble. It was just unfortunate that Dave's timing was off. Or Jonathan's.

'I meant, what's *this* all about?' Jonathan swept his hand over the papers and boxes, then added quickly, in case another bit of paper was thrust into his face, 'in a nutshell?'

'Well.' Dave sat back in his chair, feeling good, excited. 'Plumbing, for instance. Recycling our own waste, composting the crap and reusing our own water . . . Reed beds.' He leant forward again to his papers. 'I've got—'

Jonathan quickly slammed his hand over Dave's to stop him rummaging further. 'Yes. Just tell me.'

'Solar energy, watermills – the bills for this place must be enormous. You see, what they never tell you is that anything the big boys do, we can do smaller.' Dave leant forward, his nose almost touching Jonathan's. 'Wind energy,' he whispered with quiet triumph.

Jonathan released Dave's hand and sat back, looked at the papers and models and then looked at Dave. 'Have you been talking to Ewan?'

Dave was confused. 'I haven't seen Ewan this morning.'

Jonathan gestured to the mess on his desk. 'All this couldn't have taken you one morning.'

'No, I've been doing it for weeks. Thought . . .' Dave smiled sheepishly. 'Thought it would be a good idea. Maybe something for you to try. Just . . . fantasising.'

'And then Ewan said . . . ?'

'I haven't seen Ewan.' Dave frowned. What had this got to do with Ewan?

'So why are you showing me all this now? If you've been thinking about it for weeks?'

Dave had the feeling he'd done something wrong but couldn't imagine what. 'Because Margaret's just told me we're going self-sufficient, so . . .' Dave shrugged.

'Margaret told you we're going *what*?' Jonathan looked perplexed.

'Self-sufficient.'

Margaret?

Dave suddenly beamed. 'Was that Ewan's idea?' Dave had thought Margaret must have broached the subject with Jonathan. She and Dave had often talked about it, imagined it. But if Ewan had thought about it too, well, that carried much more clout.

Jonathan looked at Dave. Dave had always been genuine,

open, uncomplicated. It was true that Dave and Ewan were very close friends, but Dave would never allow himself to be Ewan's partner in crime. *Margaret* would never allow Dave to be Ewan's partner in crime. But then Dave said it was Margaret's idea . . . But Margaret had been furious with Ewan this morning, so . . . So whatever Ewan was up to, it had nothing to do with Dave or Margaret – or Jonathan's growing paranoia.

'Okay, Dave, get it sorted and . . . let's see.' Jonathan smiled. As Dave stood up Jonathan thought, If he smiles any wider his face will break. He almost laughed when Dave grabbed his hand and shook it energetically. Then a terrible thought struck him.

'I mean the plans, Dave. Just the plans. Get the plans sorted, not the actual house, yet.'

Sally whistled loudly as she saw Margaret approaching across the lawn with a tea tray. Jim quickly snuffed out the joint and hid it amongst the grass cuttings. Sean stuffed the dope tin into his pocket. The three sat looking relaxed and innocent, smiling pleasantly as Margaret drew near.

'You've made a lovely job of that lawn,' Margaret said as she plonked the tray down in the middle of the sitting trio. 'Seems a shame to dig it up after all that hard work.'

Margaret turned and made her way back to the house with three bemused faces watching her. Thirty seconds later she heard Sean behind her, running to catch up and yelling, 'Digging it up? What do you mean, digging it up?'

Margaret giggled.

Eric yelled above the noise of the polisher, 'Mind the floor, it's—'

Sean slipped onto his back, skidded the length of the hall, stood up and went into Jonathan's study.

'Slippy,' Eric finished.

Sean put his knuckles on Jonathan's desk and leant over menacingly into Jonathan's face. 'Apparently you've got to put a tick in a box, sign on the dotted line or something pathetically stupid like that.'

Jonathan, more than a little nervous, nodded quizzically.

'Cows, sheep, pigs, chickens. Miriam says,' Sean added.

'Miriam says what?' Jonathan asked. His head was reeling from the morning's events, and he still hadn't seen Sarah.

'You've got to sign; you've got to agree.'

'Agree to *what*, Sean?' Jonathan wasn't exactly *scared* of Sean, but he wasn't too comfortable being alone with him, especially when he hadn't got a clue what he was on about.

'Margaret said I've got to talk to Miriam because she'll be doing the accounts . . .'

Margaret again, Jonathan thought. What *is* she playing at?

'Miriam said I've got to talk to you because you've got the money. But all I want to do is go out and buy them. I know what I'm doing; I know what I'm talking about. Cows for the long grass, sheep for the short. At the same time, they're manuring it, saves us a lot of trouble and labour. Come the spring, weather warms up, heats the soil, we only have to plough it over, dig in the grass, along with all the cow and sheep shit that they've dumped between now and then. Perfect growing conditions – hopefully. Then move them to another field. Timing's perfect, if we do it now. So stop pissing around and give me the money. Okay?'

Jonathan, at a complete loss for something to say, was greatly relieved when Sally poked her smiling face round the door.

'And pigs, explain the pigs, Sean.'

'And pigs because I like them,' Sean explained.

'No. Pigs because they help plough up the field and then you eat them, every part, no waste,' Sally explained.

'Yeah, and that.' Sean nodded, frowning slightly.

Sally came fully into the room, stood next to Sean and smiled brightly at Jonathan. Jonathan looked at the two of them, then directed his attention to Sally. Sally he could cope with. Given the morning's events (a Ewan–organised putsch, Jonathan reckoned), Sally was probably the only person he could cope with.

'I think you need to talk to . . .' Jonathan paused to consider his surrender.

'I'm not talking to anybody else,' Sean thundered. 'I'm being passed around here like an old tea bag.'

'Ewan,' Jonathan surrendered. 'I think you need to talk to Ewan.'

'I'm sick of talking to people,' Sean continued. 'Don't like talking to people; hate fucking people.'

'Ewan's all right, Sean,' Sally soothed.

'Oh yeah, Ewan's all right. Don't mind talking to him. Ewan's not a shithead,' Sean agreed as he turned and made for the door.

Sally smiled appeasingly. 'It's all right, Jonathan, he doesn't really think you're a shithead,' she explained. 'It's just his way of saying he likes you.'

'Yeah.' Jonathan nodded. 'Everybody's got really funny ways of saying they like me.'

Eric leant proudly on his polisher, surveying his workmanship, as Sean and Sally took a run, dived onto the hall floor and slid towards the stairs.

'Don't mess with my floor!' Eric yelled.

'Well then, don't be such a twat!' Sean replied as he and Sally bounded up the stairs.

'I think it looks beautiful,' said Sarah as she descended, passing the galumphs with grace. She looked particularly beautiful herself this morning. 'Eric, you've excelled yourself.'

Eric beamed as Sarah came down to his level. Now here was someone who appreciated perfection – well, in floors, anyway.

'You haven't seen Ewan anywhere, have you?' she asked.

Eric was about to start gossiping about the morning's events: Ewan looking like thunder, Jonathan's study like Piccadilly Circus. But he was interrupted.

'Sarah, do you have a minute?' Jonathan called from the doorway of his study.

Ewan was in his room trying to rewrite his notes when Sarah entered. If he hadn't been screwing up his face in an effort to get his brain to work, he might have recognised the warning signs. Might have noticed the look of fury on Sarah's face as she walked across the room. Might have realised that her hand grabbing the back of his hair wasn't romantic. He guessed something was wrong when she slammed his face against the table. His nose bled instantly.

'You bastard,' Sarah said.

She kept hold of his hair and managed another bang before Ewan's brain engaged enough to brace himself against a third attempt. Sarah punched his head and shoulders with her fists instead, so he laid his head on the table and protected himself with his arms, waiting for her to stop. He should have expected this. Had done, but thought it would happen later – tonight maybe, or tomorrow.

'Who else did you tell? Who else besides Jonathan?'

'Er . . . Miriam and Margaret.' His voice sounded thick with blood, muffled in the table.

'So Margaret tells Dave, Dave tells Eric, Jonathan tells Sally,

Sally tells Sean, and Eric and Sean tell Nick and Jim. Thanks, Ewan. Thanks a bundle.' She stopped pounding his head and shoulders, stepped back and delivered a jabbing kick, catching him painfully in his kidney.

'The only person I can rely on, the only person I can trust, is Miriam. Miriam won't tell anyone; Miriam has a bit of respect. I should have told Miriam, shouldn't I? You did suggest that, didn't you?'

Ewan remained silently buried in the table, stiff, still, waiting for the next blow. It never came. He risked a peek over the top of his arm. She'd stopped now, thankfully, and had moved away, her back to him. Ewan hoped she might have started crying. Girls always softened when they cried. He raised his head slightly, ready to duck down again if necessary.

'I'm sorry, Sarah. I hadn't meant to; it just came out.'

'Bastard,' she said quietly. Not quite crying, but almost. Almost safe. Ewan risked sitting up fully. 'So what did Jonathan say?' he asked.

Sarah turned, half smiled, tears brimming at her eyelids. 'He offered to marry me,' she replied.

Her smile widened to a laugh but the tears started to roll. Aggression vanished, punishment over. Ewan wiped some blood from his nose with the back of his hand, and couldn't help laughing too.

'He did what?'

'I don't know what you're laughing for,' she said. 'I said yes.'

Ewan's laugh disappeared. It was the biggest punch she'd delivered. The one he'd been expecting from the first day he met her.

Chapter 5

February 1971 – seven months later

Dave wanted to be Merlin. It was quite clear. The purpose of the meeting was not so much to make surprise arrangements for the wedding, as to make surprise arrangements to dress up as knights of the Round Table for the wedding. Dave had expected reluctance, not competition.

'Merlin would be a piano player,' Eric argued.

'Merlin might not be a piano player, but he'd definitely be a musician, Dave,' Nick said.

'Well, he'd be a musician *and* lead singer, wouldn't he?' Jim added, as though it were obvious.

'Merlin *cooks* – potions and stuff,' Dave said with an insistence that bordered on petulant. 'And it's *my* idea.'

It was a typical meeting.

Miriam knew no one was going to be Merlin, but couldn't care less. She looked at Sally. Sally raised her eyes heavenwards and giggled with Margaret. Miriam giggled too.

Miriam was happy. She woke with a feeling of excitement, slept with a sense of optimism, and dealt good-naturedly with the bustle and business in between. She felt like she belonged. It was similar to how she'd felt as head girl in the sixth form, except now she thought hard about what clothes to wear. Not to look pretty – pretty wasn't necessary – but to look attractive. Miriam had also started helping outside, labouring like a navvy when she was by nature an intellectual indoor type. She had blisters, backache and bruises and a serious crush on Sally. She hoped the feeling was mutual, but didn't have the nerve to ask.

'Ewan said we should spend the wedding hiding in bags, like John and Yoko,' Sally said.

Miriam laughed. Not because she thought it was funny, but because Sally did. Dave didn't.

'Where is Ewan, anyway? And Sean?' he asked.

'They said they're too busy,' Sally informed him. 'The first proper growing year, Dave, very important.'

'Can't the farm wait for five minutes!' Dave snapped.

'Since when has a meeting lasted five minutes?' Nick pointed out.

Dave's patience disintegrated amidst the laughter. 'Can you go and tell them this is important, Nick, please.'

Miriam felt sorry for Dave; he looked beleaguered. He was no good at organising meetings, but *was* enthusiastic about the wedding. Unfortunately nobody else was.

'Can we get on with it, do you think, Dave?' Margaret said.

'I'm waiting for the others.'

'You don't think Nick's going to come back, do you?' Sally put in, to more laughter.

Dave lost it. 'That is the problem, don't you see? That is why I've had to call this bloody meeting. We've got Jonathan and Sarah's wedding to plan – and nobody is planning anything except Jonathan and Sarah!'

There was a pause.

'Okay, Dave,' Jim said. 'So Jonathan is Arthur and Sarah is Guinevere. Who would be Lancelot?'

'Ewan, of course. Jonathan wants him to be best man.'

'And who was Lancelot in love with?' continued Jim.

The room went quiet. Miriam frowned and wondered if everybody knew what she knew.

Sally smacked her hand to her head and Eric smiled awkwardly. Margaret said, 'John and Yoko bags all round then, is it?' And Jim nodded, his point made.

Dave looked at the others in bewilderment and said, 'What? It's only a theme. It's only a *story*!'

And Miriam realised that everybody *did* know what she knew. Everybody except Dave, that is.

Pooh with a balloon. Sarah lay awkwardly and in pain and stared up at the ghostly outline high up on the nursery wall.

Everybody had warned her. Everybody had told her to stick to the lower half of the walls. They'd insisted.

'Babies are tiny; they don't need stuff high – they won't see it.'

'But babies lie on their backs; they look up!' she'd wailed, crumpled in a heap on the floor, in floods of tears, knowing at the back of her mind somewhere that it wasn't *that* important but . . . And then Jonathan offered to trace it for her, if she made a template. And this morning, his tongue poking out of the side of his mouth, he had painstakingly traced the outline of Pooh with a balloon. And Sarah was happy again.

She'd sat in the rocking chair waiting while Jonathan went to fetch the paint. Unfortunately the ladder was still there. And unfortunately Sarah had suddenly decided that Pooh with a balloon was not good enough. There had to be a honey tree 'growing' in the corner, the branches splaying across the ceiling. If she could just draw it, just quickly sketch the outline for Jonathan to paint . . .

If Nick had been a fast mover he would have walked past the nursery while Jonathan was still with Sarah. He would have overheard Sarah telling Jonathan what a great job he was doing and Jonathan telling Sarah what a great artist she was. If Nick had been a fast mover he'd have been in his room, out of hearing distance of the nursery and ensconced with his beloved bass. Jonathan would have been similarly out of earshot, downstairs rummaging in the storeroom for the right shade of Pooh paint. But being so slow Nick passed Jonathan on the stairs and stopped to chat and to tell Jonathan that under no circumstances was he to go into the dining room. Jonathan knew what the meeting was about, or at least he thought he did, but was amused by Nick's sense of intrigue. Lucky that Nick was so slow, because it was then that they heard the crash, then that Jonathan knew Sarah had fallen, then that Nick discovered he could run like the clappers if necessary.

Sean noticed first. He was holding the fence post straight while Ewan hammered it into the ground. He saw something out of the corner of his eye – Jim running across the field. Behind him, in the distance, everybody was clustered around the main entrance, watching a stretcher go into an ambulance. The way he said 'Sarah' made Ewan stop instantly, follow the direction of Sean's gaze, and drop the sledgehammer. They both started running.

Jonathan felt numb, impotent. He sat in the ambulance and smiled stupidly down at Sarah's white face, holding her hand and muttering, 'It'll be fine; you'll be okay,' trying desperately to cover his fear and reassure both of them. Things had been going so well – too well, obviously. The house transformed, everybody jokily calling themselves the Tadpoles of Tadley

74

Hall and happily working together, enthusiastic, optimistic. Jonathan loved the house now – music, voices, friends, the smell of sweat and sawdust and paint, noise, chaos. Activity. Something was bound to happen; something *had* to go wrong. He'd thought it would be Ewan snapping and the wedding cancelled. But not this. He hadn't thought it would be this; this was supposed to be the *real* spring, the *real* beginning.

Nobody spoke. Their first ever willing meeting. The first time they'd all automatically gathered together in the dining room, *wanted* to gather together, and everybody sat in silence. Sean was almost in tears. Dave looked guilty, as though calling the meeting had created the fall. Miriam was white. Eric looked lost. Margaret and Nick handed out cups of tea and the others politely thanked them. They glanced at each other around the table, sipped their tea and glanced some more. Sally noticed that most of the glancing was in Ewan's direction, as they watched Ewan staring at his tea. All watching, nobody speaking.

'What do you think, Ewan?' she said.

Ewan looked up and shook his head slightly, not sure what to say. 'Er . . .' A deep breath. 'I think someone should go and find out what's happening. See how she is.'

'I'll drive you,' Eric said, almost standing.

Sally saw Ewan jump as though Eric had read his mind. 'No, I think I should go. I'll take Jonathan's car,' Miriam intervened.

Sally wanted to hit her. That was exactly what Sally hated, not just in Miriam but in all of them – pretence. Not being honest and not lying sufficiently to be accused of it.

'Why you?' Eric asked.

'Why not?' Miriam replied.

'Because Ewan should go,' Eric insisted.

'This is not the time for—'

Sally jumped in angrily. 'He didn't even see her. He didn't even get there in time. How do you think he feels, Miriam?'

Sally was raging. She wanted to bang everyone's heads together. Months she'd spent outside, freezing, sodden, over-worked and aching. Farming by moonlight, building at midnight. Sean going along with it because he was just as crazy. Sally saying, 'Come on, Ewan, let's call it a day.' Ewan grinning back, saying, 'Let's just do a bit more.' A bit more to avoid Sarah, a bit more to get over her. And now the bitch goes and falls and starts the whole thing up again. This was not the time for Miriam's bloody tact. Miriam knew how he felt. Miriam must have seen his face. *Everybody* saw his face, the look of defeat as the ambulance pulled away. Gone before he'd got there.

Miriam turned to Ewan. At least she had the sensitivity to hesitate before she brushed him off with platitudes. 'It's all right, Ewan, she wasn't that bad. She didn't look . . . bad.'

'It's not fair; it's just not bloody fair,' Sally said, forceful, impatient. 'How long does this charade have to go on?'

'Now is not the time,' Miriam said.

'So when *is* the time? When they're married? When it's too late?'

'They're not going to get married.' Jim shrugged. 'It's all just one of Sarah's games.'

'Sarah chose Jonathan, and that's the end of it,' Miriam said with what she hoped was finality.

'Oh yes, and who would Jonathan choose, given the chance?' Sally pouted.

'The same person Sarah would, given the chance,' Jim replied, looking pointedly at Ewan.

Ewan looked quizzically back at Jim, only half taking it in. Sally wanted to shake him. 'We all know, Ewan. Everything,' she said.

'Shut up, all of you,' Miriam said sharply. 'Sarah's fallen, for

God's sake; we should be thinking of her. And the baby. And Jonathan. The rest is none of our business.'

'Might already be too late,' Nick muttered quietly.

Sally watched the colour drain from Ewan's face. He closed his eyes as everyone silently stared at him.

'She wasn't that bad; it's not that bad.' Miriam's voice sounded quivery, as though her optimism was fading. She was looking around for somebody to boost it, to agree with her.

Nodding in a knowing, realistic way, Margaret said, 'She might lose the baby.'

The others nodded in agreement and stared solemnly into their teacups.

'Ah, God,' Ewan finally said, rubbing his eyes and head as though trying to focus. His chair fell backwards as he stood up. 'I'm going to find out how Sarah is, and I don't care who drives me, but somebody's got to, otherwise I'm going to drive my bloody self!'

Sally pushed Miriam out of her chair. Eric stood, but Miriam beat him to it.

Ewan felt sick and incredibly apprehensive. He put it down to worry about Sarah, but half of it was being out in the world again. He hadn't been out for months – almost a year – and certainly not in a car. The fastest Ewan went now was on a tractor. And he could see that Miriam felt the same. Both of them sat stiffly in the car, wincing as other traffic drove past, staring at strangers, feeling dreamlike, groggy, as though they'd slept too long. Neither of them mentioned it. Instead Ewan covered his nerves by ranting about the house and everybody in it. Miriam seemed happy to let him.

'I hate it. Everybody gossiping, knowing your business. It's like Maerdy. I don't know why I bothered leaving. Thought that was bad but this . . . can't sneeze without someone telling someone else and everybody saying "bless you". What's the matter with them, Miriam? Can't they survive without gossip?'

'What are you going to do, Ewan?'

Ewan knew what Miriam was asking and he didn't pause to think about it. 'I'm not going to do anything. It's like you said: Sarah chose Jonathan.'

'Did she?'

Ewan didn't know the answer to that. He thought yes and no at the same time. Thought it was either cold calculation or revenge. Or a mixture of the two. A typical Sarah thing. And, weirdly, a Jonathan thing too. Although why Jonathan should have it in for him was a mystery. Either way, it wasn't a love thing. Ewan was sure Sarah didn't love Jonathan. He was banking on it. He wasn't sure if Sarah loved *him* but – they were meant to be together. He was *absolutely* sure about that. He knew he couldn't leave.

Ewan gave Miriam a sideways look. 'Bloody Tadley. Tadpoles. Tadpoles eat each other, you know.' He laughed slightly. 'Very apposite. Whoever dreamt that one up knew what they were talking about.'

'She told you she was pregnant; that must have meant something,' Miriam reasoned.

Yes, Ewan knew it must have meant something. But it didn't mean marriage – not to him, not to Jonathan, not to anyone. It meant eleven. It meant the farm and everything that everybody was working for now. It meant replacing the Sarah obsession and the drug obsession with a work obsession. It meant something that was difficult to explain. Difficult to get the head round. Sons of miners didn't talk about grand plans or soulmates. They didn't talk about kismet or karma. Sons of miners stuck to easier subjects.

'Eric's the one – he's the worst. Don't ever tell Eric anything; it goes around like wildfire.'

'Jim said it was one of Sarah's games. What did he mean, Ewan? Do you know?'

He wished she'd shut up, wished she'd just shut the fuck up! No, he didn't know. Of course he didn't know. He wanted to, desperately. If he knew, he could do something. If he knew, he could . . . do what?

'Ewan, Jim saying it's a game – what's that mean?' Miriam persisted.

Ewan shrugged and looked briefly out of the window. 'I wouldn't listen to anyone who spent all their time trying to look like Jim Morrison.'

Miriam laughed heartily in agreement. 'He does, doesn't he? *Come on baby, light my fire . . .*' she sang in a basso profundo piss-take.

Ewan looked over in surprise. Maybe Miriam wasn't so bad; maybe she wasn't so serious. In fact, Miriam was looking quite . . . colourful at the moment, and her hair was different somehow.

'I don't think I've been happy since I've been here, Miriam,' Ewan muttered, getting as close to confessing his misery as he could. 'Spend my time avoiding you all. Pathetic. We used to be friends, didn't we? All of us? At university?'

'I used to think you were a prick,' Miriam said with relish, her laughter turning slightly hysterical.

Ewan thought about that for a second, agreed and managed a laugh. 'I thought you were a frigid cow.'

'You said "humourless frump".'

'Yeah, and that.' Ewan grinned, remembering with embarrassment the verbal drubbing she'd once given him.

Miriam fought to control the car and her cackling hysteria

as Ewan smiled affectionately and went back to looking at strangers. No, Miriam wasn't so bad after all.

Jonathan looked up and saw Ewan at the entrance of the hospital waiting room. He knew he'd come. He was glad he did. They exchanged a slight nodded greeting, Ewan continuing the curt distance as he stuffed his hands into his pockets and flopped down on a chair next to Jonathan.

'How is she?' Ewan asked flatly, stretched out, staring at his boots.

'Don't know yet; they're running tests.'

'And the baby?'

'Ditto.'

They sat in silence, both mesmerised by Ewan's waggling foot. Jonathan wondered what to say. Ewan's brick-wall mood making it difficult.

'How did you get here?' he asked eventually.

'Miriam drove me.'

'Didn't she stay?'

'Parking.'

Ewan forced his foot still by stamping his boots on the floor and sitting up. He looked vaguely around the waiting room before fixing on a nurse talking quietly to a guy in the corner.

'Well, she says parking, but knowing Miriam she'll probably hang back for half an hour or so, she's so diplomatic.' Ewan turned to face Jonathan. 'Gives us enough time to have a ding-dong argument or beat the shit out of each other or whatever it is we're heading for.'

Jonathan stared back for a couple of seconds. 'I can't imagine Miriam being *that* diplomatic,' he replied with a stab at humour.

It didn't work. Ewan wasn't joking. There was no sparkle, no smile, no twitch, just a thin-lipped stare. Jonathan couldn't believe the resentment in Ewan's face. It wasn't a game and it wasn't funny any more, and, Jonathan was surprised to realise, Ewan was more than ready to beat the shit out of him if necessary – and more than capable of doing so.

'Ewan, Sarah's not going to die, you know.'

Immediately Jonathan realised it was the wrong thing to say. Ewan turned sharply away, his knees beginning to waggle. He stood up and stared at a noticeboard, hands still firmly jammed in his pockets, his back to Jonathan. Things had changed so much since university. Their easy friendship had gone, the banter and piss-takes and close-to-the-bone digs, all impossible to maintain at competitive, jealousy-ridden Tadley. Or maybe their friendship had always been competitive, Jonathan didn't know. But he did know Ewan was winning – that much hadn't changed. And maybe it was time Ewan knew.

Jonathan looked at Ewan's back. Despite the circumstances Jonathan marvelled at how lean and strong Ewan's body had become. How fit, and healthy, and beautiful. 'Farming suits you,' he commented, and smiled as Ewan chose to ignore him and concentrate on the noticeboard.

Jonathan could put up with an argument, he could put up with a fight if necessary, be a human punchbag for all that nervous frustration – anything to be friends again. 'You are such a moron, Ewan,' he said.

Ewan's shoulders twitched. At least he was listening.

'You're so old-fashioned at heart, aren't you? All you really want is a little house, little wife, little kids, little job. You want Sarah. Mr and Mrs Hughes and baby Hughes – how romantic, how conventional. You think a wedding ring on her finger and her legs will automatically slam shut. You've lost your fantasy, haven't you? Lost your dream. You think you've lost. You're an empty-headed, brainless moron.'

Ewan slowly turned from the noticeboard. Jonathan saw the slight smile, the slight smirk beginning to form, his eyes beginning to sparkle again, the old Ewan Hughes. The old Ewan Hughes but saying nothing and waiting for the punch-line.

'A marriage certificate, Ewan. And a birth certificate with my name on. If I have children, Tadley's safe. Your vision of it is safe. *Your* vision. Safe for you and Sarah and Miriam and everybody. It's political. Just a political game. You know – politics? That stuff you're always spouting to cover up your pathetic working-class stupidity. A marriage of convenience. Didn't we tell you? Didn't Sarah mention it when she was trying to break your nose?' Jonathan's needling dissolved into a laugh. 'Couldn't you work it out, Ewan? I don't want Sarah; she knows I don't. I want you.'

Chapter 6

Chaos. Sean refused point-blank to get involved. He said somebody had to keep the farm going and besides, his pigs had more
sense than Jonathan. Margaret spent five days barking orders at
Dave, Miriam and Nick cooking in the kitchen. Eric spent five
days barking orders at Jim, Ewan and Sally cleaning throughout
the house. Meanwhile, Jonathan was ferrying Sarah's parents
and sister back and forth to the hospital and entertaining them
with a benevolence and *joie de vivre* quite at odds with the
mayhem buzzing around him.

Nobody knew why. What was the point of having a
wedding reception when the wedding had been postponed?
But Jonathan was adamant. A hundred guests were expecting
to be entertained. And no, he wasn't giving Miriam or
Margaret or anybody any lists of who was coming. If he'd
wanted to cancel it he would've done it himself. And: 'Don't
forget the ceremony in the drawing room at eight tonight.'

Ceremony? Maybe this ceremony would include a human
sacrifice – that might wipe the stupid grin off Jonathan's face.

They gathered at eight anyway. Truculent, tired but
intrigued. Even Sean came, though he was the last to arrive,
and complained the longest. They waited outside the drawing
room as instructed by the sign pinned to the door:

MAGICK TEMPLE.
Not for everyone.
Price of entry: your soul.
Do not enter until summoned.

There followed the order in which they were to enter: Ewan, Miriam, Dave, Margaret, Sean, Jim, Eric, Nick, Sally.

A gong sounded from inside the drawing room. Ewan hesitated.

'Go on,' Miriam prompted.

'How do you know that's being summoned?' he argued.

'Don't be such a sissy,' Margaret chided as she pushed Ewan towards the door.

Being 'such a sissy' was exactly what Ewan was worried about. Not that he expected anything to happen – behind a closed door, alone with Jonathan, engaged in some kind of ceremony. But since Jonathan had laid his cards fully on the table, Ewan felt obliged to react somehow – but how, he couldn't imagine. Well, he could, but . . . awkward.

Ewan tentatively opened the door to dark, murky gloom and the opening strains of some weird druggy music. He immediately felt uneasy. The only light came from two flickering candles placed in the centre of the coffee table, and pinprick glows from joss sticks dotted around the room. There was an overwhelming smell of incense, almost sickening for a few seconds. Ewan watched the shadowy figure of Jonathan moving slowly from the record player to the other side of the coffee table. He looked strange, bulky, with something covering his head; he looked almost like a hooded monk. Spooky.

Jonathan lit a taper from one of the candles and pointed it in Ewan's direction, beckoning him forward and motioning for him to sit on one of nine cushions placed in a semicircle on the floor around Ewan's side of the coffee table. Ewan sat on the middle cushion. As he did so, Jonathan lit another candle, chimed some finger cymbals, dipped his hand in a bowl and flicked some water at Ewan. Ewan looked affronted as he wiped a splash from his face. Jonathan bowed, turned and glided slowly to the gong and banged it again. As each person entered Jonathan repeated the ceremony, pointing the taper at a cushion alternately from the centre out, lighting another candle as they sat, chiming the finger cymbals, flicking water, bowing, then banging the gong, the music getting louder and more gothic as he did so.

The gloom was alleviated slightly when all eleven candles were lit and people's eyes adjusted. On the other side of the coffee table 'altar' were two high-backed chairs, covered in a heavy brocade that enhanced their throne-like appearance, towering above the coffee table and those seated on the floor. Jonathan sat majestically on one; a small wooden box was placed intriguingly on the other. Jonathan's face was solemn as he peered out from under the hood. He sat motionless and silent, secretly hoping that the music was as engulfing and disorientating as it was supposed to be. It was. They sat cross-legged, watching. All wondering what was coming next.

The music changed to insistent drumming. Jonathan swayed in his seat, backwards and forwards, picking up the rhythm of the drums, allowing his movement to increase, become circular.

'What *is* this music?' Ewan whispered to Dave, looking for distraction – Jonathan was becoming embarrassingly funny.

Dave didn't know so he turned to Sean, who was starting to drum on his legs in time with the music.

'"A Saucerful of Secrets",' Sean replied, staring wide-eyed at Jonathan.

'Pink Floyd,' Eric added as he and Sally joined in with Sean's leg drumming.

Dave and Ewan picked up on the idea. Even Miriam and Margaret started. Jim and Nick didn't. They had their own Pink Floyd fantasies and were unaware that a leg-drumming line of sniggerers was watching them. It was only when the quiet sniggering started to include loud snorts that Jim realised where he was, stopped trying to experiment with an imaginary guitar and nudged Nick. Nick nodded happily along the line, adjusted the level on his imaginary amp and clicked on his effects pedal.

The leg drumming became impossible for all except Sean as Jonathan stood, his whole body twitching and jerking in a strange St Vitus's dance, increasing the giggles from the floor. Jonathan tried to be serious and sexual but he too was giggling under his hood. He hoped nobody noticed in the gloom. This was supposed to be cosmic and moving. Sarah had insisted.

Sean thought it was. Sean drummed along and stared at Jonathan as though in a spellbound trance. Eric too was impressed. The band could do with some of these theatrics, he thought, making a mental note to discuss it with them later.

The drumming ended and a church organ swept in creating a cathedral of sound. Jonathan stood still and serious, held his arms out and announced, 'Let the communion and connection of those here present – and our beloved high priestess, who isn't – commence.'

Jonathan bowed and moved to the coffee table. He lifted up a bowl of water, held it aloft and spoke in deep, reverential tones:

'In the beginning was the Physical.
And the Physical collided with Death in order to breathe.
And Spring became possible.'

Jonathan lowered the bowl, dipped his finger in the water and splashed himself with it. The music gave his words and actions a hypnotic intensity.

'And with the Physical came the Sun and the Rain,
Who carried the Physical to the Right Place.
To warm and water it, to give emotion and intellect.
And with the Sun and the Rain came the Day and the Night,
To give movement and calm, wisdom and humour.
And Spring stirred.'

Jonathan moved round to the front of the coffee table, flicking drops of water left and right, here and there and over the watching nine.

'And the Physical met the Mother, the centre,
Who waited in the Right Place for the arrival of Spring.
And the Right Place grew,
Sprang into life from Death that held it so long.
And Music searched out the Right Place,
To give voice, inspiration.
And Music was Sharp and Soft and Fast and Slow.
And behind Music came the Wind,
To blow energy into the awaiting Elements, to set them alight.
And Spring was born.'

Jonathan swapped the water for a bowl of rose petals, which he lifted aloft before strewing around the area of the thrones, altar and seated friends.

'The plan was set in motion.
Spring danced in the Right Place.

The Right Place danced in Spring.
What was separate merged with the whole.
What was whole was made of the separate.
What was one voice now became legion,
And legion became one.
All Elements became all Elements.
And all Elements connected.'

Dave was becoming increasingly irritated. He sighed heavily as he watched Jonathan, then leant in Ewan's direction and whispered, 'I wouldn't have played Merlin in a dressing gown. I'd have made a much better costume if I'd been Merlin. And he shouldn't have a towel on his head; he should have a pointy hat.'

Ewan looked at Dave as though he were tapped. He looked back at Jonathan. Jonathan *definitely* was.

Jonathan moved slowly to the coffee table, placing his hands above the candles, making circling motions around them as if reciting a Jewish Kaddish.

'And the Sun put fire in her belly and said, "Let there be new life."
So Spring could become Summer and the seasons could begin.
And all saw that it was good.
And it was decided that the Right Place should for ever contain Spring,
and Spring should for ever contain all the Elements.
And with all the Elements the Right Place shall never die.
Let us now join all the Elements in holy matrimony.'

Jonathan lifted both arms high, his face raised to the heavens, holding the pose for a moment. 'The high priestess has spoken and this day is sacred. The high priestess has designed these tokens and they are sacred.'

Jonathan turned to the box on the chair. He picked it up,

turned back and lifted it into the air. 'These come from Sarah to you with love,' he announced. 'The high priestess has toiled long and hard and her sweat mingles with her love – so you buggers had better be grateful and bloody wear them.' He slowly lowered the box, opened it, and ceremoniously began handing a strip of intricately plaited black string to each of them, with the words: 'You are a Tadpole amongst Tadpoles.'

Ewan and Miriam looked blankly from the string to Jonathan. By the third 'You are a Tadpole amongst Tadpoles' Jonathan was finding it difficult to keep a straight face, and when Dave said in all seriousness, 'Thank you very much,' Jonathan succeeded only in nodding to the others, muttering 'Tadpole' and tossing them the remaining string bracelets. Fighting to stop the giggles, he watched their less than impressed faces.

Sally broke the silence. 'What's all this hippy-dippy shit about?' she asked, looking disdainfully at her piece of string.

Jonathan sighed and went to the record player to stop the music. 'It's a Sarah thing,' he explained. 'A wedding ceremony for all of us. She insisted we do it tonight. I don't know why. I wanted to wait but . . . She was supposed to do it; it wasn't supposed to be me. She was going to do it naked with an open robe, so that when she raised her arms—'

'Yes, thank you, Jonathan, we get the picture,' Margaret interrupted quickly. Jonathan shrugged.

'Well, I thought it was far out,' Sean announced and started clapping.

The others joined in, giving Jonathan a round of applause. Jonathan gave a slow smile, embarrassed, which broadened to a wide grin as Eric and Sean whistled loudly and the others called, 'More!'

'I'm giving you Tadley,' Jonathan said. 'It's not mine now; it's ours. Well, it will be, after the paperwork's done. And the marriage with Sarah . . . well, it's just to stop any interference from . . . anybody who should want to interfere.'

The whistles and claps grew and were joined by loud whoops and drumming feet. Jonathan started laughing. Nothing was going according to plan and everything was marvellous because of it. He felt marvellous, happy. Felt *relief* after his little 'chat' with Ewan. Absolutely nothing would change – Ewan had made that clear. In other words still (just) friends. But *better* friends now, Jonathan thought. Jonathan couldn't quite believe how good that felt, to be open, honest – and accepted.

'Congratulations,' he announced. 'We've all just got married. You may now kiss each other.' He giggled again, then stopped and shrugged. 'Ewan will explain.' Jonathan glanced towards Ewan and caught his eye. Both smiled slightly, almost sadly, their expressions more apparent as the lights flashed on. They both turned, blinked in the sudden harsh light and stared at Sarah's mother standing in the doorway.

'The hospital's just phoned. Sarah's waters have broken.'

Chaos. Everybody ran around the house, not sure what to do, not sure what they *were* doing, bumping into each other and panicking. Trying to find shoes, coats, calm.

They raced through the front door onto the driveway. Jonathan was already in his car, starting the engine, Sarah's parents and sister with him. He drove off before anybody could stop him or shout more than one word. *Jonathan!'*

'The van, the van!' Eric bellowed as they turned as one and headed for the van. They all piled in, Eric, Miriam and Margaret in the front seats, everybody else throwing themselves into the back, swearing, muttering and desperately trying to tie their bits of string around their wrists.

'Calm, calm,' Nick chanted in a panic-stricken sort of way,

before fishing a joint from his pocket and desperately lighting it. He inhaled deeply, calmed down slightly, and passed the joint around. Everybody took a drag, even Margaret.

'For God's sake, that's spooky,' Jim said. 'How can she do that? That's witchy, that is.'

'There was always a possibility that the baby would be premature,' Miriam replied quickly. Too quickly to convince.

'No, no, she's having it, she's having it while we're marrying each other – spooky. Really spooky.'

'It's a coincidence,' Ewan insisted.

'Jonathan said she wanted the ceremony tonight; Jonathan said she wouldn't wait. Why not? Because she knew, that's why not.'

'Why do you think they kept her in, Jim?' Miriam was desperate to be logical. 'They're not going to keep her wired up to monitors just for a dislocated hip and a bit of bleeding.'

'Yeah, but tonight. Everything happening tonight. At the same time. Synchronised and . . . spooky. And look! It's a full moon!'

The fear-heavy silence lasted a few seconds as nine pairs of eyes stared at the full moon.

'Definitely witchy. Definitely witchy,' Nick agreed.

'"A Saucerful of Secrets".' Sean nodded. 'What does *that* mean?'

'It means nothing,' Ewan impatiently muttered. 'It's just a record.'

'The whole ceremony thing, though,' Jim persisted to the point of irritation, 'at the same time, connection . . . blows the mind.'

Miriam sighed and shook her head. Margaret glanced at her and raised her eyebrows at the preposterousness of Jim's babbling. But secretly both felt spooked. Everybody felt spooked. Everybody absent-mindedly fiddled with their bracelets and considered the possibility of Sarah being a witch.

Of course, they weren't all allowed to stay. If they'd thought about it realistically, they'd have realised that thirteen people crammed into one waiting room for one baby was a bit much. When one of the nursing staff asked who the father was and Sean cheerily replied, 'We don't know, but we know it's not Dave,' Sarah's parents went white with shock and almost fainted. That was their cue to leave Jonathan to explain.

It was a long night and the van was freezing but nobody thought of going home. They took it in turns to go up to the labour ward occasionally to warm up and find out what was happening. Nothing was. At one point they had a game of football in the car park with an old tin can, but a security guard told them to stop it. They couldn't even get a cup of tea from the hospital drinks machine: nobody had thought to bring any money with them. A thoroughly cold, long, uncomfortable night. But one of the best. Nobody argued, nobody irritated and nobody felt out of place. They smiled warmly at each other and said little, and what they did say was affable. The van was the temple and their quiet togetherness the ceremony. Tadpoles amongst Tadpoles. And when Jonathan appeared around eight in the morning to tell them it was a boy, their marriage was sealed.

'Can we see them, Jonathan?' Miriam asked, leaning out of the passenger window.

'Sarah's with her family, and the baby's under observation so . . . maybe later.' Jonathan shrugged.

'What about just Ewan then?' Sally said. 'Can't Ewan see them? Just briefly?'

The decision in the van was unanimous: Ewan should go for all of them. Ewan nearly cried.

And later he did, slightly, as he and Jonathan stood, shiny-eyed and smiling in the hospital corridor, looking through the window of the baby unit.

'Third incubator from the left,' Jonathan pointed out.

That was all that was said for the longest time as Ewan pressed his nose and hands against the glass and stared at the third incubator from the left, inhibited joy and tears of relief threatening to spill.

A little wife, little kids, Jonathan thought, grinning with deep affection. It's true, it *is* all he wants. 'You're not going to argue with her, are you?' he asked.

'Why should I argue?' Ewan smiled, unable to drag his eyes from the incubator, unable to stop smiling.

'Because you thought she'd rejected you.'

'Oh Christ, Jonathan.'

'She had you going for months. Must rankle.'

Ewan frowned slightly and tore himself away from the third incubator from the left. He stood up straight and turned to face Jonathan. Jonathan waited for the lecture.

'Congratulations, Jonathan Jo,' he said. Ewan stood awkwardly for a second or two, his arms twitching. Then he stepped forward and threw his arms around Jonathan, hugging him hard, long and with affection. It was more than acceptance. Jonathan felt tears of joy sting his own eyes and he hugged Ewan back.

They turned back to the third incubator from the left and both smiled broadly, unable to control their inane grins.

'Congratulations, Ewan Hughes,' Jonathan said.

They went to Sarah's room together, Ewan dumping the great grin at the door. But at least he didn't mention the fact that it was a private room; at least he didn't bore with lectures on Nye

Bevan. He just stood quietly at the back of the room, playing polite patience and waiting for Sarah's family to take the hint and leave. Jonathan watched him watching Sarah. She was pale and exhausted, her eyes hollow, cheeks sunken, hair like rat's tails, talking to her mum and studiously ignoring Ewan. But her sunken cheeks were tinged with pink and her hollow eyes shone, aware of Ewan's gaze furtively fixed on her as though she were the most beautiful thing in the world. Then all change, back to normal as Sarah's family left the room and their expressions turned to petulance and mutual sulky glowers. Jonathan wanted to spit.

Sarah sat up slightly, painfully. Ewan moved forward and perched on her bed.

'How you feeling, you old witch?' Ewan sneered.

'Not so bad, thanks, you old toad,' Sarah sneered back, inspecting the string bracelet around Ewan's right wrist.

'I've seen the third incubator from the left.'

'Oh? And what do you think?'

'Not bad – pretty good. Thought of a name for it, have you?'

'Yes, I have, actually. I thought I'd name him after the events of the past week.'

Ewan sat back and curled his lips in a look of disgust. 'You're not going to call him Tadpole, are you?'

Sarah laughed, then groaned at the pain of laughing. Ewan touched her with tender concern. Jonathan watched with bemusement. All this nonsense on top and all these feelings underneath – it was absurd, and yet he envied it at the same time.

'No,' Sarah replied. 'Of course I'm not going to call him Tadpole. I thought I'd call him Chaos.'

Ewan thought about it, shrugged and tried to look nonchalant, but he couldn't help breaking into a huge grin. 'Yeah, that's about right.' He laughed. 'You're certainly very good at creating chaos!'

Sarah laughed and tried not to again. Ewan helped her out by kissing her deeply, passionately and, for the first time, publicly. Jonathan had never kissed like that. He'd never seen Sarah or Ewan kiss anybody else like that. Jonathan looked on as his envy slid uncomfortably towards jealousy.

Later Jonathan stood by the van while Ewan, his face still plastered with a broad smile, clambered into the back and into the centre of attention.

'You'd better get going, you lot – you've got your wedding reception, you know. They'll be there in a couple of hours.' Jonathan smirked.

'Oh God, yes, I'd forgotten,' Miriam said, turning to Eric to get the van started pronto. Eric was about to pull off when Sean leant over from the back and peered round Miriam's shoulder at Jonathan.

'What do you mean, *our* wedding reception?'

'You're the ones who got married. Have fun.' Jonathan banged the side of the van and laughed as he turned back towards the hospital.

'Oh no,' muttered Ewan, finally losing the smile.

'He wouldn't, would he?' Miriam said.

'Drive, Eric,' Margaret sighed. 'Just drive.'

Great-Uncle Hugh was the first to arrive. He was, in fact, early – sitting on the front steps, engrossed in last week's *Daily Telegraph* crossword, when the van pulled up. They piled out, grubby, tired, apprehensive and dishevelled. Great-Uncle Hugh didn't seem bothered; he didn't seem to be dressed for a wedding reception either – wellington boots, enormous overcoat that seemed two sizes too big and a fishing hat with attached floats. He smiled benevolently and waved his newspaper, striding over to shake their hands.

'I parked it round the back – wasn't too sure what to do with it, really. And the men didn't want to wait so . . . found some grass – it seems perfectly happy. Margaret, my dear . . .'

Great-Uncle Hugh shook Margaret warmly by the hand and kissed her cheek before leading them round to the back of the house where a horse was munching its way through the lawn by the terrace.

'A Suffolk Punch,' Great-Uncle Hugh explained. 'I was wavering between that and bees. But then Aggie said she was thinking bees, so . . . there you are. Where's Jonathan? Is he not around?'

Everybody felt safe with Great-Uncle Hugh. Ewan, Dave and Miriam remembered him from the funeral; he was a completely dotty old man who kept swigging from a hip flask – he seemed permanently nine sheets to the wind. But he was *Jonathan's* uncle, and a favourite one, so had been expected. It was the ninety-nine other mystery guests that were the worry.

Dave leant in Ewan's bedroom doorway as Ewan was dressing.

'Do you think I should cut my hair, Ewan?'

'Why? Does it need cutting?'

'It's just that Miriam's phoned her parents.'

'And?'

'There was no reply.'

Ewan stopped pulling on his purple shirt for a second and looked worriedly at Dave. 'My lot aren't on the phone.'

'Neither are mine,' Dave said. He rallied slightly. 'I've got an Auntie Betty: she is.'

Ewan continued dressing, then undressing, now unsure about the purple shirt. 'Okay, phone your Auntie Betty – see if she knows anything.'

Dave was about to do just that when, from downstairs, he and Ewan heard Sean scream delightedly, 'Mum!'

Dave and Ewan exchanged looks.

'I'll help you cut your hair then,' Ewan said forlornly, removing his purple shirt and looking for a white one.

Dave's Auntie Betty turned up with Dave's mum, his four sisters and various other relations and friends in a Morris 1100, a Humber Sunbeam and a Hillman Imp. The cars parked bonnet to boot along the path outside the house. The Tadpoles lined the steps of the house like a crumpled and skewed welcoming committee dressed in someone else's Sunday best. Dave's mum took one look at Dave, took a comb out of her handbag and tried to get Dave's hair into something resembling a shape.

It was the beginning of the Parting of the Ways.

Dave's dad turned up five minutes later in an A35 van, copper piping tied to the roof rack and a treasure trove of toilets, sinks, hinges, handles, plugs, dynamos, nuts and bolts, light fittings and batteries crammed in the back. He took out his work tools, rubbed his hands together and appeared set to demolish the house.

Dave rummaged through the van like a kid at Christmas, yelling, 'Taps! Oh, Dad, taps, just what I wanted!'

Two minutes later, Dave, his dad, his work tools and his taps had disappeared, leaving Dave's mum looking annoyed but unsurprised.

Miriam's family came next. Her mother, father and grand-mother rolled up in an immaculately clean, wood-panelled

Morris Minor Traveller. All three got out of the car and stood like royalty as Miriam approached and kissed them. Her father strode about as though he owned the place, shook hands with everybody as though they were staff, and said, 'The name's Bernard – call me Bernie.'

Nobody did.

'You'll never achieve self-sufficiency,' Miriam's father stated. 'Salt and books, Miriam, you can't survive without salt and books.' He beckoned Ewan and Eric to his car to lug a tea chest packed with salt from the back seat, while he ostentatiously opened the boot of the car to display the boxes of books.

'As demanded by your friend Jonathan's contribution list,' he said pompously.

Miriam looked at her shoes.

Miriam's mother ('Call me Sheila') filled the silence by faking a broad smile, attempting to appear 'with it' and saying, in a nervously shrill voice, 'So, are you all hippies?'

Miriam's shoulders started to shake and Sally laughed out loud.

Jim's and Nick's mothers were heard before they were seen, giving Jim enough time to grab Nick and make a bolt for it. The sound of their ferocious arguing drifted on the wind from somewhere near the bottom of the drive. Dave's Auntie Betty had never heard so much effing and blinding in her life – and *she* came from Dudley. As the open-top American car came into view Ewan assumed from the rigid, nothing-to-do-with-me expression on the driver's face that the mothers were in the back of a fancy hire car with chauffeur. But Eric explained that the driver was Jim's stepdad.

'Stepdad? He looks younger than Jim.'

'No, no, he's a good four or five years older,' Eric said. 'He's Nick's mum's younger brother. Jim and Nick are half-cousins

. . . or step-nephew and . . . Or half-step-uncle and . . .' Eric shook his head. 'It's very complicated,' he said, more to himself than to Ewan.

The front passenger seat wasn't empty either. Nick's dad had slid so far down in his seat that it only looked that way. It gave everybody quite a turn when he suddenly sat up. He looked ancient – mouselike, grey and thoroughly stoned.

Jim's and Nick's mums didn't hang around; they bickered across the drive, ignored the gawping faces, blew Eric a kiss and swept into the house as though stars at a royal premiere. Jim's stepdad did a three-point turn in seven moves, and Nick's dad slid back down in his seat and disappeared from view. They were never seen again.

Eric's parents were much friendlier. Or they would have been, given the chance. Before the van had stopped Eric raced over and pulled the van doors open, shouting, 'Wait till you see the ceilings! Wait till you see the floors! Wait till you see the size of the rooms!'

His mother shouted back, 'Wait till you see what we've brought! We've got mops, buckets, brooms, disinfectant, that new lemon scourer that you like . . .'

At the same time countless children and teenagers spewed out of the van like cramped sheep released into a meadow. The noise was deafening. Eric's dad laughed indulgently and yelled to the onlookers, 'They're not all ours, you know!'

Eric grabbed his parents' arms and practically frogmarched them towards the house, his mum and dad spluttering an affable hello and waving helplessly in greeting. Ewan and Sally watched with visions of destruction as the horde of kids, armed with footballs, headed for a winter-sown wheat field. Eric's dad seemed to know without looking. He turned on the steps, whistled and pointed to a fallow field next door. Like good sheep the flock of kids obeyed and Eric's mum and dad disappeared inside the house with Eric shouting, 'Wait till you see this floor – it's marble!'

The whole of Maerdy turned up in a coach. Or so it seemed to Ewan. His heart sank as it heralded its chugging arrival with a large Welsh dragon flag on prominent display in the front passenger window and 'Little Moscow' written on the charter board.

Everybody he'd spent his whole life avoiding stepped down from the coach, one by one, smiling and waving and flashing before him as though his life were about to end. Amongst them Mrs Pryce, the town cow, who would find out everything he'd been doing *and* tell his mam. Her son, Mad Wizzo, who still looked like a Teddy boy and still looked pathetic, and probably still sold speed. Donna Matthews, Ewan's first proper girlfriend. Her sister Diane, his first improper girlfriend and taker of his virginity. Idris Weeks, who beat him up in the third form and became his best friend. Bryn and Tom, his huge, rugby-playing older brothers, who beat him up constantly. His mother, Nesta, with her 'gang of girls', chivvying the men to put down the beer and get off their backsides, then supervising the unloading of *boxes* of stuff from the coach. Tins of baked beans, boxes of chocolate, packets of tea, jars of coffee, bags of salt, paper, pens, cigarettes, fire lighters, matches, sacks of coal . . .

'We went round the town and had a collection.' Nesta grinned.

Ewan couldn't help but smile – the steps looked like a Red Cross depot at a major disaster area.

And his dad, Gareth, looming before him, fixing him with those maddening shiny eyes, and booming in a voice loud enough for *everybody* to hear, 'God gives you the brain to go to university and you end up being a farmer?'

Ewan lost the smile but found Sally by his right shoulder, slipping her hand into his and squeezing hard.

It was nice to see his mam, though.

And it was nice to see Margaret, stumbling down the steps, screaming, 'Peter, Peter!' and weeping with joy as a taxi drew up and an old man, who looked uncannily like her, got out.

'My brother, Canada, forty-two years,' Margaret managed to blurt out, tears streaming down her face, with the biggest grin in the world as she had the life squeezed out of her by her brother's bear hug. Even Bernard (call me *pompous*) looked humbled.

Nobody turned up for Sally. Children's homes and social workers don't stay in touch, even if they are local. Sally didn't care; she was already with her family. Three sisters and seven brothers. Sally stood with Ewan in the middle of a field, surrounded by his mum, dad, brothers and the Welsh contingent. She held Ewan's hand as he tried to explain the various merits of hard wheat and soft wheat, winter wheat and spring wheat. She held his hand tighter when Gareth clapped him solidly on the back and said, 'Yeah, all bloody marvellous, Ewan, but how about we move to another bloody muddy field where you can bore us rigid about barley?'

Sally felt tears welling up alongside her anger. It was strange, unfamiliar. She swallowed hard and forced the tears down. Sally was used to anger but she wasn't used to tears.

Dave wasn't used to anyone interfering. He sat on the toilet lid, glum-faced, chin in one hand, redundant wrench in the other, and couldn't even bring himself to look in the direction of his dad, wedged in under the bath and faffing. Dave had installed four en suite bathrooms with no help from anyone (not counting Eric and Ewan, who held stuff and did as they were told). Dave's dad had looked at all four, inspected them, and even *praised* his accomplishments. So why he should feel the need to take over and treat Dave like an *apprentice* was beyond Dave. The worst of it was, Dave felt guilty. Sitting on the toilet lid, getting more and more irritated, just because his dad was trying to help. He should feel pleased; he should be glad his dad was interested and supportive. Trouble was, Dave wasn't.

Jim and Nick found Eric and his parents in the music room. Unfortunately they found their mums there as well. Jim didn't mind too much – Eric's parents were too cheerfully manic to give people time to argue. Besides, it gave him the opportunity to hold forth about his ideas.

'A studio with recording facilities, the possibility of holding outdoor concerts, providing rehearsal space for other bands . . .' Jim revelled in the nodding approval of Eric's parents, and ignored the look of doubt spreading over his mother's face.

Nick was *happy* to see his mum, despite what Jim said. Nick was even happier when his mum pulled him to one side and slipped two sweet bags into his hand.

'I know it wasn't on the contribution list,' she whispered. 'But it's a little present for now, and seeds to plant for later.' She gave Nick a sly wink and a big kiss.

Nick knew nothing about gardening so shuffled off to find Ewan while Jim launched into his painted-panel idea. This was Jim's killer innovation and he swept around the room, gesticulating flamboyantly.

'Different-coloured panels placed in front of each musician, the colours either clashing or harmonious, producing different textures of sound . . .'

Eric had heard all this before and prised his parents slowly and silently away. Nick's mum thought it sounded fab; Jim's mum thought it was bollocks. Jim found himself very much alone as he turned to deal with the mothers' erupting argument.

Margaret was having a lovely day. She sat in the kitchen with Peter and Great-Uncle Hugh, regaling them with tales of what the 'daft young things' had been up to. The more she talked the more it dawned on her that she loved her daft young things dearly. And she included Ewan in that love, despite (or because of) the sudden invasion of dozens of Welshwomen, insisting *now* was the time to add the finishing touches to the Ballroom Buffet and demanding to make themselves useful.

The Ballroom Buffet was horrendous. Ewan hated it. Outside was bad enough but at least he could *breathe*. He was wedged between his hulking great brothers on a sofa, unable to move because his mother had insisted her 'boys' sit while she fetched food for them all. Sickeningly, he'd acquiesced because he didn't want to upset her. How easy it was to slip into old ways. How easy it was for his brothers too, pressing against him like a ham sandwich.

'What's this thing then?' Bryn said, flicking at the string bracelet on Ewan's wrist and taking the piss.

'If we hadn't met your bird, we'd have thought you were turning into a bit of a poof, Ewan,' said Tom, back to the old juvenile wind-up.

'What do you mean, "turning into", Tom? He's always been one, hasn't he? Anyway, his bird looks like a boy.'

Ewan forced himself off the sofa not bothering to correct his brothers' assumptions. He'd decided years ago that things were better buttoned up and lied about. And stuff the buffet too – he wasn't even hungry. There were other ways of pleasing his mother, and reverting to old habits and trying to punch Bryn's lights out wasn't one of them. He passed Sally talking to his dad.

'How can you call yourself a socialist, Mr Hughes, when you sit there while your wife runs around fetching your food?'

Ewan had to smile at that. Sally was bloody beautiful no matter what she looked like. He passed Welshmen sitting and Welshwomen flapping around them. He knew every single one of them and they all irritated the hell out of him. Who is this party for exactly, Jonathan? He passed Miriam.

'No, Dad, Tadley is not just an experiment, and I *don't want* to work in the City!'

Us. This party is for us. Close the gates, pull up the draw-bridge and tell repressive family, old friends and past habits to fuck off! What was the point of leaving home if home was going to follow and spoil it?

He passed Sean talking to Dave – almost *crying* to Dave.

'I love my mum, I really do. She loves animals too; she patted every single cow, every single pig, with love and affection. I love her, I do – but I *don't* want her to move in. And she was threatening to, Dave; she wants to. She asked if she could.'

'What did you do, Sean?' Dave replied.

'Ran, mate, ran.'

And Great-Uncle Hugh passed Ewan, stopped him, held his arm and pulled him to the wall. 'I've heard all about you from Margaret. I shouldn't, of course, but try some of this.'

Ewan took a swig from Great-Uncle Hugh's hip flask. He was unable to figure out what it was but felt pleasantly stoned about ten minutes later.

Eric had run himself into exhaustion showing his mum and dad the house and *still* his parents were brimming with enthu-siasm. Eric needed food. He needed to stoke up before the tour of the outbuildings and farm. Everything *seemed* fine when they entered the ballroom. But halfway across the floor, Sally exploded, the room plunged into silence, and all Eric could do to cover his embarrassment was point out the ornate ceiling to his parents.

With tear-streaked vitriol, Sally gave Ewan's dad a raging piece of her mind. Gareth Hughes's arms were spread wide in an apologetic gesture; he was defenceless against a female. His eyes shone and he laughed broadly. 'Nothing wrong with being a farmer. I think it's marvellous, think it's bloody brilliant – most socialist thing he could do!'

'Well, tell him then!' Sally spat.

Eric saw Miriam looking strangely proud and Ewan grinning dopily at his brothers and saying, 'That's my bird, that is.'

Eric's parents kept their eyes on the ceiling and ignored the outburst. Eric grabbed a handful of vol-au-vents and ushered them off to explore the outbuildings and see where cheese was going to be made, and butter, where sheep shearing would take place, dyeing, spinning, weaving . . .

Eric couldn't stop. His parents didn't want him to stop. He ran from shed to stable to barn to field. He bumped into an old woman enquiring where she could set up her beehive. She listed all the things Jonathan's relatives and friends were contributing. 'Butter churns, an anvil, cheese-making equipment, farm implements, a potter's wheel, a loom . . .'

Eric listed all the plans they'd made. 'Making our own jumpers, our own clothes, shoes, linen; we might grow flax, cotton, all sorts. Experiment. Trial and error. Greenhouses, polytunnels. Leather, tanning, a blacksmith's maybe, pottery, basket-weaving, making furniture, bricks. Milling our own flour, making bread, beer, wine, whisky, bottling, preserving, pickling . . .'

Eric stopped and held his head in disbelief. He'd never ever listed the plans like this, never thought about it as a *whole*. He stood outside, still holding his head, unable to move. The beehive woman sought help elsewhere. And Eric's mum and dad did the only thing his mum and dad could do – they dashed back to the ballroom to tell everybody else.

Miriam stood supportively close to Sally at the buffet table. Not that Sally needed support – she kept giggling quietly to herself and throwing cheeky-and-proud-of-it glances at Miriam. Miriam giggled too, mainly because *nobody* was saying anything. Gareth Hughes seemed none the worse for the outburst, sitting with his family, laughing and talking. He *was* avoiding Ewan, though. Or maybe Ewan was avoiding him. Ewan was at the other end of the room, leaning against the wall by the door – ready for a quick getaway, Miriam thought as she nudged Sally and tipped her head in Ewan's direction.

Ewan saw them looking and raised Great-Uncle Hugh's hip flask in salute to Sally, a big grin plastered across his face. Sally coloured with embarrassment and giggled again. 'Ewan's mum says I don't feed him enough,' she said.

Miriam giggled. She watched her mother and grandmother sidle over.

'Miriam dear,' her grandmother said, 'your mother and I were wondering which one was Jonathan – we were hoping to meet him.'

Sally turned away but Miriam distinctly heard her laugh, and her shoulders were shaking convulsively.

'Jonathan's at the hospital, Mother,' Miriam said, cutting out the middleman and getting straight to the point. 'With Sarah, his fiancée. She's just had a baby.'

Miriam's mother looked crestfallen and said, 'Oh.'

Sally nearly wet herself.

Miriam watched her mother and grandmother drift off in search of other suitable marriage material. Both she and Sally were by now hysterical. Eventually Sally straightened herself up and looked directly at Miriam with a daring glint in her eye. 'Do you care?' she said.

Miriam knew exactly what Sally was asking – or at least she *hoped* she did. 'Not any more, no,' she said.

Jonathan arrived back from the hospital with Sarah's family. He expected laughter and celebration, but was met by silence. He stood at the entrance to the ballroom and saw Miriam and Sally snogging passionately in front of a speechless, staring crowd. From the other end of the room somebody shouted, 'Your bird, Ewan?'

Jonathan jumped and looked round as Ewan, behind him, shouted back, 'Yes, Bryn, my gorgeous, amazing, beautiful brave bird!'

Ewan took a large swig from Great-Uncle Hugh's hip flask and cackled maniacally.

Jonathan looked again at Miriam and Sally, wondering which one was Ewan's 'bird' and what on earth was going on. Then he pitched forward as Ewan clapped him solidly on the back.

'Great party, Jonathan.' Ewan beamed. 'Bloody marvellous, mate!'

Chapter 7

April 1972 – one year later

Sarah balanced Chaos on her hip and breezed gracefully down the stairs, the silk jersey crêpe softly brushing and caressing her as she moved, making her naked body beneath feel deliciously sensual. The white, rich material fell in perfect folds from her shoulders to her feet, the neckline cut low and draped to accentuate the shape of her breasts . . . Chaos's hand was placed artfully on her right breast, emphasising her sensuality and fecundity. It was a perfect dress, the best thing she'd ever made. One flick of the shoulders and the dress would fall, cascading in a silk-rich heap to the floor. Who could resist it? None of them – she'd designed it that way. Sarah giggled. No more deference, no more assumptions that she was half of something, waiting for Ewan to be asleep or out working before the dogs came sniffing – even Jim thought of her as 'Ewan's lady', *and* Jonathan, and she was *married* to Jonathan! And definitely no more uneventful domestic bliss, curled up nightly with Chaos between them like a cute and cosy passion killer. So, goodbye, 'Mrs Hughes', hello, wicked white witch bitch man-eater ball-breaker Ewan-baiter. Passion was only real passion when it was real jealousy, real rage – not fantasy, assumption and memory. Ewan hated it too, she was sure of it – even if he wasn't.

Sarah entered the breakfast room expecting to find at least Jim and Nick and a couple of chicks to compete with. There were chicks – four of them – but no Jim and Nick, no band. There were two guys, strangers, and they immediately sat up and took notice. Sarah hadn't had sex with a stranger for ages. Ewan would die at a stranger. It was the thing he loved the most. Sarah knew it, even though he'd never admit it.

Sarah smiled brightly, sang 'Good morning' and introduced herself to the guys – the band's new roadies. She plonked herself opposite the bedraggled girls, positioning Chaos on her knee like a trophy. This was going to be easy.

Jim explained the situation in the silence of the study and watched Jonathan's smile fade. He turned to look at Ewan. Ewan had slumped back in his chair, speechless and still, staring at the rain through the window. Not even his leg twitched. Jim's news was a bombshell. Jim had known it would be.

'Congratulations,' Jonathan murmured.

Jim smiled apologetically.

'The lead singer died,' Nick said – for the umpteenth time.

Jonathan nodded.

The band had only found out last night. Their new manager, Tyler, had turned up at the gig in Birmingham, over-excited and armed with champagne. The news about the lead singer was tragic, of course. But Jethro Tull needed another support band. Jim and Nick were over the moon. As were Eric and Sean – until the implications dawned. They'd be away for at least six months, possibly even a year. The loss of manpower could spell disaster for the farm and the choice was stark: the Horsemen or Tadley Hall? After a long night of discussion, Jim had elected himself spokesman. They would have to leave tomorrow.

'I'm sorry,' Jim mumbled, amazed at how guilty he felt.

'The lead singer died,' Nick said again, in case Ewan and Jonathan had missed the explanation.

Ewan nodded slightly and Jim felt worse. It must be Eric and Sean getting to him. Eric and Sean and their ambivalence, their downright lack of enthusiasm for fame, fortune and the rock and roll high life.

Dave leant contemplatively over the pen and said, 'It's only a pig.'

Miriam looked up sharply, wondering what on earth had possessed Dave to say something *so stupid* at such a crucial time.

'It might be "only a pig" to you, Dave, but I love my pigs,' Sean said with a menacing glower. He didn't get up, though. He stayed on his knees in the straw, rubbing his knuckles affectionately along the head and snout of the fat beast. The pig snorted its appreciation and snuffled its nose towards Sean.

Sally kept her eyes fixed on the instruction manual and her mind fixed on the belief that one book was not enough. One book was never enough. It took more than one book to figure out how to make a lathe, even though the diagrams were exactly the same, so . . . So far they'd managed a few chickens. Chickens were surprisingly easy. Sheep were cute, cows were big, and pigs were Sean's. So, even if Sean *was* willing, it would take at least two books to kill the pig. And possibly even three.

Dave shrugged in bewilderment. 'If you don't want to kill the pig, Sean, why have we all trooped out to help?'

Sean opened his mouth with murderous intent but nothing came out. He contemptuously ignored Dave and lovingly rubbed and smacked the pig's rump instead.

Eric turned away. He leant his back and elbows against the rails and took a diversionary interest in the sound of the rain on the corrugated roof of the pig shed. He felt like crying. And he desperately wanted to explain that Sean was saying goodbye. But Jonathan had to know first; it was the way things were done at Tadley.

'He's one of my favourites,' Sean suddenly blurted in the background. 'I've had him since he was a weaner!'

Eric blinked rapidly at the roof as Sean sprawled helplessly in the straw, overcome by sobs of heartbreak. Miriam jumped into the pigpen to comfort him. Eric surreptitiously wiped away a tear while nobody was looking. He hated it. This wasn't his scene at all. He couldn't understand why they couldn't all be vegetarians, or buy their bacon from the butcher's or just send the poor pig to the slaughterhouse like normal people. Self-sufficiency was one thing but there were limits, surely.

'It's only a pig,' Dave said again, intending it to sound sympathetic.

Sean saw red. He jumped up, knocked Miriam out of the way and practically fell over the pen rails in an attempt to get at Dave. Dave plastered himself against the side of the shed, just out of reach of Sean's swinging fists. As Sally ran round to help Miriam she dropped the book into the pigpen. The pig took the opportunity to urinate copiously over it. Eric turned and faced the scene. Pig-killing and Dave-punching were not how he wanted to leave Tadley.

'Sarah changed our clothes,' Eric blurted out, choking on his words as he fought back the tears. 'She told us how to look better and move better and be sexier. Stuff Ewan's said is in Jim and Nick's lyrics . . .'

Sean stopped swinging wild punches and turned sharply to Eric.

'Jonathan's given us a home and you've all given us energy, love and the confidence to practise and get good,' Eric continued. 'We've worked on the farm and the house, we've eaten good food and we've got muscles. We're not flabby and pasty and half-dead-looking any more; we look good, virile – sexy, Tyler reckons.'

Miriam and Sally exchanged bewildered glances and looked at Eric in confusion. Sally even laughed and queried, *'Sexy?'*

Dave kept his eye on Sean and inched towards the shed door as Sean climbed out of the pen and stumbled towards Eric, his head shaking and his eyes getting blacker. Dave didn't know what Eric was on about but was mighty grateful for the diversion.

'We're a hundred per cent better than we were before we came here,' Eric said, watching Sean's menacing approach. 'So we deserve success, yes. But it should be here, at Tadley, with all of you, with everyone. We should be a band of string-bracelet-wearing Tadpoles, somehow.'

'What are you on about, Eric?' Miriam asked.

'It's not "only a pig", it's Sean's offering; it's his gift,' Eric said.

Sean punched him. Sean was furious. Eric was sent sprawling.

'No, Eric,' Sean said, 'Jim's the spokesman, Jonathan's the boss, you're speaking out of turn, and it *is* only a pig!'

That was what Eric liked about Sean: his respect for etiquette.

It had been a good year. It really had been a good year. Ewan would have happily said so, had anyone asked. Not that anyone needed to – his mood, energy and optimism said it all. He crossed the hall with Jonathan's voice buzzing round his head:

'All Elements connected. And with all the Elements the Right Place shall never die.' It was a couple of lines from the 'wedding ceremony' that Sarah had written and Jonathan performed. Ewan would never admit that those words had struck a chord; he would never admit that he believed in them. But he did, passionately. And this past year had proved Sarah's words right. All eleven of them *had* connected and Tadley was alive and thriving. Sarah's sacrament hadn't mentioned what would happen if four 'elements' left, though, and that was what now preoccupied him.

'You're a bloody coward, Ewan.'

Sally's voice interrupted Ewan's thoughts. He looked quizzically at Sally and Dave coming towards him, then remembered Sean's pig.

'Sorry, Sally, I'm crops, not animals.' Ewan shrugged innocently, sidestepping any explanation of meetings or leaving bands – that was Jonathan's job.

'Oh, we're suddenly into job demarcation, are we? How very convenient,' she replied sarcastically. 'Sean was in tears, you know.'

'He nearly killed me,' Dave added. 'And Miriam. Then he nearly killed Eric. He nearly killed everyone but the pig. And according to *this* book we need a shotgun.' Dave held up one of three books he was carrying. 'Thank God Sean didn't read this!'

Ewan laughed but Sally and Dave didn't. They were distracted by something behind him.

'Even I can kill a chicken,' Sarah said.

Ewan did a classic double take. He turned and gave a slight, peevish raise of the eyebrows, followed a split second later by a 'what the fuck' gawp. Ewan turned fully to take in the picture of Sarah and Chaos framed in the breakfast-room doorway.

Chaos gurgled a laugh and bounced on Sarah's hip in an over-joyed greeting that only one-year-olds and dogs can do with sincerity. Sarah, in contrast, stood triumphant, half smirking and half sneering with that old love/hate look that Ewan had thought she'd long lost.

'What on earth are you wearing?' Sally asked, screwing up her face with incredulity.

'Bloody hell, Sarah, you look radiant,' Dave announced with unabashed conviction.

Ewan felt the rug being pulled from under him in massive jerks – first Jim, now Sarah. What he'd thought was a perfect relationship was about to follow the farm down the toilet. Not enough that he'd had to accept Jim and Nick as 'co-lovers'. Not enough that he'd learnt to turn a blind eye to an occasionally frustrated Eric or Sean. A new game – a new *painful* game – was being presented. He had the urge to say, 'Not now, not when everything's crumbling,' but that was the surest way of losing. Besides, it was strangely exciting.

'She's wearing an old sheet, Dave,' Ewan said, fixing his eyes on Sarah's and forcing himself to smirk. 'Just a stupid old sheet. The one Jonathan's old man died in, I should imagine.'

Sarah arched her eyebrows, nodding her head graciously at Ewan's pathetic attempt at insult.

'Well, it's a beautiful sheet. Don't you think she looks beauti-ful in her sheet, Ewan?' Dave said.

'But what's she going to do in it, Dave?' Sally asked.

Ewan almost laughed but the unspoken reply to Sally's ques-tion stopped him and the game became clear. A stranger appeared behind Sarah, holding her waist as he tried to manoeuvre his way around her, whispering in her ear, almost biting it, almost nuzzling. Whatever he said, it seemed to turn Sarah on.

'Yes, well, let's say goodbye to our guests first.' She blushed, standing aside to let four pouting and miserable girls out of the room. An unusually quiet and embarrassed Jim and Nick appeared, avoiding eye contact with Ewan as they escorted the girls to the front door. Another guy, face shining with sexual possibility, passed her, touched her, stood close by and tried to amuse Chaos by waggling his fingers at him.

It was an old game. A cutting, humiliating slap in the face, and Ewan's eyes and lips briefly narrowed. His reaction was too brief for Sarah's satisfaction. She frowned slightly as he stepped forward and removed Chaos from her arms, a broad smile growing on his face. His message was clear. 'Do what you like – I'll hold the baby.' He was bluffing. Underneath he was raging, he must be. Sarah watched Jim and Nick send the four girls on their way.

'Well, they didn't last long, did they?' she said with a smile of mock innocence. 'Hardly had a chance to say hello. Pity really, we could do with more females. Don't you think we need more females in the community, Ewan?'

'No, I don't,' Ewan replied. 'No need.'

Sarah frowned and looked enquiringly at him, inviting him to explain.

'The band are leaving,' he explained.

Jonathan followed the noise and found an ad hoc meeting taking place in the hall. Everybody was there and talking at once.

'We're not leaving,' Eric insisted to Margaret. 'We'll just be coming and going.'

'You don't think I'd abandon my animals, do you?' Sean said to Miriam. 'Besides, I've got to check now, because that pig this morning, he's won a reprieve. You can't put a pig on death row twice – it's inhumane.'

'Oh no, you can't kill that pig,' Eric joined in. 'I've grown attached to that pig myself.'

'Well, perhaps you could take it on tour with you?' Margaret suggested with a deadpan expression.

Eric and Sean seriously considered the idea. Jim and Nick and the new roadies looked alarmed.

Jonathan crumpled up his hastily written speech and surreptitiously shoved it in his pocket. The atmosphere in the hall was bristling and the voices were getting louder. Chaos was the only one who looked happy. He was taking advantage of the group gathering to practise his walking, using the various legs as staging posts. Ewan and Sarah were locked in their own argument.

'Why should we do what you want?' Sarah sneered at Ewan. 'What makes you think that what you do is the most important thing around here?'

'Because it's obvious: we've got to eat,' Ewan replied. 'Can't survive on tarot readings, can we, Sarah?'

Jonathan opened his mouth but Sally interrupted – she looked thoroughly pissed off.

'We're losing four men, Jonathan – two of them bloody useful,' she said, as if it were somehow Jonathan's fault. Jim and Nick looked affronted.

'You're not losing us; we'll just be coming and going,' Eric insisted.

Jonathan waved his hands down like a teacher engulfed by demanding kids. 'Okay, everybody, okay,' he called, trying to calm everyone. It didn't work. Sarah's and Ewan's tempers were steadily rising.

'Well then, we'll have to employ some staff, won't we!' Sarah spat.

'No, *we'll* have to work properly – won't *we*!' Ewan countered.

116

'I do work properly – it's just not good enough for you.'

'Candle-making? Tapestry? Meditation?'

Chaos fell at Sarah's feet. He'd aimed for Dave's leg but Dave had unknowingly moved. Sarah instinctively bent towards him. Jim did what Jonathan had been dreading. Jim took Sarah's side.

'Candle-making's useful. And practical,' he said. 'I mean, the generator's dodgy at the best of times.'

'The generator is not dodgy,' Dave argued, taking umbrage.

'She's bloody engraving them. Putting fancy patterns into them,' Ewan said, rounding on Jim. 'And then she's using them for her stupid incantations and meditations. Very useful. Very bloody practical.'

'Meditation eases stress,' Nick said.

'So why is she a screaming, wired-up neurotic then?' Sally asked.

'I am not a screaming, wired-up neurotic,' Sarah gasped, totally appalled. She picked Chaos up and shoved him unceremoniously into Miriam's arms.

Chaos didn't seem to mind but Miriam did. 'I don't know about neurotic but you *are* behaving like a bloody bitch on heat,' she grumbled.

Sarah continued to rage at Ewan. 'So what *is* useful, huh? How about feeding the chickens, egg-collecting, having the guts to *kill* the chickens, clothes-making, decorating, looking after Chaos, cleaning, tidying, laundry—'

'Sexual relief for the workers,' Ewan interrupted.

'Which you *love*!' she sneered as she slapped his face.

The slap echoed loudly around the hall – everybody felt it.

'Can we please, everybody, calm down,' Jonathan pleaded, wishing he could slap *both* Ewan and Sarah as they glowered furiously at each other.

Sarah's rage was too close to murderous to stop. 'You are a

scheming, manipulative bastard, who wants everything his own way.'

'*I* am?' Ewan said with incredulity at the pot calling the kettle black.

Sarah ignored him. 'You want it to be colourless, don't you? Colourless and drab and boring. And *practical*.' She mimicked his Welsh accent with disgust. 'Everything's got to be *practical*. Everybody's got to be just like you — soulless. That's what you want, isn't it? Everybody like you, without art or romance or music — you even despise the band, don't you? Go on, admit it, you think what they're doing is a waste of time too, don't you?'

'Well, let's face it, they are leaving us in the lurch.' Ewan shrugged with throwaway disdain.

'We're not leaving,' Eric started, 'we'll just be—'

'You bloody are, Eric!' Ewan shouted, suddenly losing it. 'You've gone. You've chosen. And the whole thing's fucked up. We've planted for the whole year, for all of us. Where's our manpower now? Where's our farm? Where's Tadley? It's wasted.'

Ewan had spoken everyone's mind and even Sarah shut up. Jonathan sighed with some kind of relief. The band looked at their feet. They knew it already; they'd discussed it.

Eric spoke quietly. 'We're a band, always were, you know that.'

Ewan nodded and also looked at his feet, shamed into silence by his loss of temper at poor old harmless Eric.

'We can't stop them,' Jonathan said. 'If that's what they want to do.'

Ewan nodded again. The rest of the room, though dismayed, murmured agreement.

'Anyway, we are going to be here whenever we can,' Jim explained. 'And we'll bust a gut to make harvest. I know you all think one or two of us are crap but . . . we do all want to be here, make it work.'

Ewan kept his head down but glanced up at Jim. Probably for the first time in their lives they exchanged friendly, apologetic grins.

'So,' Sarah said, looking at Ewan.

Ewan raised his head and looked at Sarah's dress; it was a beautiful dress. He looked at her in it; she was beautiful in it. 'So,' he said to her, 'You're going to have to hitch this thing up between your legs and become a peasant, aren't you?'

She paused. 'Make me,' she challenged.

'Ewan, it's raining,' Sarah complained as she reluctantly allowed herself to be dragged to the front door and out onto the porch.

'Look, over there, see?' Ewan kept hold of Sarah's hand and pointed with his free hand towards a field near the farmyard. The wet brown earth seemed to shimmer with a hazy green sheen.

'Yes,' Sarah replied quizzically, 'what about it?'

'That's my wheat growing,' he said.

'So?'

'Beautiful, isn't it?'

She sighed. 'I suppose. If you like that sort of thing.'

'I do.'

Ewan gazed out at the field, lost in a half-smiling reverie. Sarah looked at his face and realised with amazement that he really did love it. Perhaps he wasn't so soulless after all. And perhaps that was the purpose of this outing – romance from his point of view. Soft, loving walks through the wood and toast by the fire, that sort of thing. She looked back at the field and the farmyard and the land, trying to find some love for it, trying to share a common feeling, but it just looked wet. Even the idea of fucking under the rain-curtained porch seemed more slushy than sexy and not in the least bit exciting or sleazy. Love just didn't turn her on. And she was about to say so when he spoke.

'Now, look at this here,' he said, pointing to an empty flower bed in the lawn just beyond the porch.

Sarah sighed again. 'What about it?'

Ewan tugged hard on her hand and ran down the steps, pulling her with him into the rain. She was too surprised to resist.

'It's mud and manure and it's full of worms,' he shouted. 'And I'm going to ruin your dress in it!'

'Don't you dare!' she screamed as he dragged her at speed towards the grass.

Ewan swung her arm forward with such force that she was propelled beyond him, sent spinning onward and downward into the flower bed with a huge muddy splat. He wasted no time in diving on top of her, fighting to roll her over and over in the mud, plastering her hair, face, body and dress as her screams, mixed with laughter, pierced the air and his ears.

'It's silk jersey crêpe!' she raged in protest.

'Oh, what a shame,' he sympathised.

'Dry-clean only!'

'Tragic.'

She managed to get a foot into his chest and pushed him off. He staggered backwards, slipped, skidded and smacked onto his back. He lay there for a moment looking back at the house, pausing for breath before slowly getting to his feet. Soaking, filthy, with rain streaking down her dirt-stained face, Sarah took the opportunity to stand, grabbing handfuls of mud at the same time. She bent low, legs apart, manoeuvring from one foot to the other, her face fierce, ready to do battle, ready to fight back should he approach.

'You bastard,' she yelled, breathing hard. 'You were supposed to just flick the shoulders. Flick the shoulders and watch it cascade to the floor in a silk-rich heap!'

'There'll be me, Jonathan and Dave,' Ewan said. 'Jonathan's not into girls any more and you're not Dave's type.' He said 'type' as though Dave wouldn't touch such a cheap slag with a bargepole. He could still do it, still turn her on as easily as spitting.

She started throwing mud at him. The first shot splattered his face: bingo! The second hit his chest. Not so good. 'You haven't won, you know,' she raged, bending quickly to scoop up more mud. 'You haven't won. Without the band you're going to need more men. You're going to have to get more men. Harvest time, Ewan, back-breaking.'

'Well then, I'm going to have to break my back because it's going to be just me or no one!'

He said it seriously. Sarah was amazed at how serious he was. Fine. She liked a challenge. The third shot hit his groin. Funny. The fourth missed completely. She was losing her grip and he was approaching. Bastard, bastard, bastard.

Face to face, eyeball to eyeball, both breathing hard, Ewan flicked at the material on her shoulders. It didn't move. He tugged at it, managing to pull the clinging, muddy mess off her shoulders. It stuck halfway down her arms. Between them, in a laughing, non-sexy, workaday fashion, they managed to peel the sodden, sticking dress away from Sarah's body. Bunched in a heap around her hips, it finally fell with a muddy *crump* to the ground. Both looked at it with disdain: a total anticlimax. They looked at each other and shrugged. Sarah grabbed Ewan's face with mud-encrusted hands, Ewan grabbed Sarah's mud-encrusted waist and they kissed. She was about to pull him down into the empty flower bed, but he pulled out of the kiss, grinned and said, 'You know your husband's watching, don't you?'

They both turned and looked up at Jonathan's bedroom window. The curtain twitched.

Sarah laughed with excitement. 'Let's give him something to look at then,' she said, ripping Ewan's shirt off his back. Then, while trying to peel his jeans off, Sarah pushed Ewan backwards and climbed on top, and they made mad, muddy, squelchy, passionate love.

Chapter 8

September 1972 – five months later

Sarah tied her hair back with an old neckerchief, smiled down at Chaos playing on the floor and busied herself preparing lettuce and cucumber salad. She looked like a peasant, barefoot, pregnant, tired and tanned. And she felt guilty and miserable. Which was why she was making lettuce and cucumber salad. Silly, really, Sarah thought, as she finished shredding lettuce into a bowl and started slicing the cucumber, but since Ewan had said, 'Don't bother with cucumber, lettuce and things that won't keep,' she felt a compulsion to make it. Just to prove it wouldn't all lie rotting in the fields. Just to prove she cared. No tomatoes with this salad, though. She was sick to death of tomatoes. She and Chaos must have picked and washed and bottled thousands. And though Chaos was a dear little enthusiast it had taken twice as long. So the sweetcorn would have to wait till tomorrow. Which meant the peas would be a few days later than planned. And God knows *when* she'd get round to the beans. At this rate she'd be as backed up and overworked as Ewan and they'd *never* see each other – not that they had for weeks, because Ewan slept at the kitchen table. And they hadn't had sex for months.

Sarah felt a sudden sharp pain as the knife sliced into her finger. The cut wasn't too bad but blood fell onto the cucumber. Sarah stuck her finger in her mouth and burst into tears. Hormones, she knew. With Chaos it had been Pooh with a balloon and with this one it was cucumber. Cucumber and lettuce and things that won't keep. Except it wasn't hormones; it was guilt. It must break his heart to say, 'Let it rot.'

Sarah tried to pull herself together. She wiped her face with her sleeve and felt Chaos stretching up to her. 'Kiss,' he said, taking her hand and kissing the finger better. Sarah smiled, hugged him and wept.

Jonathan shuffled stiffly towards the house. He'd just finished his last job for the day: secretly tipping away gallons of surplus milk because there was no time to make butter or cheese. His back was agony, all his muscles ached and he was resolute: no more argument, no more discussion. Sometimes you just had to admit defeat, and if Ewan wanted to throw a fit – if Ewan had *time* to throw a fit – then so be it. But don't mention the milk.

Jonathan groaned weakly as he kicked off his boots and creaked into the kitchen. He lowered himself slowly into a chair and matched the tired, pain-addled faces of Miriam, Dave and Margaret already round the table. Sarah dished out a strange combination of stew and salad and put it in front of him, adding a big wedge of brick-like bread to double the appeal. Chaos did his best to entertain everybody by sitting on the floor singing and banging a wooden spoon on a biscuit tin. As usual, there was no Ewan, no Sally.

'I don't care any more, Dave,' Jonathan announced. 'I'm going into town tomorrow, and hang the consequences.'

Dave threw his spoon down, pushed his chair back and

glared at Jonathan. 'Harrods,' he said, with the same entrenched disgust as he'd said it yesterday and the day before that, and the day before that.

Harrods. Dave's argument always came down to Harrods. A deliberate dig at Jonathan's upper-class credentials. If they employed farmhands this year, what would they do next year? If they took one easy route, how many more easy routes would they be tempted to take? Would they buy a combine harvester and the diesel that went with it? Spray everything with pesticide and herbicides from a boom spray to avoid bugs and weeds? Install gas fires instead of solar panels because parts of the house got a bit chilly in winter? Get wood from a timber yard because they couldn't be arsed to coppice their own trees? *Or* get proper paying jobs and go straight to Harrods and *buy* a life because that was easier.

Idealistically it was a faultless argument, Jonathan knew. Jonathan even agreed with it. But circumstances *weren't* ideal and they had to do *something*. Ewan's carefully considered plan of working themselves to death, twenty hours a day, seven days a week for months on end, was unhealthy and unproductive – Ewan and Sally were getting slower and slower and less able to be logical, practical or willing to listen to reason.

'Four farmhands, that's all,' Jonathan said. 'Just replacements for the band, for *this* year. Next year we'll be organised.'

'You should wait till Ewan and Sally are here,' Margaret said. 'If you're going to stick the knife in, Jonathan, do it in front of them.' It was what Margaret always said. She agreed with Dave's argument that it was a class thing. While Ewan was trying to dig his way out, Jonathan was trying to buy it.

Jonathan deeply resented the idea of a class *anything*. But even so, so what? It didn't make Ewan right and Jonathan wrong. It just made Ewan unable to cope and Jonathan sitting on a perfectly reasonable solution. It was the best way to save the crops, the farm and everybody's mental and physical health.

Miriam got up from the table and filled a bowl with water. She snatched the spoon and tin from Chaos and, before he could cry, plonked the bowl in front of him. 'Less noisy, Chaos,' she said through clenched teeth.

Everyone breathed a sigh of secret relief and turned to her in surprise. Miriam's mood was uncharacteristically spiky.

'Ewan and Sally can't continue to triple-shift,' she said. 'They can't be six people. So, we either employ people and save what we can, or run out of food and buy it in later. The question is, which is the lesser of two evils? Personally I would hate to buy in food.'

'Thank you, Miriam.' Jonathan nodded at what he saw as the impartial voice of reason.

Margaret's back went up. She was tempted to clock Jonathan with his uneaten hunk of bread.

'*However,*' Miriam snapped with unusual impatience, 'give them a couple of days, Jonathan, then let's discuss it. With them,' she added, with a nod of appeasement towards Margaret.

Sarah had tried to stay out of the discussion but Chaos upended his bowl of water. Miriam stomped across the kitchen, grabbed the mop and furiously cleared up the mess. If even Miriam was on a short fuse, perhaps now was the time for honesty.

'I tried to talk to Ewan but he won't listen,' Sarah said, reddening with embarrassment. 'He won't have farmhands because he doesn't trust me. He's trying to get at me, trying to control me.' She took in the quizzical stares of everybody and tried to explain further. 'He's trying to stop me having sex. It's a game. So somebody should talk to him because . . . why should everybody else suffer?'

They were all now looking at her as though she were a

moron. Dave glared with exhausted impatience. 'Contrary to popular belief, the universe doesn't revolve around *you*, Sarah.'

'No,' she admitted reasonably. 'But Ewan does.'

Dave was at a loss as to whether it was he or she who had lost the plot. Margaret stepped in.

'Yes, well, Dave's not Ewan,' she sneered. 'And neither am I, and neither is Sally. And we're not doing this for Ewan; we're doing it for ourselves. So if farmhands are employed, you'd better employ enough to cover the three of *us* – because *we* won't be doing any more.'

If everything else stopped it would be all right, Sally thought as she picked up the sheaves of wheat *again* and arranged them in a stook *again*. If the other crops stopped growing and ripening and the animals didn't need checking, if the cows didn't need milking, the eggs didn't need collecting, the bees took a holiday and the humans didn't stop to eat and sleep and *argue,* and four extra bodies hadn't deserted and . . . and, and, and. It would be all right; it would be easy, enjoyable even. The wheat would have been harvested by now, Ewan would be happy, everybody would be celebrating and time wouldn't be ticking desperately away. As it was, the weather forecast was ominous, the grain was overripe and everybody was worn out. She watched the stook fall over, *again*. Sod it. Why was there always one? She sighed heavily.

'Ewan, Sally, it's dark! Come on!'

Dave was calling from the top of the field. Thank God. Dave the Rescuer. Sally ached, her whole body. And she was tired and hot and hungry and still raging at Miriam's pig-headedness; her back was breaking and her legs were wobbling; but if Ewan was staying out, she was staying out. But please, please, Dave, stop crawling and come on! Dave crawled. Seemed to.

'Right, you buggers!' she yelled at the sheaves. 'Sit!' She looked over at Ewan, still cutting, slow, worn out, desperate. Dave was nearly here; Dave would stop him, drag him away. And once Ewan had stopped, she could stop. Just this last stook; the rest could lie there till tomorrow.

'Come on, Ewan, your dinner's getting cold.' Dave was with Ewan now, taking the scythe off him easily. Ewan was exhausted.

Sally stood back and looked at the stook. It fell over. She felt like crying. She got angry instead. 'You can go to hell as far as I'm concerned,' she shouted at the fallen sheaves. No. Not true. She looked over at Dave and Ewan looking back at her. They were going to do it. Going to do it all, even if it killed them, because if they didn't, it would kill Ewan.

Dave and Ewan silently took over and helped her rebuild the stook. It behaved perfectly. Bastards. Sally felt like yelling, 'If you'd done as many as I have today . . . !' But she didn't. Instead she allowed Dave to put his arm round her shoulder and Ewan to hold her hand and all three of them left the field without looking back. The stook fell over.

Ewan and Sally crawled into the kitchen behind Dave, their last remnants of energy visibly draining as they said nothing and sat. Margaret quickly filled two bowls with stew and put them on the kitchen table, hovering around, wanting to do more, ready to spoon-feed them if necessary. She watched Ewan rub his eyes and try to keep awake long enough to eat. If Jonathan, Sarah and Miriam had stayed up, they would have understood, Margaret was sure. This wasn't a game. He wasn't doing this because of Sarah — well, not entirely.

Margaret glanced over at Dave sitting wearily in an easy chair by the range. Dave noticed her glance and gave her an enquiring look, wondering if Ewan and Sally should be told.

Margaret surreptitiously shook her head. No. Give Sarah the chance to stop undermining Ewan, Miriam the chance to get off the fence and Jonathan to forget his knee-jerk, reach-for-the-bank-book offers of help. And in the meantime, carry on as normal.

But Sally burst into tears.

Nobody had particularly noticed Sally drop her spoon, but everybody heard the loud bang as her head hit the table while bending to retrieve it. She looked stunned for a moment, sitting up in confusion, and then, without warning, broke down in tears. Ewan looked up, watched her tears spill and looked quickly down, getting up from the table and moving away. He put the kettle on the range, took it off again and kept his back to them. He was almost crying himself.

Margaret put her arm round Sally as Dave diplomatically looked at his hands. Sally was desperately trying to stop.

'I'm sorry, I'm sorry, I'm just a big baby. It's just . . . I'm not really crying.'

Sally looked over at Ewan but he didn't turn round. Margaret rubbed her back sympathetically; even now Sally was trying to prove her worth. Still trying to prove she was as good as the boys.

'I'm not really crying, Ewan. It's just . . . We just . . .' Sally fished for excuses.

Ewan turned to face them. 'We just need more people,' he admitted.

Margaret glanced worriedly at Dave. Ewan couldn't quit, not now. Dave couldn't argue with Jonathan *and* Ewan.

Ewan breathed in deeply, about to speak the unspeakable. 'Sarah's been saying it, Jonathan's been saying it, Miriam's been . . . wavering . . .'

Sally jumped in bitterly. 'Miriam's been a pig. If she just

turned a blind eye, it wouldn't hurt her. A measly few quid. I'd *walk* into town if necessary.'

Margaret was only half listening. She was willing Ewan not to say it. Willing Ewan not to admit defeat. It was so typical. The one time she wanted him steaming and he was too exhausted to oblige. If they hadn't run out of coffee, if she'd rationed it earlier, things would be better. 'If you had some coffee. If I got some coffee from somewhere—'

'Coffee?' Sally snorted with derision, anger soaking up the tears. She looked at Margaret as though she had gone mad. 'Coffee, Margaret?'

'Coffee's good for energy, stamina,' Margaret replied almost apologetically, suddenly feeling as stupid as Sally was making her out to be.

'I'm not talking about coffee,' Sally spat. 'I'm talking about speed!'

The silence was palpable.

Saying 'speed' was summoning the devil as far as Margaret was concerned. And the way Ewan's eyes suddenly lit up, the flush of excitement in his face, temporarily relieving the pallor of tiredness, only confirmed her beliefs.

Sally sighed angrily and put her chin in her hands. 'Doesn't matter anyway. Miriam wouldn't give me the money.'

Sally's argument with Miriam the night before had ended with Sally thumping the wall instead of Miriam and vowing never to speak to her again. All Miriam had to do was raid the petty cash and drive her into town. Sally could score some speed, everybody could work like billy-o and they'd all be happy. Nobody had to take it if they didn't want to; it was just in case people did. And Sally did. And Ewan would. And everybody else might. A few quid from petty cash and Miriam said no. Sally went ballistic. Miriam still said no. The petty cash was Jonathan's money and Jonathan's money did *not* get used for drugs. It was a house rule, and if Sally didn't like that she'd have to ask Ewan why.

Sally looked at Ewan and said, 'Why?'

Ewan fidgeted awkwardly. 'Miriam's right. If it's Jonathan's money – no drugs.'

'Why?' Sally asked again, completely stunned by Ewan's passive acceptance.

'House rule.' Ewan echoed Miriam, then shrugged. Nothing more to say, end of subject.

Sally was incensed.

Dave looked awkwardly around the kitchen, Ewan looked at the floor and Margaret raised her eyebrows. The devil refusing to rear its ugly head? She had to admire that. He could break that rule right now. Everybody knows he's tired; everybody knows he's desperate. It wouldn't take much to twist Jonathan's arm – Ewan must know that. It's not a binge with thousands of pounds; it's an expedient few quid – as Sally said. It's not *then*, to aid his self-destruction; it's *now*, to stop his self-destruction. He must know it. And he's refusing, honouring Jonathan's rule.

It was up to her then. Short-term devilment or a long-term battle. Lines had already been drawn, Margaret knew it. And she knew whose side she wanted to be on. She looked sternly at Ewan while she spoke to Sally. 'If it's *just* speed and nothing else, and it's *just* for bringing in the harvest, and it helps – I've got some money. And I can drive.'

The blackness of the night and the motion of the car was soporific. Ewan sat forward in an effort to stay awake, resting his arms on Dave's seat in front of him as he tried to wear Margaret down. Margaret was having none of it as she calmly concentrated on her driving, and kept an eye on the hooligan driver bearing down in the car behind.

'Oh, come on, Margaret,' Ewan whined.

'No. Not till dawn.'

'Dave could rig up some lights; we could clear a field before dawn,' he insisted.

Dave and Margaret exchanged long-suffering looks.

'I'm not rigging up any lights, Ewan,' Dave said.

'But we can do it now. It's possible.'

'Not till dawn. Now get some sleep,' Margaret said firmly.

Ewan sighed and sat back from Dave's seat, resisting the urge to slump into his own. He was desperate not to crash, but knew he was on the edge of it. He looked down at Sally slumped beside him, her head lolling back on the seat, bleary-eyed but smiling.

'We could see perfectly with floodlights,' Ewan cajoled.

'If it proves a point,' Sally murmured, forcing her heavy eyes to stay open.

'Oh, come on, Margaret,' Ewan persisted, sitting forward again. 'Just a little taste, just to check it, so we're ready at first light.'

'Is it the harvest you're obsessed with, Ewan, or the drugs?' Margaret sweetly enquired.

Ewan glared petulantly at her and slumped back in his seat, shaking his head and exchanging exasperated looks with Sally. Dave snorted a quick laugh and glanced at the car behind in the wing mirror. It seemed dangerously close.

'You want to pull over to the side a bit, Margaret,' Dave suggested.

'Not at all,' Margaret calmly replied. 'People should learn to have some manners.'

Ewan and Sally struggled up to look blearily out of the back window. It was something to watch, something to take an interest in, something to keep them awake.

The country lane was narrow and the car in front was slow and hogging the middle of the road. Tyler bore down impatiently. They were way late, past midnight already, and if the band wanted to make an entrance, it was useless if the others were asleep. Tyler couldn't see the attraction, frankly. Why his boys were so desperate to be with a bunch of yokels who got up at five and probably went to bed by nine, he couldn't imagine. Still if that was what the Four Horsemen of the Apocalypse wanted, that was Tyler's mission to accomplish.

'Get out of the fucking way, you stupid, dozy mad cow!' he screeched at the car in front.

'It's Jonathan's car,' Eric insisted for the fourth time.

'Can't be,' Jim replied.

'God. Women drivers! Old women drivers! Fucking morons!' Tyler continued, oblivious to the conversation in the back.

'What's his registration?' Sean asked, peering round Nick in the front seat, trying to see the car ahead of them.

'Don't know,' Eric said, 'but that's Jonathan's car. I'm sure of it.'

'So who's the woman driving?' Jim asked.

'Must be Miriam.'

'Miriam's not old.'

'Does Margaret drive?'

'Yeah, look!' Sean shouted. 'That's Ewan and Sally in the back!'

Nick slapped Tyler on the leg. 'Overtake them, Ty.'

Tyler gave him a withering look. 'What do you think I've been *trying* to do, Nick?'

★

Margaret decided enough was enough when the car behind started insistently peeping its horn and flashing its headlights.

'Okay,' she said, 'I want you to open all the windows and shout as much foul language as you can. I know it's not lady-like, Sally, but bugger it – some people don't know what manners are.'

She manoeuvred the car to one side as Dave, Ewan and Sally wound down the windows. They all stopped, open-mouthed, however, as they watched the Bentley rolling past with the band grinning, waving and yelling inside it.

'Put the wagons in a circle, everybody,' Dave said. 'It's the cavalry.'

Ewan and Sally flopped back into their seats with a sigh of enormous, heartfelt relief. The Bentley pulled up a short distance in front, and Margaret stopped the car. Eric and Sean got there first and leant in at Margaret's window.

'We've come for the harvest,' Eric announced with a huge grin.

'We've just bought some speed!' Margaret complained.

'Even better,' Sean said.

Jim made straight for Ewan and Sally's window. 'Speed, Ewan? No, mate, way out of fashion,' he gloated. 'Cocaine's the thing now.'

Sally managed a look of disdain. 'Like Ewan cares about *fashion*, mate.'

Ewan nodded in agreement with Sally, but said, 'Got any on you, Jim?'

Jim smiled smugly, was about to say yes and tell him just how much, but didn't bother – Ewan and Sally had crashed.

Dave and Margaret dubbed Tyler 'the Tornado'. After helping carry Ewan and Sally to their beds, he went back and forth to the car, single-handedly unloading a seemingly endless supply of salt, tea, coffee, chocolate, Rizla papers, cigarettes, shoes, clothes, books, presents for everybody and the band's gear. He refused all Dave and Margaret's offers of help apart from coffee and a lettuce and cucumber sandwich, and insisted he could make up his own bed if Margaret just pointed him in the right direction. Margaret never knew if he found his bed or used it, but Tyler was still whirling when she and Dave got up late the next day. He'd managed to round up a horde of helpers who were busily clearing the fields, plus a few photographers and reporters who also pitched in for an hour or so.

Ewan and Sally slept solidly till early evening. When they did put in a groggy appearance, they found the wheat had all been safely cut and stooked. And fruit and vegetable boxes were piled high and ready to be stored. A group of strangers were stripping the beans with Sarah and Chaos, and the other Tadpoles, with somebody called Tyler, were digging up the potatoes. Ewan didn't have the heart to tell them he'd planned to leave the potatoes for at least a couple of weeks longer. Instead he and Sally tramped across the field with shooting sticks, binoculars and a flask so they could sit, watch and take the merciless piss out of the band for their lack of condition. When that got boring they tried to find out what Margaret had done with the speed. And when she wouldn't tell them, they got back to work – when they weren't stopping to jump up and down and grin joyously at each other.

Later that evening the band gave an impromptu harvest festival concert in the ballroom for the other Tadpoles and helpers. It was then that the rain started. Had Ewan known that the rain would persist for weeks he might have gone round and personally kissed and hugged everybody for saving him from the nightmare of digging up mud-drenched potato fields. But people were lucky; they just had to put up with his beaming relief, constant 'welcome home' punches and endless gratitude for pitching in and saving the farm.

Ewan did feel a slight twang of resentment when Tyler was voted 'man of the match' and presented with an honorary string bracelet for having 'the most stamina, the most muscle and the most enthusiasm'. But, as he said to Sally, Margaret and Dave muttering in the corner, it didn't really matter, it was just a bit of fun and at least the crops were safe.

Besides, as Ewan discovered during the course of the party, Tyler had not the slightest interest in Sarah.

Chapter 9

'Dragons!' Chaos yelled as he ran down the corridor.

Serendipity screamed and ran after her brother with fearful delight. Ewan and Sean roared like monsters and thundered round the corner. Ewan charged at Chaos, grabbed him under the arms and swung him over his shoulder as Sean scooped Serendipity up, skidded onto his knees, half turned and fell backwards against a door. The door banged open and Sean and Dipity spilt into the room. Ewan couldn't believe his luck. It was Sarah's workroom. He'd wanted to have a look inside for months.

Eric fought to keep his hands steady as the clay wobbled erratically, spun out of control and collapsed into a shapeless lump. He gawped in shock at the arrivals in the doorway.

The arrivals in the doorway gawped in shock at seeing Eric at Sarah's pottery wheel.

'Dragon got me,' Serendipity said, in a four-year-old way of explaining the unannounced intrusion, punching Sean in the stomach to prove the honesty of her story.

Eric didn't look any happier.

'What you doing in here, Eric?' Sean asked.

137

'What does it look like I'm doing?' Eric replied, the wheel still turning as his leg pumped in irritation. 'I'm making a pot.'

'Looks like you're making wet clay to me.' Ewan laughed as he lifted Chaos off his back, stepped over Sean and Dipity and came fully into the room. He turned in a slow circle, taking in the untidy mess, which no doubt Sarah would argue was an *artistic* mess and so somehow superior. The place was crammed with stuff: pottery, paintings, bundles of material, baskets, rugs. Shelves bulging, drawers too full to close.

'Haven't you two got something better to do?' Eric glowered.

'We're waiting for Tyler.' Sean shrugged as he started wandering around the workroom.

'She's got a lot of stuff in here, hasn't she?' Ewan said to no one in particular, but changing the subject. His drug habits were of no concern to house gossip Eric. Ewan poked around the room opening drawers and cupboards, inspecting bits of jewellery and candles, flicking through half-sewn clothes. Eric's annoyance increased. Ewan had suspected it would.

'Has Sarah given you permission to be in here?' Eric asked.

'Has she given you permission?' Sean asked, staring threateningly at Eric.

'Yes. She said I could practise.'

'Practise what? Being a twat?'

Eric glared back. 'Haven't you got some pigs to slaughter, Sean?'

Sean raised his eyebrows with unruffled amusement. 'We've got Nontads for that,' he said.

Ewan looked quizzically at a long row of clay pots. He lifted the lid of one of them and peered at the gloop inside. 'Ugh!' he said as his head jerked back at the surprise smell. He frowned and sniffed again. 'Smells like cucumber.'

Chaos and Serendipity joined him as Ewan started lifting the lids of the other pots and sniffing. Sean meandered over to join the group.

'She uses this; this smells like her – apples,' Ewan said as he lifted the pot up, smiling slightly and sniffing again.

He bent down to let the kids have a sniff of mother-smelling gloop. Serendipity stuck her finger in for a taste. Chaos laughed when Dipity spat it out. Sean took the pot from Ewan to have a sniff and a taste; he nodded in agreement and smiled.

'Yeah, that's Sarah,' he said, handing the pot back to Ewan.

'You're not supposed to be in here, you know,' Eric complained.

'Piss off, Eric,' Sean said dismissively. 'We're taking an interest. You never know, we might want to throw a few pots ourselves.'

Ewan stopped sniffing and looked at Sean. Both grinned slyly before turning to look with amusement at Eric and the wheel. Eric sighed with heavy defeat as they approached.

'I hate winter,' he said, as Ewan and Sean rolled up their sleeves.

The parking ticket said it all. 'Welcome back to earth, mere mortal.' Tyler snatched it from under his windscreen wiper. The London street roared with a thousand different noises, a thousand different people were busy doing a thousand different things, and Tyler stood in a bubble of silence, a bubble of paralysis, glaring at the parking ticket as he felt his career disintegrate.

The meeting had only lasted an hour.

Tyler got into his Merc, tossed the parking ticket with disgust onto the passenger seat and thumped the steering wheel. 'Fuck it. Bastards,' he said.

He started the car, pulled out, drove about three feet and joined the slow, tedious bumper-to-bumper chug of life in the fast lane. At this rate he wouldn't be back at Tadley till mid-afternoon. If there was any point in going back to Tadley. With a cancelled recording contract the Horsemen were dead ducks. Tyler was left with two choices: sink with them or try to swim with another band. Neither prospect had instant appeal.

Tyler drummed his hands on the steering wheel, blared his horn at a slow bastard who wouldn't move on amber, and looked down at the parking ticket mocking him from the passenger seat.

'Fucking record company. Fucking power-crazed morons.'

He'd expected it, though. Punk was sweeping in and the Horsemen were dinosaurs. And they'd never really taken off, not big time. They'd done well for a while, but they were too soft – no ambition, no drive. Too happy pottering around their rural idyll with their growing band of like-minded commu-nards.

Sink or relearn to swim. Tyler sighed with disgust. Or be a Tadpole.

Sally came out of the drawing room and stood in the hall looking up the stairs, a big grin of amusement plastering her face. She watched Sean circling and bellowing, 'I'm going to turn you into statues!' as he chased the bunch of kids on the landing, his hands held up like grotesque claws, something brown and claylike covering them.

Ewan leant over the banisters and yelled, 'Sally, get back in there and burn your bra!'

Sally laughed. The women's group meeting had only been going half an hour but already she was bored. Half the women were outsiders: middle-class housewives, mums and misfits coming in from Ludlow and blaming everybody but themselves for their wasted brains. Sally had been to school with some of them – she'd hated the rich-bitch, toffee-nosed gits then too.

'They're in uproar,' she said. 'They can hear men. It's oppressing them.'

Ewan laughed. So did Hilary. She raised her eyes heaven-wards as she crossed the hall with her three girls: Imogen, Claudia and Matilda. Imogen and Claudia were similar ages to Chaos and Dipity and they ran up the stairs to join the fun. Matilda was only a year old, six months younger than Tranquillity, Sarah's youngest, and had to be carried.

'Would you mind?' Hilary called up.

'Not at all,' Ewan shouted, louder than necessary, and started to come down.

'It's so nice to trust men with our children while we sit around saying how useless they are,' Hilary bellowed, before disdainfully muttering, 'women's group!' and wrinkling her nose up at Sally.

Sally laughed. But both of them went, every week. Sally (so she said) to keep her eye on things and Hilary (so she said) to back her up when the sisterhood got rough.

Sally liked Hilary. She fitted into Tadley perfectly. As did her husband, Ray. They'd arrived during the last Harvest Festival in August, totally disinterested in the Horsemen or their music, but bursting with enthusiasm for the commune. It had become a word-of-mouth thing and a growing number of residents had arrived by the same route. Perfect Nontads, Ewan called them, but Sally thought that sounded disparaging and preferred to call them Tads.

Hilary handed Matilda over to Ewan just as the drawing-room door flew open and Sarah stormed out. 'Fuck off, you noisy lot!' she shouted, mainly in Ewan's direction.

Sean leant over the banister with his hands behind his back and yelled, 'Sorry, miss!'

Ewan grinned and said, 'Hello, sexy,' loud enough for the women inside to hear and, hopefully, have apoplexy.

Sally stifled a laugh. Sarah was raging. Not at what Ewan and Sean had said, but at Ewan holding someone else's baby.

Tyler was cruising up the M1 feeling better than he had done in years. It was obvious. It made perfect sense. Sink with the Horsemen and swim with the Tadpoles. It had been staring him in the face from the beginning. Tadley Hall was a gold mine. Could be.

Who said the Harvest Festival was just for the Horsemen? Who said they couldn't book a whole load of bands? A three-day event to rival Glastonbury. Who'd complain? The farmers. No, not necessarily. Ewan was terrified of lack of manpower. Stroke that neurosis and he'd agree to a million people if they helped harvest the crops. And if Ewan agreed, Sidekick Sally would. The other farmers were sheep. The Horsemen? Fuck them, they're dead. Jonathan? Jonathan was the boss, always was, always would be. They all said that. Would Jonathan be happy with a full-blown rock festival?

Tyler saw a sign and grinned. It was the answer to his question. 'Newport Pagnell or Watford Gap?' he said as he read the service station sign, debating when to stop for a line of coke.

Jonathan was happy when Ewan was happy. And Tyler could keep Ewan happy.

'Bohemian Rhapsody' came on the radio and Tyler sang along. Watford Gap. See if he could get to Watford Gap before the end of the song.

'Margaret.'

Tyler felt his good mood dip. He slowed down. Forget the

song; don't race till you know the reason. Can't arrive at Tadley half-cocked.

Margaret wouldn't go for it. If no Tadpoles were performing there was no point in putting on the festival. And she'd quickly point out that they had manpower; there were enough resident Nontads for the harvest already. Bloody Margaret. She had no Achilles heel. Meddlesome old bloody . . . darling! Tyler let out a whoop.

'Thank you, Margaret!'

It could be *more* than Glastonbury. Tyler could manage them! A whole stable of bands, a stable of Tadpole bands all living at Tadley and performing . . . *All living at Tadley?*

'Good grief, Tyler, where's your brains, man?'

A whole stable of Tadpole bands *recording* at Tadley. Jim was always going on about a recording studio. Now was the time to build it. They didn't need to know it wasn't for them. A whole stable of Tadpole bands, managed by Tyler, recording at Tadley and living fuck knows where – who cared?

'Fuck me,' Tyler yelled as his stomach lurched and a light in his head popped on. 'I've just started my own record company!'

The light in his head popped off just as quickly. *Ewan.*

'Bohemian Rhapsody' was finishing and Tyler had miles to go. Ewan would never go for a record company. And if Ewan wouldn't, Jonathan wouldn't, Sally wouldn't, the Horsemen wouldn't, Margaret wouldn't and blah, blah, blah, blah . . . Another career in ruins.

Tyler slowed right down and coasted over to the hard shoulder. He couldn't wait for Watford Gap; he needed coke now.

Tadley Hall could be perfect. Well, not perfect because it was in Shropshire, but . . .

Tyler took out his coke stash and fished under the seat for a road map to cut it on. Jonathan was the boss, always was, always would be. They all said that. Nice guy, Jonathan, queer as beet-root and madly in love with Ewan.

Tyler rolled up a fiver and snorted the coke. He sat up and smiled as 'Happy Xmas (War Is Over)' started playing.

Tadley Hall was a gold mine. Could be.

'So Ewan will have to go,' he said.

With one dismissive sweep of his hand, Jonathan brushed the sawdust, shavings and accumulated debris off the workbench, leant his back against it, folded his arms and looked at the table with disgust. It was crap. It was wonky. It was ten past eight, he was late for dinner and he'd wasted *another* day failing to make a simple table. How useless could he be? And how laughable?

By the time Jonathan arrived at the dining room his mood had sunk to miserable. The room was practically full and from the doorway it looked an uncomfortable squeeze. Plates and cutlery cluttered the table and the chairs were wedged so closely together they almost overlapped. Another table was urgently needed and nobody else would attempt one until Jonathan admitted defeat. Jonathan's mood didn't lift when Tyler ran up behind him and grabbed his elbow.

'There you are, Jonathan. I've been looking all over for you,' Tyler said, grinning like Christmas.

Jonathan tried not to glare. 'I was in the work shed.'

Tyler's grin turned to amused pity. 'Your table.'

'It's not funny, Tyler. It's wonky.'

Tyler shrugged as though laughter was the furthest thing from his mind. He let go of Jonathan's elbow and put his arm round his shoulder instead, moving him against the wall as more people trooped past.

'Don't worry about it, Jonathan.' Tyler smiled. 'People is what you're good at, not woodwork. Look . . .' He gestured

144

into the dining room, his sweep of the arm encouraging and optimistic. 'Yes, it's full and cramped, but it's full of happy people, not uncomfortable people. They don't care about a table. They squeeze together because they want to be together. Who created that? Who made that possible?'

'Ewan did,' Jonathan said dolefully, aware that Tyler was trying to cheer him up but succeeding only in making it worse.

'Did he?' Tyler seemed surprised. 'Oh,' he said almost with disappointment, before shaking his head and shrugging. 'Oh, I see, so that's why he always wants to get his own way.' Tyler leant in close with a strange smile on his face. Jonathan expected some snippet of gossip but Tyler stopped smiling, stared into Jonathan's eyes and said in a weirdly sexual way, 'It's your house, Jonathan. And is he grateful?'

Grateful? For a moment Jonathan was unable to follow the conversation. Tyler's closeness and unwavering gaze made him feel awkward and turn slightly pink at the cheeks. It was almost as though Tyler was guessing his fantasies. Jonathan couldn't move, couldn't think what to say. The only thing he could do was blink. And when he did, he distinctly felt the brush of Tyler's hand on his thigh. A flush of excitement swept through his body. The situation felt sexual, incredibly sexual, and yet so ambiguous and open to misunderstanding. Jonathan had never been seduced by a man before, and he wasn't even sure he was now.

'Come and sit with me, Jonathan. Let's chat . . .'

Jonathan felt himself being ushered through the dining room towards the far end of the table.

'And we can arrange the best time to level off your legs.'

Jonathan jerked to a stop, his face and neck suddenly scarlet and his mind racing. He was aware that practically the whole household was in the room. He stared at Tyler.

'Your table, Jonjo.' Tyler laughed, slapping his back. 'You said your table was wonky. The legs will need levelling. What did you think I meant?'

Jonathan found himself plonked into a chair next to Nick. Tyler sat down next to him, patted his hand and smiled with good-natured bonhomie at the people gathered around the table. Jonathan seemed stuck in a panic-stricken dream. He smiled at Chaos, sitting with a milk moustache on Miriam's lap.

'So, Dave,' Tyler said. 'What do you reckon?'

Dave looked up from his meal and shrugged happily. 'Perfectly possible, Tyler, perfectly possible.'

'Dave,' Jim joined in with concern, 'we're talking about a recording studio.'

'Yeah.'

'Well, it's complicated.'

'I did physics, Jim.'

'But it's going to take experts, isn't it?' Jim persisted.

'I helped wire a particle accelerator,' Dave pointed out, assuming that would clear up any doubts.

Nick looked about the room, wondering how to put it. 'Yeah, Dave, but have you ever been in a recording studio?'

Tyler shook his head with amusement. 'After all these years, they still don't know how clever you are, do they, Dave? Bloody clever, isn't he, Jonathan?' Tyler turned and grinned at Jonathan.

'Nobody told me we were going to have a recording studio,' Margaret said, frowning.

'What recording studio?' Sally said.

Jonathan was finding the conversation confusing. The dining room seemed particularly loud and stuffy, and to add to the panic Ewan lolloped in. Jonathan watched him breeze over to an empty chair, take the clean plate and cutlery, move further along the table and say to a Nontad, 'Excuse me, can we swap seats?' He watched the Nontad comply, pick up her half-finished meal and take her seat at the far end, while Ewan leant on Sally's shoulder to climb into the chair opposite Sarah. Ewan was so confident, so sure of his place as one of the founders.

Jonathan shook his head in affectionate despair. Tyler leant in and said, 'Not very egalitarian,' but Jonathan didn't want to hear; he wanted to watch Ewan.

'You smell nice, Sarah,' Ewan was saying, looking directly at her across the table. 'Apples, isn't it? Very nice.'

'What studio, Jonathan?' Sally asked again.

'Just a sort of feasibility study at the moment,' Tyler said, patting Jonathan's arm.

Jonathan felt the flush again, worse now with Ewan in the room. Ewan wasn't looking at him, though – too busy arguing with Sarah about apple-smelling soap and shampoo.

'If only you use it, why do you need potfuls?' Ewan was saying.

Sarah exploded. 'Have you been in my workroom?'

Tyler's voice was in his ear. 'So, you'd be all right with that, would you, Jonjo?'

Margaret's face was in his face. 'Why wasn't this discussed?'

Jonathan half turned, trying to keep one eye on Ewan and one ear on Tyler. It was impossible. Too much claustrophobia and too many things happening at once.

'If we went ahead with it?' Tyler asked at the same time as Sarah yelled, 'You've no right, that's private!' Noise was rising, Ewan was laughing, Margaret was frowning, Sally looked annoyed, Dave looked like he'd done something wrong and Tyler was close, getting closer . . .

'Yes, yes, seems reasonable,' Jonathan muttered, nodding rigidly and trying to avoid Tyler and his touch. Jonathan felt strangely treacherous. As though allowing this seduction – if that was what it was – was somehow betraying Ewan. Not that Ewan cared. He hadn't even looked over. Too busy . . . *trying to get his own way.* Jonathan frowned.

'And what are we being *private* about?' Ewan argued.

'Everybody agreed I could have a workroom,' Sarah argued back.

'I didn't agree.'

'You weren't there.'

'What do you mean, I wasn't there?'

'You *know* what I mean,' Sarah said pointedly, her eyes flicking a quick glance in Tyler's direction.

Jonathan watched Ewan hesitate and look around the room. Their eyes met and Ewan smiled slightly in acknowledgement. But it was only slight, only fleeting. Ewan smiled longer at Sarah. He shrugged at her with a sexual ease. Even the way he helped himself from the pots of food on the table seemed to be somehow sexual and directed at Sarah.

'What are you thinking of doing with the surplus crops, Ewan?' Tyler called over.

Jonathan jumped. Strange that Tyler should want to engage Ewan in conversation at a time like this. Except maybe it wasn't 'a time like this'. Maybe Jonathan was mistaken.

Ewan shrugged with disinterest. 'I don't know – don't care really.' He looked back at Sarah, the smile returning. 'So, why is it private?' he said.

'I didn't say it was private,' Sarah replied.

The same old game, the same old foreplay, the same old romance.

'But you don't want to let them rot, do you?' Tyler said.

Sarah and Ewan raised their eyebrows at each other. Both looked irritated. Both looked impatiently at Tyler. Both sighed.

Both seemed to mirror each other, like two sides of one coin. Jonathan was so jealous of that.

'No, of course not,' Ewan said. 'But it's not really up to me, I just grow the stuff. It's not *my* fault I grew too much.' He looked pointedly at Jim.

Jonathan saw the look of cruel amusement sweep across Ewan's face, the leg begin to twitch. He guessed Jim's hackles had risen. Jonathan cut in diplomatically – automatically. 'I think it's wonderful that we had a bumper harvest; we should all be celebrating, congratulating each other.'

'Absolutely, Jonathan, I agree,' Tyler said, patting Jonathan's shoulder.

Jonathan tensed. Was that sexual? Wasn't that sexual? Whatever it was, Ewan saw it.

'It wasn't a "bumper" harvest, Jonathan,' Ewan said wearily, as though it were obvious. 'It was lack of Horsemen fans.'

Jonathan felt a lurch of disappointment that Ewan thought nothing of the touch. He had no time to dwell on it, though. Jim was leaning over the table, almost out of his seat, spitting anger.

'You bloody ingrate, Ewan. Without our fans you'd be in deep shit. We provide you with labour.'

'Bollocks. Your fans' *labour* feeds your fans' *festival*. Why do you think there's a surplus? It's not our surplus – it's yours. So who do you think is in deep shit, Jim?'

Tyler leant forward and put a gentle restraining hand on Jim's arm, easing him back to his seat. 'Boys, boys,' he soothed.

'Don't "boys" me, mate,' Ewan snapped, losing the grin. 'Who do you think you are? Manager of everyone?'

Jonathan felt the sudden change in atmosphere. Backs stiffened and conversations stopped. Ewan's happy goading had turned to sudden, sullen irritation, his leg waggling impatiently as he glared at Tyler. Tyler spread his arms in a hands-off appeasing gesture. Jonathan caught Ewan's eye and gave him a 'cool it' look. Ewan peevishly turned away. But he lessened the waggle. Jonathan turned to Tyler with an apologetic smile.

It wasn't much but it was the sign that Tyler had been waiting for.

'What about your women's group, Sarah?' Tyler suggested. 'Why don't we give the surplus to them?'

Sarah shook her head quickly, slightly, and glanced at Ewan. Ewan wasn't watching, or seemingly listening, so Tyler persisted.

'The way you do with your soaps and shampoos?'

Ewan turned sharply and looked quizzically from Tyler to Sarah. 'You give soap and shampoo to your women's group?' he asked.

Sarah feigned disinterest. 'In exchange for stuff, yeah.'

'So that's why you've got so much of the stuff,' Ewan said. 'I'm not surprised you want to be private. Little bloody factory you've got going up there.'

'It's just in exchange, why not? No different from the festival.'

'Of course it is. We need food.'

'We need soap.'

'But you're making extra.'

'And you're growing extra – you just said so.'

Ewan shook his head dismissively. 'No comparison. The fans help out on the farm; they need feeding.' He turned to glare at Jim. 'When they turn up!'

Jim glared back.

Sarah leant forward. 'The women's group help out the women in this house.'

'Oh? How?'

'They help us put men in perspective,' she sneered.

'They're a bunch of bloody dykes!' Ewan shot back with contempt.

Sarah sat back. Ewan reddened and closed his eyes as Sally and Miriam glared at him. Tyler thought this was too easy. He pressed on, filling the uncomfortable silence. 'Can't you give the surplus to the animals, Ewan?'

'I've got enough for the animals,' Ewan replied through gritted teeth. He opened his eyes and glowered with emphasis at Jim. 'I *calculated*.'

Jim glowered back, ready to resume the argument.

Ewan goaded, 'Of course, what I didn't calculate on—'

Jonathan interrupted with a tired sigh. 'Oh, don't start again, Ewan.'

Ewan shot Jonathan a malevolent look, and saw Tyler pat his hand. Jim went for it.

'You couldn't calculate your way out of a paper bag, Ewan. You've never got the harvest in yourself. Ever. Not from the word go. Even before the festivals, you still couldn't do it, still couldn't hack it. Had to have us riding up like the cavalry. We saved your skin. Repeatedly.'

Margaret jumped in. 'Oh no, I'm not having that. I'm sorry, that is totally unfair, Jim.'

'It shouldn't be down to Ewan; it's a collective thing,' Dave added.

'He breaks his back year after year, while you preen around like a pop star . . .' Margaret continued.

'And Sally,' Ewan threw in, hoping to redeem himself. 'Don't forget Sally.'

'And the only reason he hasn't "hacked it" is because people like you don't do your fair share,' Margaret finished.

'No, too busy thinking about recording studios,' Sally complained. 'And what for, I'd like to know.'

151

'What recording studio?' Ewan looked quizzically at Sally. Margaret looked relieved.

'The Horsemen are Tadpoles,' Tyler explained. 'They believe in self-sufficiency, doing things themselves. So why are they bound up with the establishment, the music industry? Why don't they dump their record company, build their own studio and do it all themselves? It's perfectly possible. We did it with the Harvest Festivals; why not do it all the way?' Tyler looked at the perplexed faces around the table and smiled broadly, almost paternally, at Ewan.

Ewan brushed him off. 'Don't use my politics to justify your failure, Tyler.'

'Ewan, that's unfair,' Jonathan complained.

Ewan looked at Jonathan with surprise, then incredulity. 'Why don't they just admit it, Jonathan? They're finished.'

Jim jerked forward, leaning over the table with fury. 'Finished?'

'Dead in the water,' Ewan said.

'Oh, Ewan, come on,' Jonathan said, his patience waning.

'They're on the way out, it's obvious. Why do you think we had a surplus? Where were the fans?'

'You owe us,' Jim said, jabbing his finger in Ewan's direction.

'I owe you nothing,' Ewan spat back. 'Dumping your record company? Dumping or being dumped? Which way round is it, Jim?'

'You've always hated us,' Jim sneered. 'But you're fucking hot to take the proceeds, aren't you? Fucking hot to take the drugs.'

Ewan ignored him. 'Well, if you won't tell us, we'll have to guess. Guess that you failed, guess that your precious record company doesn't want you. That you've been well and truly dumped!'

Tyler kept his eyes fixed on Ewan but was aware of Sean

getting out of his seat. This hadn't been his plan, but this was a better one – Ewan was digging his own grave.

'And now you want to build your own little recording studio, so that you're not total failures,' Ewan went on. 'So that you don't have to drag around the country doing little pub gigs as glorious washed-up has-b—'

Ewan had no time to finish. Sean dragged him backwards out of his seat and slammed him up against the wall, cracking his back and head loudly against the wood panelling. Half the room stood up; the other half sat, frozen in horror or glee.

'Sean, there are children in the room!' Miriam shouted. She pulled Chaos towards her chest, trying to shield his face. Chaos was having none of it; he was transfixed.

Sean's face was like thunder – murderous. But he still managed to peer over to see Dipity, Tranx and assorted kids and babies sleeping soundly on some cushions in the corner. He returned menacingly to Ewan and tightened a hand round his throat.

'What are you saying, Ewan? Are you saying we're failures?'

Sally got out of her seat and stood close by. Jonathan ran round the table to join her, ready to pull Sean off.

'Sit down, Sean,' Margaret demanded with icy insistence.

Eric stared at Tyler, his face rigid, white. 'Back off, Sean,' Eric said through gritted teeth. 'This isn't right.' Tyler looked expressionlessly back at him. Nobody else was listening.

Sean continued to glare threateningly into Ewan's face. Ewan stared back, his heart thudding.

'Sean, sit down!' Margaret's voice rose, becoming more emphatic.

Ewan watched her as she left her seat and started making her way round the table, his eyes darting between her movement and Sean's terrifying glare. 'You don't want to do this, Sean,' he said, wheezing the words through his constricted windpipe.

'I don't want to do what, Ewan?' Sean replied with quiet venom.

Ewan's mind was blank with panic. 'Hit me,' he wanted to say, but knew that was stupid; that was obvious.

'Do what?' Sean demanded again, in a voice that suggested he'd dearly love to beat the shit out of him. 'What don't I want to do, Ewan?'

'Fuck up Tadley,' Margaret said. She stood behind Sean, her face and expression quite clear to Ewan. She was nodding vigorously.

Margaret's choice of language was perfect. Ewan watched Sean's face twitch. His grip relaxed a fraction.

'Are they trying to fuck it up?' Sean asked.

Ewan hadn't a clue what Margaret meant but she was still desperately nodding, so he tried to nod himself. He swallowed hard. 'I think so,' he managed to say.

'And I'm certain of it,' Margaret said.

'Okay then,' Sean announced brightly to the rest of the room. 'Whatever it is, I'm with Ewan.' He let go of Ewan's throat and punched him matily on the arm. 'So, Ewan, go on. Tell us what's wrong with the grand plan.'

Sean calmly returned to his seat as Ewan fell back against the wall. He felt breathless and wobbly and a total coward, and he hadn't a clue what the grand plan was. And worse, everybody was looking at him, including Sarah. Ewan slid down the wall and sat in a heap on the floor. Grand plan. What grand plan? Whatever it was he was going to lose now, though, lose to fucking *Jim*. Thanks, Sean.

The majority of the room sighed with relief and sat down. Jonathan gave him a weird look and started backing away, helping Margaret to her seat. Sally looked down at him.

'Bloody dykes?' she questioned icily.

Oh, not now, Sally! Ewan looked up at her. 'Some of my best friends are bloody dykes,' he replied tiredly.

Sally sneered disdainfully and turned away from him. 'Why do we need a recording studio?' she asked with a businesslike no-nonsense attitude.

'Absolutely,' Margaret agreed. 'I've been wondering the same thing myself.'

'Because we're *musicians*, Margaret.' Nick thought it was obvious, even to an old person. 'That's what musicians do.'

'No point in recording music when you're on the way out,' Eric quietly said. 'Unless the plan is for other bands to record music to give you a way back in.'

Tyler frowned, his calm demeanour suddenly ruffled. Ewan sighed with relief. Thanks, ladies. Thank you, old women and lesbians everywhere. Old women, lesbians and Eric.

'I helped with the harvest too, didn't I, Ewan?' Chaos said, breaking the silence.

'Yes, you did, Chaos,' Ewan replied and half laughed at the absurdity of it all.

Sally turned, grinned and held out a hand to help him up. He gratefully took it and kept hold as he stood and faced Tyler.

'I wouldn't object to a recording studio,' Ewan said. 'I wouldn't object to the band making records. Depending on what they exchange them for. But if you turn this place into a business, Tyler, if you turn Tadley into a record company, then I'm going to . . .' Ewan paused. He looked at Tyler shaking his head, Tyler's face insisting it wasn't going to be like that. Fear and panic swept through him. Tyler had sat next to Jonathan, smiled at Jonathan, agreed with Jonathan, touched Jonathan. Jonathan was the boss, always was, always would be. And Jonathan was staring at the table.

'You're going to what, Ewan?' Tyler asked benignly, pleasantly concerned.

Ewan didn't answer. Nothing. There was nothing he could do. Not if Jonathan agreed.

'Because whatever it is, I'll do it with you,' Tyler smiled.

Chapter 10

April 1979 – two years later

It was going to be a perfect day. The sun was breaking up the mist and the air smelt of blue skies and windless mornings. Ewan stood in the field, clutching wheat seed in his hand, debating whether to cast it. The children played in the dirt beside him, adding to the perfection, making it harder. Ewan hated mornings like this, hated perfect days. Perfect days gave a taste of how it could have been, how it almost was. They coloured his memory and brought fading dreams screaming to the front of his mind, creating instant nostalgia for a sense of well-being he didn't want to feel. How long could he hold on? Another year? Less? He didn't want to love these children, these people, this farm. Didn't want to love Tadley. Loving it made it all the more difficult to accept being pushed out and more tempting to jump and get it over with. Made it all the more difficult to go inside the house and endure the evening atmosphere of alienation, his disdainful shrugs and sneering sarcasm covering how trapped he felt and how much he had to lose.

Eight-year-old Chaos watched Ewan and shuffled from one foot to the other, unsure what to do. On the one hand it could be a meditation thing. Mentally visualising fields of splendour and abundance. A Very Important Spiritual Moment. In which case he should be quiet, still, attempt a similar level of thought-fulness and ignore the fact that Serendipity and Tranquillity had dug a rather large hole and were playing cooking with the dirt. Or Ewan was stoned and needed a nudge. Either way Sam, Joe and Max in the other fields were already halfway through their seed casting and Ewan was just standing there, clutching a fistful of seed and staring, miles away. Not throwing, not starting and not keeping an eye on Dipity and Tranx.

What to do? What to do? Chaos had never known Ewan meditate. Never known Ewan hang around navel-gazing when straightforward jobs needed doing. But on the other hand Ewan didn't seem stoned either. He hadn't seemed stoned ten minutes ago. Never usually got stoned till the evening. Chaos kicked around, wished Sally wasn't off helping with the lambing, and decided he'd give Ewan another couple of minutes before he nudged him. Then Tranx started eating her cooking, so Chaos bent down to stop her.

'No point in sowing if you won't see the harvest.'

Chaos looked up to see Ewan rubbing the seed thoughtfully in his hand. He wasn't sure what Ewan meant and assumed he was talking to himself. But Ewan turned and said, 'Is there, Chaos?' Chaos couldn't decide whether it was a stoned thing or a meditation thing. But it was certainly a deep thing, too deep for him to fathom. He shook his head in agreement anyway. After another slight pause Ewan shrugged and started casting the seed.

Sarah watched from the window. Ewan was finally moving but turning in wild circles, which worried her more. He and the children dancing around the field. Surely not seed sowing? It was too haphazard, too abandoned. Serendipity running,

158

leaping and showering seed like a trainee ballet dancer. Chaos throwing the seed behind him as though it were a wedding bouquet. Tranquillity trying to copy and throwing seed all over herself. Ewan lifting her upside down, spinning her round and shaking her, laughing. All four were laughing. Haphazard seed sowing. It was worrying. And not the time to be debating shops on the King's Road.

Sarah turned from the window and confronted Rebecca and Jackie, her business partners. She disliked them intensely but they were useful and talented and sneaky.

'I don't want to go to London,' Sarah said. 'I don't want to go anywhere particularly. I like it here. I've got children; I've got friends. Besides, I like the farm shop.'

'The farm shop does nothing. And the mail order and phone enquiries are getting ridiculous. We're getting swamped,' Rebecca replied.

'Nobody's asking you to live there,' Jackie said. 'We'll do all that for you. You just have to say yes.'

Sarah crossed to the other side of her workroom, removing the urge to look out of the window again and cloud the issue. The farm shop was a poke in his eye and the postal sales were underhand and under his nose and endlessly amusing – but a harmless accident. What money she earned was exchanged for materials and paid 'expenses' to Jackie, Rebecca and their office in Ludlow. It *was* in keeping with the spirit of Tadley and an outlet for her talents. It was *not* like Tyler's record company. *Not* like Jim and Nick's recording studio. *Not* like the growing band of business suits and employees that Jonathan was welcoming with open arms. A legitimate shop on the King's Road would be perfect but *not* in keeping. And worse, it would be away from Tadley. And it would be the end.

'But the spirit and the principle of Tadley—'

159

'Oh, here we go,' Rebecca interrupted with disdain. She hated Tadley and all the rigmarole connected with it.

Jackie grabbed the opportunity. 'The spirit and the principle of Tadley is to keep you down, Sarah, you know that. The spirit and the principle is designed to ensure your talents aren't recognised. Squandered, wasted. The spirit and the principle is a male spirit and a male principle. What are the men around here doing? Exactly what they want to do. What are the women doing? Struggling for recognition and washing socks!'

Sarah looked towards the window. She didn't need to look through it. Ewan wasn't sowing seed; he was throwing seed away. Throwing wheat seed away.

'It's not like that, Jackie,' she protested.

'It's exactly like that, Sarah.'

'You don't know; you don't live here.'

'I've seen enough. Heard enough from you. What's wrong with opening a shop?'

The same thing that was wrong with helping Tyler create an image for his new band, Pile Driver. Success. Tyler had promised her they'd be a failure, a tax loss. They'd giggled and worked on the designs for . . . minutes. She'd given them overblown warpaint, ridiculously high, spiked hair and costumes extreme to the point of depravity – a sure-fire failure. Tyler had promised. Jim and Nick hadn't. Straight in at number one, the media at the gates, a documentary crew trampling over Tadley, Ewan and the farmers going ballistic and Sarah secretly racked with guilt. That was what was wrong – it would be a success because Sarah wanted success. A shop on the King's Road would be heaven. A shop on the King's Road was what she wanted, what she dreamt of.

Sarah moved back towards the window. But maybe she'd want it more next year.

'Look, Jackie, Rebecca, all this discussion is irrelevant. The fact is we'd need Tadley capital. It would be a Tadpole label. Whether you like it or not, it's not up to me; it's a collective decision. And I know the collective decision will be no.' Sarah shrugged, smiled appeasingly, and looked out across the fields. The kids were pelting Ewan with seed now. Funny. Worrying.

The woman thought the farm shop was 'a veritable Aladdin's cave, a dream of a find'. The man thought it was a junk shop. Eric thought they were a couple of jumped-up chinless wonders and wanted to send them away with a flea in their ear. But Jonathan was serving.

Jonathan *hadn't* been serving. Jonathan had been hanging around waiting for the education officer. That was reasonable. Most of the Tads hung around the farm shop when they expected visitors. It was a long walk up the drive to the house and therefore polite. Dave had been in earlier, waiting for some guy called Gavin. It was normal, reasonable. What *wasn't* reasonable was Jonathan taking over just because this la-di-da couple were filthy rich, spoke with a similar accent and automatically turned to him.

The farm shop was Eric's sanctuary. An opportunity to gossip and chat with Tads and locals without having to take sides. Eric tried to remain neutral but it was difficult. He was beginning to see Ewan's point.

The couple were messing up the shelves. And they kept asking Jonathan the price of things. Jonathan's explanation of the exchange system was half-hearted and perfunctory. Both nodded but ignored him.

Mrs La-di-da had her eye on a couple of Miriam's jumpers, a basket of Sarah's soap and cosmetics, a silk-screen blouse, some beeswax candles and a selection of Margaret's pickles and preserves. Mr La-di-da fancied the makings of a ploughman's lunch, a pork pie and some home-brewed beer. Eric winced – farm territory.

Eric waited for Jonathan to ask if they smoked, had any news-papers or magazines, a can of petrol, wellies, spades, jacks or jump leads, a travel rug. Jonathan didn't ask. Jonathan named a price. It was low but it was cash. Eric wondered what kind of suicide mission Jonathan was on. Farm territory. A three-pronged, blistering attack. Sean, Sally, Ewan.

Jonathan took the money, aware that Eric's eyes were on him, but he waited till the couple had left before he shrugged and said, 'What difference does it make? A couple of pennies for some bread, beer, a pork pie, some cheese?'

'Well then, why do it?'

'Why not?'

Eric's neutrality disintegrated. 'Because, Jonathan, money makes people think they're important. The more they have, the more important they think they are. It makes them think they have the right to take over and dictate terms. What's important about contributing to a bank account that very few of us need or use? Tadley was supposed to be an alternative.'

Jonathan raised a disdainful eyebrow. 'You sound like Ewan.'

'Good.'

Jonathan turned with a look of haughty contempt and said, 'They're swimming against the tide, Eric; it's about time they grew up.'

'It was the profile of Tyler in the *Observer* that caught my eye,' Gavin explained as he stood, hands on hips, marvelling at the outside of the cabin. 'The way they put it, I thought it was all his idea. And to be honest, I did find it a little hard to believe, given the rest of the article. May I go in?'

Gavin moved tentatively towards the cabin, hoping the answer would be yes. Of course it was. Dave was as proud as Gavin was enthusiastic. And if Gavin liked the outside and the idea, wait till he went inside and saw the whole thing working.

'I read that you call it The Cottage?' Gavin continued, running his hand along the door and door frame as he entered. 'But it's all wood, isn't it?'

'Well, yes, technically it's a cabin. But if I said 'cabin' they'd say 'shed', and we've built sheds before. And if I said 'house' they wouldn't get involved, because obviously they've got enough to do. So I had to call it a cottage because it sounded small and possible, and most got involved one way or the other. Now that it's finished, of course, they're happy to call it a cabin and want to build more, but . . .' Dave shook his head. The arguments that could be generated over one simple cabin never ceased to amaze him.

'But?' Gavin prompted, turning the lights on and off.

'We wouldn't have the wood.' Dave shrugged. 'Well, not enough, not for a few years. Have to buy it in, and . . .' He shrugged again.

Gavin didn't follow. Dave felt obliged to explain further. 'This was all our own wood, coppiced.'

Gavin was even more impressed. He turned in slow circles, taking in the light, airy atmosphere of the place. It felt warm, cosy.

'So how much did it cost exactly?' Gavin asked as he entered the kitchen and automatically tested the taps.

'Well, nothing really,' Dave said, glowing with pride as the steam rose out of the hot tap.

Gavin looked sceptical.

'Obviously the solar batteries, photovoltaics, copper piping, wire, stuff like that, were all from exchange. Oh, and the windowpanes – we haven't got round to glass yet. But actual money? Er, nothing.'

Gavin nodded and made his way to the bathroom, checking and tapping and looking inside cupboards as he went, his enthusiasm overtaken by quick fire questioning.

'Plumbing?' he asked, lifting the lid of the toilet and peering in.

'Recycled grey water,' Dave automatically fired back. 'A reed bed system.'

'Sewage?'

'Composted. It was easier than the main house because we could start from scratch. Although at the main house we have got—'

Gavin cut him off. 'So the whole thing's solar powered?'

'And wind,' Dave explained. 'If you have a look out the back . . .' Dave started to point but Gavin had already moved that way.

'Decoration?' he asked.

'Home-made paint, natural dyes.' Dave followed like a puppy.

'Furniture?'

'Home-grown, handmade, wood, willow, wool, linen. We've got a blacksmith called Jack, who moved in from the town, funnily enough; he only lived—'

'And it stands totally alone?'

'What?' Dave was momentarily thrown by this question.

'It is completely energy efficient, relying on no outside utilities?'

'Oh. Yeah.'

'No gas, electricity, sewage or water companies?'

'That's right.'

'Totally natural products in so far as is possible?'

'Yep.'

'Dave.' Gavin grinned. 'I think you and I could do business.'

Dave was nonplussed. 'What?'

'Imagine it, thousands of people being inspired by your cottage. Exciting, yes?'

Dave hadn't a clue what Gavin was on about, but found himself flushed with excitement and nodding enthusiastically nonetheless.

As Hilary escorted the woman from the room, Jonathan could tell that the education officer was more than pleased, more than satisfied. The education officer had been positively amazed at the children's standard of achievement, Jonathan could read it in her face. Admittedly Imogen and Claudia were particularly bright, Chaos was quick and eager, and Serendipity had more nous than was natural in a six-year-old, but still, Jonathan couldn't help feeling that he'd probably found his place in the scheme of things, finally found something he was good at. A standard well above average, the education officer's report usually said, and Jonathan didn't doubt it would say that again. But this time it would be a report that included Sam and Jean's two lads. And it was Dylan and Zappa that Jonathan was most proud of.

They had arrived as a frightful pair of would-be thugs, mini Hell's Angels, or so it seemed to Jonathan, who had never come face to face with council estate, factory-fodder no-hopers before. He had never seen the inside of a state school, primary or otherwise, and was scared stiff of the little brutes, at a complete loss as to what to do with them, how to talk to them, approach them, teach them. Then Sally admitted she used to be like that. Ewan agreed he could have been like that. Dave said his schoolmates had been like that and Sean took an instant shine to them. Jonathan saw the challenge. Dylan and Zappa were going to turn out to be as hard-working, as motivated and as determined as Sally, Ewan, Dave and Sean. The trick was getting them to believe it. So far it seemed to be working.

'Are we still ahead?' Chaos asked.

Jonathan looked at him, looked at all the kids, proudly. 'Yes, you're still ahead.'

'Can we bugger off back to the farm then? As a reward sort of thing?' Zappa sweetly enquired.

Jonathan sighed affectionately. Well, it was *almost* working. 'Yes, you can bugger off back to the farm.'

He watched the children clatter out. A standard well above average, the education officer usually said. So why not a legitimate school, a proper alternative school, for outsiders as well as Tadpoles?

Dave endeavoured to herd the cows out of their winter quarters and into the spring sunshine and fresh pasture. He was distracted, though, his mind not totally on the job. His mind was more on Gavin and books. Maybe Gavin was a bit too businesslike for comfort, a bit too flash, but making a book, an *informative* book, an *instructional* book – that was what Tadley was all about. Books were what Tadley relied on. Absolutely nothing wrong with books. Books were *good*.

The cows seemed to sense Dave's distraction and were overexcited, neurotic and downright awkward. Things didn't improve when eight screaming and whooping kids descended on the shed entrance – the cows panicked, turned and tried to get back in. Dave sympathised. Now he was going to have to organise everybody. Organise the cows and organise the kids. And organisation Dave couldn't do. All he'd wanted was a quiet time to look for the argument. Books. Dave could see no argument in books. It didn't mean there wasn't one, though.

Dave started smacking the cows out of the shed again. The

kids also started smacking the cows. The cows went this way and that but not out. Dylan climbed onto the roof.

If someone wrote a book about cows and kids, Dave would certainly read it.

'Dylan, could you get down, please.'

Dylan carried on climbing, Dylan was obviously deaf.

'Dylan!' Dave pleaded. He couldn't *think* with all this distraction. One thing was certain. He didn't know how, and he didn't know why, but he just knew there was going to be an argument. He sat down forlornly on a bale of hay and looked at the mayhem in and around the shed. Dave hated arguments.

Between them Chaos and Dipity got one cow moving out. Imogen and Claudia gave a slight push and another cow followed. Matilda slapped a third cow's rump, Tranx copied and missed, but the cow obliged and moved anyway. The other cows took the hint and left with dignity. Zappa joined his brother on the roof. Dave sighed and stood up, was about to yell up to Dylan and Zappa but decided not to bother – they'd only ignore him. He followed the cows and other kids instead; they knew what they were doing.

'Books, Chaos,' Dave said as he fell in with the kids manoeuvring the cows out of the farmyard. 'Ewan reads books, doesn't he?'

'Yeah.' Chaos shrugged. 'Everybody knows that.'

'And Sally?'

'Yeah.'

'And Sean?'

Chaos thought for a second or two. 'I think he read a book once,' he finally said.

'I can read a book,' Serendipity proudly announced.

'Can you, Dips?' Dave smiled. That was the answer really. *Everybody* read books. You couldn't argue with books. Books were good.

Dave turned to deal with Dylan and Zappa, but Eric came round the corner and beat him to it. 'Get down off that bloody roof now!' he barked.

Dylan and Zappa moved themselves.

'Hey, Dave,' Eric said. 'You'll never guess what happened in the farm shop.'

Dave gave him a look. From Eric's face it wasn't going to be the arrival of the Virgin Mary. Or if it was, the Virgin Mary had arrived and started an argument.

'Whatever it is, Eric, I don't want to know.'

Eric shrugged and told him anyway.

Ewan felt tired as he approached the drawing room, his spirit dragged wearily down by the prospect of *another* meeting, *another* argument, *another* waste of time. All this palaver over a pork pie – it was ridiculous. His little squad of farmers, tight-lipped with grim-faced aggression, marched with menace behind him, practically silent in socks on a marble floor. No doubt some twat-head would accuse them of *sneaking up* on the meeting – to do what? Join in? It was pathetic. Ewan could hear Dave talking about his cabin, his voice prominent above the murmur and hum of a jam-packed drawing room. The whole house gathered – united by the prospect of a divisive show-down. Dave stopped mid-sentence, his mouth frozen and his face red, taking a sudden interest in the carpet as Ewan appeared in the doorway. That was upsetting. Ewan had no argument with Dave.

A brittle atmosphere descended as Ewan and the farmers sat. The silence was tiresome and uncomfortable till Ewan, through gritted teeth, said, 'Carry on with what you were saying, Dave.'

But Dave only managed a shrug and, 'Just a book. About the cottage. A how-to book.'

Ewan felt *so* tired.

'How much money would you get for this book, Dave?'

Tyler's deliberately provocative question raised audibly sharp intakes of breath as everybody glanced furtively at Ewan. Ewan wasn't falling for it. He looked at Tyler and smiled. It was a strange smile.

Dave struggled to explain that money hadn't been discussed. That he'd asked Miriam to have a meeting with Gavin. That the book deal was only an idea, nothing concrete – and certainly nothing commercial.

'Well, I might have a chat with Gavin,' Tyler said. 'I'm perhaps tougher at negotiating than Miriam.'

Jonathan agreed. Tyler glanced over at Ewan, but Ewan only smiled. A vote was taken. Ewan raised his hand in support of Dave's book so everybody else did. Dave looked relieved but cheated.

After a long, silent pause Ewan started. 'About the farm shop,' he said.

And Jonathan jumped in. 'Have you any idea how difficult it is to deal with you lot? With your pathetic demands and oh-so-holier-than-thou ideals? Half the people in this place are not allowed to do what they want, or are scared of doing what they want, because of you. You're like a little mafia. It was never the idea; bowing down and worshipping you was never the idea.'

Ewan answered sarcastically, 'Oh, wasn't it really, Jonathan?'

Jonathan breathed deeply, tired of it, bored. Tired of Ewan. He stared at him with something approaching loathing. 'We never agreed to self-sufficiency,' he said.

A gasp of incredulity erupted around the room, but Ewan didn't argue and Jonathan ploughed on. 'All we agreed to was doing our own thing. All we agreed to was *not* being dictated to by some top dog, power-hungry Stalinist despot. We *didn't* agree to having our ideas or potential squashed by some jumped-up little Welsh Hitler.'

Ewan's eyes narrowed.

'You might like farming, but personally I think it's shit. A lot of us do. A lot of us couldn't give a fuck about the farm, or your politics, or you really. We never agreed to live in some kind of hermetically sealed bubble, turning our backs on the world and grubbing around like troglodytes. Some people here have better things to do, things they'd rather do, things they're good at. And that means living in the twentieth century. Having contact with the outside world, with economics, business, money. Why, heaven forfend, we might even get ourselves a television. And if you don't like that, well . . .' Jonathan shrugged disdainfully and glared at Ewan.

Everyone mentally finished Jonathan's sentence and watched with silent worry, waiting for the explosion.

'Fuck you, Jonathan,' Ewan said with icy calm, an almost reasonable expression on his face. 'Let's be perfectly honest here. It's what you wanted, isn't it?'

Jonathan was disarmed; he'd expected the usual rage. The room held its breath. Sarah looked at Sally. Sally seemed strangely upset, strangely bewildered. Sally knew what was going to happen. Sarah shook her head with alarm, worried that she did too.

'Fuck you, Jonathan,' Ewan said again. 'You wanted me to fuck you.'

'Ewan, don't,' Sarah pleaded.

'And all this is because I haven't.'

Jonathan took a loud, involuntary gulp of air as his eyes darted to his feet. He suddenly felt very cold. He hadn't expected this at all.

'All this is because I'm with Sarah and you're with Tyler.'

Ewan paused slightly; he'd had enough. 'And you don't want Tyler. Tyler's not your type. I am. I'm your type. But you're so glad that Tyler gives you a blow job. So grateful for Tyler's mouth, hands – whatever, I don't want to know. So grateful for some kind of sex, affection, whatever you want to call it, that you'll do it for him, won't you? You'll push me out, won't you, Jonathan? You'll push me because you can't fuck me.'

Jonathan kept his eyes on his feet, his head shaking slightly, his face white, mouthing the word no. But it was obviously yes. Ewan almost felt sorry for him, but reckoned he'd get over it. He stood up, stretched his back slightly and looked around the room, trying to smile, wanting to lighten the leaden atmosphere and find a reason to stay.

'I suppose it makes a change for a straight guy to be victimised by a gay one, but . . .' Ewan shrugged. 'Nobody likes victimisation.' He tried to appear nonchalant but he looked wiped out, defeated.

When Ewan left, Sally, Sean and the farmers left. As did Sarah, Dave, Miriam, Margaret, Eric, all the kids and approximately fifty per cent of the room.

Sarah closed the front door behind her and went down the steps to the porch wall where Ewan was sitting. His legs dangled over the stone newel, his back to her as he looked out over his fields.

'Are you going to get stoned now?' she asked.

'Yes.'

Sarah sat down and put her arms around him. 'Good. I want to get stoned with you,' she said. 'Well and truly hammered.'

She felt the jerk of his body as he half laughed. She couldn't let him leave. Leave her. Let Jonathan win.

'I'm so stupid, Sarah,' he sighed.

'Hmm.' She had to agree with that.

'I can't do this anywhere else. They can make money any-where, set up a business anywhere, everywhere. But I can only do this here. I've got to leave and I've got nowhere to go.'

Sarah wanted to say 'London'. She wanted to say, 'Forget the farm. Let's take the kids, just the two of us, go to London and open a shop on the King's Road.'

But he said, 'I had them in my hand, had them in my hand and thought about it. Then I chucked them. Bloody threw them. I should have flushed them down the toilet. I've got to wait till harvest now.'

Sarah remembered the haphazard seed sowing and realised that meant he was staying – at least till the wheat harvest. Which was better than London because, realistically, he wouldn't think the kids were his to take.

'Want to fuck me?' she asked.

'No,' he replied, beginning to laugh. 'I can't at the moment. I've got an image in my head of Jonathan fucking *me*.'

Chaos watched them through the upstairs window. He couldn't hear what they were saying but they were laughing. Wrapped in each other's arms, friendly, close. Chaos didn't understand it. He didn't understand any of it, but if Ewan and Sarah were together, he was happy.

Chaos climbed into his bed, settled down to stare at the ceiling, and listened to the deep, unconscious breathing of Dylan and Zappa. Voices drifted up from the stairs or outside his door as people passed along the corridor. He heard Sally worrying about Ewan leaving, and Miriam reassuring her.

'He won't go; there are too many on his side.'

Chaos closed his eyes. As expected, Miriam looked in, checked the boys were asleep and closed the door. Chaos opened his eyes. Ewan leaving? He heard Dave and Margaret.

'But *I* wanted to live in it.'

'You want, Dave, but Ewan *needs*.'

Chaos frowned – Ewan needs what? Chaos was itching to get up, have a midnight ramble; he wasn't a bit tired. He heard the front door close, his mother giggling as she came up the stairs. Ewan saying, 'After all that and you're thinking of a threesome? That is *vicious*, Sarah.'

Chaos listened to them walk past. He longed for them to come in and tell him what was going on. He heard one door open, one door close. It was Ewan's door, Chaos was sure of it. His mum would be sleeping in Ewan's room. *Good*. Miriam's right, Ewan's not leaving. Then silence for a while. Silence for a long time. Chaos got up.

From his vantage point on the second-storey landing, Chaos watched Sally and Miriam go to Ewan's room. He saw Sally go in and back out quickly in surprise, pulling the door with her and colliding with Miriam.

'I'm sorry, Ewan, I thought you'd be alone,' she stammered.

'It's all right, I'm not *sleeping* with the enemy – *yet*.' Ewan laughed.

Chaos heard Sarah giggle in the background. They were stoned.

He watched Margaret and Dave join them a little bit later, Margaret emphatically announcing in the doorway, 'Dave's cabin, Ewan, Dave's cabin!' The door closed but Chaos could still hear their laughter, their voices, a vague hum in the silence of the house.

Chaos watched Jonathan and Tyler climb the stairs and walk along the corridor. They looked dishevelled, tired. Tyler waited while Jonathan listened at Ewan's door, smelling the dope. They went into the room next to Ewan's. Jonathan's room.

Jonathan bypassed the main light and put on the bedside lamp instead, keeping the room dim, the atmosphere low. He lay stiffly on the bed, stared at the ceiling and listened to the murmur from next door. Giggling, muffled voices, nothing distinct. Tyler sat on the bed next to him, a vague look of unease on his face.

'*Do* you want to fuck him?' Tyler asked.

Jonathan shook his head.

'Want to pretend to fuck him?'

Jonathan looked quizzical.

'I can't do the Welsh accent,' Tyler said, 'but I can be a pain in the bum.'

Jonathan might have laughed but just then the music started. Loud. From Ewan's room. Lou Reed singing 'Vicious'. It seemed pointed, vindictive – camp.

Jonathan sat up, closed his eyes and seethed. 'Fuck you, Ewan Hughes,' he said. He grabbed Tyler and kissed him forcefully, almost aggressively.

Tyler pulled out of the kiss and stared at Jonathan.

'Fuck Ewan Hughes,' Jonathan said, his hand still holding tightly to the back of Tyler's neck, digging in, hurting. 'Fuck him, fuck him, fuck him.'

Tyler struggled to move his neck free. Jonathan again grabbed at his mouth, swamping, angry. Tyler felt suffocated; he pulled away, sat back. 'Calm down, Jonjo,' he appealed, looking into Jonathan's face with suspicious concern.

Jonathan breathed, closed his eyes and tried to calm down. Lou Reed pumped through the wall; other voices joined in, singing along, loud, raucous, as though they were all on Ewan's side and laughing.

Tyler tried to take over. He kissed Jonathan tenderly, hoping to soften him, hoping to ease his raging humiliation. Jonathan turned his face away, sideways, up, out of reach, his eyes still screwed shut in burning anger. Tyler persisted, trying to unbutton Jonathan's shirt. Jonathan couldn't stand it. He moved away, off the bed, fast, pacing. The fact was he wanted to hit somebody, wanted to hit something, wanted to fuck *so* hard, wanted to fuck so hard that it *hurt*. Not Tyler. Not smooth and slow and sensual and . . .

Jonathan turned, pulled at Tyler's shirt, ripped it open. He pulled at Tyler's jeans, pulled, tugged, forced the bastard things open. He pushed Tyler down, sent him sprawling backwards on the bed.

'You want to pretend? Then lie still,' Jonathan demanded. 'Lie still and let me beat the/fuck the shit out of you!'

Jonathan stopped. Sudden, surprised. Tyler sat up, moved forward, grabbed Jonathan, pulled him down onto the bed and held him tightly. Jonathan buried his head in Tyler's neck, felt Tyler's body against his own, Tyler's arms around him. It was like Ewan but it wasn't Ewan.

'I'm with you, Jonjo,' Tyler gently soothed. 'It's okay, it's all right, I'm with you.'

Jonathan remembered a time way back in the beginning. *Change what you hate and don't feel guilty.* He sat up with a jerk. 'I wish you wouldn't call me that, Tyler. I really hate, loathe and detest you calling me that.' Jonathan moved off the bed to the other side of the room, away from Tyler. 'In fact, I hate, loathe and detest a lot of the things you do.'

'What are you saying, Jonj— Jonathan?'

'I'm saying I don't think you fit in with Tadley. Or rather, I think Tadley's fitting in with you, and I don't like it.'

'Ewan doesn't like it.'

'*I* don't like it.'

Tyler gave up. He breathed deeply, got off the bed and re-arranged his clothes. 'I live here; my business is here.' His face had changed; he suddenly looked hard, businesslike.

Jonathan looked equally hard as he shrugged dismissively. 'You can be paid off.'

Tyler shook his head. 'It's not as simple as that, Jonathan. Too many complications. Besides, it's not up to you. Tadley doesn't belong to you any more; it's a collective.'

'I think it might be best all round if you left, Tyler.'

Tyler smiled. 'For tonight, Jonathan. It might be best for tonight.'

Chaos sat cross-legged, peering through the bars on the second-storey landing, his leg jigging, patience waning, excitement beginning to get the better of him. Chaos loved the parties. And as soon as the music started, Chaos knew there was going to be a party. He had to be patient. When they were stoned enough, happy enough, stupid enough, they'd let him in, not worry, not bother. The timing's got to be right; the timing's got to be perfect. Sean had already gone in with a whole group, so that should speed things up, create mayhem quicker. Just wait a little bit longer.

Chaos watched as Eric staggered along the corridor carrying a tray laden with beer pitchers and bottles of wine and whisky. He kicked at Ewan's door, waiting for somebody to hear and open it. Unfortunately Eric was kicking in time to the music. Even Chaos knew that was daft.

Chaos watched Tyler leave Jonathan's room, trying to make his ripped shirt look decent. He watched as Tyler exchanged a curt nod with Eric. Tyler didn't bother opening the door for him, though. Tyler obviously wasn't going to the party. Tyler obviously wasn't in the mood. Chaos was – couldn't wait. Lou Reed's *Transformer* blaring out. Somebody let Eric in.

Wait three, maybe four, songs, then go in. They won't care.

★

Jonathan sat on the bed, listening to Lou Reed through the wall, and wondered how long this would be going on. He would have laughed at any other time, dismissed Ewan's musical 'jokes' as juvenile, pathetic. But not tonight. Tonight Jonathan was tired, and Ewan's choice seemed particularly . . . well, vicious.

Jonathan tried to get angry, but he'd had enough of being angry. He hurt, if the truth be known. Had hurt for a long time. Years. Every time Ewan looked at Sarah, spoke to her, argued with her, touched her, had sex with her, so open, so pointed, rubbing Jonathan's nose in it, laughing at him, sneering, making him feel so awkward, so uncomfortable – so jealous.

Jonathan listened as people laughed, chatted, shouted above the music, sang along with it, Ewan's room filling with the others – party time. Drugs, drink, sex, whatever. Anything goes; anything goes except what Jonathan wants. Stop it now, Ewan, please. Stop it.

Maybe Tyler wasn't the best choice, but Tyler was the only choice. And Ewan was always there, always around, lithe, sexy, horny. Horny for Sarah. Sexy with Sarah. It was okay for them, easy, acceptable. All they had to do was fall into each other's arms, kiss, grab, roll around in mud and . . .

No, no, no. What are you talking about, Jonathan? You're hurt? You're angry? Fact is, Ewan's angry. Ewan's hurt. This is no joke. Ewan isn't doing it as a joke. This is pointed, stabbing, jabbing at him, because what is Ewan supposed to do? What *should* Ewan do? What *could* Ewan do? Ewan had accepted it all along, knew all along, and Ewan never despised him, never recoiled in horror, never called him pervert, pooftah, pansy . . .

How long can you love someone? How long can you hope for the impossible?

People gathering outside, spilling out of Ewan's room,

laughing, talking, singing along to this bitchy, spiteful, nasty, love-soaked album.

Jonathan remembered a time, so many years ago. His father just died, Ewan with Jonathan, on this very bed. Ewan grabbing him, holding him, allowing him to cry. Jonathan burying his head in Ewan's neck, feeling Ewan's body against his own, Ewan's arms around him. He felt safe, warm, loved. He desperately wanted Ewan to love him. Desperately wanted Ewan to stay.

'I don't want you to go,' he'd said.

'I'll be with you, Jonathan Jo,' Ewan had replied. 'I'll be with you till it's over.'

Get over it, Jonathan.

'It's over, Ewan!' he bellowed as he kicked away a chair, pushed over the dressing table and started trashing the room.

He held the big heavy mirror in his hands, turned, lifted it and froze. Ewan, arms folded, face neutral, leant against the door frame and watched. The others were behind him, looking worried, concerned, trying to get a better view.

Jonathan suddenly became aware of the mess, the destruction, Lou Reed singing 'Perfect Day'.

'All this over a pork pie, Jonathan?' Ewan asked.

Jonathan put down the mirror, looked at Ewan, nodded and tried to laugh. He burst into tears instead. Ewan herded the others away and turned back to pull the door closed. The last thing Jonathan saw before the door shut was the quizzical expression on Chaos's face. Jonathan sat down on the bed, sang along to 'Perfect Day' and cried.

The next song played was Jefferson Airplane – 'White Rabbit'.

It meant nothing.

Chapter 11

June 1982 – three years later

'Are you ready or what?' Eric's voice crackled through the intercom.

'Ready and waiting,' Chaos lied. He stopped pacing the floor of the recording studio, took his seat at the piano stool, looked reluctantly at the keys and tried again to get angry.

Common Entrance exam. What for? Just for whose interest exactly? Jonathan's. Just for Jonathan's interest. So Jonathan could pump up his ego, boast about legitimacy and bolster the school's prospectus. Chaos was a guinea pig, an experiment in Establishment values. Or something like that.

Chaos stretched his fingers. The anger wasn't coming. And without anger, Chaos couldn't turn Eric's idea of a stupid ballad into something that meant something. 'Come out of the Tree, Dipity' wasn't meant to be soft – it was meant to be hard and fast and confusing, and whether it be out of interest, fun or posterity, Chaos was reluctant to commit it to tape till it was.

The red light went on. Chaos thought about the Common Entrance exam and knew he didn't really understand the argument. He wasn't angry; he just didn't want to sit it – he was nervous. His fingers hit the piano keys, fumbled, plonked; he opened his mouth, stopped.

Eric leant over the desk. 'We haven't got a lot of time, Chaos.'

Chaos looked at the clock – not a lot of time. Oh yeah, think about *that*. That was infinitely more annoying than thinking of doing some stupid exam. Chaos ground his teeth, jigged his leg and silently raised a thumbs–up for Eric to start recording. He picked up the pace, double time, thumped out the tune and started to pour out his anger.

> *'Come out of the tree, Dipity,*
> *Don't stare, Dipity,*
> *Share, Dipity,*
> *Explain it to me . . .'*

Halfway through, Jim walked into the studio and Nick walked into the booth.

'Come on, come on, this is not a bloody playground, you know,' Jim said.

Chaos stopped. His anger didn't.

'Shouldn't you be with Jonathan?' Jim pushed.

Chaos slammed down the lid of the piano – *guaranteed* to annoy – kicked over a microphone stand and stomped out of the studio.

Eric sighed heavily and turned off the tape. 'He's good, you know,' he complained to Nick.

'Just because he can play a piano, doesn't make him *yours*, Eric.'

Since he had decided on a short haircut and only cocaine, Nick had become something of a complete bastard. Good producer, though. Would be a better one if he listened to Chaos, took him seriously. Yes, Eric was fully aware that an eleven-year-old pop singer was more than stomach churning, but it wasn't about that. It was about practice. Get Chaos confident, get him good, then unleash him when he was eighteen, nineteen – could be brilliant. Chaos could be *huge*. And no, Eric did *not* think that just because Chaos could play the piano. But . . .

'I bet if he played bass there'd be more than a spark of interest, Nick!' Eric sneered as he left the big boys to their precious studio.

Chaos hung around the corridor and watched the 'proper' band arrive. He hadn't seen this lot before, nobody familiar, New Romantics by the look of them. He didn't bother speaking to them; he wasn't in the mood today. He felt fed up, restless, and there was nowhere to hide. More and more rooms had been turned into offices. Offices 'out of bounds during office hours'. Offices full of 'smartly dressed strangers, who walk around efficiently, drink coffee importantly and speak in perfect telephone tones', as Sally put it. Well, with a lot of swearing in between, but that was the gist of it. The truth of it too. God, if only Chaos could live in one of Dave's cabins! Life would be easy then; life would be fun.

'Why didn't you just do it properly, Chaos?' Eric joined him and complained.

Chaos pouted. He wanted to lose his temper and shout, 'Dipity up a tree! Dipity up a tree!' But he didn't. He half hoped that Eric was right and Dipity up a tree *was* tender and spiritual and cute, and not frightening and weird and confusing as Chaos thought it was.

'Anyway, haven't you got an exam or something this morning?' Eric remembered. Now Chaos was definitely ready to lose his temper. But, thankfully, somebody screamed and all thoughts of exams were over for the rest of the morning.

'It's a pig!' the receptionist screamed. 'There's a pig in the hall! Two!'

Chaos and Eric raced to the hall to laugh at the spectacle. The receptionist was standing on her desk and shouting, 'Keep still! Don't move!' to the hapless visitor poised with Dave's coffee-table book, *The Cottage*, grabbed from the stack of tastefully arranged literature and held aloft like a cudgel. Three office doors were open just wide enough to prove the cowardice of the people peering out. One woman was frozen halfway up the stairs, a bunch of files clutched in one hand and her skirt clutched tightly round her knees with the other. Two others on the first-floor landing were holding each other in alarm, ready to run up another flight of stairs if necessary. And three brave souls in the hall were slipping and sliding and wishing they knew something, *anything*, about animals as they tried to round up and shoo out three pigs, four sheep, two cows and several chickens.

There was no sign of any of the farmworkers.

Eric and Chaos exchanged looks as the drawing-room door flew open and Sarah stood there, a face like thunder and a mood for no nonsense.

'Who let these animals in here?' She didn't so much enquire as demand to crucify. A silent staring response. Nobody said, but obvious chief suspect was Sean.

Eric and Chaos knew how to deal with animals. They knew how to calm them and turn them and get them back outside. Eric and Chaos also knew how to get animals confused, nervous and crapping in panic. So when Sarah pointed an outraged finger at them and demanded that they 'Do something!', Eric and Chaos did. There was shit everywhere.

Chaos was amazed to discover that cows could open doors. Well, with a little judicious sleight of hand and a quick bang with a human backside. Sheep were very good at getting tangled in telephone wire. *All* animals seemed to respond to screams, and positively *danced* with excitement when humans noisily clambered onto desks or slammed themselves against walls and filing cabinets.

Eric was busy wondering if pigs could climb stairs. He found that if they ran fast enough – they could! The woman with the files found that *very* entertaining.

And Sarah? Sarah was beside herself with rage.

Sarah knew the car park plans hadn't gone down well, but this was juvenile, and certainly, definitely – emphatically – *not* going to help their case. If she could sack them she would; if she could kill them she would; if she could pour concrete over the whole fucking farm she would.

She managed to corner and catch two of the chickens, saw the faces of Sally and Sean in them and felt like wringing their necks. She threw them venomously out of the door and turned with murderous intent on a pig. She would have had it too – the pig took one look at Sarah's face, dithered from one foot to the other and was ready to throw up its trotters in surrender – except that Sarah slipped on manure and fell clumsily to the floor. Her smart, business-tart white dress was ruined. Shit, mud, rain, weather – more reasons why the car park was necessary.

Sarah sat on the floor and watched one of the chickens blithely stroll back into the hall. Sarah looked at it. Glared at it. Opened her mouth to scream at it. But decided it would be far more satisfying screaming at the humans. It was probably just as useless, probably just as much a waste of time, but definitely, *definitely* more satisfying. She got up and thundered out of the front door.

Chaos threw a quick wave to Eric and followed his mum.

From their vantage point on the roof, nine farmers peered

over the parapets like shadowy desperadoes. Sean, Sally, Sam, Joe, Max, Pete, Juliet, James and Emma.

Dave muttered something about losing his tape measure and slipped quietly behind the half-erected cabin. Tea. The only way Pattie knew of declaring her undying love for Dave was to make him cups of tea. The only way Dave knew how to respond was to drink it. Gallons of it. Dave's bladder was not happy. It had got to the point where he'd use any excuse he could think of rather than admit he needed a piss – again. But at least it had cured his obsession with toilet privacy and en suite bathrooms. Ewan thought it was hilarious and (secretly) incredibly romantic.

Ewan sat down on what was going to be the doorway and rested the plank of wood on his knees. He watched Sarah stomping her way across the fields, Chaos a short distance behind.

Dave reappeared, sheepishly zipping up his flies.

'Did you find it?' Ewan grinned.

'What?' Dave asked, before remembering, reddening, and making a show of patting his pockets.

Ewan's grin broadened as he pointed to Dave's tape measure balanced on the woodpile where it always was. 'Just fuck her, Dave. It's what she wants,' he said. 'Then you can get to the interesting part – constant tedious argument.'

Dave joined Ewan to sit on the unfinished cabin floor as Sarah and Chaos came closer. There was no point in getting back to work; they knew what she'd be raging about.

'Looks like you'll have time for a tea break,' Ewan said and started laughing as Dave shook his head in despair.

'Oh, don't, Ewan, please,' he pleaded.

'Do something, Ewan!' Sarah thundered when she was sure she was in shouting distance.

Ewan raised his eyebrows and grinned at Chaos hanging back a little from the scene before putting on a deadpan face and waiting till Sarah was right in front of him.

'I'm sorry, Sarah, I'm a bit busy at the minute; I'm holding a plank,' he said.

Dave turned away and tried not to laugh. Partly because he didn't want to get involved; partly because if he laughed he'd have to piss again.

Sarah slowly spat out every word through gritted teeth. 'So put the plank down.'

Ewan mimicked the staccato. 'Then we won't finish the shed.'

'Cabin,' Dave corrected.

'Whatever.' Ewan shrugged.

'You're farm manager; you're responsible!' Sarah seethed.

'Farm managers push pens, not pigs.' Ewan smiled obstinately at her.

Sarah twitched impatiently, in two minds whether to punch him or plead with him to get involved. 'We don't need the farm, you know. I can always arrange to get rid of it.'

'Good idea. Maybe we could turn it into a golf course,' Ewan said. 'That would be good for business.'

Dave snorted, got up quickly and disappeared behind the back of the cabin.

Sarah breathed deeply and tried to calm down. 'Make Sean and Sally get those animals out of the house, Ewan,' she muttered through pursed lips. 'Whether they like it or not we *are* having a car park!'

Sarah turned and stomped off. Ewan gave Chaos an 'I'm in the doghouse' look before turning away and allowing his face to fall.

★

185

From their vantage point on the roof, the nine desperado farmers silently watched the animals being herded out of the house and back to the farm by Jonathan, his assistant, Mandy, and twenty-two schoolchildren. Eric trailed reluctantly behind, turned and gave a surreptitious shrug in the direction of the roof – sorry guys, did my best. Sean raised his arms, mimed Lee Harvey Oswald and blew Jonathan's brains out.

Sally looked across the fields, watching Ewan stroll slowly towards the house, taking his time, chatting with Chaos, casually stopping to ponder thoughts. She was incensed. 'He should be up here,' she said to no one in particular.

'What do you expect him to do, Sally?' Sam asked.

'Fight!' she spat, before turning with sullen contempt and plonking down with her back against the parapet.

'The workers united shall never be defeated,' Sean chanted flippantly, leaning over the parapet. Leaning *dangerously* over to the other farmers' minds.

A few moments later Sally heard Ewan shout, 'Jump, Sean.' Sean made a huge, laughing pretence at doing so.

Sally got up and looked over the parapet. Ewan and Chaos were sitting on the wall of no man's land, the porch steps outside the house, Ewan patiently looking up, patiently waiting for Sean to fall. Sally glowered down but stepped back behind the parapet as she heard the front door open.

Sarah appeared in the doorway, hands on hips, in fresh clothes and with wet hair. And calmer. Definitely calmer because, apart from a cursory glance, she and Ewan pointedly avoided eye contact. Maddeningly avoided eye contact, as far as Chaos was concerned.

Sarah walked down the steps and looked up at the house, first floor, second floor, roof. She saw nothing. Ewan rubbed the hint of a smirk from his mouth as Sarah moved closer, tacitly agreeing the need for a powwow. Nothing was said for a while, Ewan tapping his foot and Sarah distracted by it, both trying to get their heads into 'professional discussion' mode. Chaos remained dutifully quiet next to Ewan, hoping not to be noticed, or at least, hoping not to appear to be intruding. He liked Ewan and his mum together, no matter- what they were doing. Whether they were at each other's throats or in each other's arms they always seemed *together.* Not that they'd done much of either lately.

Sarah was about to say something but looked beyond Ewan, beyond the steps. Ewan and Chaos automatically turned to look and quickly turned back. The mood changed, tensed, as Jonathan approached. Ewan fished in his pocket for his dope tin.

Chaos wasn't sure whether to stay on the wall or disappear up to the roof. Jonathan, Sarah and Ewan together, in such close proximity, that was really too intriguing to pass up. Chaos couldn't remember when he last saw *that.* But was Jonathan approaching for the powwow or the exam? Although Chaos was fairly confident in his latest 'Exams are crap because . . .' strategy, he felt uncomfortable at the possibility of having to argue with Jonathan in front of Ewan. It was, after all, Ewan's argument and Chaos wasn't too sure how that might go down. Then again, there were a group of disgruntled farmers, a house that stank to high heaven, office workers complaining, and Sarah and Ewan on neutral territory. Maybe exams wouldn't be Jonathan's top priority. Jonathan, Sarah and Ewan – together. Oh, he couldn't miss that. If necessary he'd sit the stupid exam. If necessary he'd even try to *pass* the stupid exam.

It was strange. Clipped, cold, perfunctory. If Sarah and Ewan were good at avoiding eye contact, Ewan and Jonathan were past masters at the job. Chaos had never seen Ewan roll a joint

CLAIRE DOWIE

so slowly, with so much concentration, such bent-over intensity. Nor seen Jonathan take so much interest in the view of the land, the fields in the distance, birds and aircraft flying overhead.

'The house needs clearing up,' Jonathan stated flatly, almost as though speaking to himself.

'My workers might agree to that,' Ewan replied impersonally. '*If* the car park plans are dumped.'

'We need a car park,' Sarah said.

'Not over my workers' fields.'

'You have acres of fields, Ewan,' Jonathan reasoned. 'There are fields that haven't even been cultivated yet.'

'Not yet, no, but the way things are going, we'll be having to feed the five thousand,' Ewan replied pointedly.

'But at the moment, you have spare fields,' Jonathan persisted.

Ewan said nothing and concentrated on licking papers.

'People are fed up with having to park by the post room,' Sarah tried to explain.

Ewan frowned and stopped licking for a moment. 'Where's the post room?'

'The old farm shop,' Jonathan said, and almost glanced in Ewan's direction, surprised that Ewan didn't know.

'They have to walk all the way up from the bottom,' Sarah said.

'So?'

'When it's cold, wet, blowing a gale, snowing?' Sarah thought it was obvious.

Ewan managed one derisive glance, then laughed. 'Poor babies. Poor weak-willed, lily-livered bunch of jellies.'

Sarah was about to lose her businesslike cool, but Jonathan continued the diplomacy. 'The proposed field is in a perfect position for a car park. Easy access for the house, easy access for the farm. Some of the farmworkers have cars, haven't they? The employees?'

Ewan ignored Jonathan's question as he studiously laid out some tobacco. Jonathan looked as far as Ewan's joint rolling and dope tin, but not at him. He vaguely wondered where Ewan got the dope from; it certainly wasn't home-grown.

'And then there's the visitors. What kind of image are we projecting if they have to tramp all the way up from the post room?'

'Depends what image you want to project,' Ewan mumbled, before clearing his throat and speaking with more authority. 'My workers have, under the circumstances, tried to be reasonable about the politics of the house. They have continued to provide food, even though production has had to increase. That seems reasonable – under the circumstances. However, when the house proposes to encroach onto the land, not only to acquire a sizeable chunk of it for nefarious purposes, but also to interfere with a carefully planned crop rotation system, well, it doesn't seem reasonable to them. It doesn't seem as though the house is even *trying* to be reasonable. And, as *farm manager*, I have to agree.'

Ewan looked up briefly, hoping the way he had sneered 'farm manager' had proved his contempt for the way that he'd been labelled. He then returned to his joint rolling, and spoke more quietly.

'Besides, that field is . . . My workers treat the proposed field as prime, one of the best, the main field. You may not understand it, but it's at the heart of what they do.'

Chaos watched Jonathan look over at the proposed field, frown and shake his head. 'It looks pretty much the same as any other field to me.'

Chaos held his breath as he watched Ewan stop trying to roll the perfect joint and simply stare at it for a moment, before screwing it up into a ball like rubbish.

'Yes, absolutely, Jonathan, it's just another field. One of many. And as you say, there are other fields, uncultivated ones. Okay, so they're *right at the bottom*, nowhere near the house or farm-yard, but hey, isn't that what we want? And we could start making rings of fields around the sheds, make the sheds our base, when Dave and I have built enough of them. Which we could do if everybody left me alone. So, yeah, do it. Put your car park there. Put it anywhere. Don't even ask me – I'm not interested; I'm only trying to stop them putting animals in the house.'

Ewan sighed, looked at the screwed-up joint in his hand, and shook his head. 'Thank God I didn't get round to the dope.' He then picked his Rizlas out of his tin to start all over again.

Jonathan and Sarah exchanged looks. Chaos thought they were both stupid. 'It's the first field they ever ploughed,' he told them. 'Everybody knows it's the first field. Well, I knew it was, anyway.'

'Shut up, Chaos,' Ewan snapped.

Sudden realisation smacked Jonathan and Sarah as they stared sharply at Ewan's bent head.

Chaos reddened, stung by Ewan's instant dismissal. He stared awkwardly at Jonathan and Sarah, but they were looking at each other and at the ground, hoping it might open up. They had forgotten, completely forgotten, Chaos could tell. He was glad then, glad he'd told them, despite Ewan's slap down. He wanted to tell them more, wanted to tell them everything he hated about Tadley. But he couldn't. Ewan was sitting there and it was Ewan's argument. He had to wait till he was old enough to live in one of Dave's cabins.

'Okay, let's try to compromise,' Jonathan started, feeling

totally insensitive and hoping to make amends. 'The lawn here, it looks nice, yes, but it doesn't get used much. The kids can't play on it because of the flower bed . . .'

Jonathan turned his back on Sarah as he gestured to the lawn in front of the steps, a flower bed in the middle. Ewan and Sarah looked over to the lawn and flower bed. Flowers now but empty once. Muddy once. Mud and manure and worms and rain and a dress and sex. Ewan half smiled at the memory and went back to his joint rolling. Chaos watched his mother's face tighten.

'And people sit here occasionally, but there are other places to sit . . .'

Chaos watched his mother's eyes widen, alarmed, shaking her head as Jonathan spoke.

'And we'd have to cut down the trees, but it would just be along that one side. So . . . what is wrong with a compromise solution and making this a car park?'

'Serendipity.' The word fell involuntarily out of Sarah's mouth.

Chaos frowned, Ewan's head jerked up and Jonathan turned. It was almost like the world had stopped. Chaos didn't understand. He didn't understand the way his mother looked at Ewan. Didn't understand the way Ewan blinked back, his face suddenly white. He didn't understand Jonathan's slow, dawning expression of comprehension as he looked between the two of them, then flickered a quick glance up to his bedroom window and back to the flower bed. Or Jonathan's arms reaching forward as though he wanted to touch Sarah and Ewan, but dithering and changing his mind, rubbing his mouth instead. Jonathan had said something wrong, he'd put his foot in it somehow, but Chaos didn't know how, couldn't see why, and what had Dipity to do with it?

Silence. A long, long silence before Ewan spoke.

'How old's Dipity, Chaos?' he asked, still white, still looking at Sarah.

Chaos was bewildered. Tears were rolling down Sarah's face. And Jonathan too; he looked desperately sad, desperately worried.

'Nine. Nine and a half,' Chaos replied.

'Nine and a half,' Ewan repeated, nodding with a strange expression. 'Nine and a half years.' He bent his head and slowly and carefully packed away his dope tin. He was breathing heavily and swallowing hard and he rubbed the lid of his dope tin obsessively, disturbingly.

'You've waited nine and a half years.'

When he looked up at Sarah again, he was almost grinning, trying to laugh, but tears were in his eyes. 'How about this for a compromise?' he said. 'Let's have a huge car park. One huge, gigantic car park, all over the first field and all over the lawn. We'll concrete over the flower bed and tell everybody our love's buried under it. Our love buried under concrete, eh, Sarah? That sounds poetic, doesn't it? Is that poetic enough for you? Is that romantic enough for you, or will it take something more?'

Sarah put her arms out to grab him but Ewan shrugged her off and walked away.

Sally sat silently on the roof with Sean and the farmers and overheard every word. It was over. She knew. Not just Sarah and Ewan's relationship, but the whole spirit of Tadley. She got up and peered over the parapet. Ewan was making his way round to the side of the house, to Tyler's 'off-licence'.

She followed Ewan round, keeping pace for pace with him up above, glancing over, looking down on him. She couldn't see his face; his head was down.

Dipity was dark. Curly hair and brown eyes. Like Ewan – or Sean, or Jim. Nobody questioned. Nobody looked too closely. The kids belonged to everybody. It was the only way it could work; the only way it could be equal. Chaos looked like his mum, a miniature male version of Sarah. Tranx too, blonde and beautiful. Dipity, though, was dark.

Ewan stopped outside Tyler's office and tapped on the window. 'Is Tyler there?'

Sally looked back at Sean. Sean was devastated.

Sarah sat huddled in her big office chair, her feet curled up under her, her eyes puffed up and piggy, her face haggard and her hands trembling. She stared around at the mess in the old drawing room, once a shared space, now her own office. A mixture of arty untidiness and business untidiness. She'd not really noticed it before. The phone was ringing. Sarah stared at it. And Miriam was standing there staring at her. Sarah stared back. Miriam silently put some papers in front of her. Contracts. Two. One for a record company takeover and one to put the Tadpole label on some cheap, shitty clothing that was made in Korea. Sarah stared at them. Who gave a fuck? She just wanted it to stop. She just wanted him to say, 'Stop all this and come and live in a shed with me.' Sarah was so jealous of Dave's sheds.

'He hates me now, Miriam.'

'No, he doesn't. He's never hated you.'

'He hates me now.'

'What? Over a car park? I don't think so, Sarah. I don't think he cares any more.'

Sarah looked up quizzically and found herself laughing. Desperately, hysterically – she'd forgotten about the car park. Miriam looked confused, concerned; that seemed even funnier.

Sarah's shoulders slumped, her stomach caved in and she started sobbing again.

'I've fucked it up. Fucked it all up. I wanted to tell him when I was pregnant but . . . I thought he'd laugh or sneer or say, 'How can you tell? Could be anybody's.' She wasn't anybody's. I knew, I definitely knew. Because he did that with Chaos. He wanted me to have an abortion, Miriam, I know he did. When I told him about Chaos. Okay, yeah, you know, things were . . . I was . . . a slag and everything but . . . But what if he stops loving Chaos and Tranquillity? What if he loves them less? How are they going to feel? How's Serendipity going to feel now, after all these years? How's he going to react to her?'

Miriam shook her head. She looked even more bewildered.

'What do I do, Miriam? How can I make him love me again? Should I build my own shed or give up the business and let Tyler take over completely? What do I do?'

Sarah dropped her head into her arms as her sobs overtook her.

Margaret sat close on the bed, held Ewan's hand and peered intently into his eyes. She'd sympathised, cajoled, badgered and shouted and wasn't sure if Ewan was even aware of her, let alone hearing what she was saying. Slumped on his bed in the corner, his head propped against the wall, staring at her. Could you get through to them when they were in this state? Margaret wasn't sure, but she had to do something.

She tried again. 'Ewan? Ewan, listen to me. Do this for me. I'm too old, I can't do it any longer. The garden, the cottage garden, my vegetable patch, remember? Belonged to Jack, my husband. It needs weeding, Ewan.'

Ewan stared vacantly.

Margaret wanted to grab hold of his head and bang it

repeatedly against the wall. Stoned and staring, stupidly staring. Why couldn't he have a good cry like normal people? Wreck the place like Jonathan? At least talk! This was so destructive. It had always been so destructive.

'I remember Jack,' he slurred.

Margaret sighed; it was impossible. 'You never met him, Ewan.'

'Horses . . . shoes . . .' Ewan mumbled.

'Not Jack the blacksmith. My husband, Jack. His vegetable patch. Remember? You offered to weed it.' Margaret despaired. She *was* getting too old. 'It's overgrown, Ewan. The vegetables have run to seed. It's all tangled and choking. I need you to weed it now. It's nothing to do with the house or the farm or anything. Nothing to do with them. Nothing to do with any of them. It's mine and it's dying. They'd be trespassing. Remember?'

Ewan stared thoughtfully at her, his face showing the slow, clunking chug of his brain. Finally. He was finally listening to her.

'You said "fuck you, Ewan Hughes", and that was the first time I liked you.'

Margaret smiled. Ewan returned the smile. It was a pathetic, crooked, druggy smile. But it was still a smile.

Chapter 12

September 1984 – two years later

Party time, traditionally. The late summer nights beginning to shorten. The days spent digging, picking, cutting, threshing and storing. The evenings spent hanging around the big table outside the cabins, partying. Home-made beer, wine, whisky, cider, home-grown dope. Music sometimes, laughter and banter usually, a sense of unity always. Harvest. But this year, these last six weeks? Muted, pensive. True, the farmers still gathered, still hung around the big table together, still drank, smoked, talked. But they'd avoided the main topic and kept their feelings to themselves.

For the last six weeks Sean had persevered with dope. He'd wanted something harder but the agreement had been 'no Tyler' and Sean stuck to agreements. But trying to mellow wasn't working. The anger and hurt still nagged. Sean was fed up with perseverance. He was drinking whisky. He wanted to get drunk and belligerent and morose. It was working. He started to drum slowly, rhythmically, on the table. One hand at first, flat, solid, like a clock ticking with thudding frustration, waiting to pump up the action.

It was the way Ewan had said 'going home' that had hurt.

The way he'd said 'back to my family, my community' that had cut like a knife. He had perhaps not meant it to. There had been no attack, no hint of contempt, just worry. And perhaps that was what made it worse. It sounded honest.

Six weeks ago Sean and Sally had hovered impatiently in the doorway of Ewan's cabin. Chaos was there, sitting quietly in the corner, hanging with Ewan like a faithful puppy. Sally and Sean were waiting to harvest the wheat fields, waiting for the word from Ewan, hoping for his participation. But he didn't seem to be moving, didn't seem willing. He was slouched at the table, head in hand, jigging his foot incessantly. Orgreave. Talking again about the pitched, bloody battle at Orgreave. Ewan was obsessing on it. He had been for weeks. All of it. The miners, the government, the pit closures, revenge for 1974, 'wanting to kill us, wanting to destroy us'. His dad on strike, his brothers, the whole of Maerdy. He listened continuously to Radio 4, waiting every hour for news bulletins, accosting employees for newspapers, demanding they describe the minutiae of television reports.

Sean and Sally remembered the miners' strike of '74 – and '72. Ewan had worried – fretted – then too. No different this time, they'd thought.

The wheat harvest was special. It was supposed to mean something to him, supposed to get him moving, take his mind off things. It had worked before. But Ewan said, 'I'm going home.' Sean didn't think much of it, didn't think 'now', didn't think 'today'. Sean thought Ewan meant a few days away to check on his family, for reassurance. Sean doubted Sally thought much of it either. She glowered impatiently, reminded Ewan that his dad was a bastard, his brothers were pricks, and the wheat fields were 'home'. Ewan shook his head and Sally stomped off in a fury. Ewan looked at him and said, 'I'm going

home, Sean. I'm going back to my family, my community.'
That was when it hurt. That was when Sean realised.

Sally felt the slow, steady beat of Sean's hand vibrating
through the table. Sean was sinking into the whisky and she
decided to do the same. Sally started to drum.

She'd loved Ewan as a brother, as the family she'd never had.
When he went down she'd looked after him. When he went
way down she'd fought to pull him back up. She'd sympathised
when he needed sympathy. Kicked him when he needed a
kick. And when he was better, he turned round and kicked her.
If he'd left for a reason. If he'd left because of Sarah or Tyler or
some other bastard, she could maybe have understood. But he'd
left because none of it and none of them meant anything. She'd
curled up in Miriam's arms and cried, and then wondered how
long it would be before Miriam left her.

Eric sat between Joe and Max wondering what to talk about.
He opened his mouth from time to time, but closed it again,
aware that everything had the word 'Ewan' in it. Eric wanted
to talk so badly. Nobody wanted him to; everybody walked
away. But if Eric couldn't talk it through, he was stuck with the
same thought: he was no longer in a band, no longer had a
huge, beautiful house to clean, no longer believed in the
Tadpole marriage and, like Ewan, no longer had a reason to be
there. Eric looked over at Sean and Sally and started drumming.

Margaret sat with Dave and Pattie and sipped half-heartedly
at her wine; she didn't really want it. She talked about the
imminent birth of Pattie and Dave's baby but her mind wasn't
on it. She didn't want to be with the group either but it was
better than being alone. Being alone was too upsetting – it gave
her the excuse to cry.

The cottage garden was empty. Healthy, special 'cabin crew'
vegetables ready to harvest, but empty. That must have been how

he felt. That must have been the reason. He wouldn't have left it otherwise. He seemed to love it, seemed to have bounced back. He kept saying 'cabin crew', kept insisting 'cabin crew vegetables'. Maybe he just *couldn't* harvest them. Or explain, to her, to them. She'd always seen the garden as a sanctuary, a little bit of freedom, but maybe he'd seen it as defeat, retreat. He'd needed it after the break-up, practically lived in it, hid in it, played with the kids and tried to get straight and keep straight, but . . . It was like losing a son. Margaret realised she was drumming.

The younger children ran around and played too close to the barbecue, eleven-year-old Dipity sat on Sean's roof, and, like typical thirteen-year-olds, Chaos and Zappa created a mild diversion while Dylan stole some Rizlas and a handful of cannabis. Miriam saw it all but didn't register. It was late too, way past the young ones' bedtime, but Miriam's mind wasn't on the kids – it was on her own burning sense of resentment.

To leave, so secretly, so furtively, without a word to anyone except Sean. To leave Sally and Chaos and, perhaps more importantly, Dipity. When everyone was trying to get along. When Sarah was actively trying to clean up the business and rekindle their relationship. When the consensus was to pull together and oust Tyler. To bring in the harvest without him, despite him – for him. A family member. A friend she didn't always like but had known since she was nineteen. To leave. It hurt. It felt like betrayal. Miriam started drumming.

Sarah stood under the porch, played nervously with the string bracelet around her wrist and looked over the fields towards the lights of the cabins. It was late and Miriam had promised to bring the kids back. Chaos and Serendipity she didn't mind about, and even though Tranquillity was only eight and *should* be in bed by now, Sarah had decided not to worry about it this time. But some of the house crew's kids were there and they *were* worried about it. They didn't want to go down to the cabins, didn't like mixing with 'that scruffy bunch of doped-up hippies', and Sarah was the boss so . . . But Sarah didn't want to go, not now, not yet. It was too soon, too upsetting. Too final. He wouldn't be there and her emotions were raw.

The younger children stopped playing and stood together silent and still, aware that something was wrong, something was strange. Dipity sat cross-legged on Sean's roof with her chin in her hands and watched them. Chaos, Zappa and Dylan appeared from behind the back of Eric's cabin to see what was going on.

Dave put a protective arm round Pattie and looked worriedly around the group of adults. Everybody was drumming. Hard, loud, rhythmic. And it was getting harder, louder, faster. Staring at each other, connecting with each other, threatening.

'He's coming back, you know,' Dave announced with conviction. 'He wouldn't choose Maerdy over Tadley. He hated it there, felt trapped. He told me. He felt trapped there.'

They didn't believe him, or, if they did, they didn't want to. The drumming increased to swamp Dave's voice. Dave looked at Pattie; she looked back with concern and jerked her head upward. Dave stood up.

'It's just the strike, the fight,' Dave tried again. 'Once it's over, what's Ewan going to do? Sit on a hillside and despair again? Sit on a hillside just desperate to get away?' Dave didn't know what to do. He didn't know what they were thinking of doing, but he was scared. This was ridiculous. Ewan was a mate.

Margaret's drumming stopped. Ewan on a hillside? He'd sat once, outside his cabin, sat and watched Dipity on Sean's roof. He'd just sat for ages, saying nothing, doing nothing but watching Dipity. Finally he'd said, 'It's still the same and it's still a hill and it's still sloping and it still looks like shit from on high.'

Margaret had dismissed it as druggy rambling. But he'd picked himself up after that. Got himself straight. She looked over at Dipity on Sean's roof. A sloping roof. Looking at Tadley from on high. Still a hillside, still sloping, still shit. Margaret's drumming continued harder and with more conviction.

Jonathan held Sarah's hand as they made their way across the fields to the cabins. He hadn't wanted to go, but when Sarah had gone halfway, heard drumming and come back for support, what could he do? Anyway, maybe it was time he confronted the others; maybe it was time they talked about it. The last six weeks had been strange. Everything, the house, cabins, land, all seemingly engulfed in an eerie silence. Noise, yes, but echoing, intrusive, unreal. Or maybe that had just been how Jonathan felt. Strange, Jonathan had hardly seen Ewan for years, rarely thought about him, didn't think he felt anything any more, but . . . the numbness since he'd left persisted. And the way in which he'd left – empty-handed and without warning – was a shock.

Sarah and Jonathan stopped a short distance from the cabins and watched.

Sean said it. 'Let's burn his cabin.'

The drumming increased and Dave was *really* scared; he couldn't understand it. Ewan had been on their side. He'd tried. He'd fought for them, lived with them. They liked him, trusted him. Yeah, he was a pillock at times, but . . . He was Dave's mate – he was Dave's best mate – and his family was in trouble. His family was on strike, his whole town; that was worrying, that was frightening. It was understandable.

He shouted it. 'He's coming back! He's got to!' Dave stood for a second, stared at the drummers and realised the harvest was over; Ewan had missed it. He wasn't coming back. Dave flopped down into his chair, mumbled, 'He belongs here' – and gave up. Pattie put an arm round him. Chaos joined Dave and Pattie at the table and all three cried.

Eric piled all Ewan's personal books, clothes, papers and paraphernalia in a heap in the centre of the cabin and Sean soaked them in whisky. Sally emptied another jug of whisky over the unmade bed in the corner. Margaret stood in the doorway of the cabin and fiddled with a box of matches.

The others stood around the outside of the cabin, clapped their hands rhythmically and chanted, 'Burn, burn, burn!' while the children stood apart and clapped and chanted with more fanaticism but no understanding.

Dipity remained cross-legged on Sean's roof, chin in hands, watching dispassionately.

Tranx saw Sarah pull away from Jonathan's hand and stumble towards the cabin. She went towards her mother, but Sarah didn't notice. Tranx went and held Jonathan's hand instead.

Sarah pushed Sean, Sally and Eric out of the cabin and took the matches from Margaret. She struck a match, then another, then another, then another. Margaret pulled her away. The clapping stopped.

The Tadpoles stood silently and watched the cabin burn. After six weeks of pain and bewilderment it was necessary. The funeral had begun.

Dave put an arm round Pattie and Chaos. Jonathan bent down and hugged Tranx, holding her tightly to him. Sarah and Sally grabbed each other, buried their faces in each other's necks and cried. Miriam put an arm round Margaret, Eric rubbed Sean's back, and Dipity watched from Sean's roof and muttered, 'Morons.'

Two days later six trucks arrived. The end of harvest had obviously been calculated. The drivers parked in a line by the steps to the main entrance, unconcerned that the employees had to squeeze past them. The miners didn't think they looked threatening, but maybe the attitude had become second nature. Blame the government, Thatcher, the times, the weather, the class system – whatever. Needless to say they'd been ferrying flying pickets, doing battle with police cordons and hurling abuse at scabs, and were in no mood to question what to them was politeness, and what to the employees clearly wasn't. The miners hung around the trucks, cadged cigarettes, begged cups of tea, rattled change buckets and generally made their presence uncomfortably felt. Basically, though, they just wanted the surplus. Ewan Hughes had said there would be one.

Jim, Nick, Tyler and the music crew begged to differ. Sarah, Jonathan and Miriam thought some sort of arrangement could be made. Sean, Sally and Margaret were hardly listening.

Sean, Sally and Margaret were dancing with battle-ready delight. Ewan hadn't deserted; he'd simply upped the ante with a whole new game. They started to believe that maybe Dave had been right – Ewan would come back. He was probably hiding down the drive, behind the old farm shop, smirking. Okay, so they burnt down his cabin – 'whoops, sorry, mate' – but he'd understand; he'd laugh probably, eventually.

Jim, Nick and Tyler were battle-ready but they weren't dancing. Neither were Sarah, Jonathan and Miriam. The interested parties with their differing agendas clogged up the steps at the entrance to the house.

'No. No way,' Tyler stated categorically. 'We're legally bound; we need it. It's ours.'

'But couldn't we somehow compromise?' Jonathan asked.

'How, Jonathan? The Harvest Festival starts in two weeks. Free food – it's traditional.' Tyler was adamant.

'Yes, but couldn't we share the surplus?' Sarah said. 'I

mean, they're miners; from what I've heard things are pretty desperate.'

'I don't care who they are.' Jim shrugged. 'Or how desperate.'

'There isn't a surplus,' Nick insisted. 'You keep saying "surplus"; stop thinking "surplus". Think *fifteen thousand people*. Fifteen thousand people have paid to eat free food.'

'Plus the bands, roadies, technicians – they all expect hospitality,' Jim added.

'But they're Tadpole bands,' Jonathan tried. 'They'd understand the concept of—'

'Oh, fuck the concept, Jonathan,' Tyler said. 'I've got a BBC film crew to think of. How's that going to look? Fifteen thousand fans dying of starvation on national television.'

'Okay then, okay,' Miriam said, 'what would be the financial implications of buying in the food?'

Tyler's impatience grew. 'The Harvest Festival starts in two weeks. How the hell can we arrange to feed fifteen thousand people in two weeks, Miriam?'

'You could cancel.'

'What?'

'Or postpone.'

'Over a few lazy, layabout miners? Are you mad?' Jim said, then glanced worriedly at the group of burly spectators by the trucks. 'No offence, lads, nothing personal.' He smiled.

'Sorry, did I not just say "film crew"? Did I not just say "BBC"? Are you perhaps going slightly deaf, Miriam?' Tyler sneered.

'Miners,' Sarah calmly said. 'Trendy, fashionable Thatcher bashers. How would refusing to support them affect our hot new caring, ethical image, do you think, Tyler? Particularly on TV?'

The argument continued between the music crew and the house crew. Margaret dispatched the miners to invade the house to cadge cigarettes, breakfast and donations while the matter was sorted. It might take a while; the cabin crew hadn't been called upon for their twopennyworth yet. But when they were, the argument was going to be very different – they grew the stuff; they had the power.

It wasn't Ewan, but it was Ewan's family, sort of, and that was good enough for Chaos. He had finally found something to do that felt good, felt *real*. He had been numb, bereft, and burning the cabin might have helped the others but, to Chaos, the large gaping hole that was left only emphasised the large gaping hole he'd felt for the past six weeks. Chaos had wanted to go with him. He'd begged. Ewan had refused. Chaos had worshipped him and Ewan had slapped him down, again. Or so Chaos had thought at the time. But maybe not, maybe this was the point. Maybe this was what Ewan meant. A big family out there somewhere, beyond the gates, all on the same side, all in agreement.

'And,' Ewan said, 'they have to win or there's nothing.'
Nothing.
'And I know, Chaos, because I lived there.'
Chaos and the kid crew again tried to budge one of the potato bins. It was hopeless. They couldn't even drag it as far as the storeroom door, let alone up the basement steps, all along the side of the house, around the front and to the trucks. Certainly not without somebody noticing; they were grunting too much already and they'd only managed a foot or so.
'We could take a few potatoes at a time,' Imogen suggested.
'That should give them one plate of chips before we get caught,' Dylan scoffed.

'We're going to get caught anyway,' Claudia said.

Claudia was right, of course, Chaos knew. Dylan was right too: a handful of potatoes wasn't enough. And they should have waited, maybe, till Sally sorted it out, but . . . Sally *was* going to sort it out, because this was right, this was how it should be, but . . .

'Why don't we ask the miners to help?' Dipity said.

Chaos stopped trying to budge the bin and looked at her. He hated his sister sometimes; she was far too clever.

'I don't like them; they're scary,' Tranx said.

Chaos looked indignantly at his other sister – *she* was far too weird.

Meanwhile, Dave was pacing around his cabin in a quandary. Nervous, excited and reluctant to argue. Eric was ready and willing, fully prepared to drive them if that was what they wanted. Or fully prepared to go and ask somebody who had driven a car sometime in the last five years if that was what they preferred. Either way, he was ready and willing to do *something*, Dave, but don't let her just sit there and say she's not moving!

Pattie's body hunched as another contraction swept through her. She then relaxed, sat back and smiled at Dave. She was determined: she wasn't moving.

Sally noticed that the kids were running behind the trucks bent over like squaddies in enemy territory. She saw a miner peer slyly round the side of the house, spot Sally watching and disappear again. She smirked.

'Have you any idea how many thousands we'll lose when the writs start flying?' Tyler was demanding of Jonathan.

'Why don't we discuss this inside?' Sally suggested, changing her expression to businesslike concern as she put a friendly arm round Sarah's waist and started to usher her up the steps. Sarah was immediately suspicious but moved anyway.

Sean was having none of it. 'I have not been in that house for three years, I have not wanted to be in that house for three years, and I have no intention of going in that house now.'

Sally almost kicked him. She smiled hard into his face instead. 'Okay, Sean, you guard the trucks.'

Sean could have protested. But Sally smiled even harder, raising her eyebrows in emphasis. And Sean agreed; maybe beating the shit out of Tyler *wasn't* the best form of negotiation. He stayed outside.

The kids and miners had made a couple of food runs to the trucks before Sean twigged. *The Great Escape* came to mind. He stood at the door to the house, kept one eye on the hall through the side window and one eye on the 'perimeter fence'. Any time he saw the 'enemy' approaching he whistled the theme from *The Great Escape*.

Eric had neither the time nor the inclination to wonder what six trucks were doing parked in front of the house; his mind was elsewhere. Was Dave's decision right? Was it too late? Should he tell Sarah, just in case? After all, even if a midwife *did* agree to come, she still had to come, and okay, so the hospital wasn't impossibly far, but how long did babies take? Chaos had taken for ever, but Dipity had been quicker and Tranx had slipped out like a pea through a hole in a pocket. So . . . Sarah knew about babies. Sarah knew more than Dave and Pattie anyway. And certainly more than Eric.

Eric ran up the steps to the house and was stopped by Sean.

'Miners.' Sean nodded at Eric, tapping the side of his nose conspiratorially. 'You know what to do.'

'Yeah, I've got to phone for a midwife,' Eric replied and disappeared into the house.

It was a toss-up as to whether Sean or Eric was the most confused.

Ten minutes later, however, Eric stood next to Sean with a clearer head. He attempted to fill Sean in on the events at Dave's cabin as he watched Dylan and Zappa struggle quickly along the path hefting a box of carrots, followed by Matilda picking up the many stray ones that fell.

'So a midwife's coming. Two, in fact. They didn't think giving birth in a shed was *ideal*, but . . . if it's good enough for Jesus . . .'

Between them, four miners lugged a potato bin along the path, managing to lift it and swing it into one of the trucks.

'And first babies generally take ages, no rush, no cause for alarm . . .'

Chaos and Dipity shuffled past with a big sack of onions.

'Which is good, because Sarah was busy sorting out the miners . . .' Eric stopped. 'Miners?'

'Ewan,' Sean said.

Eric opened his eyes wide as he realised what was going on. He knew all about the miners' plight. Anybody who'd been within a hundred yards of Ewan knew about the miners' plight.

'Bloody hell.' He grinned. 'Are we stealing this?'

'No, we're not stealing. It's ours,' Sean said.

'But isn't it the festival food?'

'Don't think, Eric, just fetch the farmers.'

Suspicious. Highly suspicious. Miriam stood frowning on the porch. Too many farmers and kids around, shuffling quietly in groups, trying to appear nonchalant. The miners walking quickly to their trucks – too quickly. Miriam looked quizzically at Sally. Sally looked despondent and avoided Miriam's gaze. And then the penny dropped. Sally and Margaret's filibustering, their endless talk, talk, talk and time-wasting in Sarah's office. Miriam couldn't believe their stupidity – couldn't believe Sally's. Why didn't she say? Five minutes more and . . . Miriam rubbed her head in horror. The massive financial mess simply didn't bear thinking about.

Jonathan didn't notice. He'd been elected spokesman and, although he preferred it to be him rather than Tyler, he certainly wasn't looking forward to it. He'd been reminded these last couple of days of a motto he used to have: *Change what you hate and don't feel guilty*. Oh, if only he could, he thought, if only he could.

Sarah, though, nothing got past Sarah. She came out of the house, took one look at the bodies milling around and immediately went over to the trucks to look in the back. They had loaded up a *ton* of stuff.

The farmers and kids looked at her innocently, unable to *imagine* how that food got there. Sarah knew she didn't need to lose her temper. She said it calmly. 'Take it out and take it back.'

Sally reluctantly nodded.

Chaos said, 'No.'

'Just do as you're told, Chaos, please,' Sarah said.

The farmers and miners looked to Sally for explanation. With the trucks already loaded people were reluctant to give in so easily. The kid crew were beginning to look *very* sulky and obstinate. Sally looked at her feet; she missed Ewan so keenly at that point, knew she could never take his place. Margaret rubbed her back in sympathy.

'No,' Chaos said again.

The kids bunched stubbornly around Chaos, adding their vote and hoping to make him look bigger than he was.

'You don't understand these things, Chaos,' Sarah explained, trying to soften her approach.

'What don't I understand exactly?' Chaos demanded. There was a feeling, growing from inside, coming up, Chaos could feel it coming up. From his feet? His stomach? He didn't know, but he could feel it, a conviction, *the* conviction: *Ewan's not here any more — nobody can stop me.*

'We can't spare any food; we don't *have* a surplus,' Sarah insisted, alternating her apologetic expression between the kids and the miners. 'We've got the Harvest Festival; we're contractually bound.'

'Sarah's right,' Sally added tiredly. 'I'm sorry, but there's nothing we can do. I thought we could, but we can't.'

Jonathan stepped forward. 'But obviously a financial contribution would be more than easy to —'

Chaos leapt in with an energy he wasn't prepared for. 'Fuck the financial contribution, Jonathan.'

The miners winced, er, hang on a minute.

'You don't get it, do you? You never got it.' Chaos's eyes darted with determination between Jonathan and Sarah. 'This food is Ewan's food. For his family. And his family is my family; his family is Sally's family — and Sean's and Margaret's and yours. It's your family. We're all in it together. And your "financial contribution" doesn't belong. Your money is not part of our family. We never grew it; we never loved it; we never wanted it. Ewan doesn't want what's yours; he wants what's ours. And the food belongs to everybody. So give your financial contribution to Tyler and give Ewan what belongs to us.'

'Chaos,' Sarah tried to reason, 'you don't understand the way the business operates —'

'But I do!' Chaos could feel the rage, the feeling about to explode, his stomach tightening, head swelling, blood pounding. It felt *good*. It felt *so good*. 'I understand the business better than you do. I understand what the business does. Business threw Sean and Eric out of music, it threw Margaret and Dave out of the kitchen, it stopped me playing piano. It had you, Jonathan, comparing the size of our brains with those of the outside world. It had you, Sarah, too busy to care about your own kids. When we wanted you we went to Miriam; when we wanted you we went to Ewan, or Sally, or Dave, or Eric. The business had us burning Ewan's cabin because we believed in him. We believed we couldn't do it without him. We should have burnt down the house. We should be running through there now, destroying it. Because it wants to destroy us. It wants us to be house crew and music crew and cabin crew. Oh, and kid crew, because we don't know which way we're going to run yet – shall we be rich or shall we be poor? And Ewan's told me about poverty. I've heard all about how your business creates it. It's creating it here. We're already poor; you've made us poor.'

The kids moved back a step but kept solid, giving Chaos room to expand, to grow, willing him to keep going.

'And business wants to destroy the bigger family, the family outside. These people, these guys . . .' Chaos gestured at the miners standing with bemused impatience, wondering how long before they could take off with their – preferably full – trucks.

'These guys have got to win or they've got nothing. Nothing! Can you imagine that? Can you live with that? All they've got is family, community. And business is destroying it, trying to prove its power over and over again. And you wonder why Ewan fought, and Sally fought, and the cabin crew. You pushed us out of the house and we still fought back. You pushed us into cabins and we still laugh more than you do. You tried to concrete our land and we crapped in your house. And Ewan's not even here and he's spitting in your eye. Because you are wrong. You are wrong, wrong, wrong. You want to be better? Better than family? Better than community? You can't be better. You could never be better than us. Because I know what I love, and Ewan knew what he loved, and Sally knows, and Dave, and we all know and you don't. So stuff your business and give them our food!'

Chaos glared at Jonathan and Sarah. The children glared along with him like a little pack of hungry and desperate hounds. The farmers resisted the temptation to applaud. Nobody moved. Nobody knew quite what to say. Even the miners seemed impressed. Chaos continued to glare, willing himself not to crumble, his legs beginning to wobble in the silence as he realised he'd finally said it, finally spoken. Sarah tried to out-glare him, but knew there was no way the farmers and kids were going to unload the trucks now. She wasn't even sure she wanted them to. She gave in, said nothing and turned hopefully to Jonathan and Miriam. Maybe they could find an escape route.

Jonathan tried a pathetic, 'Chaos, you're only thirteen.'

But Eric dismissed it, 'Doesn't make him wrong.'

Miriam saw it in the kids' faces, the farmers', even the miners' faces. Remove one apple from those trucks and there's going to be a riot. Bloody Ewan. No, no, not Ewan, Chaos. Bloody Chaos. A massive financial mess when they take the trucks or a massive financial mess when they destroy the house? Miriam said nothing.

Silence, impasse. Everybody looked around expectantly, nervously waiting to see how to move.

Sarah swallowed her pride and thought practically. 'We're going to have to renegotiate with Tyler, see if we can't reach a compromise.'

'We don't have to compromise,' Dipity piped up. 'Just give Tyler the business and tell him to piss off.'

Sarah looked at her in alarm. She could have sworn Dipity had spoken with a Welsh accent. She overheard Jonathan mutter, 'Double-headed hydra.' He looked at her and smiled with happy resignation.

Sally sidled over and put an arm round her waist. 'All the kids are Ewan's,' she whispered in Sarah's ear, 'every single one of them.' It was said with love, not spite. And Sean started whistling the theme from *The Great Escape*.

Chaos and Dipity exchanged looks and smiled with certainty. It seemed obviously simple to them. They looked around at the adults. It wasn't obviously simple to them but . . .

The miners looked at the group, shrugged at one another, and headed for the trucks. Nobody tried to stop them.

Meanwhile, Dave beamed with pride as he looked down at his son cradled gently in his arms.

'Can we call him Robert?'

'Why Robert?' Pattie asked.

'Because it's a normal name, a proper name, a real one,' Dave said. 'And if necessary, we can call him Birmingham Bob.'

Chapter 13

May 1986 – two years later

Chaos sat on the wall. Ludlow! It was so exciting, so strange and exotic and foreign. Shops. People going in and out of shops, big shops, small shops, looking in windows, people walking quick, some slow, pushchairs, snatches of conversation, people arguing, people dragging toddlers and shopping. People everywhere. And cars. All colours, every colour, streaming past. They smelt revolting but they were loud and fast and going places. Everybody busy, everybody moving, everybody going places. Chaos felt flushed with anticipation, high with excitement. This was something else – this was the world! This was Ludlow!

He turned to Dipity. 'How often do you come here?'

Dipity shrugged. 'Whenever I feel like it.'

Chaos was awestruck. Dipity knew it.

'Chaos, how are you ever going to leave if you don't practise?'

Chaos was caught on the hop. He opened his mouth to excuse his stupidity but closed it when Dipity jumped off the wall. 'What do you want to do now?' she asked.

Everything, Chaos wanted to say, everything that you do. He slid off the wall, half proud, half infuriated that his thirteen-year-old sister was so cool. Rambling down to town. 'Let's ramble down to town,' she'd suggested. It had never occurred to him.

'Do you want to try crossing the road?' Dipity asked.

'What?'

Dipity smiled slyly. She jumped out into the road, dodged and weaved and ran through the traffic, managing to end up safely, hands on hips and laughing, on the other side of the road. Now she was just showing off!

Chaos stepped off the kerb, stopped dead in the road, panic-stricken, fear-frozen. A car was coming at him, a big red one, coming *fast* towards him, horn blaring, brakes screeching – a terrible noise. Chaos jumped back onto the kerb, sweating. Dipity was leaning, pointedly able and smugly smirking, against a big window of some huge shop. I hate you, Dipity, you're a bitch!

'You all right, son?'

Chaos swung round to see a strange bloke in a funny hat and black clothes with shiny buttons and numbers.

'I'm just crossing the road,' Chaos blurted, aware that his voice had risen an octave and he felt like a two-year-old. He glanced over at Dipity; she'd collapsed on the pavement laughing hysterically. Chaos hoped she'd wet herself.

The man in the funny hat eyed Chaos with a mixture of suspicion and disdain, took him by the elbow and pointed him down the road a little. 'See that zebra crossing?' the man said in a mocking tone. 'Use it.'

Chaos looked. He was obviously not going to see a zebra, but he was so used to people's druggy hallucinations that he automatically nodded and shuffled the way Mad Hat pointed. Dipity was bored with her shenanigans and matched him stride for stride on the other side, pointing to a black and white strip in the road. Chaos stepped up to the kerb and dithered. The cars stopped. He grinned, raised his arms and strutted across the road like Moses parting the Red Sea.

Dipity rolled her eyes. 'You are such a moron, Chaos,' she sneered.

Chaos shrugged with the haughtiness of achievement. 'I just crossed the road, Dips. They stopped for me!'

'Yeah, aren't you annoyed?'

Chaos frowned. Annoyed? He was jumping in triumph.

'You're fifteen and you don't know how to cross a road. We know nothing. They've taught us nothing, except how to rot at Tadley. Did they ever wonder how we'd cope when we left?'

Chaos's frown increased with sudden awareness. Dipity was quietly desperate and totally right. Ludlow was the real world and Chaos knew nothing. He looked back at the traffic and the crossing. The triumph died.

'Do you know who you were talking to?' Dipity asked.

'Some guy on acid.' Chaos shrugged, knowing full well it wasn't, but he'd assumed . . . He'd assumed.

'A policeman.'

Chaos stared up the street in the direction the policeman had gone. 'The guys Ewan was fighting with the miners?'

Dipity nodded. Chaos was appalled and mechanically rubbed the invisible dirt from the elbow that the enemy had touched.

'So why are policemen here?' he asked.

'The police are everywhere.'

'Are there miners here?'

'Oh, Chaos, you know nothing,' Dipity mocked. She folded her arms and looked seriously into his face. 'Do you know how far Maerdy is? Do you know how far Wales is?'

Chaos turned away impatiently. 'I never mentioned Maerdy,' he protested.

216

'You didn't have to.'

Chaos looked back at Dipity with irritation. He hated his own transparency, hated the way everybody could read him like a book. But he couldn't stop himself.

'*Is* it far?' he found himself asking. Ewan-obsessed. Everybody knew he was Ewan-obsessed, and everybody thought he was a fool.

Dipity seemed to be galvanised into action. Her pace quickened as she marched down the road, speaking in a gabble. 'Well, I know you have to get a train . . .'

'A train?'

'And you're going to need money. You've got to learn about money, Chaos. Everything out here is money, money, money. It's all Sarah territory. Then you've got to work out how you're going to tell them, *if* you're going to tell them, *what* you're going to tell them —'

'Hang on, hang on,' Chaos interrupted, grabbing his sister's arm to stop her. 'What are you talking about, Dipity?'

'You do want to go, don't you?'

'To Maerdy?' Chaos spluttered in bewilderment. 'Yes, but —'

'So you've got to practise.' Dipity put a hand on Chaos's back and ushered him down the street. 'Now, let's go and have a look at the train station.'

Chaos blinked in confusion. This whole trip out had been a con. It wasn't a five-mile 'ramble down to town' at all. He was being bulldozed, used and manipulated. But helped. Dipity would help. Help find Ewan. Thank God. She'd have to; he knew nothing.

Chaos and Dipity turned a corner and stopped dead as a familiar face looked down at them.

Eric 'Keyboards' Morell
(Lone Horseman of the Apocalypse)
Plus Guests. Every Tuesday, 8 p.m.

'Did you know he was doing that?' Chaos asked, indignation replacing the first jab of excited surprise.

Of course Dipity didn't know. If anybody knew it would be Chaos, the amount of time he spent with Eric in the music room.

Every Tuesday, 8 p.m. Chaos wasn't sure whether he was incensed, hurt or jealous. He stepped back from the window where the poster was displayed and looked at the building. The Railway Inn. This would be a pub then. One of those places Miriam said Ewan had lived in during university. Dipity had already gone over to the doors but they were locked; no way of knowing what it was like inside. They both went back to the poster. *Eric Morell. Plus Guests. Every Tuesday, 8 p.m.*

'We'll see what it's like on Tuesday then,' Dipity said.

Chaos nodded. We certainly will, he thought. We certainly bloody will.

'Eric "Keyboards" Morell,' Dipity jeered. 'The *Lone* Horseman.' She let out a snort of derision.

Chaos smiled but he didn't find it in the least bit amusing.

Dipity didn't find the railway station in the least bit amusing. Dipity was in a fury.

'We don't want to get on a train; we just want to look at them!' she screeched. 'We won't touch them; we won't even spit at them. All we'll be doing is looking. You're charging us for the use of our eyes. It's ridiculous. It's capitalistic, bureaucratic crap!'

'Yes, but you've still got to buy a platform ticket,' the man hiding behind the window of the funny little room said with an evenness that Chaos thought bordered on sainthood.

'What about if we stand at that barrier thing and listen?' Dipity sneered. 'Will you charge us for the use of our ears as well?'

Chaos laughed. Dipity was *so cool*.

'Oh, for heaven's sake.' The guy behind them barged forward, shoving Dipity to one side. 'Give me a return to Cardiff and two platform tickets for these kids! Some of us have got trains to catch!'

'I don't want charity; charity is a means of control,' Dipity seethed. 'It's a matter of principle. I don't want someone buying them for us!'

'Cardiff,' Chaos repeated, staring at Dipity with excitement. 'The guy's going to Cardiff, Dips – he's catching a train to *Wales*!'

Jonathan sat in the study scrutinising the half-dozen or so envelopes in front of him. He knew it was pathetic; Sarah had already done it. But it had become something of a ritual, looking at the envelopes, the handwriting – pointless after two years – for both of them. But that was the trouble with rituals; they were easy to do but difficult to break. He listened to Miriam on the phone in the background. She was talking to the vet. That was worrying.

Jonathan handed Miriam the post, quickly jumped from his chair and followed her into the hall. 'Are the pigs sick again?' he asked, trying to engage her in friendly conversation.

'Yes.' Miriam rolled her eyes.

Jonathan saw her do it. He was dogging people again. Another stupid habit he couldn't seem to break.

'Romantic, isn't it?' Miriam said. 'Well, it would be if Sean actually worked up the courage to phone her himself.'

Jonathan was nonplussed. Miriam looked surprised. 'Haven't

you seen the new vet, Jonathan? She's gorgeous. It's Sean that's sick – lovesick.' Miriam laughed.

Jonathan was stunned. 'You mean the pigs aren't really sick?'

'Nothing a roll in the hay wouldn't cure.'

Jonathan's cheekbones twitched, the teeth–grinding habit.

'Is there some problem, Jonathan?'

'I thought the pigs were sick.'

'No, the pigs are fine.'

'It's been going on for weeks.'

'Yes, I know.'

'I didn't.' Jonathan looked away, avoiding Miriam's eyes. 'I am so sick of this, Miriam. So sick of this . . . place, house. I really thought when Tyler left . . . Jim and Nick, when everything went, the offices, business, school, everything . . . When we celebrated. We all celebrated, Miriam, together.'

'Well, why don't you try joining in, Jonathan? Come and milk a cow occasionally, do a spot of weeding. You must be bored stupid doing nothing.'

Jonathan sighed peevishly.

'You could help me find Chaos; I can't find him anywhere,' Eric said as he rounded the corner and came into view.

Nobody had seen Chaos all morning. Or Dipity for that matter. Simple, then. Chaos was with Dipity. And Dipity was an expert at disappearing, so no point in looking. Jonathan carried on, though, not because he was worried but because he was actually rather enjoying it. If 'enjoy' was the right word.

Everywhere was dreadfully run-down. Well, not exactly run-down, but . . . meadows. Overgrown meadows full of wild flowers, that were once productive fields. Two cows looking small and incongruous in a field that once held sixty. Three pigs snuffling amongst twenty pigpens. The actual farm was now so small, the people so few, it seemed to echo the atmosphere of the house – empty, dying. Sad, obviously, but Jonathan couldn't help feeling relieved, couldn't help feeling there was now hope.

The cabins too looked lived in, tatty. Some of them were empty but the atmosphere wasn't quite as desolate as elsewhere; there was still life, albeit quiet. Ewan's burnt-out cabin was still there, like an ugly reminder. Tranx and Matilda using the remains of the floor for a stage, putting on a 'concert'. Jonathan chatted with Dave and Margaret for a while; he hadn't done that for ages. He'd meant to, wanted to, but since they never came up to the house it had been difficult. Difficult to go down, difficult to find a reason to go. But they welcomed him, or seemed to. Margaret was getting old now, Jonathan realised, muddled sometimes, confused. Dave was the same, more or less; he talked about Robert, walking, talking, practically toilet-trained, then laughed as Robert stood and blithely wet himself. Sally said 'Hi, Jonathan' as she walked past, as though it were the most natural thing in the world for him to be there.

'Milk a cow occasionally,' Miriam had said. 'Do a spot of weeding.' Yes, but how? Jonathan had thought. Blunder in? Barge into a close-knit, tight little group, fully aware of being the outsider, the dream-wrecker? Fully aware of the silence and awkwardness that would greet him? If Jonathan had known, if somebody had told him it was just as desperate out here . . .

About two hours or so, hardly any time at all. Chaos could have done it years ago. He could have followed Ewan straight out of the gate had he known it was so simple. Thirteen. He had been thirteen, the same age as Dipity was now. Dipity's done it; he could have done it. A walk into town, a train, a bus.

'Don't be so hard on yourself,' Dipity said dismissively. 'We're here now; that's what counts.'

Chaos swallowed his self-criticism. I'm here now.

But where to begin? Maerdy was nothing like Tadley. It was an alien place, drab, dirty, dead. No big house, no farm and fields, no cabins, no music, no colour. There were houses. Lots of little terraced houses. The only big things were the mines, and the hills, green and black, looming over the town like shadows. There weren't even big shops like in Ludlow, only a few little ones. One or two pub-looking places, which weren't so small, but they looked hard and forbidding, not bright and intriguing and covered in hanging baskets like the pubs in Ludlow. Strange town, different atmosphere. Chaos and Dipity felt despondent, instinctively hating the place but refusing to acknowledge it. Where to begin?

After an age of dithering Dipity asked a passing woman where Ewan Hughes lived. The woman didn't know a Ewan Hughes, but her two friends across the road might. Chaos, Dipity and the woman crossed the road – easily, there was hardly any traffic.

'Ewan Hughes? There are two or three Hughes families, but there isn't a Ewan.'

'There *was* a Hughes family in Ferndale. But they left a few weeks ago.'

Chaos closed his eyes and prayed.

'Lucky devils! How did they afford it?'

The women launched into a lengthy discussion of empty houses, pit closures and redundancies.

'But was there a Ewan?' Dipity finally – rudely – interrupted.

'No, I don't think there was a Ewan. I can't think of a Ewan.'

The three women were stumped. Undeterred, they all crowded into a bread shop, where an assistant and two customers 'helped'.

'Well now, Nesta Hughes, she had a Ewan.'

'Yes, that's right, but he left years ago.'

'No, no, he came back.'

Chaos's and Dipity's hearts leapt.

'For about half an hour . . .'

Chaos's and Dipity's hearts sank.

'*He* was the one that was loaded.'

'Oh, *him*.'

A disapproving silence descended. Everybody knew who 'him' was. Chaos and Dipity exchanged worried looks as the six women shuffled slightly, thinking their own private thoughts.

'From what I heard he wasn't loaded at all.'

'How could he not be?'

'Well, a lot of it's on paper, isn't it? And, apparently, they sold the business soon after, so they were obviously in trouble.'

'Their "trouble" would be luxury around here.'

'Down to his last Porsche, I suppose.'

'I wouldn't buy another Tadpole product if it were free.'

'Disgusting.'

And then Chaos and Dipity found six pairs of eyes staring at them, daring them to admit that the Ewan Hughes they hated was the Ewan Hughes Dipity and Chaos were looking for.

Nesta Hughes was pleased to see them, though.

'Well, look at you,' she said on the doorstep, staring mainly at Dipity. 'I know who *you* are.' Nesta was fighting back tears, so Dipity didn't question the stare.

There was no Ewan, no sign of Ewan, no news of Ewan.

Nesta Hughes explained why when they were in the kitchen of the tiny house and out of earshot of Ewan's dad, Gareth.

'Ewan tried to strangle him.'

Dipity giggled nervously. She couldn't imagine Ewan being violent.

'Ewan did what?' Chaos asked in amazement.

'I had to pull them apart,' Nesta explained.

Desperate times. The strike in full swing, money practically non-existent. Ewan's brothers, Bryn, married with four kids, and Tom, divorced with three, both debt-ridden. The Tadpole empire huge, famously everywhere and fabulously wealthy. Gareth had often mentioned it, thought of phoning, begging. Gareth's pride wanting Ewan to make the move, spare them a thought. And Ewan did, seemingly. He turned up on the doorstep. Gareth asked how much money he'd brought and found out it was nothing. Ewan was penniless. His dad went mad and Ewan went for his throat.

Chaos nearly cried.

Dipity wanted to run. She wanted to get far away till the feeling of rage passed, till she could swallow it all down and forget about it.

But Nesta said, 'It surprised Gareth. Ewan was never like that, not like his brothers. He would just disappear and stew when he was younger. He was always odd; hide for hours he would. Bury his feelings.'

Dipity jumped. She felt a sudden lurch in her stomach as her leg kicked out in an involuntary twitch. Nesta smiled oddly, stared at her like she did on the doorstep – *I know who you are*. Dipity looked quickly to Chaos, a safe face, a familiar face, someone she knew about, some*thing* she knew about. He didn't look like Ewan at all.

Jonathan put down the receiver in his study and immediately thought, How's Sarah going to take it? He sat for a few minutes, staring at the now silent telephone. If Sarah's going to be cross, have answers ready for why she shouldn't be. The kids have to spread their wings sooner or later. This is their first flying lesson – a bad choice of flight maybe, but their choice.

As he made his way up the stairs he thought she might be intrigued and interested after the initial surprise. As he made his way along the corridor to Sarah's workroom he hoped that she would be proud. Proud that Chaos and Dipity were so independent and their hearts were in the right place.

At the back of his mind, though, Jonathan thought it was sad. Sad that they'd gone, sad that they'd felt the need to go, and sad that Ewan wasn't there. It had been the first question he'd asked. 'Is Ewan there? Can I speak to him?' And as he knocked on Sarah's door he realised that would probably be her first question too.

Jonathan stood nervously in the doorway of Sarah's workroom, a slight, crooked smile of apology on his face – don't shoot me, I'm only the messenger. Sarah looked up from her sewing machine, stopped working and smiled at him.

'I've just had a phone call from Ewan's mother —' Jonathan tentatively started.

'No!' Sarah screamed. She flew out of her seat and punched him in the face.

Jonathan was caught completely off guard. He might have been unsure how Sarah would react, but he *had* expected to tell her first.

'Don't tell me – I don't want to know!' Sarah shouted as her knees buckled and she sank to the floor. 'No, no, no,' she repeated, desperately shaking her head and refusing to listen to anything he might try to say.

Jonathan bent down and tried to pick her up. This was not what he had been expecting at all.

Chaos and Dipity were quiet on the train home. They looked out of the window for most of the journey, lost in thought.

They felt like seasoned travellers now. Acted like it too. The thrill of the outward journey had gone. The panic and the hand-holding when the train pulled out. The open-mouthed awe and excitement as the world sped by. The terrified scream and grab for safety when another train suddenly whooshed past. The fearful moan in the sudden darkness of the tunnel. The adventure replaced by confusion and despondency.

Chaos was glad of the quiet; he didn't feel like talking: too much to think about.

'So the idiot's not at Tadley Hall, then?'

That was what Gareth had said. That was *all* Gareth had said, about Ewan. Pit closures, redundancy, poverty, dole. Gareth talked a lot about that. Debt, despair, decay, depression. People stuck in houses they couldn't sell, in an area that had no work and no hope. All of them too old to change, too beaten to try and too young to die with dignity.

And it was all Ewan's fault.

Gareth hadn't said that, but Chaos thought it was somehow linked in Gareth's mind that way. Chaos wanted to hate him for it, but couldn't. He saw Ewan in him, heard Ewan in him, could see the similarities in thought, in politics. But where Gareth talked about fighting the government, Ewan had talked about ignoring the government. Gareth said what *they* should do; Ewan had said what *we* should do. Gareth wanting money. Ewan not wanting money. And both of them had lost. 'And they have to win or there's nothing.' Chaos hadn't fully understood it at the time. He understood it now. Maerdy with nothing and Tadley with everything and both exactly the same. And it *was*, somehow, all Ewan's fault.

'Why didn't you tell Gareth about the food trucks, Dips?' Chaos asked.

Dipity stirred from her reverie and shrugged. 'Didn't want to.'

226

Chaos nodded.

'Why didn't you?' she asked.

'I was going to – I wanted to – but Ewan's voice came into my head and said, "Shut up, Chaos," so I didn't.'

She grinned. 'Yeah, right, don't tell the bastard anything.'

Dipity returned to gazing out of the window, suddenly aware of her automatic Ewan-speak: 'keep it buttoned and lie if necessary'. She held on to the grin but she was confused. She'd thought Sean was her dad. Her urge to blow everything up, to bang everyone's heads together, to be so exasperated that she had to get away and hide, that had come from Sean, surely? Ewan liked people. He was sociable, always in the midst of things, belonging. He wasn't an outsider. He was a piss-taker and a druggy but not an outsider. Dipity felt the lurch in her stomach again. A piss-taker and a druggy. Her own defensive disregard for Tadley and everyone and everything in it frightened her now. She recognised it, or thought she did. So where was he? Why hadn't he come home? Dipity wanted to cry. She turned and beamed broadly at Chaos.

'I loved Gareth's telly, though, didn't you?'

'Oh yeah, his telly was so cool!' Chaos enthused, matching Dipity's grin.

'Sorry we're late.' Sally grinned. 'We had to have a meeting about the meeting.'

Jonathan assumed he must look how he felt – a complete prat sitting alone at a big table in a big room, slowly concluding that nobody gave a toss. Twenty minutes late. Twenty minutes of discussion down at the cabins. Jonathan scrutinised the cabin crew's faces as they came into the dining room, trying to work out who was for and who was against. For or against what? Just entering the house presumably; everybody cared about Chaos and Dipity, Jonathan was at least certain of that.

They sat around the dining-room table, just like old times, before the Tadpole empire took off. Well, no, some were missing: Jim, Nick, Tyler – Ewan, obviously. Some had been added: the kids, Pattie, Sam, Jean, Jack, Hilary, Ray. But at least the original Tadpoles had come home – if only temporarily. Miriam and Margaret automatically sat in their traditional positions; Jonathan couldn't help but smile at that. And Sarah would come, eventually. Although Jonathan wasn't sure if that was a good thing, not in the state he'd left her, white-faced and brittle. But she'd refused to explain, refused to discuss it, preferring to go back to her sewing machine as if nothing had happened.

'We weren't sure whether it was right to discuss Chaos and Dipity before they got back,' Sally explained. 'Some of us were against it.'

Jonathan nodded. Not against him, then, nor against entering the house. He scanned the silent faces, wondering what conclusion was reached at the meeting about the meeting. Nobody started so Jonathan didn't. Robert did instead; he sat on Dave's knee and started singing what Pattie finally deciphered as 'I'm a little teapot, short and stout . . .' Jonathan listened and hoped it wouldn't be too long before Eric got back with the wayward travellers.

Chaos and Dipity's apprehension dissipated as soon as they came within earshot of the dining room. Nobody could be angry, not while they were all laughing and singing 'Incy Wincy Spider'. No major argument then. But when Eric opened the door the last thing Chaos and Dipity expected was a round of applause.

Jonathan too was surprised. It seemed spontaneous, started by

Margaret, or maybe Dave. Jonathan joined in, applauded along with everybody else, cheered along with everybody else. Robert pulling him back into the group and Chaos and Dipity completing it. I love you and miss you, Ewan Hughes. We all do.

And they all did. Everybody wanted to know everything. Chaos and Dipity were unable to answer all the questions as they came flying from every direction. Questions asked with affection. Answers demanded with love and concern. A painful pause as Gareth's 'welcome' to Ewan was recounted. No hint of resentment as they wondered where he was now, what he was doing, how he was doing. A shared groan of familial doubt when Dave suggested Ewan might finally be completing his degree. An enthusiastic nod and agreement when Sally reckoned he was happily working on a farm somewhere. Laughter when Sean admitted he was waiting for news of Thatcher's assassination by organic carrot. And silence as one by one they noticed Sarah standing in the doorway – not everyone had been singing nursery rhymes.

'Ewan said we should turn our backs. Do it all here, be it all here. That does not involve leaving Tadley and ending up in some godforsaken hole in Wales. For whatever reason.'

Jonathan could see that Sarah was still rigid, her mood instantly infecting everyone as her long-repressed fears hovered just below the surface.

'I could've told you he wouldn't be there; you only had to ask,' Sarah said. 'You didn't have to leave.'

'We didn't leave; we were just visiting,' Dipity explained. 'We hadn't even meant to go – we just . . . got on the train.'

'By accident really,' Chaos added.

'Well, you don't just get on a train. You stay here; you live here,' Sarah insisted with a strange flatness to her voice. She moved fully into the room and sat at the table. But it was at the

229

corner of the table, her seat pulled back and apart from the group.

'Sarah —' Jonathan started.

'No.' She cut him off. 'We can't do it if we water it down.'

Jonathan gently persisted. 'Sarah, we've been sitting here for the last two years like the lord and lady of the manor. I don't think that's what Ewan had in mind.'

'Then we'll change it. We'll go and live down in the cabins.'

'That's not what I meant.' Jonathan glanced awkwardly around the table; everyone was staring at Sarah, aware that something was *very* wrong. Jonathan couldn't explain, not with kids in the room, not when everybody's mood had been so buoyant and there was a chance to heal wounds.

'Chaos and Dipity wanted to go,' he continued in as calm a voice as he could manage. 'And we have to respect that. We should even have helped them with that. I don't think anybody's really thought it through, not properly. They've never been out of Tadley, Sarah, and that's appalling, a horrific mistake.'

'Not a mistake. Not a mistake at all,' Sarah went on with the same flat intransigence. 'We don't know what's happening out there; we wouldn't know what they were getting into. At least at Tadley they're safe. We all are.'

'But, Sarah, you've got to agree that they should go out and learn about the world,' Miriam protested. 'It's only natural.'

'And they should be allowed the freedom to choose,' Dave added.

Sarah rounded on him. 'To choose what, Dave? Ways of killing themselves?'

'Don't say it, Sarah, don't even think it,' Jonathan quickly hissed as Dave blinked in bewilderment.

'Don't say what? Don't think what?' Chaos asked.

But Sarah did think it, couldn't help thinking it. A vague worry that had started two years ago. Nagging persistently when her letters were returned to Tadley. Becoming a desperate concern when the miners' strike ended and she'd got in touch with Jim to find out, put out feelers, make enquiries. Sarah closed her eyes as she heard Jim's voice sharper in her mind now than the day he'd sneeringly agreed with her. 'Wouldn't surprise me at all if Ewan had overdosed in some gutter somewhere.'

Sarah wiped the thought, opened her eyes and stared around the table. But her face said it all. The adults stared back, formulating their own fears.

'Don't say what? Don't think what?' Chaos asked again. 'Don't say "Ewan was wrong"? Is that what it's about?' He felt the atmosphere tense. Feelings being covered up and thoughts being buried. He'd had enough of it. 'Because I don't understand what you're saying. One minute you say we've got to do what Ewan said, and then you say forget about him.'

Chaos looked at them. Nobody wanted to say anything; nobody wanted to answer, just Sarah shaking her head and Jonathan grinding his teeth and all the others as confused and bewildered as he was but thinking something else.

'Okay then, I'll say it. Ewan was wrong. Ewan could have helped Gareth and Nesta. He could have helped his brothers. He could have helped the whole town. And he didn't. He talked about family, but he didn't care about family. He didn't give a toss.'

Dipity looked at Chaos with surprise, shock even, but at least it was something concrete to argue with. 'What are you saying, Chaos?'

'He could have helped them.'

'He did help them.'

231

Chaos shook his head.

Dipity notched up her anger. 'He sent them food.'

'That wasn't good enough. He knows it.'

'That's all he had.'

'No, it wasn't, Dipity,' Chaos sneered. 'He was rich – we were all rich. He was just too stupid to know what to do with it.'

Dipity was outraged. 'Are you blaming him because of what Sarah and Tyler and Jim and Nick did? Are you blaming him like those idiot women in Maerdy, Chaos?'

Chaos nodded.

'He gave them food,' she insisted, unable to believe her brother's stupidity, her brother's treachery. 'He gave them what he had, what he loved. We agreed, Chaos. *You* agreed. Everything else was hers and he didn't want what was hers; he hated what was hers.'

'But they didn't and he knew that; he knew that because he'd lived there!'

Chaos felt everyone's eyes boring into him as he paraphrased Ewan's own words to denounce him. He hadn't wanted to, hadn't meant to, he loved Ewan, but he felt tired, depressed. And Maerdy – Maerdy had nothing; he'd never seen 'nothing' before.

'Ewan can't change the world, Chaos,' Eric gently chided.

'He didn't even try.'

'He changed my world,' Margaret said with a look of disapproval that Chaos had never seen before.

'And mine,' Sally added with equal coldness.

'I was a servant, housekeeper, nothing,' Margaret went on, glancing slightly at Jonathan.

The others nodded, staring at Chaos, all against him. The whole room was against him.

'Oh, that's all right then, is it?' Chaos spat. 'So long as *we're* all right, the rest of the world can just go fuck itself. That is exactly how Ewan thought, and that is exactly how wrong he was. His own family. He didn't care about his own family.'

'You know nothing about his family,' Sally said.

'I went there; I saw them.'

'Well then, you know nothing about Ewan,' Dave said with an aggression that was very rarely seen. 'And you know nothing about life, or being working class, or being poor, or being desperate. All you know about is the respect that's being afforded to you right now. All you know about is equality and freedom and the right to your opinion. The right to sit at a nice table in a nice house with nice people and have your voice heard. And you've got Ewan to thank for that, so shut up, Chaos, because you're well out of order!'

'Okay, so what do we do then? Stay here and don't go out? Don't find out how other people are living?' Chaos protested.

'Yes, Chaos.' Sarah stared strangely at him. 'Because as soon as you go out there, you start to live like them and that helps nobody.'

'Oh yeah, right, we should live here, shouldn't we, as Jonathan said, like lords and ladies of the fucking manor,' Chaos sneered.

'I meant we should all live together,' Jonathan attempted to explain, trying to ease the tension. 'Not harbour ridiculous grudges about "house crew" or "cabin crew". We should live like family again, like we used to. Like Ewan wanted, all in it together. *We* should be family.'

'So what did Ewan think about this family? The same as he thought about his real family – nothing. Don't give me this shit, Jonathan. Don't make out everything's going to be cosy and rosy if we all just pluck chickens together. Miriam said we should learn about the world. And I'm learning. I'm learning that Ewan did nothing!'

'Don't you say that!' Sarah exploded, rising from her chair and lunging towards him. 'Don't you ever say that!'

Chaos was shocked as Sarah started hitting him about the head and face. He'd never been hit before.

'He might be dead, Chaos – he probably *is* dead – and you're saying he did nothing? You loved him. You bloody loved him. You believed in him and understood him and worshipped him.'

Sarah continued thumping as Chaos raised his arms to protect himself and pressed his head against the table.

'Don't say he did nothing. Don't sit there now and say it was all a waste. He was your hero. You've got to remember him like that and honour his memory. Don't sit there and blame him and say he did nothing because I ruined it. Don't ever say that!'

Sarah stopped then, calmed down and went back to her seat as if nothing had happened. She ignored the fact that the room was silent and still and staring at her. Ignored the fact that Dipity was in tears. Ignored the fact that Chaos was peering out from under his arms with the thought burning in his head, as it burned in everybody's head, He's probably dead.

'He didn't do nothing, Chaos,' Dave said quietly. 'He did what he could and he did what he believed in.'

'And he stuck to his beliefs,' Margaret added.

'The only problem was that not everybody shared those beliefs,' Sally muttered.

'With an organic carrot. Thatcher assassinated with an organic carrot, you see if I'm not wrong,' Sean said with burning conviction as he jabbed his finger aggressively in Chaos's direction.

Chapter 14

March 1988 – two years later

'"Welsh Rabbit"!' Alan called out. The audience groaned. Chaos grinned and ducked his head under the lights to peer out from the stage. Alan did the same thing every Tuesday. He loved 'Welsh Rabbit'.

Chaos couldn't understand why a jokey, throwaway song should mean so much to him. It was only a piss-take, a poke at Jefferson Airplane, *White Rabbit*, Tadley, Ewan, himself and the band. Alan's only explanation was a quote from the song, *Go ask Ewan, I think he'll know*, which, to Chaos, was no explanation at all. Especially since Alan refused to come to Tadley, even for a visit. Alan said he wasn't interested, hated farming, hated the idea of communal living, hated Jefferson Airplane and insisted, mockingly, that the rest of the band's set was 'shite' by comparison.

'But that's our encore,' Chaos protested with mock hurt. 'Do you mean you want us to finish?'

'Yes!' shouted Alan.

'No!' shouted the crowd.

'Oh, could we?' Eric pleaded with feigned exhaustion, shaking his soaked hair towards the crowd. He was drenched in sweat. They all were, band and crowd. The Railway Inn was bulging with bodies and, with dozens more turned away, it was obvious that the band had outgrown the small back room. Next stop the Tadley Hall ballroom probably. But not yet. The atmosphere here was too good, the sardine experience too exciting. Besides, Alan might not go to Tadley and Chaos liked him; he took the piss.

Gary played the opening bass line of 'Welsh Rabbit' and Sean came in with the drums, Eric picked out the guitar solo on the keyboards and Chaos grinned. Sure enough, just as he opened his mouth to sing, '*One field is for barley*' Sean, Eric and Gary changed rhythm and slammed into 'When Will the Sky Touch the Earth?' Chaos laughed – at least the band were tight!

'*You're postponing my destiny. Don't prolong my agony . . .*'

The crowd cheered. Alan booed.

Dipity stood on the table at the back of the room and watched. Chaos sang with anger, spit and deep, deep, sarcasm. Good. Dipity loved this song; it was her favourite.

'*Strip your soul bare and show me that you care. I don't want to wait any longer than I have to . . .*'

Eric had written it as a love ballad. Chaos read it as a frustrated scream about the slowness of his world-changing plans. The compromise had created a hard, slamming, change-my-world love/hate song. Dipity thought it was fabulous. To her it was about Ewan's relationship with Sarah – the need, the destructiveness, the waste. But then, to Dipity, everything the band did was about Ewan. It was the reason for the band – to find him.

'*Calling, I'm crawling, waiting to fall . . . somewhere.*'

Dipity shrugged her arm away with irritation as she felt someone tugging at her sleeve. The tugging persisted, ruining her enjoyment. She glared at the guy shouting up at her.

'You owe me some money.'

'What?' Dipity scowled, her attention alternating between the out-of-place stranger who looked vaguely familiar and her brother spitting his anger out on stage.

'Two returns to Cardiff and extra for the bus fare.' The stranger grinned. 'Tyler and the Tadpoles in London said they'd never heard of you.'

Dipity remembered then. Steve Jenkins. Platform tickets. A late-thirties jerk in a business suit. But: 'He must be all right, Dips – he's going to *Wales*.' Dipity had scrawled down Tyler's address, promising Steve he'd be repaid. A total bluff, of course, but she didn't think she'd see him again.

'Bastards,' she spat and climbed off the table to talk to Steve Jenkins properly.

'You and Whose Army?' This was the one, the favourite, the one the crowd loved most.

'Turn it round, go upside down,
You can't give what I throw away.
Lying flat with your weight on my back.
But when I push through,
I'm going to jump all over you.
Turning up with who? You and whose army?'

The crowd surged forward, the front row belly-wedged against the stage, heads bobbing, faces flushed, eyes excited, the chorus bawled out. Chaos-written.

'Throw away what they say,
Find another game to play.
Give away what they give,

237

Find another way to live.
You and whose army? You and whose army?'

Written with guilt, love, anger, resentment, fear.

Eric watched the transformation with pride. Chaos had soaked it all up, probably from birth: the Harvest Festivals, the band practices, the jams, the rehearsals, the recording sessions – watched, copied, soaked. A little bit of every band and singer he'd seen. And although Chaos was obviously a natural, he was clumsy sometimes, fake and inexperienced. During this song, though, the pose went, and the performance changed into something real and serious and exciting.

'Poverty is history,
For me, for you, I'm going to screw
That crap to the back of my mind.
See you rot in hell,
Going to make you crawl and spell,
M-o-n-e-why? You and whose army?'

This was Chaos being honest, rallying the troops, the battle cry to . . . what exactly was never explained in the song.

'Throw away what they say,
Find another game to play.
Give away what they give,
Find another way to live.
You and whose army? You and whose army?'

But Chaos seemed older than seventeen, more knowing than a dumb teenager who just wanted to get laid. He seemed as keen as Eric, as crazy as Sean, as musical as Jim and Nick, as sexy as Sarah, as open as Dave, as energetic as Sally, as generous as Jonathan, as wise as Margaret, as logical as Miriam, as arch as Ewan. And the crowd loved him. In a couple of years Chaos was going to be huge, unstoppable. Given the right management, publicity and record deal – the image of Tyler sprang into Eric's head – and Chaos would be gone. Eric played a couple of bum notes before forcing himself to stop analysing and worrying and just feel proud.

We won't lose Chaos – Chaos *is* Tadley. Chaos is *the* Tadpole.

Steve Jenkins sat in the relative quiet of the bar, eager to prove himself. He dismissed the money owed as 'exchanged' for interesting stories on dull trains: two kids searching for lost heroes and fighting the dragons of modern society – sort of.

'So why did you come?' Dipity asked, sitting opposite with a slight smirk flickering at the corners of her mouth.

'Here? Curiosity,' Steve replied. 'I wanted to see what the pair of you were up to.'

'So you knew it was Chaos then? In the band?'

'I've been following you.' Steve looked sharply at Dipity, realising that sounded wrong. He reddened slightly. 'I mean Tadley, not you personally. I've been following Tadley for years.'

'Why?'

Steve shrugged again, his embarrassment level soaring as Dipity's smirk grew. 'Just interest . . . the town's always been interested in Tadley.'

Steve was aware of appearing middle-aged – a lawyer with a midlife crisis and a messy divorce. But he *was* intrigued by Tadley. He'd followed events there since the seventies, through press reports and gossip in town. Then he met two overconfident, highly sociable, precocious little adults with frighteningly naive, childlike ignorance on a station platform in Ludlow. Genuine products of a life at Tadley Hall. A part of his youth was at Tadley – a huge sex and drugs party, years ago. It had been the highlight of his life, and Steve had hankered after it ever since.

While the band were pumping up their egos backstage, Alan took the opportunity to squeeze to the front of the hand-clapping, foot-stamping, chanting crowd. His ambition – no, his *right* – was always to be dead centre, front row, directly facing Chaos. One day he was going to get up and stand next to Chaos, out-sing him. Maybe one day replace him – just for this one song. This one song belonged to Alan; it didn't belong to Chaos. Chaos had everything and knew nothing. Alan seethed with resentment.

A cheer went up as Gary strolled back on stage, followed by Sean and Eric. Gary played the opening bass line of 'Welsh Rabbit' and Sean came in with the drums. Eric picked out the guitar solo on the keyboards and the crowd started 'hippy piss-take' dancing. Chaos reappeared. Alan grinned.

'You rich, smug, have-it-all bastard!' Alan yelled and sang along with Chaos and the rest of the room.

'One field is for barley,
And one field is for wheat,
And the garbage that they feed you
Isn't fit for you to eat.
Go ask Ewan, if life is sweet.

And if you go chase the rabbit
Down a mineshaft, you will fall,
Because the answers that they give you

Are all written at the hall.
Call Ewan, he's heard it all before.

When the farmer throws the seed down,
And tells you he's got to go,
Tear down the office and the business,
Seize the house and the studio.
Go ask Ewan, I think he'll know.

When Merlin, dykes and allies,
And Horsemen live in sheds,
And His Lordship's going backwards,
And the white queen's lost her head . . .'

Dipity heard the end coming as it reverberated through the wall to the bar. Chaos bellowing: *'Remember what the drummer said.'* The crowd roaring back: *'He's not dead. He's not dead.'*

Some of the regulars in the bar quietly sang their own version: *'Kill the singer dead. Kill the singer dead.'* Dipity looked round at them and grinned. She hated 'Welsh Rabbit' too. Well, she didn't *hate* it, but she did hate it being the standard encore. It wasn't supposed to be public. It was a private song, a Tadley song, a Tadley joke. Now it was a band and fan joke. Stuck in one night because the band ran out of songs but not energy or ego, encouraged by Alan's weekly requests, and rendered obligatory by the crowd's compulsion for pathetic idiot dancing and tuneless bellowing. Dipity finished her drink, grinned at Steve Jenkins and stood.

'Have you got a car?' she asked.

'Yes.'

'Good. Fancy a fuck?'

Steve nearly spat his drink out in surprise. 'What?'

241

'Fancy a fuck?'

'Dipity, you're only fifteen!'

'So?'

'I'm nearly forty.'

'So?'

'Dipity?'

'So, "No, thank you, I'd rather not," would have done.' Dipity laughed. 'Except that you would but it's not acceptable in polite society. Coming to Tadley then?' She didn't wait for an answer; she turned her back on Steve Jenkins and marched out of the bar. She had party people to organise.

The van, crammed with bodies and equipment, sputtered its way along the country lane in a stench of exhaust fumes, cigarette and dope smoke, beer breath and stale sweat. It was definitely illegal – the van and its contents. And conspicuous. It was a miracle the police hadn't stopped them yet. If only the other cars would over-take or leave a decent gap or pretend not to be involved – any-thing rather than chug behind like a sad and slow army convoy.

'Not Quite Newts?' Gary suggested.

'The Amphibians,' Eric mused.

'The Post-Apocalyptic Pigs,' Sean sneered.

Eric considered it.

Sean glared. 'We'll stick to the Lone Ranger and His Three Temporary Tontos,' he said.

Eric glared back. 'We can't. As I said at the time: it's tempor-ary.'

'And not your band any more,' Sean sniped.

All three threw a slight glance towards the back of the van. It seemed obvious to Sean that it had become Chaos's band, so why they were trying to think of names for it was beyond him, particularly since Chaos clearly couldn't give a toss.

'Chaos, Two Losers and Not a Bad Bass Player,' Sean said, turning to look out of the side window, obviously hoping the conversation was dead.

Gary was determined *not* to let the conversation die. Chaos might just want to be known, but Gary wanted to be famous. A black outsider in white Ludlow. A member of a band whose other members knew each other inside out and backwards. The first newcomer to a house whose inhabitants seemed to think and breathe as one. Security would only come with success. And Gary was determined this band was going to be successful – but *not* as Tontos.

'I still think we should exploit the Tadpole connection,' Gary said. He stared at the road through the windscreen, knowing the atmosphere would change.

It did. Eric tried to distract himself by cleaning the windscreen with the back of his hand. The kids in the back of the van tuned in. Sean scowled.

'No.'

'But you are still Tadpoles, aren't you? Technically?' Gary asked with mock innocence.

Sean sighed obstinately. Eric couldn't stop himself. 'By rights, we're *more* Tadpole than Tyler. We're true Tadpoles. Total Tadpoles.'

'We are *not* Tadpoles,' Sean said.

'Yes, but—' Eric said.

'That Tadpole crap finished years ago, so just leave it, Eric.'

'All I meant was—'

'Leave it.'

'It was our ceremony,' Eric persisted. 'We were the ones who were married, not Tyler.'

'All right, Eric, look . . .' Sean pulled the ragged old string bracelet off his wrist, wound down the window and threw it out of the van. 'We've all just got divorced. Okay? Now shut the fuck up about Tadpoles.'

Sean realised what he'd done. Or rather the icy silence from the back of the van told him what he'd done. Sean felt a dozen or so pairs of eyes boring into the back of his head, led by one particular pair of cold, accusing, humourless eyes.

'Stop the van, Eric,' Sean sighed.

Everybody piled out and began the hunt for Sean's bracelet.

'You don't think he's still wearing his, do you?' Sean said as Chaos glowered at him, illuminated in the headlights of the convoy of cars behind them. Chaos walked away in disgust.

'All right then, all right,' Sean called after him, fully familiar with Chaos's unbending Ewan obsession. 'Frog. How about Frog? Bigger than Tadpole, better than Tadpole, but still Tadpoles at heart. And he'll know then; he'll know it's us but grown up a bit. How about that?'

Chaos turned, shrugged, and rejoined the search. Gary smirked, patted Sean on the shoulder and started looking for the bracelet.

Not that it was lost. It had caught on Steve Jenkins's windscreen wiper, but Dipity's priority wasn't to tell everyone to stop looking. Her priority was to tell Sean, with a venomous hiss, to repair it, replace it, ask Sarah to remake it, but never, ever discard it, chuck it, treat it with contempt or forget the connection. Dipity was, if anything, worse than Chaos. It wasn't symbolic – it was personal.

Sean's only defence was to mutter gruffly about insular lives creating neurotic kids and squeeze the string back onto his wrist. Even so, he was still barred from the van. Whether he joined another car or walked home, Chaos and Dipity neither knew nor cared. Dipity returned to Steve Jenkins's car and Chaos took Sean's seat in the front of the now quieter and less boisterous van. The convoy chugged onwards to Tadley and everybody turned the word over in their minds and thought the same thing.

Frog. It sounded crap.

It was a repeat. A taste of history. The stew was simmering, the bread buttered, salad and snacks laid out and the party upstairs was in full swing. Margaret sat with Dave at the kitchen table as they idled over their coffee and watched the kids invade the kitchen. 'Grandchildren' she called them, secretly.

Oh, the party wasn't huge. It wouldn't last weeks either. But Margaret knew it was the rebirth of Tadley, a new generation, and it was happening in the same way: music, drugs, sex and strangers. They came because of Chaos and the band, just as in those years they'd come because of Jim and Nick and the band. But now it wasn't just sex and ego. Chaos wanted their bodies, yes, as did all the kid crew – running around like rampant rabbits with a deadline, as Margaret put it. But Chaos also wanted bodies to farm and repair and repaint and rebuild. And a lot of these kids were willing, more than willing. It was the reason they stayed.

Chaos sprawled on the floor of the dimly lit drawing room, the conversations around him nothing he could join – cinema on his left, football on his right and a place called Coronation Street behind him. Sarah dropped half a dozen condoms into his lap and Chaos looked up and glared. A girl about twelve feet in front of him who *had* been giving him the eye now turned to talk to Eric and some guy. Chaos momentarily forgot his wrath and looked twice at the guy. He assumed he recognised him from the Railway Inn but . . . that didn't seem right somehow.

Chaos returned to his irritation and brushed the condoms

aside with disdain. It was the typical Tuesday lull. The half-hour or so of parental concern before the adults pissed off and let the kids relax. Sarah walked amongst them, dispensing condoms with fanatic zeal while everyone pretended sex was the last thing on their minds. Sarah was so embarrassing and so *straight*. Absolutely no drugs whatsoever and only safe sex, she insisted. Jonathan too was bumbling around, peering at kids and worrying about drugs. It was irritating and unnecessary. Soft drugs only, Dipity's rule. Although Dipity's definition of 'soft' changed weekly, depending on her mood and the person she was chasing that evening. But Jonathan and Sarah didn't need to know that. And Jonathan and Sarah didn't need to know that Chaos and Dipity had decided there had to be a Ewan. If Tadley was going to work at all, there had to be a Ewan. With drugs and messy, unsafe sex if necessary. Without them, preferably.

'Who's Eric talking to, Jonathan?' Chaos asked as Jonathan stumbled past.

'Some guy called Steve. They're talking about the good old bad old days of . . .'

Chaos didn't hear the rest. The girl from earlier suddenly jumped on top of him, invaded his mouth and vision and started snogging him. He didn't complain. When Chaos came up for air he noticed that Jonathan and Sarah had joined Eric and the Steve guy. They were all sitting in an animated huddle on the sofas, talking about the good old bad old days of . . . what? The guy was laughing, pointing around the room. Sarah's hands were covering her face with good-humoured embarrassment, Eric got up and did an impression of collapsing on the floor, Jonathan winced and shook his head as though affectionately remembering something awful. Chaos looked around for Dipity, but couldn't see her. The good old bad old days of . . .

'I'm sorry,' he said to the girl, 'I just remembered something I had to tell Eric.'

Chaos got up to join the group. Ewan. The good old bad old days of Ewan, it had to be. The Steve guy was something to do with Ewan.

Dipity was downstairs. She stood silently watching. Unable to do anything, because she didn't know what to do.

Dave dabbed TCP onto Alan's battered face, while Margaret put a bowl of stew in front of him, even though Alan had insisted he didn't want any.

Alan seemed ashamed and somehow incredibly young. The other kids in the kitchen pretended not to notice, quickly and quietly taking what they wanted and making themselves scarce. It seemed that fights with parents were embarrassing and private and getting beaten up by your dad was nobody else's business. Dipity was disturbed. It was a long walk on a cold night and though she was pleased Alan had come to them, the reason why made no sense to her. Everybody else seemed to understand. Dave and Margaret understood immediately, even though they'd never met Alan.

When Alan started to eat his stew, Dipity could stand it no longer. She wanted explanation, understanding. She wanted to make sense of this stupid, stupid world. Dipity grabbed Margaret's hand and pulled her out of the kitchen, spitting whispers behind the door and taking a crash course in conventional lifestyles and nuclear explosive families.

Dave, finding himself alone with Alan and stuck for a suitable conversation, asked Alan what he wanted to do now.

'Call Ewan,' Alan replied.

Dave frowned. 'Is that your mate? Is he here at the party or do you want to phone him?'

'Call Ewan, he's heard it all before,' Alan repeated.

Dave recognised the words then: 'Welsh Rabbit'. A shaft of hope jabbed up from his stomach. 'Do you know Ewan?' he asked excitedly. 'Our Ewan? Ewan Hughes?' Ewan in Ludlow? Living, hiding, just down the road? But 'Welsh Rabbit' was a private song, a Tadley song, and Ewan didn't know it. Dave was bewildered. Alan looked up at Dave, the first time he'd looked at anyone since he'd arrived.

'Ewan *Hughes*?' Alan said. 'Ewan *Hughes*? Fucking hell,' he whispered. '*You and Whose Army*? Ewan Hughes' Army. Fucking hell!' Alan shouted as he got out of his seat and started dancing excitedly up and down the kitchen. He sang raucously, '*Go ask Ewan, I think he'll know!*'

Dave realised with disappointment that Alan *didn't* know Ewan, but did, annoyingly, know 'Welsh Rabbit'. Private stuff seeping out of Tadley. Annoying, bloody annoying.

'Ewan Hughes' Army!' Alan grinned excitedly.

'Welsh Rabbit'. Dave smiled back. Merlin. Bloody annoying *and* embarrassing.

Chapter 15

August 1991 – three years later

'*Margaret's getting older, Margaret's getting colder.*'

Chaos quickly closed the ballroom doors and prayed nobody had heard Sean singing his latest 'composition'.

'*Come back, you bastard, and say goodbye. Come back, you bastard, before she dies.*'

Gary put his hand over his mouth as his shoulders started to shake. Chaos openly giggled. Gallows humour. Fine for the band, but the Frogspawn wouldn't laugh.

'We can't sing that, Sean,' Eric gasped.

'Why not? It's a message, isn't it?'

'It would kill her.'

'All right then . . .' Sean started again, his foot pounding like a heartbeat on the bass drum.

> '*Margaret's getting older,*
> *Margaret's getting colder,*
> *Come back, you bastard, and say goodbye.*
> *Come back, you bastard —*
> *Oops, too late, she's dead.*'

Chaos collapsed in hysterics at one of the tables.

Dipity poked her head round the door and glared. 'We need this room for a meeting. Urgently.'

'You and your bloody meetings. And your bloody urgency.' Sean scowled. 'Can't we just bloody rehearse?'

'Not if you're singing that rubbish, no,' she said, pushing the doors open fully and standing back as a stream of Frogspawn poured in.

Sean played a drum roll and bounced his sticks off the cymbals in disdain – one flew into his face and nearly had his eye out. It didn't help Chaos control his laughter. Nerves. Chaos was a bag of nerves. The tension at Tadley was getting unbearable as the Harvest Festival approached. Sarah had pulled out all the stops and pulled in all the favours. Simultaneous radio and TV coverage, the biggest crowd so far, huge publicity, high expectation, months of preparation, interviews, appearances and promos.

All because of Margaret. She was dying. And she wanted to see Ewan. They'd tried everything, looked everywhere they could think of. Contacted Maerdy, old friends, relatives, looked up old university people, scanned phone books, the electoral register, even the death register. Nothing. The Harvest Festival then. If Margaret could just hang on till after the Harvest Festival, maybe Ewan would hear and come back, just once, for her.

Chaos calmed down and watched as Matilda and Tranx helped Margaret to a seat. She was thin and wasted and bent, but struggling on and smiling. Panic washed over him and the thought flashed that maybe Margaret would die before the festival and stop the pressure. It was an awful thought. Chaos wiped it away and directed his growing anger towards Dipity. The band should be practising. Practise, practise, practise. The better Frog were, the longer Margaret would live, and the more likely that Ewan would hear and return. Totally irrational, he knew, but

Eric and Sean felt the same, and Gary understood. This gig had to be brilliant.

After a lot of irritating faff and appeals for quiet, Dipity started. 'Jonathan, you are a liar, a coward and a traitor.'

Chaos sighed heavily.

'That was a nice, dramatic opening statement, Dipity.' Jonathan smiled. 'Would you like to qualify it for us?'

'Your bank accounts—'

Chaos raised his eyes heavenwards.

'Have you been hacking again, Alan?' Miriam interrupted. 'We've told you – no hacking.'

'I was looking for Ewan,' Alan said.

'In Jonathan's bank accounts?' she retorted. 'I don't think you'll find him there.'

Chaos joined in the laughter. Alan and his computer – he was such a twat. He'd hacked into the Tadley accounts and the Frog accounts, despite the fact that they were open on Miriam's desk any time he wanted to look at them. Then he'd tried to redeem himself by hacking into Tyler's Tadpole accounts. Admittedly, Chaos had wanted to know what was in them – but even so, Alan was still a twat.

'Explain it, Alan. Jonathan's bank accounts,' Dipity said above the laughter.

Chaos watched Alan fumble and stumble as his pile of computer printouts took on a life of their own. The top page slipped and the whole lot followed, unfolding into a heap on the floor.

'A lot of it is cross-referenced,' Alan stammered as he stepped on and ripped a long strip of animated paper.

Chaos looked over at Dipity, hoping his expression was clear. *Your boyfriend's a twat!* Although Dipity was so private, Chaos wasn't even sure if Alan *was* her boyfriend.

'Jonathan's got property. Everywhere,' Dipity announced.

'And the proof is in there . . .' She waggled her finger at the mess
of paper that Alan was fighting. 'Somewhere.'

As Chaos turned in surprise to Jonathan, Dipity turned to
Chaos and smugly stuck her tongue out.

'Well, not quite *everywhere*, but yes, I have, some,' Jonathan said.
'But I don't see how that makes me a liar, a coward or a traitor.'

Dipity glared as though it were obvious, but Chaos couldn't
see it. 'You're a liar, Jonathan, because you kept it secret and kept
it for yourself. Which makes you a coward, because you've never
risked anything for Tadley; you've always had a safety net. And
that makes you a traitor, because Tadley has just been a plaything
for you, a hobby to keep you amused.'

Jonathan shook his head and smiled, as though his memories
were anything but amusing.

Dipity went on. 'All in it together, Ewan said, but you were
never in it, ever.'

Chaos finally saw Dipity and Alan's point. Yep, that seemed a
reasonable argument, but so what? Who cared now? They had
plenty of money for their own property. Lots of properties.
Money was coming out of their ears. Dave, Pattie and Sally were
at this moment buying property in Mablethorpe. And that was
only the first of many.

'What was I supposed to do with it, Dipity?' Jonathan asked.
'What would you have done? Then? What would *Ewan* have
done?' he added with sarcasm.

Chaos frowned and saw Miriam roll her eyes. She was equally
disdainful of their 'what would Ewan do' mantra. That was irritating. Now Chaos would have to take Dipity's side.

'You could have used those properties, Jonathan,' Dipity
argued.

'How?'

'For Tadley. For the collective.'

'We didn't need them,' Jonathan said. 'We lived here; we didn't want to live elsewhere.'

'You could have sold them.'

'For what? Money? Tadley's never needed it. Whether we liked it or not Tadley has always made money. It's always been a success. But we never expanded – *Ewan* never thought of expanding. So what would Ewan have done?'

Margaret laughed. 'Ewan would have sold all the properties and smoked, swallowed and snorted the profits,' she said.

Jonathan grinned and nodded his head, which irritated Chaos more.

'He never jacked up, though,' Margaret said, suddenly serious and shaking her head towards Sarah. 'He never injected.'

Chaos felt a wave of cold panic roll through his body.

'With all those properties, Jonathan, you could have given one to Ewan. Then we'd know where he was,' Dipity hissed through pursed lips.

'If I'd known he was going, I would have done, Dipity,' Jonathan hissed back.

Chaos's panic turned to waves of nausea. Poor old Dipity, she felt just as scared as he did. Her 'urgent meeting' was stress coming out sideways.

'And he had a strong constitution, always up for work the next day . . . Well, almost always. There were a couple of hairy moments, but he came through . . .' Margaret said, her words trailing off.

'Can we get back to work, please?' Chaos tried not to whine as he swallowed hard. 'With all these new-found properties, we've got to find Frogspawn to put in them.'

Jonathan turned to Chaos and smiled slightly, as though about to say something, but Miriam stood up. 'Ewan's bank account, Alan!' she shouted. 'Have you hacked into that?'

Alan looked unsure whether Miriam was accusing or enquiring, but seemed to decide it was a stupid question either way. 'Ewan Hughes hasn't got a bank account!' he scoffed proudly.

'Yes, he has,' Miriam said, pushing her seat back and marching towards the door. 'Or at least he did have. I opened it for him.'

Alan stared at the screen, his image of Ewan unravelling before his eyes. The fortune that had amassed in Ewan's account during the Tadpole years was huge.

'Did he know about this?' he asked.

'He agreed to it, signed for it,' Miriam said.

Alan looked as if he'd been smacked in the face. Miriam wanted Alan's image to crash completely. She hated it – it was out of all proportion and wasn't even Ewan any more.

Alan stared at the screen a while longer, his brain computing the information. 'Brilliant,' he finally said with a huge, triumphant grin. 'He hasn't touched it.'

True, the amount hadn't changed since Ewan went missing; the account was still dormant.

'He's probably forgotten about it,' she explained.

'Forgotten? About this much money? Brilliant.'

Miriam sighed. 'I meant he probably doesn't remember that he had an account.'

'Brilliant.'

'Not brilliant, Alan, it was the middle of an argument and he simply signed out of petulance. Not brilliant at all.'

'No, Miriam, that's brilliant. That means he didn't want it then and . . .' Alan nodded towards the screen. 'He doesn't want it now.'

'It means he doesn't know he's got it.'

'Brilliant.'

'How the hell is that brilliant?' Miriam snapped.

254

'He's not allowing the capitalist game to get to him.'

'No, too busy playing his own stupid games. And making everybody's lives a misery in the process!'

The kids' crazy hero–building exasperated Miriam. Alan, who had never met him. Chaos and Dipity, whose memories were arrested at thirteen and eleven. The Frogspawn, listening to Chaos's lyrics and Alan's interpretations of them.

'Ewan wasn't a revolutionary, Alan. He wasn't a hero, saint, visionary or . . . anything. He was an awkward, irritating pain in the neck half the time.'

'Brilliant.'

'How is *that* brilliant?'

'Gives us all hope,' Alan blithely replied. 'Any other accounts?'

'You do know that he might not have touched it because he can't touch it, because he's—'

Alan cut her off. 'You can't say that, Miriam – it's not allowed.'

Miriam thought about arguing but gave up and despaired instead.

'Would he have any other accounts?' Alan asked again.

'I've no idea.'

Alan returned to his keyboard and started searching. Miriam watched as a picture of Ewan downloaded onto the screen.

'Don't mind that,' Alan said, 'I put that there.'

Miriam *did* mind. It was a photograph from university. 'Ewan didn't steal, Alan.'

Alan was not in the least perturbed. 'Yes, he did. He stole Sarah from Jonathan. He stole Tadley from him too. Brilliant.'

The excitement was mounting. Sarah's checklist crumpled up under her hands as she leant over the desk, her eyes fixed on the TV in the corner, brought in specially to monitor the festival coverage.

'*The A49 is at a standstill. Ludlow is gridlocked. Police estimates put the crowd at a hundred thousand.*'

Steve Jenkins stood behind her, his hand up her skirt, his fingers jabbing inside her. She wanted to say 'harder' but didn't. She wanted to say 'rougher' but didn't. He'd only apologise, spoil it, and getting him this far had been an achievement. Sarah's fault really; she wasn't his type. Sleazy, furtive sex didn't come naturally to Steve; he was too polite, too romantic. But at least he was a start.

Sarah's hands smoothed out the crumpled checklist, trying to cover up her sexual frustration.

'*It is absolute chaos. The organisers have wildly underestimated. But the crowd's Dunkirk spirit and "all in it together" sense of community are making this festival an event.*'

The Harvest Festival was going to be a success. And a huge part of that success was down to Sarah. Her years of sexual and social liaising and working hand in glove with Tyler were finally paying off. And all for Ewan. Ironic really.

Sarah closed her eyes and felt her checklist rip under her hands as she started to slip into the fantasy. She stopped herself. Move on. No fantasy, be real. She would still get off, still reach orgasm. It wouldn't be explosive but it was a start. Sarah forced her eyes open to stare at the TV.

A bright-eyed, grinning, cheeky face stared back at her. A face on a badge. *I'm looking for Ewan*, the badge read. White words encircling his face.

Sarah exploded.

'It's only a photograph,' Dipity sneered.

'*My* photograph.'

'My—' Dipity bit her tongue. 'Natural father' she wanted to say but knew it wasn't worth bringing up *that* little can of worms, not while Sarah was raging.

Sarah had her hand out, as though the confiscation of Dipity's and Alan's badges would wipe away the thousands of others they'd made.

'We were only doing it for Margaret,' Dipity said.

'How are badges going to help Margaret?' Sarah demanded.

Alan and Dipity glanced sideways at each other. They weren't, of course.

'My mum had three children by three different guys — we don't know who. None of them were her husband, though, because he's gay.'

Dipity couldn't help but turn to look at the TV. She felt compulsively drawn to it. Chaos was being interviewed, sounding proud that Sarah was a slag. He looks good on TV, Dipity thought. Mention Margaret, Chaos. Call Ewan.

Everyone on the TV was wearing badges. They'd become the symbol of the festival. Ewan had become the symbol of the festival.

'We only borrowed the stupid photograph; we put it back, no damage done,' Dipity said, turning back to her mother.

'That's not the point and you know it,' Sarah snapped.

'Okay,' Dipity sighed petulantly. 'We didn't mean to steal and I'm sorry we didn't ask.'

Dipity pouted and tossed her badge into Sarah's outstretched hand. Alan did the same. Sarah studied the badges, smiled at them and pinned one onto her blouse and put the other in her pocket. Dipity glanced sideways at Alan. He grinned.

'We used to get stoned. We'd sit amongst the crowd, him and me and Sally, pass the joint around and laugh at the band. Eric and Sean and Jim and Nick. Jim particularly. We'd laugh a lot at Jim.'

Margaret dreamily reminisced as Tranx gently parted her hair and fashioned two plaits entwined with purple ribbon. Margaret had made an extra effort to dress up for the festival. She wanted to be colourful; she wanted to look festive. Tranx had patiently helped her. It was traditional – Harvest Festival, Margaret would go psychedelic. 'Proud to be mutton,' Margaret would announce if any outsiders gawped.

'The first ever proper festival, I dressed up as a hippy chick and we danced together, though Ewan was totally stoned and both of us had left feet. I never approved of drugs, but . . . a little bit of dope, on special occasions . . . And he hated Jim. Sally did too. We could never have children, Jack and I.'

The bed and dressing table looked out of place with the rest of Margaret's immaculately clean and spartan cabin. Rainbow clothes, diaphanous scarves, chain belts, bangles, beads, slides, rings and make-up cluttered the area around which Margaret sat and Tranx laboured. Tranx would clear it all up later, after the gig. Margaret usually cleared it up herself, before the gig, but . . .

Margaret had said she could walk to the stage but everybody knew she couldn't, even Margaret. Matilda brought the horse, a wagon filled with cushions hitched behind it. Dylan and Zappa sat in it, waiting patiently. Loads of time yet, whenever she was ready. Frog weren't due on for an hour.

Chaos retched into the toilet. He had nothing left to bring up. Sarah rubbed his back.

'It's a normal gig, just slightly bigger,' she reassured him. 'And nerves are good. You're better when you're nervous.'

Chaos stared into the toilet and nodded miserably. No matter what he did, or thought, or anybody said, he couldn't shake the fear. Fear of what? The crowd? TV cameras? Margaret? Ewan?

The message. If he could think of a suitable message to send Ewan he wouldn't have this fear. *Margaret's getting older, Margaret's getting colder* . . . They couldn't sing that. He'd feel like a twat.

Chaos got up and went to wash his face in the sink. He stared into the mirror above it. He looked awful – white face, black circles and frightened rabbit's eyes staring back.

TV cameras. Wait for a close-up. 'Ewan, come home – Margaret wants you.' Simple. Do that. And if it ruins the song, so what? What are you singing for anyway? *Wants* you or *needs* you? 'Ewan, come home – Margaret needs you.' Better. *Needs* you is better, more urgent. Quick, simple, and not too embarrassing.

Chaos looked at his mother and smiled, assuring her he was okay. 'Nerves under control,' he said.

'Nerves are good. Controlled nerves are better.' She smiled.

Chaos went to the door and opened it. The family milled around the dressing room. Not just the band but Dipity, Imogen, Sally, Dave, Jonathan . . . the old Tadpole family – well, almost. Margaret would be on her way.

'A hundred thousand people, Chaos.' Claudia grinned triumphantly.

His stomach churned and his face whitened. He turned and ran back to the toilet. Chaos retched. Sarah rubbed.

It was a beautiful day, the colours of the people as bright as the sun. So many people. Margaret couldn't believe the numbers. It was like gravity had punched a hole and sucked the world into Tadley. Except here at the cabins, where there were only ghosts and memories. Dylan and Zappa helped her onto the wagon, arranging the cushions around her. Tranx and Matilda smiled at her and guided the horse.

'Take me the long way,' Margaret said.

Music in the distance – not Frog, some other band. Fields in the distance no longer green. A multicoloured tent city, bright tepees and painted buses towering over bog-standard khaki and military green. Tents just big enough for lovers next to square-like-a-house brown canvas next to translucent polythene held up

259

by sticks. Orange and blue tents with plastic windows that looked city-dwelling stupid. Garish temples to travelling decked with signs and symbols of peace and love and frogs and tadpoles. Naked toddlers with painted faces dancing below trees while grungy parents with dreadlocks swayed in the branches and picked apples. A field of potato pickers with calloused hands and broken backs and colourful clothes singing to the music and chatting and digging. Beans being stripped and peas being picked and wheat being threshed and milled and turned into bread and everyone smiling brighter than the sun.

Margaret rode through the crowds like the queen of the festival. The crowd parted to let her through. Kids behind the wagon tramped along, some dancing, some clapping, some stoned. All wearing badges and all following a little old lady in crazy clothes who looked beautiful. Margaret felt beautiful. A smell in the air of food and dope and sunshine. The sounds of music and laughter and chattering. Tadley covered in colour, and the colours moving and shimmering.

A smiling girl jumped onto the wagon and unpinned her badge. She handed it to Margaret. 'Do you want me to pin it on for you?' the smiling girl asked.

Margaret looked down at the badge, studied it for a long time. *I'm looking for Ewan*. Margaret smiled and handed it back.

'You have it, love. I've already found him.'

'This one's for Ewan,' Chaos mumbled nervously.

'Ewan who?' Eric cued into the microphone.

Jump! Chaos ordered himself. Jump over the nerves and bloody do it!

'*You and Whose Army!*' Chaos yelled. He jumped.

The band kicked off. Loud, raucous. The masses below exploding in a deafening cheer.

'*Turn it around, go upside down . . .*'

He felt it then, growing from inside, coming up. Chaos could feel it coming up. From his feet? His stomach? He didn't know, but he could feel it. The rage. The feeling about to explode, his stomach tightening, head swelling, blood pounding. It felt *good*. It felt *so good*. No more vomit, no more diarrhoea, no more uncontrollable shaking and pacing and woolly-headed, numb-skull panic. It was happening, it was working, and it was going to be more than all right . . .

'*You and whose army? You and whose army?*'

Halfway through the set.

'*You're postponing my destiny . . .*'

A few more songs to go.

Margaret was at the side of the stage. The family gathered around her chair, her brocade-covered throne. She was okay; she was smiling. There was plenty of time yet to give the message. *Ewan, come home – Margaret needs you.*

There had been no close-ups. Not between the songs. There had been plenty *during* the songs. Chaos had a camera practically shoved up his nose *during* the songs. But not between. Chaos *had* thought about stopping mid-song, when the camera seemed too close, intrusive, but why ruin the song? Why ruin the atmosphere? The atmosphere was electric, brilliant. One hundred thousand people swayed and sang along. All faces turned to him, one big family from beyond the gates, all on the same side, all in agreement.

Sean, Eric and Gary kept looking at him, waiting for it. The Message. They hesitated between songs, nodded their heads in the direction of the microphone. Eric had conferred with him quietly. 'Do you want me to do it?'

'No, I'll do it. Plenty of time, plenty of time.'

Margaret looked good, better, healthier. Better than she had for months. She was sitting in the wings, holding Dave's hand, the family around her. She was going to live for ever. She'd even got up a couple of times, wiggled a little dance. Dave had laughed, held her. The family was smiling, dancing. The gig was perfect. The crowd was in heaven and Chaos was God. Plenty of time yet . . .

'Waiting to fall . . . somewhere.'

'Thank you.' Margaret smiled. Chaos felt guilty. But there was still the encore, and doing it just before 'Welsh Rabbit' would be perfect.

Frog hovered in the wings, huddled in a little group away from the others, waiting for the calling and clapping to gather momentum. Chaos rubbed sweat out of his eyes, rubbed a towel over his hair and neck, and felt Sean, Eric and Gary glowering at him.

'I'll do it over the intro,' Chaos promised.

The glowers didn't lessen.

'Do the intro, and I'll come on and say it, I promise!'

Eric pointedly disregarded Chaos and turned to Sean. 'I'll do it over the drums,' he said.

Sean nodded.

'They won't do a close-up on you,' Chaos argued. He felt two inches small and a complete bastard.

The four turned in unison and looked over at Margaret. She sat quietly, still holding Dave's hand.

Sean took Chaos to one side and put his arm round him. 'Do it, Chaos,' he threatened. 'Remember who she is and what she wants and what we're selling out for. Do it over the intro or *I'll* do something. And it won't be pleasant.' Sean 'affectionately' slapped Chaos's head and returned to Eric and Gary. 'Right, I think we're ready,' he said.

Chaos listened for a few seconds to the loud, insistent chanting — the momentum had gathered to fever pitch.

Gary walked back on stage, followed by Sean and Eric.

Chaos turned to smile at Margaret.

Dave was leaning forward, bent over her body, holding her, his face twisted, contorted. Tranx falling onto her knees beside her. The family moving, turning, huddling round her, their faces bewildered, tight. Dipity staring at him. Dipity was the only one looking at Chaos. Her face said it all. *Margaret's dead.*

Gary played the opening bass line to 'Welsh Rabbit' and Sean came in with the drums. Eric picked out the guitar solo on the piano. Chaos blinked and felt the leaden weight of his mind closing down. He automatically turned away from Dipity and walked back on stage.

The microphone was a long way off. The stage seemed huge. The band played the intro. Everything slowed down, slow motion, slo-mo. The crowd roared. Slow, muffled cheering, whistling, applauding. Applauding what? Margaret dying? Not now. Don't die now. You can't die now; it's a brilliant gig.

Chaos made it to the microphone. Got to give the message or Sean will beat me up.

'Ewan . . .' What to say?

The music behind him went awry, the familiar tight sound unravelling. The piano plonked. The bass ran out of run. Only the bass drum remained, pounding through the monitors like a heartbeat. Sean's foot automatic, thumping the bass drum. Chaos turned and saw Sean, Eric and Gary looking into the wings. What to say now?

The microphone, huge in front of him.

'Ewan . . .' The only sound was the bass drum, still thumping.

'Ewan . . .' Speaking in time to the bass drum. Speaking in *rhythm*, for God's sake!

'Ewan . . . Margaret's . . .' Too late. No point now.

'Margaret's getting older, Margaret's . . .' Sean sang. The words cut painfully through Chaos's leaden head.

'No, fucking hell, don't!' Chaos yelled. The microphone. *'Ewan!'* he called.

'Ewan . . .' Who was that? That wasn't Chaos.

'Ewan . . . Ewan . . . Ewan . . .' In time to the bass drum, calling in rhythm.

'Ewan . . . Ewan . . . Ewan . . .' The crowd. Chanting. Picking up and chanting.

A sea of faces chanted at him and a sea of arms jabbed the air, stabbing towards him in rhythm. In rhythm with the word; in rhythm with the drum.

'Ewan . . .' *Come back you bastard!*

'Ewan . . . Ewan . . . Ewan . . .'

★   ★   ★

Memories of a dream or some weird trippy experience like the clouds turning to monsters or spiders in the bed. Reality buried with a year of living rough and a need to reinvent. The reality wasn't even real *now*, coming at him through the TV, Chaos and Sean and Eric and a black guy he didn't even know but felt he ought to just because he was there with them, in front of him, calling.

People in the pub drunkenly normal, the panic and sweat only here, at this table in the corner, in his head. Maybe there's really football on the telly and this is a flashback, a trip, a spiked pint. Spiking his life, because it's too good, too cosy: Caroline and the kids and the dignity of being Ian Field, being Dad sticking food on the table – not much food but it means a lot.

The old dream–trip memory too strong. Chaos and Sean and

Eric and Tadley and trying to scan the crowd, the wings of the stage, trying to see some old faces. The temptation too great to ignore and too frightening to watch at home. But *just* songs, singing, pride in Chaos, good lad, well done, nice to see you grown, not Ewan, Ewan, Ewan like a Nuremberg rally, the pub swaying, the room blurring and his new life melting.

There were a hundred opportunities to tell Caroline the truth and in six years he never took one. He can't go home. How can he go home? What's she going to say apart from 'liar'?

Nothing weird or druggy; this is actually happening. The TV is calling and Caroline's at home watching the same thing, seeing Sarah's photo of him, making the connection: Ewan Hughes. She doesn't know Ewan Hughes, remember that. It's only the badge, a picture, the photographic similarity she's seeing. That's all she knows. Like when the radio called 'Ewan Hughes' Army' that day and lightning shot through him but Caroline carried on washing up and even joined in with the chorus.

So, bluff, truth or denial when she stands with her hand on the doorknob and threatens to reject him? He could tell her the truth about all of it except Dipity. And eventually it would come to Dipity. How could he be honest about that?

Chapter 16

September 1994 – three years later

12 a.m. London

'We're not a cult,' Chaos insisted. He paced the floor of the hotel room, his every word and movement recorded by the FFC – the fucking film crew. Chaos hated hotels. He hated stupid questions too.

The FFC had been following him for the past week. A documentary. Sarah's idea. Everything was. Even Jake. Jake was Chaos's minder, counsellor, friend and driver. A twenty-eight-year-old teetotal ex-junkie grungy anarchist who ran Chaos's life with military precision and refused to take a detour to Matlock. Chaos was spoiling for an argument but the FFC were filming. Jake sat to one side and watched, waiting for Chaos to explode.

'You all wear badges,' Callum O'Connor said.

Callum O'Connor. A gentle Irishman with a gentle Irish lilt that made his probing and prying appear reasonable and any adverse reaction to it thoroughly unreasonable. Even Jake felt guarded.

'Not everybody wears them,' Chaos argued.

'Most.'

'Only some.'

'And everybody says, "What would Ewan do?"' Callum smiled and waited for Chaos to deny it.

Chaos stopped pacing and threw a malevolent glance towards Jake. Jake interpreted the glance as *Ewan would drive me to Matlock.* Jake folded his arms and looked apologetic but stubborn.

'We're not a cult,' Chaos repeated and started flicking channels on the TV. Flicking channels was all he could do. He couldn't smoke, snort, drink, fuck or argue – well, he could, but that was what Callum O'Connor and the FFC wanted.

Chaos just wanted to go to Matlock, Old Hill Farm. Marcia lived there. Of all the girls Chaos had sex with – and Jake reckoned it was hundreds – Marcia was the only one Chaos really wanted. Jake felt for him but hurtling up the M1 from London to Matlock and then hurtling back down again, just for a couple of hours of sex, was stupid to Jake's mind. Even though Tranx lived there too. And of all the girls Jake had sex with – and Jake reckoned it was two or three – Tranx was the only one Jake really wanted.

'Look, Ewan's just an idea, an image,' Chaos said as the film crew recorded every flick of the channels. 'He's the absent emperor. Frogspawn have to learn to agree on what's best for everybody. And "what Ewan would do" is what's best. It's not about him.'

Callum O'Connor blithely continued. 'So do you think he's still alive?'

Chaos flicked to a snatch of himself performing with Frog. He grimaced and turned over.

'You've had sightings, haven't you?' Callum went on. 'Videos and photos sent to you?'

Chaos watched a busty vampire lady sinking her teeth into an Edwardian gentleman. He flicked.

'Thousands, from what I've been told. Any of them him?'

Football. Tedious. Chaos flicked back to the film.

'Some lookalikes are accusing you of harassment. Surely only a cult would be obsessively searching after ten years?'

The busty vampire lady got a stake through her heart. Chaos flicked to a darts match. 'Those people aren't Frogspawn. They're . . . well, I don't know who they are, but they're not us.'

'The press call them Chaotics.'

'Whatever. We're Frogspawn and to us he's just an image, nothing to look for.'

'Must be difficult to live up to that image,' Callum said. 'To be Ewan Hughes but merely a mortal version. Can you imagine what it's like if he is still alive? Must be hell.'

'Worse than this, do you suppose?' Chaos snapped as he pointed to the intrusive camera. Jake sat forward but Chaos flicked back to Frog and grimaced.

Callum looked hurt. 'You agreed to this.'

'Hmm,' Chaos said. He turned to glare at Jake. *Take me to Matlock, you bastard.*

6 a.m.

Chaos woke with the usual thought. Where am I? He didn't know what time it was, but it seemed early and he could hear Jake's voice.

'Sheffield's exciting because it's a whole street, so if we can get it to work it would be really cool. And of course, inner city – we've never tried inner city before. Apart from Jonathan's houses and flats, of course, but they're more . . .'

'Salubrious?' Callum's voice, still prying, questioning.

'Awkward,' Jake corrected.

Chaos opened one eye, then closed it quickly. Jake was

leaning on the window sill at the other end of the room, keeping the FFC's backs turned. God, Chaos thought, don't they ever sleep?

'So why is Chaos going?' Callum asked.

'He wants to; it's Dave's project and he wants to see Dave and Pattie. And it's on the way to Mablethorpe.'

Chaos sneaked his arm behind him and felt the empty bed. He was still in London. No Marcia, no sex, no fun. Maybe they could squeeze in Matlock this afternoon. It wasn't far from Sheffield.

'So why Mablethorpe?' Callum asked.

'Kate Morris is interviewing him there. She wants to get the *feel* of a Frogspawn home.' Jake laughed. Chaos nearly did too. He'd met Kate before – she was a jumped-up, pompous bitch, who waved her long fingernails around as though she were an artist, but in fact she had all the creativity of a toad.

'Why not interview him at Tadley Hall?'

'Because Sally's at Mablethorpe. Most of the original Tadpoles are scattered now – new farms, houses, shops – so it gives Chaos the opportunity to visit them . . .'

To visit *them* but not Marcia. And originally it was supposed to be *just* Marcia. An opportunity to escape Central Office, the maelstrom of Tadley with its backbiting and infighting and factions and frictions and a hundred different *crews*. Black, beautiful Marcia. Chaos would happily have sex with her till his dick dropped off, given half the chance. He would even fall in love with her if he could. But Marcia was in Matlock and he was all over the place. 'Oh well, if you're going travelling . . .' Sarah had said and arranged a full-blown promo tour to everywhere *but* Matlock, with a documentary crew in tow 'just to prove we're *not* a cult'. Although Chaos had a sneaking suspicion they were – with Sarah as cult leader. Not that Chaos was paranoid, but his mother seemed terrified of him doing a Ewan and becoming a cabin-dwelling farmer with Marcia holding his hoe.

Chaos realised he was grinding his teeth. He also realised the room had gone silent. Jake had stopped talking; Callum had stopped prying.

Chaos wondered what was happening. Shall I wake up or shall I carry on sleeping till Jake tells me they've left? Trouble was he was busting for a piss. Would they film him pissing? Would they film him naked? Would they ever explain to him why this whole stupid rigmarole was in any way interesting? Would they film him going back to Tadley and strangling his mother? Probably yes, yes, no, yes.

Still silence. Can't lie here for ever. Breakfast TV. The FFC filming another fucking film crew – bizarre. Chaos opened one eye and came face to face with the camera.

'Good morning.' He smiled brightly.

8 a.m.

Breakfast TV. The biggest waste of time ever. But they did play ten seconds of the new video – so that's all right then, Sarah.

10 a.m.

The FFC clambered into the back of the car. Jake started the engine and Callum started again. Questions, questions, questions. It was going to be 'keep it buttoned and lie if necessary' all the way to Sheffield. Chaos batted the replies almost automatically.

'You were talking earlier about fatherhood, Chaos,' Callum said.

'No, I wasn't.'

Callum ignored him. 'Do you ever think about your own?'

'My own what?'

'Your own father.'

'What about them?'

'Don't you ever wonder who he is?'

'I know exactly who they are, all seven of them. I've got four mothers as well. Well, three now. It just happened to be Sarah's womb that I lodged in for nine months.'

'Do you think Ewan Hughes was your natural father?'

'Some of the people I live with had really shitty childhoods. I never did, because not one of my eleven parents had that much power or that much pressure.'

'But do you think Ewan Hughes was your natural father?'

'For all I care, I could've been a virgin birth,' Chaos said. 'But I don't think that's likely.'

Jake laughed uproariously. Chaos gave him a look.

'Now let me ask *you* a question, Callum,' Chaos said. 'Why do you keep going on about Ewan Hughes?'

'Because Ewan Hughes is what your career is built on. And it's the mysterious Mr H. that captures my imagination. You're just his singer.'

Jake put Nirvana in the cassette player and played it *fucking loud* all the way to Sheffield. Chaos didn't hear any more questions and the FFC took the hint and took a break.

2.15 p.m. Silver Street, Sheffield

Jake drove round the corner and there it was. Crowds, fans, cameras and reporters. Who leaked? Chaos and Jake exchanged looks – Alan on the Internet. He could have at least warned them! Jake jumped out, climbed over the bonnet and opened the door. Chaos breathed deeply and got out of the car. He was immediately swamped.

'So, what's the idea, Chaos?' Some microphone shoved under his nose.

'Just a row of houses. The council was going to demolish so

we bought them. The idea is some guinea pigs do them up and live in them, collectively.'

'What's the catch?'

'Three or four of them are going to have to earn a conventional living so that the others can maintain the houses and vegetable gardens. And look after the kids, of course, and educate them.'

'What for?'

'As an experiment.'

'You're experimenting with people's lives?'

'Yes.' Chaos grinned and tried to push his way through the crowd towards Dave, Pattie and the huddle of nervous people waiting on a doorstep. A group crowded in and screamed 'Sell-out!' into his ears. Chaos assumed they were Chaotics. Others jabbed pens into his face, yelling for autographs. Somebody kicked him on the shin, somebody else pulled his hair and another microphone banged into his mouth and split his lip. 'Are you a communist?'

'Communism and capitalism are two sides of a coin. Frogspawn don't use coins; we use people.'

'What's going to happen when you fail?'

'Either we could all fail together or I could do what the other experimenters do – blame the powerless.'

It was impossible. Nobody was letting him through. Jake was doing his best to get him forward but if anything he was going backwards. And the FFC were useless, more concerned with protecting their precious camera and microphone and getting a clear shot – revenge for Nirvana obviously.

'Why are you doing this?'

'Because I already live in a mansion, I don't want six cars because I can't drive and I don't know what else to do with the money.'

'So you're just giving it away?'

'I'm not giving it away. I'm putting it in the pot, the same way all Frogspawn who earn money put it in the pot. Money earners are the beginning; moneyless people are the result.'

'Isn't this just a publicity stunt?'

'Hopefully, yes.'

'Can you stand back please; we're pensioners and my wife's just had a new hip!' the old man bellowed by Chaos's left elbow. Chaos looked at him in alarm but it seemed to work. People automatically stepped back a pace, enough anyway for the old man and woman to grab Chaos by the arm and lead him through. Nobody, it seemed, wanted to push and shove an old couple. Chaos looked back at Jake. They both laughed in bewilderment but they made it to Dave's doorstep.

'I'm George,' the old man said, 'and this is my wife, Rose. We hate to intrude but we wondered if we could have a word with you.'

4 p.m. Milton Road, Sheffield

There was now no way they'd get to Matlock. And they were going to be late for Mablethorpe and Kate Morris would be in a mood, but what the hell – Milton Road was brilliant. Absolutely brilliant. George and Rose were right: it was exactly what Chaos wanted. The old couple's road was a normal road, ordinary. Better houses and bigger gardens than Silver Street but not inordinately so. The point was, though, it was working, and it was the residents of Milton Road who were making it work.

'We tore down the fences between the gardens about ten years ago now,' George explained as Rose handed him a cup of tea and Chaos looked at the huge strip of well-cultivated and productive land, with the chicken coop in one corner and the fenced-in goats staring back from another.

'And of course we've also got allotments,' Rose added.

'And we're old,' George said. 'Most of us are pensioners, lived here years, so we all know each other, get on, and being pensioners we've got time to potter.'

'But we've still got our old skills, do you see?' Rose added. 'Electricians, plumbers, brickies – and all the women sew, cook, knit. We turn our hands to most things, really. Well, we grew up during the war: that's what we did; that's what we do.'

Chaos and Jake exchanged grins. They couldn't believe it; it was so brilliant – so *possible.*

'Thing is, though,' George said, scratching his nose with embarrassment, 'we've only got our pensions, and this new technology palaver, solar energy and what have you, well, of course we've read about it, talked about it, but . . .'

'And then Martin, our grandson, mentioned you . . .' Rose added.

'Of course, I can't say we're too keen on your music,' George said.

'Martin is, though. Martin likes you,' Rose quickly added.

Chaos and Jake grinned.

'You don't have to like our music,' Chaos said. 'But if you help Dave at Silver Street, I think we could help you.'

'Solar panels?' George asked.

'Solar panels.' Chaos nodded.

Now Rose and George exchanged grins.

'And, knowing Dave, you'll also get compost toilets and a reed bed water recycling system.' Chaos smiled.

'Oh, I don't think we want to go that far.' George frowned.

'No, I like my creature comforts,' Rose added.

'Well, it's perfectly possible,' Jake imitated in his best Brummie accent. 'Perfectly possible.'

'But next time, George,' Chaos said, 'don't push through the crowd, especially with Rose's new hip. Just phone or write us a letter.'

'Rose hasn't got a new hip,' George admitted.

'I'm quite happy with the old one,' she added.

8.30 p.m. Mablethorpe

The lounge was supposed to be quiet, private. Kate Morris was not to be disturbed. Kate Morris wondered why nobody seemed to understand that. Bad enough that Chaos had agreed to be filmed by her crew only if Kate Morris agreed to be filmed by Callum O'Connor's crew. 'Exchange' Chaos had called it — the little prick. Bad enough that Chaos was two hours late, and *then* wasted another half-hour of Kate's time by saying hello to everybody. Not to mention the stragglers, popping their heads round the door and interrupting *just* as she was about to start. But now some bloody toddler had wandered in and Chaos was positively encouraging him.

'Hello, Benny,' He grinned, mid-interview, spreading his arms for the brat to run into.

Kate Morris was losing her cool. 'Is nobody looking after that child?'

'Yes, I am,' Chaos said.

Kate wanted to hit him. 'I meant, who does he belong to?'

'Well, he could be one of mine, I don't know.' Chaos shrugged.

Kate Morris watched the little brat climb all over the little prick and fiddle with the microphone. 'Isn't indiscriminate fatherhood rather irresponsible?' she snapped.

'Not really. We've all been tested for Aids and VD,' Chaos said, peering round Benny's body while helping the sound man rescue his microphone.

'I was thinking more in terms of the mother's position.'

'They've had tests too,' Chaos said.

Kate narrowed her eyes. He knows full well what I mean, she thought. It was typical. He was an awkward, unprofessional prick, refusing to take her seriously – worse on his own ground than in a TV studio. In fact, this horrible little farmhouse just about summed him up – shambolic and undisciplined. The lounge a mishmash of colour and style, thrown together and totally uncoordinated. Cushions clashing with other cushions, curtains clashing with rugs. Clutter and primitive craft and creaky furniture. And the whole thing looking absolutely splendid on the monitor. Kate wanted to spit. She turned to her researcher and jerked her head towards Benny. The researcher stepped forward and smiled at Chaos, opening her arms. Chaos lifted Benny into them and smiled back, his and the researcher's eyes locking for too long. Kate was incensed. *Don't get all sexy with my researcher, you jumped-up little tart – she's just a fucking researcher!*

'You've got kids, haven't you, Kate?' Chaos asked when the researcher had disappeared with the brat. 'What do you do with them? Boarding school? Nanny? Must be awful; you must miss them. You should have brought them with you. We like kids.' Chaos sat back and grinned.

Smug bastard, Kate Morris thought. 'We were talking about Frogspawn,' she said, trying to get back on track.

'Yes.'

'Don't you think that collecting the socially excluded or those on the margins of society—'

'Collecting?' Chaos queried.

'I could hardly call it "employing" could I?' Kate pointed out.

'How about "working with"? How about "sharing with" or "living equally with"?'

'My point is,' Kate tetchily continued, 'aren't you just helping prop up the government by dealing with a problem that they should be tackling?'

'If I don't believe in God I'm not waiting for a miracle, am I?'

'Meaning?'

'Meaning why should I expect the government to be interested in anything I'm doing?'

'What you're doing is quite clearly politically motivated.'

Chaos looked slightly confused. 'I think you're missing my point, Kate.'

'Or would you classify yourself as an anarchist?'

Chaos laughed dismissively. 'Did you phone a stranger this morning to ask them what you should wear today?'

Kate felt herself redden. She'd spent ages deciding what to wear today – smart but casual, professional with a hint of maverick, serious but colourful. 'I asked if you were an anarchist.'

'I'm answering.'

'What has what I'm wearing got to do with—'

'What you're wearing is irrelevant, but you still wouldn't phone a stranger about it.'

Kate opened her mouth to argue. What she was wearing was certainly *not* irrelevant. Her job depended on what she wore – how could she possibly maintain her professional status in *jeans*!

'And the government are strangers. So why ask a stranger how you should be educated, what sort of job you're allowed to do, what sort of money you have to have, who you should have sex with, what drugs you can take . . .'

Kate got the point and reddened even more.

'Do you know, I never knew drugs *were* illegal?' Chaos laughed. 'I was brought up by criminals, apparently.' He shook his head as though that was the most weirdly amusing thing he'd ever heard.

277

'So you think drugs should be legalised, do you?' Kate asked, desperate to get him on *something*.

'Are you mad?' Chaos laughed again and folded his arms, daring her to ask what *that* meant.

Kate Morris rubbed her temples and signalled a break. She'd had enough. She didn't like him. She didn't like them. And she didn't like this. She needed some Valium.

'You may be popular at the moment,' she quietly sneered as her cameraman stopped filming. 'But Frogspawn can't last and then where will you be? You'll be the loser.'

'I can't lose, Kate, I'm just the singer,' Chaos quietly sneered back. 'Besides, there's thousands of Frogspawn. And thousands of losers can pack quite a powerful punch. Now, does everyone want coffee?' Chaos called with a grin. Smug grin, Kate thought.

Everyone nodded and Kate watched in astonishment as Chaos got up to make some.

10.30 p.m.

Nobody had moved much after their evening meal and the dining room was still full of people talking, smoking and drinking. An acoustic band played in the far corner and the atmosphere of friendly relaxation reminded Callum O'Connor of his favourite pub with his favourite friends. Chaos had finally relaxed. Callum was pleased. The camera rolled, the microphone discreetly hidden. Chaos was drinking, and he'd kept disappearing. So whether he was drunk or stoned, Callum wasn't sure, but Chaos had forgotten about the camera and his tongue was loose – and it didn't occur to Sally to stop him.

'You know what Alan said, Sally? He said I shouldn't be living at Tadley; he said I should leave Tadley. Can you believe it? He said since they were generating their own income, and since they were full and didn't need Frogspawn, I was contributing nothing and should leave. And you know what? Dipity just stood there and didn't say a word, not one word. I was so angry. It's just so . . . it's getting so . . . And the point is, Sally, Alan's doing nothing. He just sits at his computer all day; he's not contributing. But, apparently, waffling with a load of bozos and making up lies about Ewan is somehow important. You know what he wants? He wants us to organise demonstrations and riots. He wants all the Frogspawn to march on Downing Street, bring London to a standstill. He wants everything to be . . . chaotic. He says . . .' Chaos pulled a blithe, butter-wouldn't-melt Alan face. '"That's what Ewan would do." Ewan wouldn't do that. Ewan wouldn't do that and Dipity knows it.'

Sally frowned, agreeing with Chaos. 'So why is Dipity going along with him?'

'Because she's obsessed. Because I told her this whole stupid Ewan thing should be dumped and forgotten about.'

'And she doesn't want to forget about him.'

'She believes in Ewan Hughes' Army; she thinks it's real.'

'Or she just doesn't want to forget about Ewan. Be fair, Chaos,' Sally said. 'It's important to her.'

'Oh, so you're taking her side?' Chaos pouted.

'I'm not taking anybody's side,' Sally protested. 'I don't know what's happening at Tadley. I just know that Dipity's . . . obsession is understandable. I never knew my dad but I still want him. And Ewan was a good father. He was to you, sort of.'

Chaos turned away. 'Bloody fathers,' he muttered. 'She's better off without him.'

Sally ignored it. 'What does everybody else say?'

'I don't know; everybody's really cagey. Sarah doesn't even know what's happening because she's too busy trying to kill me. And Jonathan won't say anything to anybody because he's got a new boyfriend and he wants everyone to like him. It's getting seriously ridiculous. I'm beginning to hate going home.'

'You know you can always live here.'

'But if I'm not at Tadley I don't know what's happening, and Alan is completely out of his box.'

'So maybe you should get Alan to leave.'

'I can't. I haven't got the power.'

'Well, if you haven't, Chaos, who has?'

Chaos looked at her; Sally already knew the answer. They shook their heads helplessly and said it together. '*Ewan Hughes.*'

12 a.m.

Chaos and Jake went to Matlock. Sally 'remembered' to tell Callum O'Connor about an hour later – unfortunately she couldn't remember the address. Or the phone number.

Chapter 17

February 1998 – four years later

Stupid awards ceremonies. Stupid crowds behind stupid barriers and stupid police and a stupid red carpet and stupid photographers and stupid cameras and stupid microphones. Of course cameras and microphones – there were always cameras and microphones. And Chaotics, hurling abuse as usual. Chaos looked the other way – if it wasn't for them, and of course Alan, he wouldn't even be there.

'Well, here's a turn-up! What brings Frog to such a prestigious event? Hoping to win something?' a stupid woman with stupid hair asked, shoving a stupid microphone into their stupid faces. Chaos wasn't in the best of moods. Neither were the band. They put on their most glaringly false showbiz smiles.

'I did it to please my mum,' Chaos said.

'I did it to please his mum,' Gary said.

'I did it because I used to please his mum,' Eric said.

'I did it because his mum used to please me,' Sean said.

'I'm his mum.' Sarah smirked.

The band and Sarah entered the hotel. This was stupid.

'This is stupid, Sarah,' Chaos muttered, keeping a look of

casual enjoyment on his face as they ploughed into the throng of singers, musicians and assembled bigwigs.

'As stupid as those Chaotics?' Sarah quietly hissed. 'We've got to get them off your back, Chaos.'

'And get the media on our side,' Chaos sneered, knowing what her agenda *really* was. With a Labour landslide anything 'different' was on shaky ground, and the media were keen to bury those who didn't toe the party line. And Frogspawn didn't toe the party line. And Chaotics didn't toe *anything* – diehard anarchists with a love of destruction. The two groups were poles apart, but that didn't stop the press linking them. And it didn't stop Alan. Chaos was sure Alan was a Chaotic, even if he did deny it. And Alan was a twat, so, if attending this God-awful shitfest wound Alan up, that was fine by Chaos. Even so, it *was* a God-awful shitfest!

'Anyway,' Sarah said, 'Jim and Nick are going to be here.'

'I don't care. I don't want to see them.' Chaos scanned the faces around the foyer, despite himself.

'Oh, I think you do, because come Monday, they're going to be working for us.' Sarah stood with her eyebrows raised, waiting for the penny to drop. The band perked up, their eyes lit up, and suddenly life wasn't so stupid after all.

'Have we bought Tadpole?' Chaos asked, hardly able to control his excitement.

Sarah nodded and smiled. 'Don't you want to gloat?'

'Oh God, yes, I want to gloat.' Eric laughed.

Sarah smirked and tapped Eric affectionately on the chest. 'You see, I told you to trust me.'

Chaos was startled by Sarah's gesture. That was *way* too sexual to be just 'old friends'.

'What about Tyler?' Sean asked, rubbing his hands with glee.

'No, Tyler's something in computers now.'

'What in computers?' Sean wondered. 'A virus?'

And then, oh happy day, Jim and Nick appeared in the foyer. The band stood and gloated.

Three hours later the tedium-fuelled alcohol consumption was taking effect. The singer who had earlier won Most Promising Newcomer was whispering something very lengthy and erotic in Chaos's ear. It sounded remarkably similar to what Sean had decided, *loud and graphically*, Sarah and Eric were doing in the toilets. Chaos didn't know whether to laugh or cringe, but certainly all thoughts of sex with the Most Promising New-comer took a dive. Sarah and *Eric*?

So far Frog had won nothing. They hadn't expected to; the music industry *hated* them.

Then the tedium turned turtle.

Chaos was only half listening to the announcement.

'And now, to present the award for the group who you the public voted best band, please welcome the man who you the public voted best prime minister . . .'

It was the music that made Chaos go cold – a snatch of 'Things Can Only Get Better' filled the room.

'Bastards!' Eric muttered through tight lips.

They'd been set up. New government, New Labour, every-thing fresh and optimistic and 'Cool Britannia'. A golden oppor-tunity for Frog to join the Establishment and go corporate. Chaos stared at Sarah. Receiving awards from famous-for-their-tits celebrities was one thing – but the prime minister? That wasn't attacking Alan and the Chaotics, that was betraying Frogspawn. Sarah looked mortified. 'Maybe you won't win,' she said.

The applause for the prime minister was way over the top. Everybody there knew what was coming, knew Frog had won, knew Frog had been set up.

'Did you know about this?' Sean hissed at Jim.

'We didn't even know *you'd* be here, let alone him,' Jim said, jerking his thumb towards the stage.

'I've been so looking forward to this.' The prime minister grinned. 'Because you know, not only do I like this group of boys as a band, but also as a symbol of a new Britain, where diversity creates unity . . . a new, caring, sharing Britain, one of partnership and endeavour . . . Inclusion. Cohesion . . .'

'Well, I'm not going up,' Sean said, sitting forward and taking a large gulp out of his glass.

Chaos looked around the room. Press photographers were already jockeying for position. Cameramen were closing in on the table. There was no exit marked 'dignified'. If they went up and shook his hand it would be a public signal of support for Blair. If they stayed put it would be two fingers to public support for themselves. Who to say 'fuck you' to? Chaos could hear a Welshwoman's voice in his head: *'I wouldn't buy another Frogspawn product if it were free.'* A few seconds to choose, and their choice about to be captured on live TV. Either way they were compromised.

'Tapped,' Nick leant forward and muttered in Chaos's ear. 'I reckon you're tapped.'

'What?'

'And the winner is . . .'

'Your phones must be tapped,' Nick said.

'Frog!'

'Fuck!' Chaos could be seen mouthing as the spotlight and camera hit the table and the room exploded into deafening applause. They weren't being applauded for winning, Frog knew that.

The band looked at Tony Blair's grinning face as he stood expectantly on the stage, inviting them to make fools of themselves either way. Sean sat. Eric sat. Gary sat. Chaos stood. 'You coming?' he asked the others.

'Don't sell out, Chaos,' Sean threatened. 'Not again. Remember Margaret?'

Chaos went alone, making his way through the tables towards the stage. The cameras zoomed in and the flashbulbs flared; the media were about to have a field day.

Chaos stepped onto the stage. The room went silent as all the money-grubbing arse-lickers and corporate dogsbodies waited to savour the moment. The prime minister smiled and extended his hand. Chaos smiled back, hand extended . . . Here it comes, any second now, front-page picture, top story on the news: 'Blair and Chaos Working Together', 'Chaos Embraces New Labour Government', 'Frogspawn Flounder – Chaotics Betrayed'.

Chaos moved his hand up, avoiding Blair's outstretched hand; he moved it up to Blair's shoulder, jabbed his finger into his collarbone and pushed Blair backwards. 'We don't need you,' Chaos said with a caustic grin. 'Why don't you go home and spend more time with your family?'

Chaos grabbed the award and quickly turned to the microphone. 'On behalf of the band I'd just like to thank all Frogspawn everywhere. This is for all of us. I'd like to thank the public for voting. And I'd like to say a special thank you to Sarah – I think she knows why.'

He left the stage and returned to the table as the rest of the room turned to uproar.

'Well, there goes Middle England,' Eric said.

'Better than losing what we got,' Gary said.

'You dumb fuck, Chaos.' Sean grinned. 'We are in *big* trouble now.'

Chaos gave Sean a look that was less than pleased.

'Here, you take this,' Chaos said to Sarah as he handed her

the award. He bent over and whispered venomously in her ear, 'And shove it up that well-worn cunt of yours!'

Chaos sat down, beamed a smile around the room and waited for the flak.

'You stupid moron!' were Dipity's words of greeting. 'The mainstream liked you and the underground listened to you. The only people listening now will be Chaotics!'

Chaos found out later that she'd burst into tears. While the others had gathered round the TV and laughed or cheered, Dipity had burst into tears. So unlike Dipity. But now she raged, five inches from his face, while the majority of the household clustered in the hall and quietly looked on. Chaos thought she'd been on Alan's side, a Chaotic. Obviously not.

'They could have lived with us, could have accepted us. They wouldn't call themselves Frogspawn, wouldn't be seen dead near a collective or a commune, but they'd watch you on the telly, they'd nod and smile and agree with you, make a cup of tea, have another biscuit and carry on with their lives. If pushed, they might say, "Yes, Chaos is all right, he's fun, he's entertaining. *And he's harmless.*"'

Ewan Hughes' Army. Dipity was actually a member, a true believer in Ewan Hughes' Army. Probably the *only* member. Not the enemy, not on Alan's side at all.

'And now what? Now what are they going to think? When the Establishment *really* has a go at us? You've ruined it. You've just given Chaotics the nod, the go-ahead. You have wiped out all Ewan's work because you were too stupid, too egotistical to walk up, *ignore* the handshake, *ignore* Blair and accept the stupid award with dignity.'

All Ewan's work. That was so like Dipity.

Chaos opened his mouth to explain but Alan stepped

forward, beamed a big smile and enthusiastically shook his hand. That was so like Alan. Chaos closed his mouth and said nothing. The flak had started and things could only get worse.

The news pictures on the TV had looked the same for the past month. The same people, same badges, same demonstration descending into riot and black-clothed police wielding shields and batons.

'*For the second time this week, the demonstrators attempted to stop the City . . .*' the news reporter announced.

Chaos, Dipity and Alan stared at the screen like pathologists studying a disease. Stop the City. It could've been stop the road-building, or stop the traffic, or stop the petrochemical companies, or the agrochemicals, or McDonald's, Nestlé, the World Bank, Third World debt, landmines . . . could've been anything, but today it was Stop the City, again.

'You've got to stop this, Alan; this is ridiculous,' Chaos said as he watched a car being pushed over onto its roof.

'Out of my hands, mate. Chaotics are on their own.'

'Somebody's organising them.'

'Yeah? Well, sorry, *I* don't have access to the prime minister.'

Chaos grimaced a hate-filled smile and Alan's smirk grew.

'What's the matter, Chaos? Isn't this what you wanted?' Alan taunted.

'You little shit.'

'Oh, I wouldn't blame Alan if I were you, Chaos,' Dipity sneered, looking daggers at both of them. '*Alan* wasn't the one who started it.'

Chaos glared at Alan. 'Yeah, but somebody's running with it, aren't they?'

'You saying it's me?' Alan glared back.

'Yeah, I'm saying it's you.'

'Prove it.'

'Badges, Alan. As the news keeps *helpfully* reminding us, they're wearing badges.'

Dipity rounded on him. 'And everybody knows they're your badges, Chaos. Everybody knows they're Frogspawn. Pawns of the Frog.'

Chaos wanted to punch her. And would have done if he wasn't certain that she'd punch him back – harder.

'What are you doing about Third World debt, Chaos?' Alan mocked. 'Poverty? Starvation? Torture under military dictatorships? Arms, weapons supplied by this country, by America, by other western governments? What's your line on that, oh Mr Holy One? Maybe they're wearing *your* badges to attract *your* attention. Saying "Hey, bozo, what about this?"'

Dipity watched with disgust as Alan, once friend, once ally, now total dipstick, came close and grinned into Chaos's face.

'You are so parochial, Chaos, so insular – you always were. So long as *we're* all right, the rest of the world can go fuck itself. That's what you think, isn't it? *We don't need you.*' Alan mimicked, jabbing Chaos provocatively in the chest. 'Perfect, Chaos. Ewan couldn't have done better.'

Chaos punched him. Dipity was pleased – one down, one to go.

As Chaos left the TV room he passed the open door of one of the upstairs offices. Steve Jenkins was on the phone, arguing.

'Of course he's not conspiring to incite a riot . . . No, not civil disobedience either . . . Okay, look, if you can prove a link between Chaotics and him, then we'll talk about conspiracy . . . They have absolutely no grounds . . . Is the *real* Saint Michael responsible for Marks & Spencer?'

★

Chaos walked further along the corridor and poked his head round the door of Sarah's workroom. Sarah wasn't in there, but loads of other people were. Alan crew. It was like a factory. Everybody busy making badges. New designs, new logos. Chaos's face and *We don't need you* now the design of the new badge. And the old badge had been updated to *We're looking for Ewan.*' Everybody in the room was wearing both.

Chaos met Val on the stairs. He smiled. Val was good, Val was sexy, and for once she wasn't pregnant.

'Hi, Val.'

'Can't stop now, Chaos,' she gabbled as she passed. 'Forty-nine allotments have been served with eviction notices, Princes Risborough and Peterhead have been refused planning permission, and Oldham council's suddenly refusing to sell. The phones are ringing non-stop. You'd better avoid the office workers; you're not exactly Mr Popularity.'

Chaos saw Monkey in the hall. Monkey informed him that Silver Street in Sheffield had had bricks through their windows. Kate Morris was preparing an hour-long defamatory TV special. Dave had discovered a couple of recruits installing bugging devices in the new Cumbria project, and Zappa had been arrested for attacking a *News of the World* reporter hiding in his cowshed.

'You moron, Chaos,' Monkey added. Monkey was one of Dipity's crew.

Miriam was probably the only one unruffled by the crisis. Chaos watched her from the doorway. With her head bent over her books, in earnest concentration with the straights in the suits, all Chaos could see was her hair – it was going grey.

Good to see her back at Tadley, though, even with grey hair. It would be nice if she looked up and smiled; it would be nice to say hello. Chaos hadn't seen her in years. Miriam travelled even more than Chaos and their paths never quite crossed. She wandered the country, going from home to home, checking accounts, number crunching, teaching and reteaching her maths-minded Frogspawn pupils. The Finance Fanatic they used to call her. Genius they were calling her now.

Tax and VAT inspectors were crawling over every house, every farm, every one-man venture conducted in a Frogspawn affiliate's front room. But if the government wanted fraud or bankruptcy they were barking up the wrong tree. This wouldn't make Miriam's hair turn grey; this wasn't a crisis: this was vindication.

'Don't just stand there, Chaos.' Miriam looked up and complained. 'At least go and make us some coffee.'

Chaos hadn't seen her in years and that was the welcome he got. His heart sank. She turned her head slightly and scratched her greying hair, making an OK sign followed by a V for victory. Chaos smiled and nodded. I wish you were my real mother, you little genius, he thought as he wandered away to make her some coffee.

Chaos's smile was short-lived. There was no respite even in the kitchen. Jonathan and Sarah followed him in and Sarah dumped a pile of newspapers onto the table.

'Read these,' she commanded.

'I don't want to read about any more drug busts, lies, sleaze stories or Chaotics,' Chaos tetchily replied.

'Well read this.'

'Child Sex Abuse in Frogspawn Home' read the headline on the top of the pile. Chaos stared at it in horror.

'Still mad at me now?' Sarah asked.

Chaos ignored the question and scanned the article. 'Is this true?'

Jonathan was on his way to Bishop's Waltham to find out. 'I don't know yet, but if it is, thank God we're being investigated.'

'I'll go with you,' Chaos offered.

'No, you've done enough damage,' Jonathan replied. 'I think it's best if Brian and I go alone.'

Chaos thought an openly gay couple entering what was bound to be a media frenzy was asking for trouble, but he kept the thought to himself, especially since Jonathan was in such a foul mood.

'We've got to be seen to be helpful, Chaos, and wrong. This is serious.'

'*Wrong?* You don't believe this abuse thing, do you, Jonathan?' Chaos argued.

'Yes. Actually I do,' Jonathan said. 'But, more importantly, everybody else will. So what *you* need to do is give a press conference to thank the social services.'

'Thank them?'

'Yes. Let it be known that we're happy to have them inspecting our homes; let it be known that we're cooperating and that any help or advice they give would be more than welcome.'

'I can't do that!' Chaos protested.

'You have to. Otherwise they'll take the children away.'

'But they're only doing it to get at us.'

'Yeah, well, they've got us.'

Chaos glared but it was quite obvious that Jonathan was far too enraged to back down. Chaos turned to Sarah instead. 'This is all your fault. You and your stupid awards ceremonies.'

'And your last two albums have re-entered the charts, and

the single's gone back to number two, despite the radio ban,' Sarah informed him.

Chaos tried to look contemptuous but couldn't help his eyebrow twitching with interest.

'And all the guys at Bishop's Waltham have volunteered to live elsewhere during the investigation for the sake of the children, and to help the authorities, and to try to *un*tarnish the Frogspawn image. So the single might make it to number one now, mightn't it?' Jonathan added sarcastically.

'I didn't mean it like that,' Sarah muttered petulantly.

'No, I'm sure you didn't,' Jonathan sneered, marching out of the kitchen as though there were a bad smell in the air.

Sarah and Chaos exchanged sullen glances and stared in silence at the coffee-maker.

'The last *two* albums?' Chaos finally asked, his eyes still rooted to the pot.

'The last two.' Sarah nodded, equally fascinated with the steaming hiss and drip of the coffee.

'We must be doing something right then.'

'Absolutely,' Sarah agreed, perking up but lowering her voice to a conspiratorial whisper. 'Actually, business is booming. And not just the record sales. The shops, organic boxes, books, recruits . . . everything.'

Chaos managed to drag his eyes from the coffee pot to look at his mother. 'So what do we do now?'

'As Jonathan said – press statement.' Sarah smiled.

Dipity scowled as she read through Chaos and Sarah's notes, her pen crossing out and crossing out and crossing out, the aggression seeming to grow with every stroke of the pen. Chaos and Sarah stamped their feet and blew into their gloved hands, pulled their coats further around them and watched Dipity's pen and Dipity's scowling face and wished they could bale hay, push a plough or go indoors. It was freezing and they felt more than stupid standing in the middle of a field doing nothing but look conspicuous and cold. But if Dave had found bugs in Cumbria, maybe Nick had been right about being tapped.

'*I* want, *I* think, *I* believe – Christ, Chaos, you are a moron,' Dipity sneered as she continued to decimate the press statement he and Sarah had so laboriously worked on. She looked up. 'You know that Alan is going to be incredibly important in all this, don't you? Without computers and the Internet, we don't stand a chance.'

Chaos nodded peevishly.

'And if he knows it's your idea, he might just want to fuck it all up,' she added.

'It's not his idea – it's mine. And who knows Ewan better than I do?' Sarah said.

Dipity thought about it and nodded. Alan would go for that. It seemed reasonable. She screwed up the paper and stuffed it into her coat pocket. 'I'll write the statement; yours is crap. But' – Dipity looked with challenging delight into Chaos's face – 'you've got to read it and *believe* it.'

'Well, here comes my comeuppance,' Chaos thought as he reluctantly nodded.

A stark, functional room in a stark, functional London hotel. The conference room was big, blandly beige and brightly lit by harsh strip lights. No windows, nothing reassuring, nothing to look at and think, Hmm, that's interesting, that makes me glad to be here. Nothing to look at but rows and rows of seats filled by rows and rows of reporters, photographers, cameras. A sea of microphones and tape recorders all pointed one way, towards the table. A safety table, put there in an attempt to protect the chair behind. One chair, in keeping with Frogspawn tradition. Nobody special. No heavies, no hand-holding, no entourage, just Dipity, Sarah and Jake, standing unobtrusively against a wall, staying out of it.

Chaos blinked at the salvo of camera flashes as he entered from the ante-room. He took in the sea of expectant faces and smiled automatically, then forced his face straight. Flat. Stay flat, Dipity's orders. Chaos took the chair, stared at the papers clutched like a lifeline in sweaty hands and cleared his throat, forcing his face not to smile.

'What's the idea, Chaos?' a journalist shouted out.

The traditional start. Chaos flicked a quick glance at the guy, nervously checked Dipity's expression and started reading in as flat a voice as possible.

'First of all I speak on behalf of the thousands of Frogspawn up and down the country. We would like to thank the social services, Inland Revenue, health and safety executive, the police – in particular the drug squad and the fraud squad – the press, radio and TV networks, MAFF, the Soil Association, the RSPCA, the NSPCC, the Schools Inspectorate, the Registry Office, the secret service and any other government department that I may have omitted. We are indebted to them all for the interest that has been taken in our homes and their concern for our well-being.'

Some of the journalists laughed. Chaos wasn't sure if it was at the absurdity of the list or glee at the hell that Frogspawn had been put through.

'Once these inspections have finished, we hope to be allowed to continue our lives independently and without help from the state.'

Chaos looked up briefly and licked his lips – his mouth was dry. 'Secondly, I personally would like to offer an apology . . .'

Microphones and tape recorders lunged forward and Chaos

lifted his face for the cameras to get a good shot. Dipity would be annoyed but he couldn't help it – habit.

'I apologise to Ewan Hughes for breaking his rules and I apologise to Frogspawn for letting them down . . .'

The press groaned.

'The circumstances of my behaviour were unfortunate and I don't think either Tony Blair or myself should have been placed in such a position.'

It wasn't good enough. They wanted more.

'What about the Chaotics, Chaos?' somebody shouted.

'Chaotics fight the opposition. Frogspawn turn their backs,' Chaos automatically replied.

A journalist scoffed. 'Oh, come off it, Chaos, you punched the prime minister.'

Murmurs of laughter rippled around the room. Chaos blinked slightly and looked over at Dipity. She was shaking her head. *Move on, move on!* Chaos stared down at his paper.

'So are you admitting you're a Chaotic?' another reporter asked.

'Are you the Gerry Adams of anarchists?' somebody shouted to a wave of laughter.

Chaos gritted his teeth and read on.

'Thirdly, Ewan Hughes believes democracy means choice. Democracy should allow us the choice to live without money. And to live without the benefit of mainstream society. Ewan Hughes said we should turn our backs. If people want to join us, Frogspawn will help them. If not, Frogspawn hope people will turn their backs on us.'

The press quietened down and frowned, exchanging wary glances. What was this?

'Fourthly, as a spokesperson for Frogspawn I have found it difficult to turn my back, so I've asked what Ewan would do, and the answer is to quit being a spokesperson. So that is what I'm going to do.'

Chaos looked up; the journalists looked back. They hadn't got it.

'Thank you,' Chaos added, signalling the end.

Still blank confusion.

'So, what are you saying, Chaos?' somebody asked.

What am I saying? What *am* I saying? It hit him then. This was no help; this didn't help. Dipity's words. Sarah's idea. Chaos still felt scared. He still felt guilty. Maerdy had nothing, Ewan was probably dead and all his dad could say was, 'So, the idiot's not at Tadley.'

'I'm quitting, you tossers!' he jeered as the anger welled up and walloped into his head.

The room sat up, the atmosphere lit up, the cameras rolled, photographers flashed, microphones and tape recorders surged. Dipity closed her eyes and wanted to spit. Sarah stepped forward in alarm, her head shaking slightly, muttering, 'Don't crack, Chaos, don't.'

Chaos cracked, loud and long and just like performing, but not rehearsed and not rhyming.

'I said, *we don't need you*, and I meant it. I was happy to say it. I never believed in Ewan Hughes. I wanted to – I tried to. But I only ever wanted to beat him. I only ever wanted to show him what he *should* have done. Your world is shit and your governments are shit and I would love to be Chaotic. I would love to physically fight on behalf of people who can't fight. I would love you to call me criminal for breaking the law in the name of justice. I wish I was Chaotic. I could've smashed Tony Blair's head into the floor. Any members of the Establishment, anybody with any power, line them up and I'd cheerfully punch their lights out. Because they are what killed him . . .'

Chaos wanted to wail. He wanted to fall apart like a baby. Nothing he did was good enough. Nothing he could do would make amends. Ewan Hughes was never coming home. And, famous though he was, Chaos couldn't raise the dead.

'But I can't. I can't be Chaotic. I've got to turn my back on you. Give up everything I love because of you. Because I don't want to lose. I don't want to be dismissed as an idiot. I've got to disappear because Frogspawn are winning. And I want them to carry on winning and prove Ewan Hughes right . . .'

Because Ewan *was* alive. He was alive and well and living in Deptford. He had kids that he loved more than Chaos, a lover that he loved more than Sarah, and a life that he loved more than Tadley. Chaos had been given pictures, information. About four years ago. Callum O'Connor and the FFC had been due to start filming – such bad timing, no time to think. He and Jake had driven secretly, sat in the car one rainy afternoon and spied on him. Ewan. Older, fatter, greyer, but obviously Ewan. He looked so ordinary. They'd watched him come and go. Caught glimpses of life through his window. And neither of them could move. Neither of them could say a word. Then or since. Ewan was alive but Ewan Hughes was dead.

'We are not miners. We are not miners fighting to keep what you gave us, fighting for an existence that you created for us. You can't take away jobs we've turned down, money we don't worship or a community you haven't built. All you can take away is me. And I've just done that for you. I don't want your world. And you know what? A hell of a lot of people don't want it either!'

Chaos knew before he even hit the door to the ante-room that he'd fucked up. If the media had shown their feelings they would have cheered. They had enough to hang him.

★

One week later one thousand three hundred and sixteen Frogspawn had been arrested for possession of drugs, seventy-seven for failure to register a birth and one guy for sex offences, and both the single *and* the last album were at number one. Chaos heard the news while harvesting leeks in Margaret's old vegetable garden.

Chapter 18

July 2000 – two years later

Josie Spencer couldn't believe what was happening in front of her; it was senseless. Just before dawn, the motorway practically clear, plenty of space and absolutely no reason for the Range Rover's sudden acceleration and last-second attempt to overtake.

'Oh my God,' she gasped.

She watched the Range Rover clip the car's rear wing, watched the car surge with the impact and slew left, crash into the barrier, flip upward into the air and career over the edge of the flyover. She watched the Range Rover drive on, registration obscured. She fumbled on the passenger seat for her mobile before it even occurred to her to stop.

Stuart yelled 'Fucking hell!' as Andy slammed on the brakes. They watched open-mouthed as the car tumbled over and over from the flyover above and landed on its roof in the field next to the road. Stuart and Andy jumped out and ran to investigate, stopping a few feet away as countless film images of exploding cars deterred them. They looked at each other and looked at the car, ugly and somehow comic like an upended tortoise, but silent, lifeless, dead. The silence even more potent amid the rustle of the breeze through the wheat.

Andy inched behind as Stuart moved forward and crouched down, twisting his head to see inside the upside-down mangled wreck. Two guys. Both dead. Seemed dead, must be. Stuart bent further in, twisted his head more.

'Fucking hell,' he whispered. He looked over his shoulder at Andy.

'One of them looks like Chaos.'

Sean, still bleary-eyed and half asleep, was looking out of the window as he pulled on his shirt. He automatically leapt for the phone when he saw the police car. He loved the old gatehouse. It was like living in a sentry box.

'Jill, Jill,' he urged his sleeping lover, 'wake up! Come on, we're being busted.'

While Sean waited for someone at the main house to answer the phone, it occurred to him that the police must know by now that Tadley was drug free. It also occurred to him that one police car with two police officers in it wasn't going to be a bust.

Tadley woke to the blood-chilling scream coming from the drawing room downstairs and echoing around the quiet house. It was Sarah. Eric and Jonathan held her. Dipity refused to believe it.

'He's in Brighton,' she repeated, over and over, her body rigid and her head shaking. 'He's in Brighton till Thursday.'

Then the phones started ringing.

Nobody mentioned Jake.

'Chaos is dead,' the newsreader announced. *'Reports just in confirm that he was involved in a fatal car accident in the early hours of this morning. Preliminary enquiries by the police suggest drugs may have been involved.'*

★

300

Jonathan felt numb. Everything seemed to be moving in slow motion, somewhere over there in the distance. Sarah had been his concern. She was safe now, sedated, her speckled grey hair visible above the lump of bedclothes she was curled under. Eric sitting on the bed, with her. And Brian with Jonathan. Jonathan could feel him, near, behind him or beside him, somewhere. He couldn't look at him, though; Jonathan couldn't look at anybody.

Jonathan came down the stairs, a lot of stairs; they seemed to go on for ever. He saw Matilda down below. Matilda seemed small in the hall, turning in circles, like a fly around a light bulb. 'Tranx,' she was saying, 'I've got to go to Tranx. Her brother *and* her lover . . .'

Jonathan thought of Margaret. Tranx always reminded Jonathan of Margaret. He saw Val down below, coming out of an office, way down below, Val talking to Matilda, stopping her turning, saying to Matilda, 'He was going to see Marcia.'

Jonathan felt a surge of air entering his body, and his head jerked back hard to receive it. He felt like he'd been punched. He thought of Ewan, staggered backwards up the stairs and thumped down.

He was going to see Marcia.

'After announcing his decision to quit Frog two years ago, Chaos had not been seen in public . . .' Blanket coverage. The radio announcer stumbling through, hoping for any snippet of information.

'Chaos continued to perform at Frogspawn festivals around the country. It is believed he may have been travelling between concerts when his driver, a drug addict, so tragically lost control of the car. Eyewitness reports that another car was involved in the incident are being investigated . . .'

Dave walked out of the kitchen. Pattie watched him go.

'Dad?' Robert said, wanting to do something, anything.

Pattie shook her head. *Leave him*, her expression read. *Let him be.*

Dave stepped out of his cabin. He ignored the other cabin dwellers milling about in their doorways, ignored the sound of a dozen radios disturbing the morning birdsong of the Cumbrian countryside. He started working, continuing the construction of another cabin. Accident or not, there was nothing to say. Accident or not, the cabin had to be built. Chaos had been desperate as a kid to live in one of Dave's cabins. He never did.

'Why?' Sally screamed down the phone. She didn't know who she was talking to, and didn't care: it was a connection to Tadley, that's what counted, and that was her immediate response. 'Why? Why now? Everything was clean; everything was legal. They couldn't touch us; they had no reason to!'

Sally took the phone away from her ear. That was why. She'd answered her own question. They couldn't get him any other way. She thought she was going to fall. Keep the anger or I'm going to fall. Sally replaced the receiver. She didn't know who she was cutting off, didn't care.

They've killed him because they couldn't touch him – couldn't touch us.

The phone rang; Sally mechanically picked it up. Yell at the bastards, tell the press to fuck off, keep the anger going, keep the anger. Sally listened for a few seconds. 'Miriam?' she whispered as she fell, collapsing on the floor and weeping, the receiver clutched tightly to her ear.

'Have they killed him, Miriam?'

The TV blared in the corner. Alan was engrossed in his computer but glanced from time to time at the pictures, pausing occasionally to hear what was being broadcast. Dipity stood behind him, behind his chair, a perfect position for both screens, her body still rigid, her face taut and white and blank. The TV warming to the topic, full of enthusiasm for the entertaining air space. Digging up anything they could find. The news presenter expressionless. An obituary before breakfast.

'There had been much speculation as to Chaos's state of mind when he announced his decision to quit Frog. Insiders claimed he was under enormous pressure in the weeks leading up to the announcement . . .'

Chaos's face loomed onto the screen. Alan glanced at it. Dipity stared at it. The press conference outburst, a bit of it. The famous bit, the done-to-death bit.

'I said, we don't need you, and I meant it. I was happy to say it . . . Your world is shit and your governments are shit and I would love to be Chaotic . . .'

Chaos on TV. Alive again. The media churning it out. Like they churned it out before.

'I wish I was Chaotic. I could've smashed Tony Blair's head into the floor. Any members of the Establishment, anybody with any power, line them up and I'd cheerfully punch their lights out.'

Edited, cut up, designed to show Chaos as anarchic. The effect had been negative. Negative for the Establishment. Chaos, Frogspawn, and even Chaotics had stuck to the plan and gone underground. And Chaos became the hero, an absent alternative. The public loved it. Dipity loved it. Chaos hated it. But the Establishment got the message and stopped advertising for them, stopped showing the clips. Till now. Why now?

Dipity looked at Alan's screen. Words, words.

Chaos assassinated.

Alan thought nothing less, and now was the time.

Go ask Ewan, I think he'll know.

The website was buzzing and Alan was in charge. He tapped out his message for the Chaotics; they'd know what it meant.

Rabbit shafted. Seed's been thrown. Call Ewan. Answers written at the hall.

Dipity watched. Her eyes blinking slowly at the two words. *Chaos assassinated.*

When did it all become so serious? When did her brother become such a threat? He only wanted to get laid; he only wanted to show off – she'd thought. Take it seriously, Chaos; Ewan's out there somewhere and I want you to find him.

Chaos assassinated. The Frogspawn had multiplied. Alan and the Chaotics had been brought into line, houses cleaned, drugs swept away, sex taken seriously and Chaos silenced. But he'd remained popular, remained in the public mind. The public beginning to change their minds, think differently and agree with him. *Chaos assassinated.*

The TV coverage was endless, the newsreader expressionlessly spewing the old line, the well-trodden track of lies and twists. The track Dipity had thought they'd abandoned as counterproductive.

'Although Chaos was a popular and successful lead singer with Frog, it was his membership of the subversive Frogspawn cult which caused controversy. The cult, led by anarchist Ewan Hughes, believed to be Chaos's father, was often at odds with the authorities and proved unpopular with the general public, many of whom denounced Chaos for using his celebrity status to entice the young into anarchy.'

A snippet of the Callum O'Connor documentary. Chaos alive on the TV. Alive in Mablethorpe. Chaos talking to Kate Morris.

'There's thousands of Frogspawn. And thousands of losers can pack quite a powerful punch.'

Chaos talking to Sally.

'He wants us to organise demonstrations and riots. He wants all the Frogspawn to march on Downing Street, bring London to a standstill . . .'

The word 'moron' jumped into Dipity's head the way it always did when she saw this clip. Don't think that word, she thought as one tear spilt over her eyelid.

'He wants everything to be . . . chaotic . . .'

And the bit that poleaxed him, the bit Chaos screamed 'Bastards!' at – Chaos pulling a blithe, butter-wouldn't-melt-face: *'That's what Ewan would do.'*

Chaos assassinated.

Why are they doing this? Why are they showing this? Where are the clips of him on *Top of the Pops*? On *Jools Holland*? Where are the clips of the Harvest Festivals?

Rabbit shafted. Seed's been thrown. Call Ewan. Answers written at the hall.

'Don't send it, Alan. It's what they want,' Dipity muttered, wiping away the one tear.

Alan ignored her. Sent it.

The TV was on at Old Hill Farm in Matlock. The sound wasn't blaring; it was muted. The residents who were gathered were watching the same thing Dipity watched, but they didn't want to hear it loud. They wanted the news to seep in quietly. They didn't want it to disturb Marcia. Didn't want Marcia in the TV lounge. They didn't want *Tranx* to disturb her.

Tranx was on the phone, her eyes on the TV screen, smiling every time Chaos's face appeared.

Tranx was disturbing the residents of Matlock.

'Zappa, you're paranoid, you're getting paranoid . . .'

Tranx was calm, unbelievably calm. Just another little crisis. All these phone calls, they were just the usual Frogspawn panic.

'How could they possibly know? Only Marcia and I knew . . . Because he phoned her last night . . . They can't possibly bug

305

every single phone, you idiot. No, Zappa, it *looked* like an accident because it *was* an accident . . .'

The residents of Matlock half watched Tranx and half watched the TV. A woman, 'Josie Spencer – eyewitness', was explaining about the Range Rover, recounting what she saw: '. . . *clipped the car, drove off* . . .'

'"*Welsh* Rabbit", Zappa, "*Welsh* Rabbit". The rabbit was Ewan, not Chaos . . .'

The residents of Matlock wondered why Zappa and Tranx were debating the meaning of 'Welsh Rabbit' at a time like this.

'The answers were written at *Tadley* Hall not *White*hall, you know that . . . Of course there's no point in everybody going to Tadley, but why London? Well then, Dylan's an idiot too, but if you like I'll ask Chaos when he gets here'

The residents of Matlock looked at Tranx with serious concern. They distinctly heard Zappa scream, '*He's dead!*' down the line. They shuddered when Tranx replied, 'They're just late.' They all jumped up and ran to her when Tranx paused to stare at the mangled wreck on the TV screen and passed out.

Alan wrote the next part easily, his fingers automatically tapping out the words he'd written so many times before.

> *One field is for barley,*
> *And one field is for wheat,*
> *And the garbage that they feed you*
> *Isn't fit for you to eat.*
> *Go ask Ewan, if life is sweet.*
>
> *And if you go chase the rabbit*
> *Down a mineshaft you will fall,*

Because the answers that they give you
Are all written at the hall.
Call Ewan, he's heard it all before.

When the farmer throws the seed down,
And tells you he's got to go,
Tear down the office and the business,
Seize the house and the studio.
Go ask Ewan, I think he'll know.

When Merlin, dykes and allies,
And Horsemen live in sheds,
And His Lordship's going backwards,
And the white queen's lost her head,
Remember what the drummer said:
He's not dead. He's not dead.

Then the explanation for any idiots who weren't familiar with
his interpretations.

The government is safe and laughing in the barley. They have killed Chaos
in the wheat field. The wreck is in a wheat field. Switch on your TV — see
it and believe. They are now feeding you the garbage of propaganda, lies
and misinformation — every Chaotic knows there were no drugs; every
Frogspawn knows Jake was clean. Listen to the news; listen to the lies —
hear it and disbelieve. Then ask, is life sweet? Chaos has been assassinated,
is that sweet? The seed has been thrown. Now is the time to go. Tear down
offices and businesses, seize the Houses of Parliament and the TV studios.
The lordships and queens of the Establishment want to go backwards and
destabilise Frogspawn; they have lost their heads. If you want Chaos to live,
prove Frogspawn isn't dead.

Dipity stood behind Alan and read it all as he typed. She didn't have the energy to contradict him. The mangled wreck was on the TV screen and Dipity was thinking of other things.

Birmingham New Street Station was filling rapidly. More so than the usual rush-hour crush of commuters. Many people standing around the concourse weren't business-suited, weren't briefcased and mobile-phoned and hurrying to catch trains. They were standing, silent and patient, waiting to become a sizeable mob.

The buses into Birmingham city centre were a nightmare. People were refusing to pay and some bus drivers were refusing to move. The drivers that were moving were carrying sardine-wedged passengers – and they weren't always sticking to the route. The streets of Birmingham were more crowded than usual. Thousands of people were walking towards the centre, towards the train station, the coach station, the bus station, towards the motorway.

The TV cameras and the press were moving towards Birmingham New Street Station. The police were too.

What was happening in Birmingham was also happening in Manchester, Sheffield, Liverpool, Cardiff, Edinburgh, Exeter, Brighton, Norwich, Leeds . . .

The local stations were easier. The Chaotics, Frogspawn, Frog fans, Chaos lovers, supporters, sympathisers, conspiracy theorists and ghouls overcame the ticket problem by their sheer weight of numbers and simply got on the trains.

Thousands of people were trying to get to London.

A mob of reporters was already gathering outside Jonathan's old London flat in Ridgmount Gardens. The doorbell rang incessantly, the telephone rang incessantly. Imogen and Claudia ignored them both. They were watching their world crumble on the TV.

The television showed aerial shots of the M40. The motorway was chock-a-block. One way. The London way. And it wasn't just cars – it was walkers too. As soon as the newsreader said 'near Oxford' Imogen and Claudia knew it would be Dylan's farm. The line of multicoloured, tiny bobbing dots walking along the hard shoulder of the motorway would be the inhabitants of Dylan's Great Milton farm. And, as the helicopter flew further along the M40 towards Horton-cum-Studley . . . Zappa's crew, doing exactly the same thing.

Imogen and Claudia held each other as the newsreader informed them, and the helicopter showed them, that it wasn't just Dylan and Zappa's crews who were motorway walking. And it wasn't just the M40.

'They're coming,' Imogen said.

'Alan's Welsh Rabbit,' Claudia said.

Imogen and Claudia looked at each other and shook their heads in despair.

Chief Superintendent Gordon was in charge of operations at Whitehall. They'd expected trouble, they'd expected people, but not this many, not this soon. And many of these people *weren't* Chaotics. Many were genuinely bewildered and grief-stricken mourners. It wouldn't look good when the rioting started. Chief Superintendent Gordon's only hope was to staunch the flow. He spoke to anybody with a microphone and camera.

'The Metropolitan Police appreciate that this is a tragic day. However, London is not the place to express that tragedy. The Chaotics have always been a volatile group and we don't want trouble. So I'm urging anyone thinking of coming to London to turn round and stay in their homes.'

'The Chaotics have always been a volatile group.'

Dipity snapped. They were *expecting* it. The amount of police

309

around Whitehall, Trafalgar Square, Westminster – they'd expected it, planned for it. It made sense.

Dipity seemed to explode into action. She pushed Alan out of his seat. Alan let her do it. Let her do whatever she wanted. After all, Chaos was her brother and Alan had already done what he needed to do.

Dipity sat in front of Alan's computer screen, her leg pumping with energy and her eyes blinking rapidly as tears of rage blurred her vision. She wrote:

STOP! IT'S WHAT THEY WANT. THEY'LL SEND IN THE ARMY. EWAN SAID: TURN YOUR BACKS. CHAOS SAID: TURN IT ROUND. DON'T FIGHT. IT'S WHAT THEY WANT. DON'T PLAY THEIR GAME. PLAY FROGSPAWN!

Dipity sent the message, leapt out of the seat and ran through the house. She careered down the stairs, out of the door and down the drive. People were gathered at the gates. She knew they'd be there. A camera, a microphone. She knew there'd be cameras and microphones.

Dipity grabbed a microphone and screamed into the camera.

'I'm Chaos's sister, I'm Ewan Hughes' daughter, and neither of them wants this. They both know this will destroy us. This is what the Establishment wants. Please turn your back. Please go home. Their weapons are useless if we don't fight. If we *don't* fight. Chaos told you. Don't turn your back on Chaos now. He died because we were winning. Frogspawn. Ewan Hughes' Army. *Turn it round, go upside down*. We've got to keep on winning. We've got to win by silence, inaction and self-sufficiency. Win as family, as Frogspawn, on Frogspawn territory. Go home, please. For Chaos.'

She knew she'd lost. She knew it was too late. She also knew that if Ewan was still out there, and they knew where, he'd be next.

A reporter took the opportunity. 'Why does everybody think he was assassinated?'

Dipity glared at the reporter. It was so obvious. 'Look at the police presence, look at what's happening in London, look at the TV, the radio, see what they're saying. Everything is organised. They're prepared. They knew it was going to happen.'

The reporter shrugged with confusion. 'From what I've seen and heard this morning, it's the Chaotics who were organised.'

Dipity stopped jittering. Her body calmed, her blood ran cold and an old image jumped into her head. It was of Alan poking Chaos in the chest, saying, *'We don't need you.'*

Dipity blinked once, turned her back on the reporter and the crowd around the gate and walked slowly back to Tadley.

Thousands of people never made it to London and had to content themselves with rioting in their home towns.

London itself was like a war zone. The prime minister briefly announced that, although it wasn't a crisis and everything was under control, if it persisted he'd have no option but to send in the army.

*   *   *

Ian Field was listening to the news on the radio when his head started spinning and his legs went from under him. He nearly fell off the scaffolding. He would have done if another brickie hadn't managed to grab him. He said he was okay but the whiteness of his face and his trembling body spoke otherwise. He took the rest of the day off.

'Flu,' he told his partner, Caroline. 'I think I'm getting flu.'

He could feel her accusing eyes on his retreating back as he stumbled up the stairs of their little terraced house in Deptford. He could hear the TV blaring in the background.

'I'm Chaos's sister, I'm Ewan Hughes' daughter, and neither of them wants this . . .'

He wanted to give in, lie on the landing and wail like a banshee. But not in front of the kids, and Sally was there, he'd seen her, on the edge of his vision, sitting on the living-room floor and looking like Dipity, watching her half-sister calling. His two worlds colliding, not sure which he was in, but he wanted to curl up with Caroline and die with Sarah. This is not supposed to happen; it's not supposed to be like this. Sarah. He almost heard her scream on the scaffolding.

If he could make it to his bed, find safety and privacy. But Caroline would follow. No privacy any more. Nowhere was private except the bathroom at midnight on New Year's Eve for a couple of drunken sentimental tears.

Make it to the bed, vomit it all up and to hell with what Caroline thinks. Burn the bridges. She knows anyway, unspoken knowledge, and it doesn't seem that important any more. If he could crawl under the bedclothes, let his head quietly and privately explode . . .

He heard the bedroom door opening, felt her presence in the room.

She sat on the bed and looked at the thinning grey hair that was visible above the lump of bedclothes he was curled under.

'Are you going to get in contact?' Caroline asked.

'No,' his muffled voice replied.

'Why not?'

'Because it's over.'